REPARATION
A STORY OF HOPE

JOSEPH F. MURRAY

REPARATION: A STORY OF HOPE
Copyright © Joseph F. Murray, 2021.
All rights reserved.
Interior Design: Jennie Lyne Hiott
Copyright inspires creativity, encourages the sharing of voices, and creates a vibrant civilization. Thank you for purchasing an authorized edition of this book and for complying with copyright laws by not reproducing, scanning, or distributing any part of it in any form, electronic or mechanical, without written permission from the author, except in the case of brief quotation embodied in critical articles and reviews.

This is a work of fiction. The names, characters, places, and incidents are products of the writer's imagination or are used fictitiously and should not be construed as real. Any similarities to persons, living or dead, actual events, locale, or organizations is entirely coincidental.

DEDICATION

I am so happy and honored to dedicate this book to my wide and best friend, Barbara. I am so appreciative for all her help, advice, and correction she has given me. After I completed every chapter, she patiently listened to every read as I read it to her, offering advice and comments whenever needed.

God has truly blessed me with her. No husband could ask for a better wife and friend. We have shared everything together since we've been married, and I am happy to share this novel with her.

Thanks Barb for standing by me. I can't tell you how much your constant support and encouragement have helped me throughout the writing of this book.

I love you.

ACKNOWLEDGEMENTS

The entire concept of this book would not have been possible had it not been inspired by Jesus Himself. Many months ago, I kept getting the thought of writing a book. After much prayer and discernment, I made the decision to go forward with the project, even though I had never written a novel before. As I began writing, most of the words, ideas, and concepts came to me without thinking. As I look back to how quick and easy it was to complete the book, there is no doubt that it was only through divine inspiration that this was possible. I will always be thankful to the Lord for all that He has done for me, and I hope that the message in this book will be well received.

It is with sincere appreciation that I acknowledge Reka Montfort for all the support, technical help, and advice given. Anytime I needed help, she was always willing and ready to assist. Reka spent countless hours assisting me throughout the writing of this book. From the very simple to the more complex problems, including all the formatting she did. Her help was invaluable to me, and without it, this novel would never have been possible. Thank you Reka for putting up with me and never complaining when I so often messed up. I've come to realize what a special friend you are. From the bottom of my heart, thank you so much.

Last, but not least, I would also like to acknowledge and thank Mary and Dave Barnes, two of my closest friends, who were also such an encouragement to me. They always took time to critique and listen to every chapter as soon as it was finished. They are true friends. The help and support given me is so appreciated.

CONTENTS

Prologue
Chapter I
Chapter II
Chapter III
Chapter IV
Chapter V
Chapter VI
Chapter VII
Chapter VIII
Chapter IX
Chapter X
Chapter XI
Chapter XII
Chapter XIII

PROLOGUE

Two huge, yellow, bloodshot eyes pierced out over the darkness as Azazal surveryed over his domain. Silhouetted by the dim light of the moon, you could see him perched atop of the water tower located at the far edge of town. This was no ordinary demon. The creature was huge compared to all of the sentinels under his command, who were scattered over the entire town of Clarksville.

His face was hideous, deformed and scared, indicating he had been in many battles. Huge black wings, looking like the consistency of steel, wrapped around his body, ready to protect him from any danger. What appeared to be slime oozed from his nose with every breath he took, and the scent of sulfur was present.

A slight smile emerged from Azazal's face as he gloated at the chaos and despair he had caused throughout the town. Azazal knew that his work was almost complete. Just a few more odds and ends to shore up. Just a few more obstinate people to death with. Then, he could focus on the Seminary.

PROLOGUE

Yes, the town was almost ready. Most everyone had succumbed to the influence of the demons that constantly attached themselves to their weaknesses. Most everyone, except Fr. James O'Malley, the pastor of St. Andrews Catholic Church, Claudia, and Frank Bogan, who own and operate a small coffee shop, Mrs. Johnson, who refused to leave Clarksville after her husband died years ago, Maggie Saunders, who for the past 22 years has volunteered to housekeep and cook for Fr. O'Malley, and a dozen or so other people, including Joshua Donovan.

The night was cool and damp, and the town was dark… exceptionally dark. Almost all the streetlights were out, broken or never replaced. Even the houses were dark, even though it was still early evening. Due to a mandate by Mayor Talon, all businesses were ordered to close at 6:00pm because of looting and vandalism that has plagued the city for months. One lone streetlight illuminated the broken sidewalk as Joshua Donovan slowly walked home from his work at Buzzy's Gas Station, one of only three gas stations still operating in town. Buzzy's was only two blocks from where Josh lived, which allowed him to easily walk to and from work.

Josh walked slower than his usual pace, almost as if he was carrying a thousand pounds on his shoulders. Although it had only been six months since the attack at the seminary, he still couldn't get it out of his mind…not so much as to what happened to him, but more as to what was still going on in that place.

St. Andrews Church always had a light on, as Fr. O'Malley wanted to keep the church doors always open for anyone who wanted to pray. Unfortunately, most of the time the church stood empty, except for a few who still attended Sunday Mass.

As Josh passed the steps of St. Andrews, he paused, something was not quite right. Yet all he could detect was a slight scent of sulfur in the air. The same scent he had so often smelled at the seminary. Josh was sure that evil was present.

"Who's there?" Josh yelled, turning around to see if someone was behind him.

Then, out of the corner of his eye he thought he saw something black whizzing through the bushes on the empty lot across the street.

"Hey...who's there?"

Nothing, absolutely nothing. Perhaps it was just the wind, he thought. Yet an eerie feeling crept along his spine.

His house was only a few yards away and he was anxious to get home. Fr. O'Malley, who had an empty apartment above his house, had offered it to Josh months ago. The house was connected to the church by an enclosed atrium, which allowed for quick entrance to the church, especially during inclement weather.

Despite his eerie feeling, Josh was not too concerned, as he often felt uneasy whenever night fell upon the city. Still the smell of sulfur was present, more present than before. *What's going on*, he thought. No sooner had that thought passed his mind when another flash of black whizzed past him. Then it was gone, and so was the smell of sulfur.

The demon who had been assigned to spy on Josh, rushed back to Azazal. "He's going straight home tonight," the demon reported in his high-pitched voice.

"He didn't go into the church?" asked Azazal

"No Master, directly home."

"Hum!" Azazal mumbled as he scratched his head. "Maybe we're finally getting to him." A slight smile emerged across his face. "Get back to him and don't let him out of your sight. Keep attacking...keep attacking."

"I will master, but I can't get too close. His guardian is powerful."

PROLOGUE

"So are we," screamed Azazal. "Now go!"

As Josh reached his home, he used the outside stairs, as he most often did, so as not to disturb Fr. O'Malley. Josh was breathing heavily, steam emitting from each breath as he reached the top of the steps. He was still shaking from what he had just experienced. Catching his breath, he quickly looked around before entering his kitchen door. Tears welled up in his eyes.

"Oh Jesus," he said in a low prayerful voice. "What's happening? What's happened to our world? To our country? There's so much evil, so much immorality in this city...Where have all the good people gone? Oh, dear God, help us...help us..."

Josh unlocked the door, entered the kitchen, and went directly to the sink for a drink of water. After taking off his jacket, throwing it toward the hooks on the wall and missing them, he continued into his small, cramped living room. Looking up, he froze in place with an astonished and frightened expression on his face. Instantly falling back, flipping over a chair behind him, he huddled in the corner of the room, stunned by the light emitting from the figure standing in front of him.

"Joshua, don't be afraid," the Lord said.

At the exact moment that the Lord spoke, a tremendous light burst from every window. The light was brighter than any light man had ever seen. The force of the light, bursting from the house, was as powerful as a bomb exploding, with the force of wind and fire as it shot forward in every direction.

Every demon in its immediate vicinity was immediately disintegrated. Others, further away, were fleeing as fast as they could fly, only to have their wings destroyed as the flames of light caught up to them. The screams of demons were horrendous as they fled to their leader, Azazal. Those who were foolish enough to look back were immediately blinded, and losing control, crashed to their demise. Even Azazal, who was miles away, was knocked off the water tower he was perched on. Not having time to react, he flipped and tumbled toward the ground. He, along with dozens of other demons, ended up stunned but protected by a huge hill as the light passed over them.

"Master, master!" The demons of confusion screamed. "What's happening? What's happening?" Almost instantly, they were joined by many others producing screams and ungodly screeches of confusion. Azazal, recovering from his fall and clearly shaken, grabbed the demon nearest to him. Clearly infuriated, he crushed the demon and threw it into the others gathered at his feet.

"Quiet!" he blasted.

The silence that followed seemed like an eternity. Finally, Azazal mumbled in almost an unintelligible voice. "It must be Him. It must be the King of Hosts…" But why? Why would he himself come to this city? His thoughts lingered as the demons reassembled waiting for their next order. Azazal immediately sent two of his fastest messengers to go for reinforcements, as most of his army had just been instantly destroyed. They flew off, away from the city remembering to fly low. Grabbing two of his sentinels, Azazal commanded them to find out exactly where the light had come from.

"But Master," screeched the two sentinels. "The light…the light will destroy us."

"Go you stupid fools!" screamed Azazal. "Go, get out of my sight," as he lunged forward to grab them. But they took off before Azazal could finish his command. As they flew to the top of the hill, the light struck their wings. Before they could redirect themselves down, they were burnt to a crisp. Azazal went crazy, frothing at the mouth and screaming out every obscenity he knew. All the time trying to grab and stomp on demons who were now scattering in all directions.

Of course, no living creature had even seen the light. No one, except for the demons and the Lord's Angelic Guardians who now surrounded the house. Angels of all sizes and ranks. Most dominant were what appeared to be military angels, dressed in various suits of armor with huge swords firmly grasped in their hands. Clearly, no demon would ever think of approaching the house, not to mention the town, as long as the Lord of Hosts was present.

"Joshua," the Lord repeated, *"It is I... Jesus. Do not be afraid."* Slowly the light faded, and Josh could clearly see the Lord.

"Come sit with me. I have much to tell you."

Although Josh was shaken, a deep feeling of peace came upon him. Getting to his feet, he approached Jesus and immediately fell to his knees.

"Please Jesus, forgive me. I'm not worthy to be here in your presence. I'm just a sinner. Just a simple person."

"Please Lord..." he began to say, when Jesus interrupted him. Reaching for his hand and helping him to his feet, a calmness that Josh had never felt before came upon him.

"Was it you Lord, who I saw so many years ago when I was just a kid sitting in church?"

Smiling, Jesus said, *"Yes Joshua, it was I."*

Josh sat on his couch, pushing aside pillows and some clothes that were usually collected there. The Lord likewise sat on a chair close to him, took his hand and began to talk.

"I have heard your prayers and many others."

Josh was not listening. He couldn't help staring at Him. All that was going through his mind was how human Jesus looked. How beautiful His face was and how calming His blue-green eyes were. Actually, Josh thought He looked almost exactly like a famous portrait he had seen years ago. Jesus was wearing what appeared to be an off-white cotton homespun hooded shirt, similar to what we call a sweatshirt, loose slacks of the same color, and sandals completed His wardrobe.

It was then that Josh noticed the wounds clearly visible on His feet and the nail holes in His hands. A shudder of sadness rushed over Josh as he involuntarily pulled his own hand away from Jesus.

"Don't be sad, my son. My sufferings were for you and for all people who believe in me. Now, are you ready to listen?

"There is much to tell you and much to ask of you. There is so much evil in this world. Men and women have sinned and have given into temptation. Governments are corrupt. Many in the holy city of Rome have succumbed to Satan's temptations. Much immorality is taking place all over the world. Many priests have fallen and are committing atrocities of abuse and sexual pleasures. Men have mocked the saints, mocked me and my Mother.

"Churches have been desecrated and burned to the ground. False idols and prophets have been venerated and worshiped. Satanic rituals are taking place throughout the world. And yet, even the messages and appeals through the many apparitions I have given to the world have been scorned and disregarded by many. Yes, even the Miracle of the Sun at Fatima, documented and witnessed by over one hundred thousand people, was denied by many, and now almost forgotten.

"My Mother and I have been warning of these dangers and have been pleading for repentance for decades. Our hearts bleed with sadness, yet these sins

continue. We weep for the millions and millions of babies who have been aborted and robbed of their precious lives."

Josh continued to stare at Jesus as tears began to well up in his eyes.

"Now the time has come for Judgement. Yet, my Mother pleads with me to give this world one last chance to repent and to accept my love. Had it not been for her and for the many prayers and rosaries that have been offered up for the repentance of sinners, this world would now be under my Judgement." Jesus wiped the tears from Josh's eyes. Then, to Josh's surprise, He took his hand and held it tight.

"I have accepted my Mother's plea and have decided to give the world one more chance to change their ways. Therefore, I have come to you. I am asking you to deliver my final message to all of mankind. It is my hope, my final plea, the last chance for men and women to repent, to put aside their evil ways and to unify my Church with love." Releasing Josh's hand, Jesus stood up.

"It is my hope for all to be with me in Paradise, yet so many have refused my invitation. So many have turned from me and have embraced darkness. My Church remains divided, which offends and hurts me."

Jesus looked closely into Josh's eyes.

"Will you accept this cross and deliver this final message to all who will listen?"

Josh was clearly shaken, with tears again welling up in his eyes.

"Oh Lord, of course I will do anything you ask, but... but how? How will I ever be able to help anyone to repent when so many have already refused to listen? Who am I Lord? I am nobody. I'm..." Jesus interrupted Josh before he could finish.

"I have chosen you before you were born. I have watched you grow and turn from evil time and time again. I honor the rosary that you and your mother have said every day. You are my choice and that is all you need to know."

Josh remembered how faithful Mary was when she was asked to be the Mother of God.

"I will do whatever you ask of me," Josh said in a soft voice. "But Lord, I need your help. Please help me, and...where do I begin?"

"You begin with this city. Satan is using it to launch his attack against my Church. Once it is under his control, he will use it to conceal his plans to convert and deceive many seminarians and priests into his evil ways, not only in this city but throughout the world."

Jesus stood up and slowly walked to the window. His light was still bursting forth from His presence.

"Joshua," said Jesus as He turned to face him. *"This will be no easy task. You will suffer much. It will be a heavy cross that will be hard to carry. You will be attacked by many, by evil spirits and Satan himself. You will be shunned and called the antichrist. It is for this reason that I will empower you with my Holy Spirit which will protect you and enable you to prevail against all the powers of hell."* Jesus moved closer to Josh and sat down next to him on the couch.

"I will have two of my most powerful warriors surround you with their protection. Their names are Kapriel and Lancer. They will be with you always. Nothing will be able to destroy them, nor will any harm befall you, so long as you are surrounded by their protection. In times of danger, stand close to them, as you will be surrounded by an invisible shield that Satan

PROLOGUE

himself will not be able to penetrate. This will infuriate evil and cause them to attack you with other strategies."

"Be aware of those that will have a red glowing mist around their head. Only you and your guardians will be able to see it. No man, no evil spirit, not even Satan will be aware of this mark. This gift will allow you to see those sinners who belong to Satan and are under his control. Be aware that they will be difficult to help. Nevertheless, it is my desire that all, even these sinners, will repent and accept my love. Do not divulge your knowledge of this mark to anyone, lest it be ineffective."

Jesus continued as Josh sat listening carefully to every word.

"There is one more gift that I will give you. Use it wisely, as many will condemn you because of it. As I empowered my apostles to heal, I also empower you with this gift. Ask anything in my name and it will be given to you. Use it only for the purpose of saving souls, for the purpose of strengthening faith, and to help the unbelievers believe that my message is real... Again, use this gift wisely so that souls will be saved and converted."

Josh continued to sit, although in a state of almost disbelief, trying to absorb everything the Lord had said. For a long time, he could not speak or perhaps did not want to speak. Finally, he found enough courage and began to ask all sorts of questions.

"Jesus, what about Satan and all his evil spirits around this place, and around the world? How do I deal with that?"

Jesus answered with a smile and with a commanding voice.

"Prayer and repentance will crush this evil. Therefore, I am pleading one last time for men to change

their ways. You must lead them back to me. You must give them hope. And you must show them the love and mercy I have for everyone.

"Tell them to repent and to change their evil ways. Teach them the power of prayer. Unify men and my Church that I established so long ago. Too many have broken away from it. Again, my son, this will not be an easy task. Men's hearts are hardened and often blind to truth. I will give you insight into many things that will help you accomplish these tasks. Remember to trust in me always, especially when darkness is present and when hope seems impossible. And know that I will be with you always."

Suddenly the Lord's voice changed to a stern and commanding tone.

"Remember to tell all men that Judgement is near...Very near..."

Josh asked many other questions, many of which Jesus answered and many of which Josh was told that it was not for him to know. In all cases, Jesus answered with a loving and caring voice, assuring Josh that he had nothing to fear and that his protection would be with him always. Hours passed, but time appeared to be non-existent. After all was said, Josh moving closer to the Lord, placed his head on Jesus's lap and quietly fell asleep.

There were no dreams, no nightmares, as he usually had, no worries, no anxiety. Nothing, except peaceful sleep.

With that, the great light was gone.

PROLOGUE

CHAPTER I

The Beginning

(22 Years Earlier)

Joshua Donovan was born on January 12th, in the year 2019, in the small, quiet town of Jinksville, South Carolina. At one time, Jinksville had a population of about 25,000 people. Today, due to the declining economy and closing of many businesses, there are less than 6,000 people left, most of which have lived in Jinksville all of their lives.

Prior to 2017, it was a typical small town, with busy streets, Walmart shopping, several hair salons, barber shops, several movie theaters, coffee shops, and numerous bars, pubs, and restaurants. Of course, Jinksville also had all the public services one would expect to find in any town or city, such as schools, fire, hospitals, postal, sanitary, and public word services. Today, unfortunately, it is quite different, with few businesses and shops left. Those that are left have been reduced in size and personnel.

CHAPTER I

Mathew Donovan worked for the Jinksville Postal Service and was one of the few postal men left who preferred to walk his daily route. Knowing just about everyone in town, he was affectionately known as "Matty," and always had a lollipop or a piece of candy for the many kids that greeted him.

"Here comes the mailman, go out and get the mail," one of the neighbors said to her two boys who were waiting anxiously by the window. Opening the door, they ran out to greet Matty.

"Well, there, how are you guys doing?" Matty asked. Without waiting for an answer, he handed them two envelopes. "These are for mom," and reaching into his candy bag for two lollipops, "and these are for you." Looking up he waved to Mrs. Simpson as she waved back, all the time continuing onward for his next delivery.

Josh's mother, Joan Donovan, worked part time in the Wilcox General Store, the only one in town still in business since the pandemic hit in the early 20's. Unfortunately, the town, like so many in the country, had been devastated by Covid-19, and all the shutdowns, which caused so many businesses to close and so many people to seek more lucrative business opportunities elsewhere.

Joan was a real gem for Peter Wilcox, who owned the store. He lost his wife several years ago to cancer and depended heavily on Joan who practically ran the entire place. Although she worked long hours and was not paid very much, she was nevertheless thankful that she was one of the lucky few who still had a job. Despite the hardships caused by the pandemic, Matty and Joan Donovan remained in Jinksville, and weathered out their difficulties as best they could.

When Josh was six, his parents enrolled him in St. Ann's Catholic Grammar School. Being their only child, they had saved for years to afford this expense. From the time Josh entered school, it was obvious that he was above average.

As a first grader, he could read and spell at the third-grade level. Additionally, to the amazement of his teachers, he could recite the "Hail Mary" and the "Our Father" without missing a word. Of course, Josh was no stranger to these prayers, as his mother began to teach him how to pray from a very young age. She would say the words and he would repeat them until he eventually knew them by heart.

By the time Josh was seven and in second grade, he could say the entire rosary, although at this age he did not know all the mysteries associated with each decade or fully understand the meaning of each prayer. As time went on, he and his mother would say the rosary together every night, although sometimes, especially after a hard day at school, Josh would fall asleep with the beads still in his hand. Whenever this happened, his mother would assure him that his angel would always finish it for him.

Josh continued to outshine and surpass his classmates. Although only in second grade, Josh could now read at a six-grade level. He was exceptionally good at spelling and soon became the second-grade spelling bee champ.

Unlike most of the kids, Josh loved his religious class, as he knew by heart most of the prayers being taught. On one occasion, Sister Margaret called Josh into her office. Meeting him at her office door, she said,

"Joshua, I hear you can say the rosary all by yourself. Is that true?" Josh nodded his head, acknowledging he could.

"Well, that's wonderful. And who taught you all the prayers you know?"

Josh, not paying too much attention to her question and concentrating more on the fish tank in the corner of her

CHAPTER I

office, mumbled in a soft voice, "My mommy. We say prayers every night. Daddy does sometimes too."

Sister Margaret led Josh over to her desk, and after he sat down asked,

"What else does Mommy teach you?"

"Mommy teaches me to be good in church and not to talk." Then, looking back at the fish tank, he continued, "and when the priest holds up the bread, that is the best part."

"What do you mean that is the best part?" Sister Margaret asked. Josh turned and directly looked at Sister Margaret.

"Mommy says that this is when Jesus comes to us."

Sister Margaret smiled. "Is there anything else your Mommy teaches you?"

"Oh yes," Josh replied in an exciting voice. "Mommy teaches me how to read in my books, we sing songs, and spell words…and I know prayers to say before we eat. Daddy plays ball with me, and I can catch now. Daddy also lets me help him build stuff in his shop. Daddy's helping me build a sailboat so I can sail it in the creek this summer."

"Oh, how nice," replied Sister Margaret.

Smiling, she reached for a piece of candy from the bowl on her desk and handed it to him. "Thank you, Joshua…you can go back to your classroom now."

Just before leaving her office, he suddenly turned and blurted out, "I can also say the Pledge of Allegiance!"

Nodding her head to approve, she replied in a kind voice, "That's wonderful…that's wonderful Josh."

"Can I come back and look at the fish?"

"You certainly can. Would you like to feed the fish for me every day?" Josh broke out into a huge smile and nodded vigorously.

"Good," Sister Margaret said. "Come by every day before you eat lunch."

The Donovan's always attended Mass at St. Ann's Church every Sunday, followed by a delicious breakfast at IHOP. This was a tradition that would go on for many years. Joan was more religious than her husband, or at least she appeared to be, perhaps because of her openness with prayer. She was always praying for some special cause or for someone in need. She attended morning Mass every day, prior to work, and always brought Joshua, even as an infant, along with her. When Josh started school, he was still able to continue to go to Mass with her, as Mass ended at 7:30 AM, which still left thirty minutes to spare before school started. This practice would continue all throughout his schooling and well into most of his adult life.

Josh told Sister Margaret that he was taught to be on his very best behavior whenever he was in church. His parents insisted that when he was in church, he was to respect others by not talking and not to cause any kind of disturbance. By the time Josh was six, he was pretty sure what was expected of him.

On the second Sunday of Easter, the Feast of Divine Mercy, toward the very end of Mass, while Josh was sitting quietly in his pew, something caught his eye at the front of the church. Standing up on the kneeler and stretching his neck trying to get a better view, he began to stare intensely at the statue of Jesus just to the side of the altar.

It was a common statue that can be found in many churches, especially ones built in the earlier years. This was the typical Jesus statue, long hair and beard, red and white robes, standing with his head bowed down, with his hands and palms outstretched to his sides. Josh's mother, noticing him staring at the statue, gently pulled him down to his seat and quietly reminded him to pay attention.

CHAPTER I

"But, mommy," Josh replied, "Jesus is smiling at me." Joan pulled Josh closer to her and whispered,

"I know Josh, Jesus smiles at all of us."

"No mommy, he's looking at me...and smiling! Jesus is looking at me...Mommy look!" And with that, Josh stood up on the pew and pointed directly to the statue. "Jesus is smiling at me," shouting loud enough that most everyone heard him.

Almost instantly, people looked at the statue and then immediately back to Josh who was still pointing. To them, the statue had not changed and still showed its sad expression on its face.

Joan and Matty were mortified. Some of their friends that were sitting close to them were smiling to assure them not to worry. Jenny Preston, one of Joan's best friends who happened to be sitting next to her, gently grabbed her hand and assured her not to worry.

"It's no big thing. You know kids. He's just a child," she said

Joan smiled back with a nod but could not hide her embarrassment. Of course, not everyone was smiling, especially Father Baxter, who was celebrating the Mass. No, he wasn't smiling at all, nor was Josh's father who was yanking Josh down to his seat as fast as he could. Leaning over close enough to bite off Josh's ear, Matty said,

"Not another word...not another word...hear me!"

After the final blessing, Matty grabbed Josh by the arm and practically dragged him out of the church. Once everyone had passed and said their polite hello's, Matty knelt with his face almost touching Josh's.

"Listen to me," his father said in a stern voice. "Jesus loves all of us and smiles at all of us. Do you understand?" But before Josh could answer, getting angrier, Matty stood up and continued,

"I never want you to disrupt anyone in Mass again. Not ever again. Never! Jesus smiles at us from Heaven, not from statues. Do you understand me?"

With tears in his eyes, all Josh could do was to nod his head up and down, acknowledging what his father had said. Josh knew his father's anger, especially his rule about not disturbing anyone in church. Beginning to cry, he huddled behind his mother's dress.

"Don't be too hard on him Matty," his mother pleaded. "Remember he's only seven, and you know the imagination seven year old's have."

Matty looked at Josh, then back to Joan.

"Well. Well, he's almost eight, but I suppose you're right…" Looking back at Josh, he confirmed his words. "But never again, understand?"

It wasn't so much of a question, but more of a command. And Josh knew it. The anger in his father's face faded, and as far as Matty was concerned that was the end of it. Little did he know that was just the beginning. As Josh walked slowly to the car, he knew that whether he ever saw the statue smile and look at him again, he would never tell anyone about it. And he never did.

Several small red bloodshot eyes were fixed on Josh as they tried to decipher what had just taken place. Of course, they were not in church when all this happened, as too many angelic angels and guardians were present. It was then that they noticed something very unusual.

Following the people out of the church was a large band of angels and guardians who were now surrounding Josh and his family.

"What's going on?" Jarell asked his companion. Denzil, the larger of the two demons, simply shrugged his shoulders as if to say, "I have no clue." Each demon looked dumbfounded as they had never witnessed this before. The question lingered for some time. Finally,

CHAPTER I

Denzil spoke. "Get closer to them and see if you can hear anything."

Dodging between parked cars, trees, and shrubs like a black mist passing through and around these objects, Jarell stopped just close enough to hear. Unfortunately for him, he was almost instantly spotted by two guardians. The angels drew their swords to attack, but before they could strike, the demon flew off like a slingshot, not daring to look back to check if he was being followed.

"What did you hear?" asked Denzil.

"Not much," replied the smaller one, completely out of breath and thankful that he had not been pursued by the two guardians.

"But I heard his father scold him. Not sure what all the fuss was about but something about Jesus smiling, and I think I heard something about a statue."

"A statue..." repeated Denzil. "Doesn't make sense... but still all these guardians...something is up. We best tell Belzar about this," the larger one said, as they flew off to report their findings.

Belzar was a high-ranking demon who oversaw all the towns in this area of the country. In fact, Belzar once served under Azazel until he was promoted due to his cunningness, deception, and effectiveness in causing souls to fall. Priests and seminarians were his specialty. In fact, he had already deceived two priests from the Archdiocese of Virginia since the time of his promotion.

It took almost twenty minutes for the two demons to find Belzar, as he was nowhere in the vicinity.

"Master, master," the demons screeched out as they reached the cave where Belzar had stationed himself along with some of his generals, captains, and numerous field sentinels.

"Well, what do you two screw-ups want?" Belzar asked. But before they could answer, he continued, "I told you to stay in that lousy town until I returned with more sentinels."

"But master!"

"But what?" screamed Belzar.

"Well…" Denzil hesitantly said, "There was a host of angels and warriors coming out of the church today. They surrounded the Donovan kid and his family."

"And? What about it?" Belzar asked, annoyed at their hesitance.

"We've never seen anything like it," replied the smaller demon in his squeaky voice. "I heard them talk about Jesus smiling and something about statues."

Immediately after he said this, both demons began to tremble, feeling quite stupid and seeing the anger beginning to well up on Belzar's face.

"You left your post to tell me about smiles and a statue," Belzar hissed.

Having trouble controlling himself, with slime and sulfur frothing from his mouth, he commanded,

"Get back to that town NOW you fools!" But before the two demons had a chance to fly back, they heard,

"WAIT! WAIT."

Slowly Belzar walked around them in a circle. Eventually he sat down, silent. All eyes were fixed on him. Finally, looking at the two demons, he gestured with his finger for them to approach him. As they walked cautiously closer, Belzar asked,

"Who is this Donovan kid?"

Brief silence, then the larger demon said,

"We don't know. He's nobody special, but he goes to church every day."

Belzar slowly looked up and appeared somewhat interested. "Every day…! He goes to church every single day," he thought to himself.

"How old is this kid?" Belzar asked aloud.

CHAPTER I

Immediately Jarell, the smaller of the two, answered anxiously, "seven years old," glad to finally provide an answer.

"Seven...you said seven years old...?"

"SEVEN YEARS OLD," Belzar repeated in an almost an unintelligible voice. Now the sulfur and slime were freely flowing. His eyes widened to reveal a deep red-yellow color and his nostrils flared open as if he was not getting enough air.

"You idiots...you idiots!" he screamed out. "Why do I always have so many idiots serving me?"

The two demons began to step back away from Belzar, clearly recognizing the fury he was expressing toward them. Turning, they began to run to avoid Belzar's grasp.

"He's no threat to me! You idiots! Not at his age. Tell me about him when he has hair on his balls. Now, get back to that stinking town and continue to destroy souls."

Embarrassed and mortified in front of the rest of the demon sentinels, they flew away as fast as they could, all the time cursing Belzar for making them look like fools.

"He'll be sorry for that," Denzil screamed out to the smaller one. "Just you wait and see. He'll be sorry."

Once they left, Belzar began to calm down, releasing the nervous tension from all the others still watching him. Sitting down, he finally broke from his irritated disposition and blurted out in a mocking tone,

"Seven years old. Smiles and statues..." With that he began to laugh and was quickly joined by all the other fools.

Years passed, and Josh grew in size, strength, and looks. By the time he was in eighth grade, he was quite a handsome boy. Brownish-blond hair and a fantastic build for an eighth grader. He could thank his father for that, as they would run together for at least five miles, every Saturday. Additionally, they faithfully worked out daily with the weight set that Josh received on his tenth birthday.

Josh had remained faithful to his prayers and attended daily Mass. He would often sit in front of the statue of Jesus, but no one ever paid very much attention to him. The exception was when he received his First Holy Communion and his Confirmation. These were the only times that he brought attention to himself. His parents and Father Baxter noticed that he was intensely staring at the statue of Jesus for an exceptionally long period of time, but unlike the first time when he brought so much attention to it, he never said a word to anyone, nor did anyone say anything to him. Nor did they have to, as they could clearly see the broad smile on his face.

Josh never forgot to say his rosary, now fully comprehending the meaning of each mystery, and understanding the significance of each prayer. Often, he found himself saying two rosary's a day, one immediately after morning Mass and the other after dinner, along with his mother. All too often, it was Joan, not Josh, who would now fall asleep with the rosary beads in her hand.

Josh had noticed that something was not quite right with her. She appeared to always be tired and had reduced the amount of social work she was involved in. Nevertheless, she continued working at the Wilcox General Store and for the most part, her daily routine appeared normal. Matty, on the other hand, was never more fit and active than ever before in his life. Every Saturday, before his run with Josh, he would help Joan out by unloading suppliers delivered to the Wilcox Store. As time went on, it became harder and harder for Joan to do heavy lifting. She often had to use a pole with squeeze fingers to reach items high on the shelves.

Mr. Wilcox, now in his eighties, only came to the store to say hello and distribute paychecks. Joan had hired her

CHAPTER I

friend Jenny Preston, several years back, to help take up the slack since Mr. Wilcox was no longer able to work. Between Joan, Jenny, and Josh helping part time and now Matty's help, they appeared to be doing just fine, except for worrying about the future of their employment once Mr. Wilcox passed.

In one aspect, eighth grade was relatively sad for Josh and for all those who worked and taught at St. Ann's Grammar School. This was the last year before the Archdiocese closed the school due to lack of monetary funding and the decline of available nuns to help run the school. Eight years ago, almost every grade was taught by the good sisters. Unfortunately, there were only two left, with all other grades being taught by lay teachers.

Additionally, it was upsetting to the congregation, as their pastor, Father Baxter, was retiring. He had been pastor of St. Ann's for the past fourteen years. Father Dennis would take over his position as of July 1st. Father Hugh, fresh out of the Sacred Heart Seminary, located in Clarksville, N.Y. arrived four months ago to fill in the void. When he arrived, he was warmly greeted by Fathers Baxter and Dennis, as well as by all the staff, including old Mrs. Bogart, who did all the cooking for the priests.

"Well, if you'll excuse me," she said after first meeting Fr. Hugh, "I have to attend dinner." With that, she briskly walked away thinking to herself, "Strange...I don't think I like him. Besides he smells like sulfur."

Father Baxter also felt somewhat uneasy. Something just didn't seem right with Fr. Hugh. He appeared to be somewhat distant. Somewhat different. For one thing, he didn't even take the time to pop his head into the church when he arrived, nor was he the least bit interested or impressed with Father's Baxter's Garden or the magnificent cross that was sculptured in Italy.

In fact, the only thing Father Hugh showed any interest in was his desire to train and coordinate the Altar Boy Program.

Little did they realize that evil had just stepped into St. Ann's. Evil that had just arrived from an evil seminary.

No doubt that the declining economy and the continuing effects of Covid-19 were critical factors in the schools closing and in the decline of church attendance and financial support. The less obvious reason for all this occurring was the satanic attacks taking place all over the city. Most especially were the attacks toward the church and particularly those against the youth.

These demonic attacks were having a devastating effect on the city, especially on those who had little or no faith to begin with. Most obvious were the effects of the lies, deception, and sexual temptations that were targeted on the teens, and most especially on those attending high school.

To make matters worse, there were reports of sexual abuse taking place in the church with some altar boys. Although no names were ever mentioned and the reports were very sketchy, any concern went directly to Father Hugh, who assured that these allegations would be thoroughly investigated. Father Baxter, now in his late seventies, had absolutely no clue that this was occurring, nor did Father Dennis.

Year by year, more and more demons had descended on the town of Jinksville. Denzel and Jarell, who had reported to Belzar years ago about Josh, were now too busy to worry about him. They had been promoted to a higher rank, as they had proven to be quite effective in coordinating attacks on young kids and the many drunks that could be found throughout the town. Their strategy was to constantly bombard the kids with demons of immorality, deaf and dumbness, deception, lust, and

CHAPTER I

fornication. By constantly attacking them, they hoped that the kids would succumb to their sexual desires. All they really had to do was to convince one or two to succumb and the rest would follow, as they knew how effective peer pressure could be.

As for all those poor souls that had succumbed to alcohol, they were mercilessly attacked by specialty demons. The demons of alcohol and despair were extremely successful. Already over the past three years, a half dozen souls had taken their own lives.

Despite the hard times that most businesses were experiencing, four bars, two pubs, and one night club remained open. And not only open but thriving. One did not have to look far to find some drunk passed out laying on some sidewalk or another hulled close to a fire burning in an empty oil drum, totally intoxicated and surrounded by swarms of black figures dodging all around them. Especially upsetting was the large number of high school kids that frequented these places. Making the almighty dollar was always the reason why these establishments looked the other way when it came to underage drinking.

"Let them in," whispered the demons of deception and greed. "After all, these kids need some kind of release and won't cause any trouble."

The demons continued to whisper in the ears of those checking ID's.

"Besides…the more people in this place, the happier you will make your boss…he doesn't care …all he wants is to keep this place open and to make money." Greed chimed in. "And don't forget, the more people in this place, the more tips you will make…Let the kids in…let them in…"

Of particular sadness was the fact that no one seemed to care. Not one adult, not any of the owners, not the police, who often stopped in to have a drink or two after their shift was over, and not even some parents who apparently had little concern as to what their kids were up to.

Mack's Bar and Grill was especially frequented by many of the high school seniors. Every Friday night, you could always find the regulars drinking themselves silly until eventually piling into someone's pick-up truck, speeding through town, yelling, and carrying on as if they had no worry in the world or could care less about anyone or anything.

Saturday night was another story. Not only was this the place to go, but a great hang out for underage kids wanting to drink, dance, and have a good time. Mack Robinson, a single father and owner of the place, would always have a D.J. from nine to midnight on Saturday nights. By the time nine rolled around, you could always find dozens of students along with the senior jocks of the school, lining up at the bar ordering beer to take back to the tables where their girlfriends were eagerly waiting for them.

Music was loud and dancing was popular. Not only popular but close…very, very close, and encouraged as if there was a contest going on. All the time being supervised by dozens of red glowing eyes watching their every move.

Theodore John Robinson, T.J., as they all called him, was Mack's son, and was the quarterback for the high school football team. He was no stranger to his dad's bar. Matter of fact, Mack encouraged T.J. and his football friends to hang out and to drink there, as opposed to somewhere else. He felt that if they were going to drink anyway, why not at his place where he could more easily keep an eye on them.

Of course, this brought smiles to the warped faces of the many demons dodging in and out of the place. Successful were the demons of Confusion, Deception, and

CHAPTER I

Lies. Their influence had been quite effective in messing up Mack's mind and rationalization.

Additionally, because Mack himself was almost always drunk, he had little to no idea what was going on at his bar, not to mention what his son was up to. Needless to say, drinking was a problem in the town of Jinksville.

Father Baxter, now in the early stages of Parkinson's, was often found asleep in his office. Nevertheless, he remained fairly active, spending a lot of time instructing Father Dennis on everything that had to be done, especially on the financial situation of the school and church.

It was on a sunny June day, just a few weeks after Josh had graduated from eighth grade, and one week before Father Baxter left St. Ann's for his retirement, that he invited Josh to join him for prayer in his private garden. Father Baxter referred to the garden as his "Holy Place" to pray. Josh was thrilled just to be able to enter the garden, as it was off limits to most everyone except for the holy sisters, the priests, and of course the gardener, who also served as custodian for the church and school. The garden was located between the back of the church and the side of the rectory, accessible from either entrance from both buildings and from the huge iron gates located at the far north end. The garden was absolutely beautiful, enclosed between the two buildings, surrounded by an eight-foot stone wall, matching the same stone on the church and on the rectory.

Throughout the garden and along its pathways were gorgeous colorful flowers of all kinds. But the highlight of the garden was a ten-foot cross of Jesus, located at its center. A quick glance of the statue would lead anyone to believe that the figure hanging on the cross was real. It was donated by a wealthy parishioner, who had it custom made by a famous sculptor in Italy and shipped to the parish eighty-two years ago when the church was built. Surrounding the cross were beautiful red roses that Father Baxter planted when he first came to the parish and personally cared for. Directly in front and close to the cross was a kneeler, and behind that was a hand carved wooden bench where he would sit for hours praying.

"Come sit with me," Father Baxter said to Josh. "Let's say a few prayers together for Father Hugh, our new priest."

"Sure," Josh replied.

After saying a prayer or two, Father Baxter turned to face Josh. "What do you think about going to public school next year?"

"Well... since St. Ann's doesn't have a high school, I guess I don't have much of a choice. Guess it will be ok."

Father Baxter put his hand on Josh's shoulder. "Listen son. You know there will be all kinds of people you will meet. Some good, some not so good. Most won't have the faith and prayer convictions you have, so, well...don't get discouraged if you find some who don't believe as you do. Most importantly," he continued, "try not to be pulled into things, especially things that might pull you away from the Lord. You know what I mean Josh, sex and all that stuff."

"I know Father. I'll be careful," as he glanced up at the cross. They sat for a while not speaking. Finally, Father Baxter broke the silence.

"Josh, have you ever thought about becoming a priest?"

Josh mumbled out a little nervous chuckle. "Father, I'm... I'm not holy enough to become a priest."

"What do you mean you're not holy enough? You say your prayers, you go to church, you hardly ever get into trouble. Not real trouble that is. Of course you can become a priest. Listen to me Josh, one doesn't have to be holy as

CHAPTER I

the saints to be a priest. You just need to love God and be willing to serve Him. Do you know what I mean?"

"I guess so," replied Josh. "I'm willing to do all that and I really love Jesus but sometimes I really screw up."

"What do you mean you screw up?"

Josh was a little embarrassed but had no difficulty talking to Father. "Sex...Sometimes I sin."

"Josh, we all are sinners, every one of us."

"Yeah, I know...but, I mean...well...sometimes I think about sexual things, sometimes I fool around with myself...you know what I mean. I've told you about this in confession."

Father Baxter put his hand on Josh's shoulder. "Don't ever let that stop you from serving the Lord. He certainly understands and especially understands, at your age...you're just a young boy experiencing many changes in your life and body that are absolutely normal." Taking a quick breath, he continued.

"Now I'm not giving you a green light with all of this, remember God wants us to try to be our very best always, but He certainly understands that we will sometimes mess up. That's why He suffered and died for all of us and why He is so merciful. So don't be too hard on yourself, ok?"

"You know Josh, a lot of people believe that holiness is just living a life without sinning, or at least without much sin in their lives. That's true, but it's much more than that. I believe that holiness is also when a sinner is willing to repent every time they screw up. Always picking themselves up, time and time again, no matter how many times they mess up. That's the really hard thing to do. It's easy to despair, to give up or not even care. Try not to get discouraged, but to keep picking yourself up time and time again. And...I think that's what makes a person a saint, and in reality, what makes us holy."

Josh listened intently. Finally, he said to Father Baxter, holding back his tears, "I will really miss you Father."
"Me too Josh, me too."

Unable to control the tears flowing down his cheeks, he hugged Father Baxter, as he knew the elderly priest was very sick.

"Thanks for letting me pray with you in this garden." Josh stood up and slowly began walking toward the gate.

"Any time, any time. Oh, by the way, I've told Fr. Dennis that you can pray here anytime you want."
"Thanks Father, it will always remind me of you."
"Now, don't forget to think about the priesthood."

"I won't forget, I think I would really like that." Just before Josh reached the gate, Father Baxter yelled out,

"Josh, by the way...Did you really see the statue of Jesus smile and look at you so many years ago?"

Josh stopped dead in his tracks. Turning to face Father, he said,

"What do you think?" Waiting a few seconds, Father Baxter replied,
"Yes, I think so."

Josh looked intently at his old friend and simply smiled with an expression that lit up his face. Then he turned and left without saying a word, nor did he have to, as the answer was plastered all over his face. Closing the gates, Josh walked away, and that was the last time he would ever see Father Baxter alive again.

CHAPTER II

JINKSVILLE PUBLIC SCHOOL

By the time Josh was 15 and entering into ninth grade, St. Ann's Grammar School was converted into a small hospital and ambulance center to serve the people of Jinksville and the people in the neighboring towns. The church remained open as did the rectory. The convent, located next to the church on Elm Street, also remained the property of the Archdiocese and was turned into a shelter for the homeless.

Jinksville Public High School included grades nine through twelve. The school was located almost directly across from St. Ann's Church, separated by a two-lane highway…if it could even be called that, as few cars and trucks now traveled it due to the construction on Route13. In fact, due to its infrequent use and its deteriorating condition, it was now referred to by most everyone in town as "Pothole Road."

When Josh entered ninth grade, he was as excited as ever. He was looking forward to meeting new teachers, changing classes each hour, and especially meeting new friends. Now that he didn't have friends as St. Ann's, but

CHAPTER II

because he just wanted to make new ones and probably more so, because he carried the stigma from his experience with the statue with him throughout grammar school. Josh was not embarrassed at all about this. In fact, he always felt that he was so fortunate and blessed, even though no one believed him. As far as everyone else was concerned, he had simply made up the story about the statue to get attention. He recognized later that most of his classmates at St. Ann's were not very friendly toward him. Perhaps some disliked him because he was well liked by all the nuns and priests. Perhaps they thought that he was somehow above them. Perhaps they simply were jealous, especially about his experience with the statue. In any case, he was looking forward to new experiences and making new friends.

Rebecca Flowers had taken a liking to Josh the first day she met him in home room, as he took a liking to her too. They had sat next to each other and were partners in Chemistry class, and over time they would become good friends. That was just fine with Josh. Friends were what he wanted, nothing serious. Just good friends.

One of the first things Josh noticed about public school was the total lack of prayer or religion. This should have been obvious to him, but after eight years of beginning every school day with a prayer and seeing a crucifix in every room, it was a little hard for him to adjust.

To compensate, while in home room waiting for his first class to begin, Josh would reach into his pocket, hold his rosary, and say a little prayer to himself. "Dear God, this is a new day, a new beginning and a new commitment to you. Please bless me and this day, Amen."

Josh loved his classes and loved all the new experiences he was exposed to. But as he walked the halls, getting familiar with the school's layout and poking his head into the various rooms that he was going to have classes in, he felt somewhat uneasy. Something wasn't quite right, and he thought he smelled something putrid, although he had no clue what it was. Little did he know that the school was infested with demons perched on every ledge or railing throughout the school. Most flew around following any student that was an easy target.

Large demon sentinels guarded the outside entrances. They would report to the demons inside as to how many angelic angels had entered the school each day and were ready to battle if any real danger came upon them. Denzil and Jarell were made aware of what was going on at the school and were constantly planning new cunning attacks on those students who would be most susceptible. So long as there was an angel protecting a student, the demons were helpless to interfere, unless some kid would falter and give into some temptation. Sex was the greatest weapon they used against so many young and vulnerable kids. And it showed, as so many had black demons clinging to their backs, with their fangs sunk in deep, rendering their angelic angel guardians helpless.

However, none dared to attack Josh. Coming directly from church, he was carrying Jesus with him, after receiving communion every day. All they could do was to curse him and hope that somehow someone would cause him to falter.

One of the courses Josh signed up for was shop. After explaining all the safety rules and regulations of the shop that everyone had to follow, his instructor pointed out some of the many projects the students could make, none of which interested Josh.

"Mr. Holloway, do you think it would be alright for me to build a picnic table and bench set?" asked Josh.

CHAPTER II

"Son," Mr. Holloway responded, "those kinds of projects are mostly reserved for the older students who have more experience than beginners.

"But Sir," Josh continued, "I'm not a beginner. My father and I have a shop at home, and he's taught me to safely use most tools, even power tools."

His teacher hesitated for a minute. "Well, if you think you're up to it, go for it, but check with me each step of the project, and especially before you use any power tools."

"Ok, I will!" Josh eagerly replied. Thinking to himself, he immediately thanked the Lord. Seeing this exchange, all the kids in the class gathered around Mr. Holloway, each simultaneously begging him to build various projects.

Looking at Josh, Holloway said in a somewhat excited tone, "Now see what special favors cause."

"Ok...Ok...Everyone...Just be patient. I'll get to all of you," he said addressing the class. And he did, spending the rest of the period helping each student with their desired project. Mr. Holloway was thrilled, as he never had so much enthusiasm in his classes before.

Josh had never had Physical Education class in grammar school. At best, they would shoot baskets during recess or just play stupid games. Most of the time they would just hang around until the half hour was up. Needless to say, he was excited to have this new experience, and who wouldn't be at his age.

The first day of gym orientation, he was assigned a locker and a uniform. It was made clear that it was to be worn, whether or not you were participating in activity that day. "Who would not want to participate?" Josh thought to himself. However, he quickly learned that there was a group who always wanted to make trouble, mock someone's ability, bully someone, or better yet, cut class to smoke a joint or two.

Josh was relatively shy, especially undressing in front of anyone. After all, he had never done that before except at home as a very young boy. During his first day of gym, one week later, Josh quickly changed into his gym clothes, as he was excited to get into the gym. However, he purposely put on his gym shorts over his underwear. There was no way he was going to strip naked in front of everyone.

After gym, entering the locker room, he quickly realized that everyone was taking a shower with no concern or embarrassment at all. For the first time in his life, he felt like everyone else and somehow, as he stripped down and joined his classmates in a large open shower, he felt a feeling of normalcy. A normalcy that he had not felt all through grammar school, a normalcy that would allow him to grow and to accept his calling in life.

The demons, who were waiting to pounce on Josh, were infuriated, as they thought he would succumb to their sexual temptations, especially seeing so many naked bodies. After all, they had been successful with others, why not him. But their ideas continued to prove useless against Josh.

Entering his sophomore year, Josh was well liked by most everyone, especially the girls. He had continued to mature, gain strength and muscle, and continued his workout schedule of lifting weights and running each day. He certainly had the body and looks that one would die for. Josh only lived two miles from school. Because his mom was sick and could no longer drive him, he ran the two miles each day. After school, he would lift weights with the guys for a half hour before heading to the Wilcox store for work.

Although Josh had hoped to play football this fall, he realized that it was impossible so long as he had to work.

CHAPTER II

Times were tough and his family needed the extra money. Additionally, any activity after school was not really an option at this time, so long that his mom was sick. Joan had to occasionally miss work which only made matters worse. Unfortunately, she appeared to be getting worse each month.

"The doctors don't know what is wrong with me," or at least that's what she said to Josh. "Just tired...but nothing to worry about."

Josh was no fool, he could read between the lines and see the sad expression on her face that she always had trouble hiding. Matty just sat with his head down and said nothing most of the time. Joan had her good and bad days. Thank God, they were mostly good.

Before long, football season came and went, and so did the school year. There were only two eventful moments that occurred. The first was a fire that broke out in the chemistry lab. No one was hurt, but because of the toxic chemicals, the school was closed for two weeks. Secondly, just before spring break, Philip Cockley ripped open his arm and had to have one hundred and thirty-two stitches. Evidently, just after the second period started, he was running down the empty hallway toward the men's room which was located directly at the end of the hall. Without stopping, he stretched out his arm to push open the door. However, he must have forgotten that the door opened out, not in. Placing his hand on the glass window, located in the middle of the door, his arm went through, cutting it to shreds. Phil was back at school within two weeks, and as you might expect, every window in the men's and women's bathroom doors were boarded up until they could be replaced with solid wood doors.

Over the summer, Joan's cancer appeared to be getting worse. She and Matty had hoped that her treatments would be successful. Remission evidently wasn't going to happen. Josh spent most of his summer home, caring for his mom. Between him, his dad, Jenny, and several other friends, Joan was well cared for.

The Donovan's had always attended early Mass on Sundays. Unfortunately, church was no longer an option for Joan as she was too weak to make the trip. Matty, who was just clearing Joan's breakfast dishes, turned to Josh.

"Why don't you go to the eleven o'clock Mass. No sense both of us missing."

"Ok, think I will." Although he could walk to church, he wanted to drive as it was still new to him. "Can I take the car?"

"Be careful," Joan shouted out in a weak voice.

"I will!" And off he went.

Arriving at Church, with five minutes to spare, his eyes brightened up. Rebecca Flowers was walking into St. Ann's along with her parents.

"Hey Becky," Josh called out, running up to catch her.

"Mom, Dad, this is Josh... You know, my friend from school."

"So glad to meet you," Josh politely said.

"Go ahead in," Becky said to her parents. "We'll find a seat in a minute." Both looked at each other with a surprised look.

"I didn't know you were Catholic?" stammered Josh, but before he could get the words out of his mouth, Becky was saying to him,

"I didn't know you went to this church. I've never seen you here before."

"Yea, I usually go to early Mass."

"Cool," Becky said. "Now we have something else in common."

After Mass, Josh offered to drive Becky home. Before leaving they sat for a while and talked about their new shared experience. Becky did the most talking. She told

CHAPTER II

Josh that her parents had separated some years ago and she was now living with her mother. She said that although she was baptized and raised Catholic, they did not attend church often. On special occasions, her mom and dad would attend church together, although she never did tell Josh what these occasions were. "Weird," Josh thought to himself.

Josh had no hesitation talking about Jesus and the faith he had. However, he never mentioned the statue, the prayer garden, or his desire to someday become a priest.

"I really envy you Josh. You have such a strong faith, I wish I had it."

"You can," Josh eagerly replied. "Jesus gives all of us faith. All we have to do is to be open to it."

Becky felt a little embarrassed. Although she was a Catholic, she really had no idea what he was talking about. "Yeah…but…I don't even know what that means."

Josh did not want to evangelize to her, nor was he going to. Instead, he simply said, "It's really easy. Just be sorry for your sins and put Him in charge…in the center of your life. That's basically it. He'll do all the rest." Little was said as he drove Becky home. Josh could see she was deep in thought.

"Hey, Beck…I have several good books you might want to read. I'll bring them to school with me next week."

"I'd like that…I think I'd like that a lot."

Summer came and went quite fast. He saw Becky as much as he could, and when that was impossible, they would talk for hours on the phone. What had begun as a simple friendship, now was developing into something deeper. Although Josh had not changed his mind about the priesthood, the more he saw Becky, the more confused he became.

There was no doubt about it; he was liking her more and more. There was something about her. Something about her that mesmerized him. He loved her smile, he loved how easy it was to talk to her, to be with her, even if they just sat and studied together without saying a word. Was it something he was inwardly looking for? Was it love? And yet beyond all these feelings, his love for the Lord and his desire to serve Him, never faded.

Junior year arrived. New teachers, new classmates, new courses, and always lots of homework. This year, Josh had two free periods which was great because it allowed him to do his homework at school, leaving him plenty of extra time to help his dad out with mom. The bonus was Becky also shared one of those free periods, giving them time to study together.

Realizing that the football season had already started, Josh was pretty down. He had hoped to be able to join the team this season. He certainly had the ability and skills needed. A favorite pastime of his was to go to Central Park on Sundays with his dad and pass and kick footballs back and forth. This was sort of a tradition they had done since Josh was a very young boy.

One Sunday afternoon, Coach Patterson happened to be driving past Central Park. Out of the corner of his eye, he thought he saw Josh Donovan playing ball with someone. As he slowed his car down, closer observation revealed that it was indeed Josh. However, what caught his attention was how skilled he appeared to be.

When Josh passed the football, he was impressed as to how accurate the pass was. Over and over a perfect spiral in the air. His catching skills were no less impressive, especially when he would "go long" and make a spectacular catch. The icing on the cake was the distance and accuracy of his kicking abilities. "Shit," coach Patterson thought to himself, "he can kick that damn ball further that any of my players can. Hum..." he thought. He'd give T.J., his starting quarterback, a run for his

CHAPTER II

money. After exiting his car, he approached Josh and his father.

"Hi!" Josh yelled out in a loud voice as he spotted and waved to Coach Patterson. When they were close enough to one another, Josh made the introductions.

"This is my father, and dad, this is Coach Patterson. He coaches football and wrestling at school."

"So glad to meet you, Mr. Donovan."

"The pleasure is mine," replied Matty.

Patterson continued, "I happened to be driving by and couldn't help but see you guys playing. Josh, you have some great ability. I don't think I've ever seen someone kick and pass as good as you in a long time."

"Thanks," Josh replied in an embarrassed tone.

"Listen. Next year I'm wondering if you might consider joining," but before he could finish, Josh interrupted.

"Coach, I would love to but…I can't. I have to work after school and on Saturdays."

"Oh," replied Patterson in a surprised and disappointed tone.

Josh's father appeared to be somewhat embarrassed as he knew Josh loved the sport and wanted to play dearly. "He's only working because he knows how desperately we need the extra money," Matty thought to himself. He should play and why not. Every kid should be able to play if they want. Looking at Josh and then back to Patterson, Matty said…

"Coach Patterson, right now things are a little tough at our house. My wife is sick, and things are a little tight financially, but I'll talk to my wife. Perhaps we might be able to work something out."

Patterson, reached for Matty's hand. "So sorry about your wife, but I sure hope you can work something out for Josh. It would be a crime to let his talent go to waste."

Matty, taken back a little, nevertheless smiled as they shook hands and parted. Josh was ecstatic.

"Do you really mean it? What about work? What about the extra money? Would mom have to hire someone else?"

Matty interrupted, "I didn't say yes. I just said we would try. We'll think about it and maybe we can figure something out. Maybe…We'll see. Right now, we have to get back to Mrs. Preston so she can get back to her own place."

Jenny Preston had agreed to stay with Joan while Josh and Matty took a well-deserved break. Getting into the car, Josh couldn't keep the smile off his face, although, deep down, he knew that it was probably impossible. Matty was thinking the same thing. "How will we ever be able to swing this? Damn, I shouldn't have said anything." Quickly glancing over at Josh and seeing the excitement on his son's face, he continued to think, "We just have to make it work."

Every day at school, Josh and Becky would sit together at lunch, along with the rest of the regulars at the table, most of whom were girls.

"Hey lover boy!" T.J. yelled from across the cafeteria. "Come sit with us, or are we not your type?"

Jokes like this caused everyone to laugh, while Josh, embarrassed as he was, would just hold up both hands as if to say "I can't help it…Come rescue me."

Understanding what he was gesturing, T.J. and a few other football players would come and join them, pushing and making room for everyone to sit. The group became regular every day. Sex was a common topic among most of the teens. The guys had little hesitation discussing their so-called "love life," whether it was true or not, and their various personal escapades. The girls weren't as open as the guys were but always eager to listen.

CHAPTER II

Unfortunately, this was a great time for temptation to zero-in on the weakest of the group. Although no one could see them, the lunch table was surrounded by red bloodshot-eyed demons savoring over every word spoken. Josh really loved this time of day and thoroughly enjoyed taking part in all the conversations; but unfortunately for him, these were also some of the times that he felt most uncomfortable and was most vulnerable.

Josh was no prude but was shocked to hear some of what was discussed, and even embarrassed. When topics of sex would arise, he felt tremendous peer pressure to participate. However, he never gave into the dozens of attacks he was receiving and would always make some excuse to leave.

"Where ya going?" T.J. blurted out.

"Nowhere really," Josh said.

"What's the matter, don't you want to listen? Might learn something." Laughter broke out as Josh stood up to leave.

"Actually, no. I don't want to listen and I'm sure you guys can't teach me anything I don't already know."

"Wow." T.J. managed to say, but the smile had left his face along with most of the others.

Becky grabbed him by the arm.

"Wait Josh. They're just messing around," but Josh continued to leave. Becky swung around on her seat to follow him. "Wait up," she yelled. "Wait for me."

"Let him go," someone yelled out. "He's just a pussy. I bet he doesn't even know what he has between his legs," another shouted. Again, laughter broke out.

"Hey, bro…" T.J. yelled as he stood up. "Come on back. We're just joking with you. Come on man, don't be a jerk." But Josh had already left the cafeteria.

Unknown to everyone at school, Josh still attended morning Mass every day. After Mass, he would faithfully

REPARATION: A STORY OF HOPE

visit the garden, and after saying his rosary would hurriedly exit through the gate, crossing Pothole Road with ten minutes to spare before his first class started. He wasn't ashamed, yet he wasn't publicizing it and he did not know what he would ever say if ever confronted about his churchgoing. The other guys were already on his case about him not wanting to talk about sex, and he couldn't handle that situation other than walking away.

Yes, he loved Jesus very much, but, thinking to himself, "How do I tell everyone I hang around with that I'm thinking about becoming a priest. I haven't even told Becky, nor my parents yet... I don't even think the guys in school know I'm Catholic..." Then, mumbling to himself, he said, "No problem in a Catholic School, but here in public school...No way...At least not now."

Becky finally caught up to him.

"Don't pay any attention to them. They're just idiots." Looking at her they both began to laugh.

"Yea, I know, but...I just don't like their filthy mouths. All they want to talk about is sex." Becky nodded in agreement.

"But don't you ever think about it?" she asked.

"Sure, all the time...not really...but...well...I mean sure, I'd like to have sex but I want to wait. If I get married." Josh bit his lip the moment the words came out of his mouth.

"What do you mean...? IF you get married??"

"I mean when and if I find the right person. I just think it's right to wait...You know what I mean"

"Yea, I guess so," Becky mumbled. "Unless... somehow I fall madly in love with the right person."

The little demon huddling close by her smiled, showing his hideous pointed teeth. "I know *exactly* what she means," the demon thought to himself. "I have my work cut out for me, but before I'm finished, they'll be shacking

CHAPTER II

up with each other just like all the other fools in this school are."

Christmas came and went, with spring quickly approaching. Becky hoped that Josh would ask her out on a date, but so far, no luck. Although Josh wanted to date her, the conflict was still there, and he didn't want to lead her on if indeed Jesus was calling him to the priesthood.

"Can't we just be really good friends," he thought to himself. Day after day, week after week had passed and still no date, not to mention all the good times they missed at Mack's Bar and Grill. So far that was OK with her since Josh was not dating anyone else, not yet at least. Nevertheless, she was going to date him, even if she had to ask him out herself.

Two twins, Billy and Michael Costello enrolled into school shortly before spring break. Everyone liked them immediately as they were fun to be around and appeared to be down-to-earth guys. Both played football at Williamsburg High and wrestled and were county champs in their prospective weight class. Obviously, Coach Patterson was anxious to sign both up, as they would be a welcome asset to the teams.

It just so happened that Billy and Michael's parents opened a coffee and bakery shop right off Main Street, and it wasn't long before this was a popular stop after school, which helped contribute to their already growing popularity. Not only were Billy and Michael popular with all the jocks but were also quite a hit with most of the girls, giving Josh a run for his money.

"He's not the only one with good looks," whispered Susan Smith to Becky, as they stood at their hall lockers eying all the popular guys passing by.

"I'm going to have that one," remarked Susan, as Billy Costello passed by them.

"Why not his brother?" asked Becky.

"His brother...not a bad idea. Think I'll just have to have them both," she said with a smirk on her face. Becky wasn't impressed.

"By the way," Susan hurriedly asked. "Are you going to Mack's Grill this Saturday?"

"Maybe," replied Becky, thinking to herself that she wasn't going to go if she had to go alone.

"Why don't you ask Josh? You know, no date, just have him come along with us and have some fun." Becky thought to herself that it wasn't a bad idea.

"Maybe I will, maybe I will…"

Friday was a rainy day. The regular gang, now including Billy and Michael, were in the cafeteria having lunch together. The group had become so large that they had to push two tables together to fit everyone. Josh, still very depressed about his mom and about not getting the OK from his dad about football yet, had a worried frown on his face. He had prayed about it every day, but so far, no response. And he really didn't expect one anymore.

Becky, noticing Josh's demeanor, picked up her tray and pushed herself next to him. "What's up?" she asked.

"Nothing really."

"Well, you look like you're down in the dumps."

"Yeah…guess I am, a little."

"Anything I can do to cheer ya up?" as she wrapped both arms around him.

"No not really," Josh replied, as Becky continued hugging him.

"Hey!" pushing back from him, "I have a great idea. A bunch of us are going out to Mack's Grill Saturday. You know, T.J.'s dad's place. What about coming along with us?"

Hesitating a little, and just before he began to speak, Becky said,

CHAPTER II

"Not a date. Just friends getting together. Please? Pretty please?" she insisted as she looked deeply into his face.

Although Josh wanted to date her, there was always that inner conflict between dating and the priesthood. "Only one way to find out," he thought to himself.

"Yeah, I think I would like that. Not a date…Right?"

Becky was thrilled. "We're going to have a great time Josh, not a date, just friends. Do you want to meet us there?" Becky asked.

"No…I don't even know where the place is," although thinking to himself, he had a pretty good idea where it was. "Can you meet me at my house? We'll just go together."

"No problem," Becky replied, "I'll meet you at your house around eight."

"OK. Sounds good to me," as both headed for their next class. Becky was ecstatic, practically dancing and twirling down the hall to her next class. No sooner had she entered the room when she ran up to Susan Smith with the news.

"You'll never guess!"

"Never guess what?" asked Susan.

"Well…guess who's going with me to Mack's Grill."

"NO!" Susan replied with bulging eyes and a smile from cheek to cheek.

"Yup…Josh. He's going with me."

"Did you ask him, or did he ask you?"

"He didn't even know we were going. How could he ask me? I asked him."

"Oh my god. Your first date with him."

"It's not really a date, we're just friends."

"Yeah right." Susan said with a grin on her face.

"In any case, he's going and I'm meeting him at eight." Smiling and walking slowly to her seat, Susan looked back over her shoulder and said,

"I'll be watching, you lucky dog. I'll be watching…" and Susan wasn't the only one that would be watching. So would a couple of dozen red bloodshot eyes.

Becky arrived at Josh's place right at eight on the dot. Josh's parents were excited for him, as he had never really dated before. "It's not a date," Josh repeated, at least a half dozen times to his mother. Luckily, this was a good day for Joan. She was dressed and not only feeling pretty good, but even was able to say her rosary.

"Well, in any case," Joan said, "Date or not, have a great time and be sure you tell me all about it." Matty simply shook his head.

"Leave the boy alone. Enjoy yourself, and be careful. Oh, and one other thing. Could you guys walk if it's not too far? I'd like for your mother not to have to worry about you driving."

"But, DAD!"

"JOSH," Matty said in a stern voice that basically meant there would be no discussion.

"OK," Josh said, as he let out a huge breath of annoyed but understanding air.

Although Josh had gone out with girls before, it wasn't anything like this. Most of the time his dating was in groups, such as the Friday night block dances the town sponsored, which didn't really count. These block dances were held for all the high school students, from 7:00pm to 10:00pm, in the school parking lot. This was a great time for the kids to get together as a group and have a good time, dancing and listening to loud music. Of course, the guys congregated to one side of the lot while the girls gathered opposite them; close enough to look at each other, but far enough away so that neither group could hear each other's intimate conversations.

CHAPTER II

Few actually danced, but that didn't matter to the school chaperones, as they were happy the kids were off the streets and not drinking. Little did they know that immediately after the so-called dance ended, many of the kids headed out to the numerous bars and clubs that looked the other way when it came to checking IDs.

Josh had a tight, nervous feeling in his stomach as Becky drove up the driveway. Before she had a chance to get out of the car, Josh was already out the door to meet her.

"Aren't you going to introduce us?" Joan called out as she and Matty stood at the kitchen doorway?

Trying his best to hide his embarrassment, Josh yelled back, "Oh Yeah…this is Becky."

"Hi!" she said waving at them while handing Josh the keys.

"Would it be alright with you if we walk? My mom…"

"Sure, it's fine," Becky interrupted before he could finish. "It'll be fun."

But before Joan had a chance to say another word, or ask any questions, they were already well on their way. All Joan could do was to wave.

"I was just going to tell them to have a good time."

"Yeah…right" Matty responded, with a smile on his face. There was no doubt in his mind that she had a million questions to ask, and knowing her, she would not hesitate to ask them.

With his arm around her, he closed the kitchen door and walked inside. Sitting down on the couch, Joan had a contented smile on her face, knowing that Josh was happy. Matty, on the other hand, was simply content to know that Joan was feeling better than she had felt in weeks.

Mack's Bar and Grill was less than a half mile from Josh's house. However, it was on the other side of the train tracks, an area that Josh hardly visited. Passing two blocks, then crossing under the tracks, through an old brick tunnel, containing one dim light bulb, through an open field, up over a hill, and finally through a thick grove of pine trees, they arrived at Mack's somewhere around 8:45pm. Josh was somewhat taken back by the number of parked cars and bright lights surrounding the place, as if it was Christmas, and the loud music blasting out.

"Not what I expected," he thought to himself.

Becky and Josh walked in and were immediately greeted by a bunch of kids from their school, some of which Josh recognized immediately.

"Hey Bro!" T.J. shouted, as he waved them over to their table. "Glad you made it. We were just about to order pizza. How 'bout you guys?"

"Sure," Josh replied, pushing his hair out of his eyes, while pulling up two chairs to join the group. Some of the guys had dates, but most did not. Susan, who had already arrived earlier, couldn't keep her eyes off Josh. He was wearing dark blue tailored jeans, a black belt, an open neck white button-down shirt, and black running shoes, and of course, no socks. Becky, noticing Susan staring at Josh, kicked her from under the table.

"Hey, Susan," she said. "I see you are here with Billy." Putting her arm around Billy, Susan grinned.

"Yeah! And we're going to have a really great time, aren't we Billy?"

Billy looked surprised, but was grinning from ear to ear. "We are?" He asked as if he had no idea what she was inferring.

T.J. introduced Josh to everyone he didn't know, including his date Debbie Hastings, who was practically hanging all over him. Becky evidently knew everyone made Josh feel a little self-conscious.

CHAPTER II

"What ya want to drink?" asked Michael, who was also there by himself. "Oh, never mind..." as two pitchers of beer arrived at the table.

"Complements of Susan," the waiter said. One of the guys that Josh didn't know began to pass around glasses for everyone. Before Josh could say anything, his glass was already poured.

"Here's to Susan!" T.J. toasted. And with that, everyone lifted their glass and began to drink, including Josh.

Three pizzas arrived and the beer was flowing. After two more pitchers of beer, most everyone was happy. Really happy. Many in the group were going up to the bar and returning with hard drinks.

"How 'bout a whisky sour?" Billy asked Josh.

"You've got to be kidding, he doesn't want that," T.J. insisted. "Have a Jack on the rocks, now that's a man's drink."

"No thanks, I'm good with beer." Josh had just finished a gulp when Becky stood up, grabbed Josh by the arm, and said, "Let's dance."

Before Josh could respond, Becky had already pulled him up to his feet and was dragging him onto the dance floor. Josh, who was not used to drinking, was having a great time. The music was loud and fast as they joined the others on the small dance floor at the far end of the bar. Josh's head was spinning and all he knew was that he and Becky were having a great time. This was a new experience for him, and, at the moment, he didn't have a care in the world.

By 10:00pm, there were so many people on the dance floor that it was hard to see who was dancing with who, and in reality, no one cared. Every couple of dances, the group would return to their table for more beer and snacks. Josh, like most of the guys, was sweating and had opened his shirt like everyone else. The cool air felt good on his chest.

"I'll be right back, don't go away," Becky yelled over the loud music to Josh.

He watched her walk towards the lady's restroom and planned to take a minute to just relax at the table himself. Before he got completely off the dance floor, he felt a tug on his arm.

"Oh Josh, it's a slow one…dance with me! Becky won't mind…"

Without resisting, Josh came back on the dance floor and moved close to Susan, holding her tight and began to dance. Now, for the first time in the evening, the demons who had been watching Josh closely moved in to surround them. It only took a few minutes before Susan began her advances. First, slipping her hand under his open shirt. Then moving closer to his face, teasing him with her lips and all the time whispering sweet nothings in his ear. Likewise, her demons were hanging all over her.

"Go for it…get closer to him…He's loving it…get closer… touch him…touch him," they all were shouting into her ear in a rhythmic sequence.

Josh, somewhat stunned, pulled his head back to avoid her kiss.

"Don't you like this?" Susan whispered to him.

Moving even closer and sliding her body up and down on his with the rhythm of the music, one hand dropped to caress his butt, while the other remained under his open shirt. Josh's head was spinning. He was almost in a daze. Never being in this situation before and not knowing exactly what to do in front of all these people, he just kind of stood there and did…nothing. Suddenly Josh caught sight of Becky returning from the restroom. Josh yelled out and waved.

"Hey, Beck! We're over here."

CHAPTER II

"I see you guys are dancing," she said as she joined them on the dance floor. There was no jealousy or concern. She knew they were just having a good time. However, seeing the stress on Josh's face, she asked,

"You alright, Josh?"

"Yeah, no problem... I just have to take a wicked pee." Without wasting a second, he headed for the men's room, with his head still spinning from the beer and staggering all the way.

"You guys OK?" Becky asked.

"Yeah, no problem. I don't know what's got into him. Guess he can't hold his liquor...Hey, I gotta take a pee too. Be right back," Susan said.

Becky had no clue what had just happened between them, nor did anyone else as they were all too busy dancing, drinking, and making out. Returning to the table, Becky immediately jumped into the conversations around her while waiting for Josh.

As Susan approached the rest room areas, two of T.J.'s friends were just coming out of the men's room.

"Hey guys, do me a favor. Don't let anyone in here until I come out."

Both looked at Susan with envious eyes. "You got it"

Susan thanked them with a huge smile and proceeded to open the door to the men's room.

Josh was just finishing splashing water on his face when he caught sight of her.

"What's the matter Josh? I know you were enjoying our little dance." Not wasting any time, she stepped closer to him, placing both hands under his shirt. "Come on Josh, I know you want this."

Struggling a bit, and moving away from the sinks, she continued her advances, hanging all over him. Suddenly after a few seconds, she slowly began to unbuckle his belt while dropping to her knees. Josh leaned back against the wall, as if it was an invitation for her to continue.

Demons were everywhere, dodging in and out all around them. A larger demon clung to Susan encouraging the advances she was making. Their hideous faces gleaming with smiles as they contemplated what was about to happen. Waiting for Josh to decide if he was going to cave into Susan's advances, the guardian named Kapriel stood helpless, watching another large demon approach Josh, ready to sink his fangs into him. The demonic attacks were now bombarding him from all directions. Then something strange happened.

When Josh closed his eyes, he clearly saw the statue of Jesus he had seen so many years ago. The statue turned to look at him; this time however, it was not smiling, but had tears running down its face.

"STOP!" Josh yelled out as he grabbed Susan's hand just before she was about to unzip his jeans. "GET OUT OF HERE!" he screamed, angry and with tears in his eyes.

Susan, shocked and furious at him, stormed out the door, followed by her two bewildered guards. Demons scattered in all directions trying to avoid Kapriel's sword. By the time Josh left the men's room, most of the demons had already been annihilated into fiery ashes. Some of the more fortunate ones escaped. Josh was more upset with himself for letting things go so far, than he was with Susan, although he was pretty pissed at her too.

After collecting himself as best he could, and without stopping to talk to anyone, he headed for the table and grabbed Becky by the arm.

"Were leaving."

"What's wrong?" she said. "What's wrong Josh? What's going on?" Without saying a word, he continued to pull her toward the door. Becky could clearly see that he was upset, but what she didn't know was why!

CHAPTER II

"I'll tell you all about it as soon as we get out of here." There was also something else that was troubling Josh. He swore that he had felt something hanging on him throughout Susan's assault. Something heavy, yet he saw nothing. There was also something else...he thought he smelled something putrid, not the usual smells that come from public restrooms, but something else. And then it hit him. He smelled sulfur...putrid sulfur.

Just before they were about to leave, Susan burst out of the door. Standing on the steps with about a half dozen guys behind her, she quickly gave Josh the finger while screaming.

"I hate you! YOUR NOTHING BUT A DAMN QUEER FAG." Immediately turning to go back in, everyone began to laugh. The last thing Josh heard her say was, "Where's Billy and Michael?"

The few demons that had escaped flew directly to Denzil and Jarell to make their report. Petrified, because they had lost so many sentinels, they feared for their lives as they knew how much Denzil and Jarell wanted to crush Josh ever since their encounter with him so many years ago. They had never forgotten how humiliated they were made to feel by Belzar. They had plotted and maneuvered to destroy Josh for so long since then. Finally, their opportunity had come when Josh had agreed to party at Mack's. This was their chance. They could continuously tempt him all night and once he was drunk, they were sure he would let down his guard, allowing himself to be seduced.

Over a dozen seduction demons had been ordered to specifically attack Josh at every opportunity. Unfortunately for them, he had never succumbed to them or to Susan's advances.

"He's not like the others… he's not like anyone else," the demons reported.

"There were times that we thought he would submit. He certainly looked like he wanted to, but he never did…and besides, we all felt threatened by his guardian."

Denzil, now furious, screamed out, "You felt threatened??? You had over a dozen of my best! And you felt threatened by ONE guardian?!?"

"But Master…" Another demon began to speak, but before he had a chance to finish another word, a quick swipe of Denzil's hand sent him flying into oblivion.

"Sir," another brave demon politely said. "Something happened just before she got his pants down."

"What could have possibly happened?" screamed Denzil.

"Sir, we don't really know… all we know is he suddenly stopped her, and then we were fighting for our lives. His guardian is no ordinary guardian. He has the strength of ten of us, maybe twenty"

"Maybe thirty," another demon added.

"Don't be a fool! No guardian has that kind of strength."

"But Master…" several other demons began to say.

"BUT MASTER WHAT?" Denzil screamed out, interrupting them before they could finish.

Remembering what had just happened to the brave demon who dared to speak out, they simply said nothing. However, it was obvious to all the attackers who had just escaped that Josh's angelic guardian was indeed no ordinary guardian and did have the strength of at least twenty of them…or more.

Denzil and Jarell were even more furious that they had once again failed to defeat the Donovan boy. Their breaths were like fire, their eyes burning red, nostrils wide and sucking in air, expelling slime and sulfur.

CHAPTER II

"Master, Master…" one bold demon finally spoke out. "We can still defeat him. He's heading home on foot, and he has to pass under the tracks through the tunnel at Jinksville crossing."

"So, what about it?" Jarell questioned.

Somewhat sarcastically, Denzil asked, "Why do you think we can defeat him at the tunnel when you idiots couldn't do it at the bar?"

The brave demon continued. "Sir, we can attack him from each end of the tunnel at the same time. They won't be able to escape, and his guardian, no matter how strong he is, won't be able to defend Josh while at the same time attacking all of us. THEY WILL NEVER KNOW WHAT HIT THEM. Once his guardian is destroyed, we can attack the Donovan kid continuously…we could even show ourselves to him, scaring the shit out of him… and I guarantee, his faith will be destroyed after we are through with him."

Hmm! That just may work. "Is anyone with him?" Denzil asked.

"Just Becky Flowers, but her guardian is no match for all of us."

Smiles were on all their faces. "What's your name?" asked Denzil to the brave demon who had just outlined the plan.

"Arequeet, Master."

"Well, Arequeet, you have just been promoted to Second Lieutenant, and will lead this attack." Sixty red, bloodshot-eyed demons immediately flew off toward the tunnel, led by the smiling overconfident Arequeet.

Josh and Becky were just passing through the pine trees. Standing at the top of the hill, they could see the lights of the town just beyond the tracks. The night was clear and warm, silhouetted by a full moon. Josh had already given her a full account of what had occurred on the dance floor, and in the restroom, except for the vision of the statue. By the time they descended the hill and crossed the field, he had just finishing telling Becky all about his devotion to Jesus, his praying the rosary each day, starting from when he was a child, his routine of attending daily Mass, and the times he spends in the church garden every day before school.

"I know it sounds crazy to you, but I know I'm different. I know you won't understand, but now I know that Jesus has been calling me. He's been calling me ever since I was a child." Just before they entered the tunnel, they stopped. Josh could clearly see that Becky was upset.

"Don't cry Beck," holding her tight. "I never wanted to hurt you…I just wanted to be friends." Tearfully, Becky listened as he continued to open his heart to her.

"All my life I have tried my best to surrender to Jesus. But, then then I met you… and as time went on, I really have come to love you." Trying to hold back his tears, he continued. "I love your smile, I love your laugh, I love to be with you. And yet… I love Jesus more… if I didn't, you would be the one that I would love to spend the rest of my life with."

Becky was now sobbing openly.

"Oh Josh…why didn't you tell me this before?" she managed to mumble through her tears.

"I don't know. I tried. Maybe I wasn't sure what Jesus wanted of me. Maybe I thought that the party tonight would change everything. Maybe I was scared of losing your friendship, I don't know… but something happened to me tonight that helped me understand what my calling in life truly is, and I know now that it's the priesthood."

Not able to say another word, she simply looked at him and followed him into the tunnel. No sooner than they had reached the center when the tunnel walls began to shake.

CHAPTER II

There was a horrendous loud rumbling noise, as if a freight train was passing over. The noise was deafening, and loose bricks began to fall from various places from the ceiling. The light, now blinking, was swinging wildly back and forth until it hit the wall bursting in pieces.

Josh and Becky dropped to the floor, hulled together along the side of the tunnel wall, protecting themselves as best they could from any falling objects. Becky was screaming while Josh tried his best to pray, trusting and hoping that they would get out alive.

Little did they know that a huge spiritual battle was taking place all around them. As soon as they had entered, the demons began their assault. Kapriel, who was guarding Josh, and Reece, Becky's guardian, instantly had their swords drawn and were slashing demons as fast as they were attacking them from both sides of the tunnel. Both guardians were standing next to Josh and Becky with their wings outstretched, protecting and covering them like an umbrella.

Wind was blowing through the tunnel like a tornado and the sounds of demons screaming and bursting into fiery ashes was deafening. Josh thought he could see a red glowing mist at each end of the tunnel. Little did he know that what he was seeing was dozens of bloodshot, red evil eyes.

As the battle continued, Arequeet started to get nervous. He was losing demons faster than he could count. His plan might have worked except he had underestimated the strength of Reece, Becky's angel. As small as he was, he proved to be a freeze fighter. The other major flaw in Arequeet's plan was that he had forgotten that the Lord of Hosts always comes to the assistance of His faithful. He had heard Josh's plea for help and had dispatched dozens of angelic warriors, who were now surrounding the tunnel, literally blocking Arequeet's army from escaping, while at the same time, slashing them to pieces. Arequeet was correct. They never knew what hit them. Unfortunately, as it turned out, he was predicting his own demise instead of theirs.

Within minutes, the fight was over. Josh and Becky, shaken but completely unhurt, helped each other up and ran out of the tunnel. As they exited, Josh looked over his shoulder for the freight train that he assumed had caused all the noise and damage. Even though he could clearly see up and down the entire length of the tracks, no train was in sight. In fact, no train had been on the tracks in over a year.

By the time they reached Josh's house, they were completely out of breath. Joan and Matty had gone to bed with only the dim porch light greeting them. So much had happened in the past few hours that neither of them knew exactly what to say. Finally, Becky broke the silence. "What just happened to us?" she asked.

"I really don't know, but I think I have an idea..." Josh was about to tell her when Becky interrupted.

"Listen, Josh. Something happened to me in that tunnel... I don't know what it was, but I know everything will be alright. You know how much I care for you, how much I love you, and I want you to know that I will always love you. I will always be your friend, no matter what you do. I can't believe I'm saying this. An hour ago, I was ready to never speak to you again. But now... something... something I felt... something in the tunnel changed me. Anyway, I hope you know that what I just said is real and comes from my heart."

Josh didn't attempt to respond. Rather he just held her tight, believing with all his heart that the Holy Spirit had moved in Becky, giving her strength and understanding.

CHAPTER II

Monday morning was another beautiful spring day. Just before school started, Josh, as usual, was leaving the church garden. However, this time Becky was watching and waiting for him on the other side of Pothole Road.

"Hey, what are you doing here?" asked Josh.

"Just thought I'd meet you and walk you to your homeroom. Hope that's OK."

"Sure is," Josh happily said.

As they sat in homeroom, waiting for their first class to begin, Josh noticed that T.J. and several others were staring at him in a very odd way.

Josh thought to himself, "Perhaps they are mad at me over the party incident with Susan. Did they really think I am gay? Not that it matters. Was it something that I am wearing, or something else?" Not paying any more attention to it, he got up as the bell rang and headed for his first class.

All through the morning, Josh experienced cold or even dirty looks from most everyone. Bewildered and concerned, he had no idea what was going on but would soon find out during lunch. Josh was running late so most of the regulars were already seated by time he arrived.

However, today, the regular gang was not sitting at the same table. T.J. and a couple of his football friends were at one table. Susan, accompanied by several of her close friends, were sitting close to the windows overlooking the parking lot. Becky, who just arrived, chose to sit with the rest of the regular gang, opposite from where Susan was.

As Josh came in, he immediately got in line to get his food. No sooner had he stepped out of line looking for a place to sit, than T.J. began his verbal assault.

"Hey, bro! Go over and sit with the girls...We don't sit with queers!"

"Yeah, queer boy! Don't come anywhere close to us," another friend of T.J.'s shouted out. Susan and her crowd began to laugh, accompanied by the jeers and middle fingers of many others. By this point Josh had walked over to Becky's table.

Still holding his tray, T.J. stood next to Josh with his face way too close and yelled out so that everyone could hear, "What's the matter, bro? Couldn't get it up with Susan or were you waiting for some guy to…"

Not waiting for T.J. to finish, Josh shoved his tray into T.J.'s chest, knocking him back across the table, spilling food and drinks everywhere. Immediately, T.J. was back up on his feet joined by several of his buddies, ready to pounce on Josh. Before the brawl could begin, several teachers were already between them, stopping anything that was about to happen. T.J. was livid, cursing and blasting out obscenities of all kinds.

"Who started it?" asked one of the teachers.

"Josh did. I never touched him," T.J. exclaimed.

Becky chimed in, "Yeah, but you were mouthing off… egging him on."

"Go to the principal's office," the other teacher said to Josh.

"This isn't over queer boy," T.J. yelled as Josh left the cafeteria. "This isn't over by a long shot!"

For a moment there was silence. Then Becky stood up screaming out so everyone in the room could hear.

"YOU STUPID IDIOTS! HE'S NOT GAY! HE'S NOT GAY! HE JUST WANTS TO BE A PRIEST!"

Becky caught up to Josh just before he reached the office, but before she had a chance to say anything, another teacher, exiting the office, jogged up to him.

"Josh, you're wanted in the office."

"Yeah, I know. I'm on my way."

"No," the teacher said. "It's an emergency… something at home."

Flying through the door of the office, Josh yelled out,

CHAPTER II

"What's wrong? What's wrong.???"

"Josh, you need to go home immediately."

"Oh my God…it's mom…it's my mother."

Barely had he said those words when he was already out the door running home as fast as he could. Approaching his house, he could see flashing red and blue lights from several police cars. Running up the steps, skipping two at a time, he rushed into the living room. Seeing his mother laying on the couch, he quickly knelt beside her. "Mom, are you alright? What's wrong?" Then, looking around, he asked, "Where's dad?"

"Josh… Josh… he's gone," his mom managed to say. Joan was crying uncontrollably. Jenny Preston quietly explained.

"He was hit by a drunk driver while walking his route. The police said that he didn't suffer… he was killed instantly." Josh couldn't believe his ears. Welling up with tearful emotion, he burst into tears. Crying his heart out, he hugged his mother. Jenny tried to console them, but they both continued to sob together. Their hearts were broken. The hardest part was that neither one had a chance to say goodbye.

The funeral was simple and the internment private. As expected, the church was completely full, as Matty was well loved by so many. To Josh's surprise, so many from school also attended, including most of his teachers, Becky, Billy, Michael, Coach Patterson, even T.J. and all the regular gang.

After the funeral Mass, T.J. made it a point to talk to Josh. "Hey Josh, I'm really sorry about your dad. And… I'm sorry about last week in the cafeteria. I'm an idiot. But I'm really sorry about all of it."

"Yeah… me too," Josh replied.

"No, I mean it. And about that gay stuff. That was out of line...we didn't know you wanted to… well, you know the priest stuff… just want you to know we're cool with it. Susan is a jerk."

"Don't worry about it," Josh said. "No problem."

They pounded knuckle to knuckle as T.J. got in his car heading home. Josh stood for some time looking down the road as the car disappeared. Thinking to himself, "I don't really care if you think it's cool or not. But I'm glad you do…"

Josh was out of school for a full week helping his mom settle the estate and completing all the odds and ends that came up with the funeral. As it turned out, Matty had excellent life insurance and to Joan's surprise, he also had mortgage protection insurance, making the house free and clear in the event of his death.

The next few months were hard for both of them. Although it was so difficult to adjust to life without Matty, their faith kept them strong. Josh kept remembering the picture titled "FOOTSTEPS IN THE SAND." He visualized Jesus carrying him and his mom throughout these difficult days. And indeed, Jesus did. Good news came that Joan's treatment appeared to be working. Her doctors reported that her blood counts were normal. She was finally in remission!

By the time Josh returned to school, the year was just about over. One month to go, school will be out and summer awaiting them. Things were quite different for Josh from the last time he was at school. No more dirty looks and comments about being gay. As a matter of fact, most everyone treated him as if that incident in the cafeteria never took place. The old gang was back to their regular table. Even Susan had rejoined them, although her presence was somewhat strained. Josh and Becky

CHAPTER II

continued to hang around with each other with their friendship growing stronger day by day.

Of all the things Josh noticed that was different was the curiosity that so many had as to his decision to become a priest. To his amazement, he wasn't ridiculed or laughed at. In fact, it was just the opposite. Questions about Jesus, about prayer, about church and the Catholic Mass were typical topics that he was asked about, especially during their lunch times together. And of course, questions about being celibate were the favorites of the guys.

Something else had changed in the school. No one of course recognized it except for the large demon sentinels guarding each entrance of the school, and of course Denzil and Jarell. To their bewilderment, more and more angelic angels were entering the school each day with fewer demonic victories reported, all because one boy had the courage to hold true to his convictions.

Summer flew by. Joan remained in remission and even returned to work, but only for a few days a week. The mortgage was paid off and money wasn't a problem as it had been before. Josh no longer had to work, although he did throughout the summer to keep busy and to be as helpful as he could. Joan made it absolutely clear to Josh that Matty wanted him to play football his senior year.

"This was what your father and I discussed," she said to him. "We were going to tell you as soon as summer started. But with everything happening, dad never had the chance…"

"Mom, I'd like to be with you and continue working."

"YOU WILL NOT," she emphatically said. "I plan to go to every home game, even if I'm in a wheelchair. Do you understand me?"

"Yes ma'am," Josh replied with the biggest smile on his face. A smile that he hadn't had in such a long time.

REPARATION: A STORY OF HOPE

Practice began two weeks before school started. Josh was thrilled to be a part of the team and so was Coach Patterson. It wasn't long before everyone realized just how skilled Josh was, T.J. included. And that was when the problems began again.

Everyone was working hard to impress Coach Patterson. Of course, their goal was to make varsity, first string. Unfortunately, no matter how good T.J. performed, Josh clearly was better. Billy and Michael, along with several others from the cafeteria group were also star players and expected to make varsity. The two weeks of August pre-season training was hot and grueling and by time it had ended, Coach Patterson was pretty sure who his starting team would be.

The topic of conversation in the cafeteria was usually centered around football. Most everyone was excited to find out who had been selected to start next week's opener. Josh was very laid back and hardly took part in the football conversations. He could tell T.J. was upset, extremely upset. Had it not been for Josh, T.J. was a shoo-in for first string quarterback.

The day finally came. After Friday's practice, the list of varsity starters was posted along with their respective positions. While the players were showering and changing in the locker room, one of the guys yelled out,

"Hey…the list is up."

Almost immediately there was a crowd pushing and shoving to see if their name was among the lucky ones.

Scanning down the list and not finding his name as starting quarterback, TJ's temper flared. "Son of a bitch! Son of a bitch!"

Josh was still showering. Still fuming, T.J. popped his head into the shower area.

"What's the matter, bro? Don't you want to know if you're starting Saturday?"

CHAPTER II

Turning off the shower, Josh answered, "Not really. Whatever Coach wants is good with me. I'm just glad to be on the team."

"Oh yeah, sure you are. Thanks to you, I'll be sitting on the bench all season."

"Listen, T.J., this is not about you and me."

"Don't think it isn't," T.J. quickly added. "If I have to break your arm, I'll be playing one way or another."

"Sorry you feel that way," Josh said as he continued to dry himself off.

Walking away, T.J. shot back, "I'm not sorry at all."

Time went quickly. Practice was grueling, but before they knew it, their first game had arrived. Josh was nervous as the game started but quickly settled down. As promised, Joan, along with Becky and the gang, were all cheering him on. The crowd went crazy as they usually do when the home team wins. Coach Patterson was thrilled with his first win of the season, 21-0.

There was quite a celebration afterwards, horns honking, banners flying, and kids cheering and screaming in congratulations to the winning team. Many of the kids, along with Josh and Becky, ended up at Pizza Hut, celebrating the team's victory. T.J. and Debbie, Billy and Susan, and Michael and his date, Sara Wilson, were at Mack's Bar and Grill getting plastered and thinking nothing of it. As the three of them sat at their favorite table, something was whispering in T.J.'s ear, giving him an idea… an idea that just might get him back on the first string.

"Hey," T.J. said. "You guys love me right, and feel the same as I do about Josh stealing my position? Right?" As expected, Michael and Billy agreed.

"Yeah man, what about it?"

REPARATION: A STORY OF HOPE

"Well..." T.J. said in a long drawn-out tone. "I was just thinking... It would be a shame if Josh got hurt during practice. You know, sometimes quarterbacks get sacked unexpectedly...and accidents *do* happen. It really would be terrible if he was unable to start in next week's game."

Smiles came across their faces. Looking at each other and being quite proud of their leader, they picked up their mugs of beer and toasted. "Here's to Josh's 'accident'."

Practice went as usual until Wednesday. Pouring rain would not stop Coach Patterson from having practice. As expected, the field was a muddy mess and players were slipping and falling everywhere. This was T.J.'s perfect opportunity to follow through with his plan. Pulling Billy and Michael aside, T.J. gave them the go ahead.

As soon as the ball was hiked to Josh, Billy allowed Michael to rush by him, slamming into Josh with all his might. They both went crashing into the muddy grass. Josh's arm twisted under him and immediately the sounds of pain were heard by everyone. The athletic trainer wasted no time calling an ambulance.

"WHAT THE HELL WERE YOU THINKING," Coach Patterson screamed into Billy's face holding him by his face mask.

"I couldn't help it, Coach. I slipped on the mud and couldn't make my block." Disgusted but satisfied with his response, he let go of him.

"PRACTICE IS OVER," he yelled out so that every player, including some bystanders, heard him. Frustrated and beside himself, the only thing he could say was, "Go get showered, NOW! And get out of my sight."

Josh was back in school the following day with only a bruised elbow. Luckily for him, the doctors felt that it would heal fairly quickly, but unfortunately he would not be able to play in Saturday's game.

CHAPTER II

"Coach," Josh pleaded, "let me place kick for extra points. I wouldn't even have to touch the ball."

"There's no way," Coach Patterson said. Josh was persistent, and along with T.J., who had just entered the office, they both finally persuaded Patterson to agree. T.J. would quarterback, and Josh would do the extra point kicking. Both were happy.

Saturday was another home game. Everyone was there cheering the team on. T.J. had not performed as well as he or Coach Patterson expected. With one fumble, resulting in a touchdown for the other team, three sacks, and several overthrown possible touch-down passes, he was not happy with himself. Nor was anyone else.

Throughout the entire game, Jinksville High was behind. As soon as they scored, the other team would edge ahead. Going into the last minutes of the game, Jinksville was behind by one point. Josh made a spectacular onside kick, giving Jinksville possession with only seconds to play. Rather than hoping for a Hail Mary pass from T.J., Coach Patterson asked Josh if he thought he could make the 53-yard field goal needed to win the game. As the ball went sailing through the air, you could hear a pin drop until it passed perfectly between the goal posts.

Pandemonium broke out. Josh was hoisted on shoulders and carried off the field as fans went crazy, clapping, yelling, and cheering celebrating their victory.

"Oh, my Lord…If Matty could have only seen this," Joan thought to herself. The only exception to those who were not celebrating were Billy, Michael, and T.J., now, more jealous, and angrier than ever.

Josh's elbow healed faster than expected, allowing him to play in every game. T.J. periodically substituted for Josh, giving him an occasional rest during the games. Coach Patterson offered T.J. the position of linebacker, but he was too proud to play anything other than quarterback. Consequently, he sat on the bench most of the season, brewing and becoming more bitter with the passing of every game.

The rest of the season went quickly, with no serious injuries. It was the first time in fourteen years that Jinksville High not only had a winning season, finishing with a record of 7-1-0, but also won the State Conference Championship. Everyone in the school, including the principal, who usually was not overly enthusiastic about sports, was excited and so proud of the team's accomplishments. Throughout all the excitement and compliments given, Josh never took credit for anything. He would always credit individual players, or the team's defense or the strength of their offense for their accomplishments. Undoubtedly, this was one of the reasons why he became so popular.

Before long, all the fall sports had ended. Christmas break was over, and spring had once again arrived. Most of the seniors were looking forward to graduation. Becky and Josh had not seen much of each other over the last couple of months. Practice every day, studies, and helping at home as much as he could, left little time for Becky or for that matter, anything else. In truth, Josh thought that this was probably a good thing as it would make their goodbyes easier. She would soon be off to college and him off to some seminary.

By now all the kids in the lunch group had grown very close. They had shared their stories, joys, laughs, and even tears with one another for close to four years. As they gathered once again, sitting at their regular table, one thing was very different. Susan, T.J., Billy, Michael, and their girlfriends sat by themselves. In fact, they hardly spoke to anyone in the regular group, and T.J. didn't speak to Josh at all.

CHAPTER II

The entire situation with football, the incident with Josh and Susan, the drunken parties that T.J. hosted, all the sex stuff that was constantly going on throughout the year, and to a degree Josh's moral influence that had such a positive effect on so many, drove a wedge between T.J., his friends, and Josh's. What no one realized was just how much hatred T.J. had for Josh, and how envious he was of him. And no one was aware that he was so adamant about getting his revenge. No one except the demons that were constantly clinging to him and whispering into his ear.

Three weeks before graduation, Joan's blood count went off the chart. Her cancer was back. Josh was devastated, especially since it had been less than a year since his father had died. Joan remained strong and positive and had tremendous support from neighbors and friends. This helped to relieve some of the pressure from Josh and enabled him to continue with school until graduation. Now more than ever, he was spending considerable time in the church garden, praying before the huge cross of Jesus.

Word had leaked out that Josh went to Mass every morning and then to the garden each day before school. This wasn't a problem for anyone as they all knew of his plans for the priesthood, and most were very supportive of him. However, for T.J., everything about Josh was a problem. He couldn't get football out of his mind. He kept thinking over and over, "I could have had a football scholarship if it weren't for that son of a bitch. He doesn't even want to go to college to play football. I do! And yet I can't, all because of him." The more he thought about it, the more infuriated he got.

Denzil and Jarell were well aware of what was going on and were also infuriated that they had once again failed with Josh. They themselves, along with dozens of demons, including masters of hatred, jealousy, revenge, anger, deception, and lies, were constantly surrounding T.J., day and night, tempting and encouraging him to get revenge.

Football wasn't the only thing T.J. was upset over. Now he had to sit throughout the graduation ceremony listening to all the praises Josh would receive about his 4.0 grade point average he had maintained over the past four years and watch as he received academic awards and trophies for his football accomplishments. Athlete of the year. Student of the year. Bullshit. It was all bullshit as far as T.J. was concerned, and if he had his way he would.

THEN, it hit him. It was almost as if a light bulb went on, or more likely, the demons finally got through to him. He knew exactly what he was going to do. All he had to do was to get a little help from Billy and Michael.

Graduation day finally arrived. The ceremony would begin at 10:30am. It was decided by the graduation committee that the diplomas would be handed out immediately after the speakers and last would be the athletic awards and special recognitions. This was a little different from the usual sequence, because Coach Patterson, who would be presenting the awards, would be arriving late, as he was out of state due to his brother's death. Becky and her family would pick up Joan and bring her home after the ceremony. Josh planned to go to early Mass and spend extra time in the garden. That would give him plenty of time to get to the school auditorium and be seated well before the ceremony began.

After Mass, Josh entered the garden, knelt and began to pray. His prayers focused on his mother, but he also prayed specifically for Becky and T.J.

"Please Lord, heal my mother...if it be Your will. Thank you for Becky and for our friendship. And bless her, especially as she goes off to college. And Lord, bless T.J., please take the hatred from his heart. Forgive me if I've

CHAPTER II

done anything to offend him and forgive him. I ask forgiveness for all of us, Amen."

After a few more minutes of silent prayer, Josh got up, slipped on his graduation gown, and headed for the iron gates. As Josh opened the gates to exit, T.J., Billy and Michael burst in, blocking his way.

"Where do you think you're going?" T.J. blurted out.

"What are you guys doing here?" Josh asked with a surprised and concerned expression. "We're here for revenge, you son of a bitch!" And with that they began their merciless attack.

Josh didn't know what hit him. A quick knee to the groin sent him to his knees, and before he could recover, T.J. kicked him in the face. Two front teeth went splattering out with blood everywhere. All three began to punch and kick him. Billy centered on his face and soon his nose was broken with multiple deep cuts to his chin and forehead. It didn't take long for both of his bloody eyes to swell up and close. Michael was kicking him in his groin and legs and then landed a crushing blow to his knee, which they were sure they heard it break.

T.J. moved to Josh's outstretched hand. Picking up his foot, he stomped down as hard as he could, crushing the bones in his fingers. Not satisfied with destroying one hand, he repeated it to the other. Watching Josh lay broken and bleeding, he said in as ugly and sarcastic a voice he could, "Now let's see you pass that perfect spiral."

"Let's get the hell out of here," Billy shouted as the three of them bolted toward the gate.

"Wait," T.J. suddenly said, "one more thing."

He quickly ran back to Josh, unzipped his fly, and pissed all over him. Feeling a sense of accomplishment, they headed off for graduation. Little did they know that this attack would change their lives forever.

And of course, there were others who felt a great sense of accomplishment.

Congratulations, dancing, laughter, and a feeling of ecstasy came over all the hideous demons that had also participated in the assault.

Josh, barely conscious, could just about see the cross of Jesus at the other end of the garden.

"Please Lord, help me…help me…" he mumbled through his broken and bloody mouth.

Slowly and painfully, he began to drag himself to the cross. Using his elbows and as much of his arms as possible, he agonized slowly forward, following the path of flowers that led to the cross. Not being able to see much, he just kept struggling forward until he finally reached his destination. The pain in his hands and body was unbearable, yet he somehow pulled himself far enough up so he could touch the feet of the statue. Exhausted and overwhelmed with pain, Josh just closed his eyes as he reached up and placed both of his broken hands on the feet of Jesus.

It was already 10:15am, and the graduation ceremony was about to begin. All the kids were lined up ready for the procession into the auditorium, all except Josh. Becky along with several others kept looking for him and asking if anyone knew where he was. Finally, the music began, and the procession started. Everyone walked in and took their assigned seats. No one was more surprised and concerned about not seeing him than his mother, who was sitting to the side of the auditorium in a wheelchair. After a brief welcome, the principal began her speech.

Josh was not fully conscious or aware of anything much, except for the pain in his body. Then it happened. Feeling the actual flesh of the feet of Jesus, warm blood

CHAPTER II

from the cross began dripping and flowing down through Josh's fingers and arms. Then, everything went blank.

Kapriel had not stood by idle. He had continuously fought off dozens of demons and was assisted by other Heavenly warriors while the attack took place. Dozens and dozens of demons were obliterated into fiery ashes. But, according to the rule of Heaven, no supernatural being could interfere physically with worldly matters. They were there to guide and protect from demonic attacks only. As much as Kapriel wanted to, he could not physically stop the attack.

"Hey Josh, wake up," Father Dennis said as he began to shake the boy on the ground. "Wake up! You're going to be late for graduation." Josh's eyes opened. Father Dennis, now looking at his watch hurriedly said, "You're already late. Hurry up and get over there."

Josh stood up, and to his amazement was fully healed, with absolutely no signs of blood or bruises on him. Not wasting any time, he bolted through the gate, all the time praising Jesus and thanking him for such a miracle. Father Dennis simply sat down on the bench in front of the statue, scratching his head wondering why Josh would fall asleep on such an important day.

Rushing into the auditorium, the graduates were already lined up, receiving their diplomas. One by one as their names were announced. Josh bolted up the stairs onto the stage just in time to be handed his diploma.

"Glad you could make it," the principal said quietly to him as she handed him his certificate.

Taking it from her, he turned toward the audience as they applauded. His mom was overjoyed but thinking to herself that she would kill him for being late. Becky had such a big smile on her face that it was almost contagious. T.J., Billy, and Michael had already received their diplomas and were sitting side by side in the front row. All three sat with their mouths wide open. The disbelieving expression on their faces was hard to describe. Beginning to shake with fear and wanting to escape as fast as they could, they somehow remained frozen in place with their eyes fixed on Josh, not knowing what was in store for them. As Josh slowly walked past them, he paused. Looking at them with a sincere expression, he leaned over and in a very quiet voice said, "I forgive you…and so does Jesus."

Almost immediately, the three of them reacted. Billy burst into tears, regretting what he had done. Michael, holding his head down, was also sobbing as he asked the Lord for forgiveness. As for T.J., he visibly was affected by the miracle he had just witnessed and was truly sorry for what he had done. Sitting with his head held back, he also had tears streaming from his eyes, all the time thinking to himself, "God is real…God is real…and I hope He will forgive me."

After the ceremony, when his mom and everyone had left, Josh and Becky headed to the church parking lot where Josh had parked his car.

"Did you really fall asleep as you told your mom?" asked Becky.

"Yup…You might say that. But that's not the whole story. I promise, someday I'll tell you all about it." And many years later, he did.

"So, what's next?" Becky asked.

"Well, I was planning this fall to go to Sacred Heart Seminary, in Clarksville. It's in Upstate New York. But with mom's cancer… I don't know. I'll just have to put it on hold."

"Why Clarksville?"

"Father Hugh suggested it to me. Had no other place in mind, so why not? Besides, he went there and promised to put a good word in for me. What about you?" Without waiting for an answer, Josh continued,

CHAPTER II

"Guess you're off to college. Did you finally settle on South Carolina University?"

"Yeah. I really like the campus and they offer exactly what I'm looking for."

"Sounds great."

They stood for some time staring at each other, but neither one could not find the right words to say. Finally, Becky broke into tears as she hugged Josh.

"No tears! Come on Beck, you promised."

"Yeah, I know, but we may never see each other again."

"No way! Of course we'll see each other. You know where I live. It's my home forever." However, Josh was not really sure that would be the case.

Driving home, they reminisced about so many of their past experiences. The time they first met, the lunch gang, their so called 'dates,' all the parties, the football games, the experience at the tunnel and so much more, all accompanied with tears and laughter. Pulling up to Becky's house, they again fell silent.

Becky struggled to look directly into Josh' eyes. "I love you Josh. I always will. No matter who I meet, or where I am, I will always love you," then she hesitantly added, "as my dearest friend."

"And I will always love you Beck." They hugged each other for their last goodbye. Just before she opened the car door, she handed him back the spiritual books he had lent her so long ago.

"Thanks, you will never know how much these books have helped me."

"Keep them! Besides, who knows? Someone else may need them some day. Perhaps your son."

Exiting the car, after taking a few steps, she turned. Choking back tears, she managed to say, "Friends forever."

Josh, now struggling to hold back his tears and making sure Becky did not see them, mumbled back, "Right… friends forever…" And with those two words, she watched him drive away.

Two and a half years passed by, and on a cold winter night, Josh's mom passed away. Josh had been caring for her all this time, working at the Wilcox General Store, as much as he could to make some extra money, while attending to all the other household chores, repairs, and bills that had to be taken care of.

Becky was now well into her junior year of college. They tried to keep in touch as much as possible through letters and occasional phone calls. However, Josh noticed that as time went on, their correspondence was becoming less and less frequent. In fact, he hadn't seen her in over a year. She, along with her parents, had moved to California. He kept remembering what she had said when they last parted.

"We may never see each other again…" Maybe she was right. And then again? Who knows? Time would tell.

By the time spring had arrived, Josh had tied up all his loose ends. He sold his childhood home and donated the money to St. Ann's Church, with the stipulation that the garden would always remain and be cared for as Father Baxter once did. That was a promise that Father Dennis would not be able to keep. After driving around town, taking a last look at the familiar places of his youth, including Becky's old house and his, he drove back to the church to say his goodbyes. The last thing he did before he left the town of Jinksville, was to visit the garden one last time.

Walking slowly around the garden, through the maze of paths and flowers, he eventually reached the cross.

CHAPTER II

Looking up at the suffering figure, he couldn't stop the tears from flowing.

"Dear Jesus, I love you so much," he whispered to himself in a soft voice. "I will never be able to thank you enough for the miracle you gave me. Thank you for my mom and my dad, for Becky and for the wonderful friendship we have, thank you for my life and for this opportunity to serve you."

Kneeling down and looking intently at the crucifix, recalling his trauma in the garden and the blood of Jesus that healed him, he began to sob uncontrollably. Finally, as the tears subsided, he prayed once again. "Please Jesus, forgive T.J., Billy and Michael. Bless them and bless me. Give me strength and help me to serve you all the days of my life." Josh knelt on the kneeler for quite some time in silent prayer. Finally, getting up and approaching the iron gates, he looked back one last time, he smiled, and with a glowing expression on his face, he drove away, headed for Sacred Heart Seminary, at the young age of 22.

CHAPTER III

THE SEMINARY

Sacred Heart Seminary, located in Clarksville, Upstate New York, was one of the most popular and productive Catholic seminaries in the United States. It was established for the formation of candidates for the Catholic priesthood. Unfortunately, as interest in the priesthood and religious life declined throughout the world, more and more of these institutions were closed. At one time in its early history, over two dozen priests were ordained yearly. Fortunately, or maybe not so fortunate, Sacred Heart remained open throughout the years….

The campus, located on three-hundred acres of beautiful rolling hills, streams, and densely wooded forests, was built in 1894. Five beautiful buildings were constructed of massive stone, taken from the hills of Pennsylvania, with impressive stone walls surrounding the entire campus.

Most buildings are inter-connected with various enclosed archways, and underground bricked-walled halls that resemble medieval tunnels. As you walk up the steps of the main building, you enter through two massive wood doors displaying the carving of Christ and his Twelve Apostles. No expense was spared to create one of the most beautiful and detailed wood carvings in the world.

REPARATION: A STORY OF HOPE

Entering a circular lobby, one is greeted by stone statues of the Twelve Apostles, chiseled out of the walls, magnificent portraits and stone sculptured figures that adorned every hallway. The gothic style of the lobby is impressive. The ceiling is huge with pointed arches, and high vaults, with the center illuminated by a massive circular stained-glass skylight. The main hall leads directly to the small church enclosed within the building. Although on a much smaller scale, the church was constructed somewhat in the gothic style. Its arches are not as massive as in the lobby, but are also quite impressive. It too is adorned with pointed-arched windows and has numerous cravings throughout its walls.

Under the church, accessed by a dimly lit stone circular staircase, similar to the medieval tunnels, is what looks like a small chapel. It is evidently used for special occasions and is off limits to everyone except for priests and senior seminarians. The main office and various other rooms, designated for administrative use, are situated off the circular lobby. To the left of the lobby is a beautiful library, with its interior walls and bookshelves made of beautiful aged red mahogany, surrounded by small circular gothic rose windows. The remainder of a large wood cross that once hung on the south wall is now only visible by its faded outline. To the right of the lobby, off a winding hall are the dormitories, where each of the twenty-five rooms now house two seminarians, a most unusual concept. Another small building, located just behind the church, houses the priests, and has a spare room reserved for an occasional guest. This seminary was once the pride of Clarksville. Many parishioners would attend Sunday Mass there until the church was closed to the public in the early seventies.

CHAPTER III

Josh took his time driving there, arriving in Clarksville in two days. The first thing he noticed as he got out of his car and looked around was the poor condition that the campus was in. It was nothing like the brochure that Father Hugh had given him. The grass needed cutting, weeds were everywhere, and although it was spring, little to no flowers were seen. Additionally, the buildings almost looked abandoned, as there were vines growing up over most of the walls, some doors and windows boarded up, and additionally some buildings needed desperate repair.

In front of the steps leading to the main building was what looked like a small circular garden with a statue of the Sacred Heart in its center. It had been neglected for years. Some of the stone benches in front of the statue were crumbling and the right hand of Jesus was missing, evidently broken off long ago.

Josh wondered why such a beautiful campus be so run down. Surely the Church must have enough money to maintain such a historic place. Trying not to pay too much attention to the deteriorated campus and buildings, Josh was nevertheless optimistic as he pulled open the massive wood door. Entering the circular lobby and before he had a chance to look around, the front door slammed shut behind him with such force that he literally jumped two feet. Looking behind him, Josh couldn't see the two small demons that had just scared the life out of him.

"We'll be seeing a lot of each other," said the smaller of the two, as they flew past him into the main office. After regaining his composure, he marveled at the beauty of the architecture that surrounded him. As he stretched his neck back looking up, he heard a voice coming from the office.

"Come in Josh. We've been expecting you."

The two demons that entered when he did retreated to the far upper corner of the wall as they caught sight of Kapriel, Josh's guardian. Massive in size, a full seven feet tall and looking like the strength of twenty, they immediately knew he was no ordinary protector. Kapriel stood directly behind Josh with his massive wings protecting him from all directions. Looking up at the two petrified creatures who were now pushing themselves further back against the wall, the message was clear: Don't even think of messing with Josh if you want to see the light of another day.

Father Gerald greeted Josh with a smile, eyeing him from head to toe. "Fr. Hugh tells us that you want to be a priest."

"Yes, sir, I…" But before Josh had a chance to finish, Father Gerald interrupted.

"Well, you're at the right place. We'll do our best to prepare you for everything you will need to know. We have accelerated our college program to allow you to complete your degree requirements in two years. With some hard work, you'll be ordained in no time at all."

"I thought the process would take years?"

"Possibly, but someone with your academic abilities, I'm sure it won't be too long before we can get you ordained."

Josh was ecstatic. "That sounds great! I'll work extra hard."

"I'm sure you will," Father Gerald said with a weird smile on his face.

Standing up and turning away from Josh, he continued to speak while fussing with something on the bookshelf. "You know Josh, we prepare our priests to be very liberal. We must be willing to discard many of our traditional values to fully serve today's society. In fact, many of the things we were taught as young children are not as true as we were once made to believe.

"Of course, we always discern what truth is to be able to make sound and accurate decisions. That's one thing

CHAPTER III

that has made this place so successful. But enough of my philosophical ideas for now! You must be starving."

Calling another priest who must have been waiting outside into the room, Father Gerald said, "Father Jim, would you please show Josh his room and give him a quick tour of the place after lunch."

Unbeknownst to Josh, and everyone in the town of Clarksville, the seminary was no longer a Catholic seminary. In fact, it had been closed and sold by the diocese years ago, along with its three hundred acres, to Anthony C Wadsworth. The Church had no idea that Wadsworth was a billionaire atheist who openly displayed hatred for the Catholic Church. Although no longer a Catholic seminary, everyone in the town thought it still was operating as such. And that is exactly what the new owner and Father Gerald wanted.

Father Gerald was no ordinary priest either. In fact, his real name was Hubert Holland, now going by the alias Father John Gerald. He was defrocked and excommunicated by the Vatican years ago for his anti-Christian ideas, his pro-abortion views, and most of all for molesting dozens of altar boys. There was a big scandal over his molestations and a lot of pressure was placed on the Vatican. Somehow, he avoided prosecution and was secretly relocated to some small parish in South Africa. Time passed and eventually he disappeared, only to mysteriously reappear as head pastor of the seminary, thanks to his lifelong friend Anthony C. Wadsworth.

Of course, Father Gerald knew full well that his plan was to have Josh, as well as all the others in his charge, ordained as soon as possible. If one could even call it ordination. Yes, they would be ordained, but not by a Bishop within the Catholic Church. Their ordinations would be administered by some defrocked priest posing as a Bishop.

Sacred Heart Seminary was now a facade for the training of men to rebel and eventually bring down Christianity and to perpetuate atheistic beliefs and hatred for God. In fact, it had become an evil den whose leaders had the mission to indoctrinate young men into rejecting the teachings of Christ, the Church, and Christian religions at large. Father Gerald and his so called 'priests' would not hesitate to use any means necessary, such as lies, falsities, drugs, addiction, tranquilizers, brain washing, and even torture to achieve their goals.

A plan was set in motion years ago to destroy the faith of the laity through sexual scandals and abuse within the churches throughout the world. Although this had a devastating effect on many good clergy and Catholics, something more drastic had to be done if they were going to convert the entire world. When Satan realized that his time was running out before this mission could be completed, a far more effective strategy had to be enacted. After much planning, Azazal and his army of demonic generals conceived a plan that would build on the sexual abuse already going on throughout the world but would be far more effective.

The strategy was to attack the very heart of the Church, the Vatican, and yes, even the Pope himself. If they could get mass numbers of religious priests, bishops and cardinals, to rebel, to defect, to spread false dogma, and even to commit sexual atrocities, especially against young children, then the seeds of defection would begin. This along with the hundreds of illegitimate so-called 'priests,' ordained from various seminaries throughout the world, would contribute even faster to the demise of Christianity. They would infiltrate every parish and soon out-number legitimate ordained priests.

Even better, once they achieved this within the walls of the Vatican, it would create such a snowball effect that

CHAPTER III

masses of the faithful would not only defect from the Church but would lose faith in the Pope and God Himself.

Unfortunately, the problem for the demons was that there weren't enough priests and religious that could be deceived and manipulated to rebel in the first place. Consequently, some thousands of illegitimate priests, loyal to their plan, were needed. What better way to produce them than to falsely ordain dozens of men each month, through various so-called 'seminaries' throughout the world.

It was decided that Clarksville would be the perfect prototype and place to begin. A small city, easy to convert, isolated and far away from busy cities where the training of large numbers of men would go unnoticed, especially by the Catholic Church, and yet close enough to New York City where they could send their seminarians to experience firsthand sin and evil that was rampant there. The icing on the cake was that Clarksville already had a seminary that was thought to still be a legitimate institution of the Church. Once the experiment in Clarksville was successful, the plan would be reproduced throughout the world.

Josh's roommate was just a young eighteen-year-old teenager who had been at the seminary for only six months. He had been in and out of foster care all his life, abandoned by his sixteen-year-old drug addicted mother at birth. Beginning life as an addicted baby, he continuously struggled for happiness, being shuffled from home to home, and from school to school. Barely finishing high school, he succumbed to the only thing that gave him pleasure and hope, even if it was false hope. He emerged himself into drugs until one day he found himself on the street. A perfect candidate for Father Gerald.

"Hey, glad to meet you! I'm Josh."

Sitting on the side of his bed with his head held down in his hands, he looked up. "Yeah, I'm David."

"Guess we'll be rooming together," Josh said. "I just got here today. Came all the way from Jinksville, South Carolina. Where are you from?"

David hesitated. "Everywhere... nowhere. Never had a permanent home. Foster care. You know, all that crap."

"Sorry to hear that." Changing the subject, Josh inquired, "So…what's it like here?"

"I really can't tell you. It's…weird," David said. As Josh started to unpack, David continued in a soft voice, still not looking directly at him.

"Quite frankly, most guys here act as if they don't even want to be a priest. Like I said…weird. I've only been here a short time myself. Half the time, I'm afraid to ask any questions. I keep telling them I don't want to be a priest, but they insist that I'm going to become one. A 'special kind of priest', they say."

"A special kind of priest…what does that mean?"

"I have no idea. I've told them that I'm not really into religion but all they keep saying is that it doesn't matter. One way or another, I will be a great help to them."

Josh stopped unpacking. He swung the only straight back chair around and sat down, listening very carefully, more confused than ever.

"Another thing, as I said, I was never into religion, but a few of the foster homes that I lived in were pretty religious people. They went to church regularly, sometimes I went with them. I don't know much about church, but I do know that that cross in the front is not supposed to be hanging upside down."

Josh looked at David more confused than ever.

"What do you mean…upside down?"

CHAPTER III

"Well, I snuck into the chapel some months ago. It's underneath the church and I noticed the cross was hanging upside down. Everyone was chanting weird sounds. It scared the crap out of me. The funny thing is no one saw me, but I felt as if a dozen eyes were staring at me. Again, weird." Not able to decipher what David had just said, Josh asked another question.

"Did you see anything else? What about any unusual smells?"

"Oh yeah, funny you ask that. The smell of sulfur is all around here. They say it's from the stone that this place was constructed of."

Josh found this more than interesting, and he was sure that those smells were not from the stones. Taking it all in, Josh sat quietly for some time. Finally breaking the silence he asked, "Are you Catholic?"

"Not really. My record says that I was baptized Catholic, but I never received my First Communion nor was I confirmed. Matter of fact, I think I don't think I've ever been in a Catholic Church, other than this place. Only been in church a few times. In and out of school and barely finished my high school degree."

"How the heck are you here studying to be a priest if you're not really a Catholic???"

"Don't ask me," replied David. "I told you, Father Gerald picked me up from the streets. I was half out of my mind with drugs. When I finally came to my senses, I had already been here for two weeks, and it took another two months of rehab to get me straight... and I'm still not really thinking straight. And if you really want to hear something strange, ever since I got here, most of the time, all I can think about is sex. Before I came here, that was never really on my mind. My whole life was consumed with drugs, and money to pay for them. Sex was on the backburner through most of that."

REPARATION: A STORY OF HOPE

Before David said another word, the six o'clock bell rang. At exactly 6:00pm every night, the dinner bell would ring, summoning everyone, including the so-called 'priests' to dinner. Obviously, no one wasted any time to respond. Sitting in the center of every plate was a paper cup containing four pills. Pink for anxiety, blue for immunity from sickness, yellow for all the daily essential vitamins, and white for retarding their sexual urges.

None of the seminarians knew exactly what the pills were for. The truth was that only the yellow pill was a legitimate vitamin supplement. The pink and blue pills were tranquilizers that were used for persuasion and control, and the white pill was given to enhance sexual drive and urges. David picked up his cup.

"Here's to us."

Just as Josh was reaching for his pills, his cup suddenly blew off the table, spilling its contents on the stone floor and disappearing into one of the many floor drains located throughout the room.

"Oh well, we'll toast tomorrow."

The first thing Josh noticed was no blessing before the meal. Asking the person sitting next to him why there wasn't a blessing, he was told that it was up to each person to say their own, as they were told that everyone was unique and had their own kind of prayer to say. Again, confused but not paying too much attention to it, he simply said his own blessing and proceeded to eat his meal.

It didn't take Josh long to make friends at his assigned table. It consisted of younger seminarians who had been at the facility for a year or less. Most of the conversations centered on food, family, towns they were from, and to Josh's utter surprise, not only girls, but boys as well. Not a word about God, religion, or the seminary itself.

Josh thought to himself, "This is almost as bad as it was at Jinksville High… I'm not sure I'm in the right place."

CHAPTER III

As they finished eating, another bell rang, indicating one hour of free time.

Just as Josh got up from the table, some guy sitting behind him, presumably a second- or third-year candidate, walked up to Josh, and putting his arm over Josh's shoulder whispered in his ear, "My advice is don't take any of the pills if you want to keep a clear head...except for the white one...That will give you a 'hard-on' lasting all night."

Before Josh could even respond, the kid disappeared into the recreation room.

It was a beautiful spring evening. Rather than joining most of the guys for TV or some other form of recreation, Josh decided to spend some quiet time by himself. Stepping outside, he walked over to the dilapidated statue of the Sacred Heart of Jesus and sat down on one of the stone benches that was still in usable condition. Sitting for some time, he could feel his head spinning in confusion. Trying to rationalize all that had occurred that day, he could not come up with any clear justifications for anything he had heard or experienced.

"Jesus help me, this isn't anything that I expected," he thought to himself. Suddenly, he felt a hand on his shoulder.

"You best come back inside. We don't like any of our boys to go outside after dinner."

"Sure," Josh quickly responded. "Sorry."

"No problem," Father Gerald said as he accompanied Josh back inside with the others.

Everyone was just leaving the recreation room as Josh arrived. Realizing that the hour had already gone by, he decided to spend a little prayer time in the church before turning in. As he headed for the church and seeing Father Jim, he called out to him.

"Hey Father," getting his attention. Josh asked, "What time is morning Mass?" Hesitantly, Father Jim responded.

"Oh! We do not have morning Mass. It's too hard to fit into our busy schedule. Just on Sundays." Without waiting for another question, Father Jim walked away.

"What kind of place is this that doesn't have daily Mass?" Josh thought to himself as he headed to the church. Josh walked slowly through the hall that led to his destination. Taking his time to admire the various sculptures on the wall, he quickly turned around, feeling that he was not alone. Seeing nothing, he continued toward the church. Again, he suddenly stopped, realizing that he was definitely not alone, yet not a person was in sight. Then, before he took another step, he could smell it…sulfur. And it wasn't coming from the stones. It was all around him.

Recalling the times in Jinksville High, the time in the men's room with Susan at Mack's, the night in the tunnel with Becky, and his recent conversation with David, he was sure Evil was present. Quickly saying a prayer to dispel any demons, he entered the church. Kneeling, he began to pray. As he prayed and glanced around the church, he noticed that all the statues had been removed from their stone pedestals. In fact, there were no statues at all in the church except for the stone sculptures carved in the stone walls.

There was a large cross at the front of the church, but here again one could only see the outline of what once the figure of the crucified Christ was. Nor was there a lit Sanctuary Lamp anywhere, indicating the presence of the Blessed Sacrament. This really didn't matter to Josh as he knew Christ was always within him. Yes, something is wrong here and Josh set his mind to figuring out what exactly it was the next day.

CHAPTER III

Josh had a little trouble finding his way back to his room, but after a few wrong turns he was safely in bed, quietly saying his rosary. Finishing it, he turned toward David, whose bed was on the opposite side of the room, to stay goodnight. However, before he could utter a word, he noticed David's hand moving up and down under the covers accompanied by an occasional moan of pleasure. Rolling over, without saying a word, Josh closed his eyes ready for another day.

Early in the morning after shaving and showering and directly after breakfast, Josh was at Father Gerald's office, only to discover that he was not in the seminary but would be back at noon. On the dot of twelve, Josh was knocking on his door.

"Come on in," a loud voice erupted from the other side of the door. "Oh Josh. Good to see you. So, what can I do for you?"

Sitting down, Josh started his inquiry.

"Do you have a few minutes to give me?"

"Sure, what's on your mind?

"Well Father… I know I've only been here for a day, but there are some things that just don't make sense to me."

"Like what?"

"To start, I was wondering why is this campus so run down, like the garden and broken statue of the Sacred Heart. I would think that the Church would want to keep it looking beautiful if nothing else, for the glory of God."

"Go on," Father said.

"Also, why are there no formal prayers before and after meals and why do we have to take those pills?"

"Anything else?"

"Another thing that I can't understand is why there is no daily Mass? I for one would like to receive communion every day. I also noticed that all the statues have been removed from the church as well as there is no Sanctuary Lamp. I know there must be a good reason for all of this, but I just would like you to explain it for me, if you would."

Father Gerald sat back in his chair, readjusting himself as if he was a little uncomfortable. Cracking a smile, he said, "There are good answers for all of your concerns, and I will be happy to explain everything to you."

Of course, inwardly, he was fuming, raging mad, and it took everything he had to control his outrage. "Who the hell do you think you are, coming in here only after one day. Give me three weeks and I will have you eating out of my hands," he thought to himself.

"Now where to begin… First, we are trying our best to raise money to improve the campus, fix the statue, windows, and broken doors. Additionally, our groundskeeper who volunteered his services for many years, passed away last spring… God rest his soul.

"Unfortunately, our diocese has given us as much money as they can spare, and quite frankly, if I must choose between cutting grass and pulling weeds, or paying for good teachers and food to feed everyone, I will choose the latter. As for prayers, before and after meals, remember I told you yesterday that we are very liberal. We feel that meaningful prayer should come from within, it should be personal and from the heart, not necessarily as a memorized standard prayer. Therefore, we ask everyone to pray whatever is on their hearts. Of course, not everyone may do it, but this is what we encourage and hope everyone will do." Taking a deep breath, he continued.

"Now, as for the removal of the statues in the church… we had them removed a few years ago to be completely refurbished and hope that we will soon have them back in place. Because of our financial situation, it has taken longer than anticipated…

CHAPTER III

"What was your other question? Oh yes, the sanctuary lamp. Of course, it is not displayed as currently the Blessed Sacrament is not present. But I can assure you that you will see it lit every Sunday when Mass is said. Last, we are trying our best to have daily Mass once again. You must realize that besides myself, Father Jim is the only fully ordained priest here. The others are close to ordination and only have less than a year before they will be ordained. Until then, Father Jim and I are usually up at five and in town helping with the many needy. So, as you can see, it's quite difficult for us to get back for early Mass. We do apologize, and hopefully will be able to resolve this in the very near future."

Father Gerald was quite proud of himself in the way he had answered all of Josh's questions. Of course, unknowing to Josh, they were all lies. Leaning back in his chair he concluded,

"Well Josh, I hope this answers all your concerns, and please feel free to come back again if you have anything else on your mind." Standing up they shook hands as he quickly escorted Josh out of the office.

Retreating to the library, Josh sat down in one of the overstuffed chairs directly in front of the fireplace. A million thoughts were going through his mind, but all in all he was fairly satisfied with the answers he was given. Because the lunch hour was just about over, Josh remained in the library for some time contemplating what he had just heard. Getting up, he headed for his next class, then suddenly he remembered. Father never mentioned anything about the pills. Oh well, he must have forgotten.

Three weeks passed and during that time there were only two mornings that Mass was celebrated, and several times, Sunday Mass was replaced with a communion service. Time went quickly, but many questions remained.

Josh had made quite a name for himself in those first few weeks. Some really liked him, mostly the newer seminarians who had yet to receive their full indoctrination. He was especially liked by his close friends who he had secretly told not to take the pills. Others liked him for his many inquisitive questions he always asked during class. Unbeknownst to everyone, he had formed a small prayer group that prayed the rosary every day. He became good friends with his roommate David. They would sit for hours and talk. Jesus, church, and the bible were topics often discussed. In addition, he taught the rosary to him and all the others in his little prayer group.

On the other hand, others disliked or perhaps even hated him, especially the ones who were threatened by his morality and spirituality. Most of all he was despised by all his teachers and senior seminarians due to his constant questions and rebuttal on spiritual matters and church dogma. Josh was always posing an opposite point of view which infuriated his teachers, sometimes making them look like fools, especially when they had difficulty defending their views. The truth is Josh only wanted to learn and explore truth and the only way he knew how to do that was to ask questions and debate various points of view. Unfortunately, no matter how sincere he was, he was considered a troublemaker and a threat to their establishment.

On Monday, June 12th, just as Josh started his fourth week, three young men entered the 'seminary'. Father Gerald gloated. "Three more seminarians. Three more future priests indoctrinated to hate the Church." All three were given the same introductory talk as Josh had received.

CHAPTER III

Overhearing Father Gerald's conversation, he repeated the same promises that he told Josh, especially how talented they all were and how quickly they would be ordained.

Josh couldn't believe his ears. It sent chills up his spine. Thinking to himself, I guess everyone is as smart and capable as I am. What a load of crap. As the three were shuttled off for a tour of the seminary with Father Jim, their thoughts were all the same, "All we want is a place to stay. We never said anything about becoming a priest."

However, what really changed the mood of the day was during dinner with the three new guys and some of the senior seminarians. Much of their conversations was overheard by Josh.

Jay Reynolds, one of the three newcomers, was kicked out of catholic high school when he was fourteen. Fortunately, his mother enrolled him in public high school but after graduating, his life took a dive. Getting into drugs and sex, he ended up on the streets of New York City for five years.

The other two were brothers, who appeared to be around twenty, and grew up in an abusive home. Spending a good many years in orphanages, they never experienced the love and security that a normal childhood would have given them. Consequently, as one might expect, they appeared to be mad at the world and didn't care about anything except themselves.

All three however, were more than happy to accept Father Gerald's offer to join the seminary, if for no other reason, they had three square meals and a place to sleep every day. As Josh glanced over at their table, he couldn't believe his eyes. Yes, the cup of pills was once again at everyone's plate, but to his surprise and horror, only white pills occupied the cup this time, and not just one, but three or four.

One of the senior seminarians, who everyone called "Bull," a name given to him because of his well-hung testicles, noticed Jay was refusing to take his pills. Walking over to him he said,

"What's the matter, my brother? Looks like you don't want to take the pills."

"No. I don't. I don't take anything if I don't know what I'm taking. Too many bad experiences, you know?"

Standing behind him, Bull blurted out, "Here we go fellas, another troublemaker!"

"No! I don't want to cause any trouble. I just don't take pills, especially when I don't know what they are for."

"Well, everyone here does, and so long as you're here, you will too."

By this time, Bull was joined by two other seniors, Jared VanNess, who everyone called Spike, most likely because of his hair style, and Rex Hamilton. Both brutes were feared by most of the newcomers. They were exceptionally cruel to them. Before anything else was said, Bull pulled Jay's head back while Spike and Rex held him down. Forcing his mouth open, he dumped the pills down his throat. Releasing him, everyone joined in with laughter, as they headed back to their tables.

Jay, screaming mad, let out a few choice curse words, but was quickly encouraged to sit back down, reminding him that he might be back on the streets if he caused any more trouble. Suddenly, all three, being quite irritated, turned and walked back to Jay's table. Pushing others aside, Spike and Rex sat down on each side of Jay while Bull sat directly across from him.

"Look, I don't want any trouble," Jay said, expecting some sort of altercation.

"Neither do us," Bull said. "But, if you're not a good boy, we'll have our way with you. You know what I mean. We'll have our way with you."

CHAPTER III

While they were speaking, Rex placed his hand high on Jay's thigh while Spike grabbed his crotch. Startled and fuming, Jay tried to get up, but Bull grabbed his wrists while the other two pushed him back down. Squeezing even harder, Spike said,

"We're not kidding. You understand us, we're not kidding. And tonight we'll teach you a lesson you'll never forget."

While all this was happening, Josh was eating his meatloaf that was served every Monday night for dinner. After a few bites, and seeing everything that just took place, he dropped his fork spitting out his food. Standing up, choking, and coughing, he headed for the nearest restroom.

"You OK?" David asked, smacking him on the back while following him out.

Once out of the dining hall and out of sight of everyone, Josh stopped his pretended choking and grabbed David by the arm.

"Let's get out of here. Quick to the library, no one will be there now."

David hurriedly followed him like a puppy dog not knowing what the hell was going on.

Entering the library, Josh looked around to be sure they were alone.

"Listen to me," Josh said, "I've been telling you for weeks that something is not right here. This place is no seminary."

Again, looking around to be sure they were alone, he pulled David close and sitting down began to explain.

"Listen to me, and don't interrupt. You know those pills that I told you not to take, especially the white one."

"Yeah," David quickly said. "I haven't taken any of them like you told me."

"Wait just listen to me," Josh continued. "I saw the pills in the cups for the new guys. They were all white, three or four of them. No other pills. Just the white ones… the sex pills. Then, as I began to eat, those three thugs came back to Jay's table, and began to molest him."

"Oh, come on," David said. "Molest him?"

"I'm telling you! I saw Rex caressing his thigh while Spike was whispering in his ear. Next thing I saw Spike was grabbing the guy's crotch and squeezing hard."

Davis just looked dumbfounded.

"The poor guy tried to get away, but they just held him down. He couldn't move. And another thing. They said that they were going to teach him a lesson tonight that he would never forget."

"That doesn't mean that they were molesting him."

"Yeah, then why did they say they would have their way with him tonight?? Come on, David! Think straight. Why else would two guys be caressing another guy's thigh and touching his crotch?"

David's mood changed.

"I've seen a few things going on in some of the rooms and even been invited to join, but that's not my thing. Just chalked it up to being gay. Who am I to judge?" David continued, "But abusing and molesting guys…? That's something different."

"Look, there's a lot crazier stuff going on here, but I don't have time to explain it all to you now. I just know we need to get out of here… and soon."

"Let's go talk to Father Gerald. He's been good to me and I'm sure he will clear all of this up."

"I have already talked to him," Josh said as he dismissed David's suggestion. Looking at David's downcast face, Josh continued,

"I don't care what Father Gerald says. Something is not right in this place. Nothing but sex and lies all day long.

CHAPTER III

Every day I pray and get the same message... 'Get out, this place is evil...' The thought is always there. Get out."

David looked at Josh again in a bewildering expression. "You might be right, but, but evil? Don't really know what that means. Maybe it's just a few guys that are out of line."

"Pay attention to everything," Josh said. "Why would anyone be given these pills in a seminary? And why would any administrative head allow sexual activity to go on? That's the last thing we need in the Church. I'm telling you something's not right. Come on David! Really think hard about it."

Their conversation was interrupted by the bell indicating that dinner had ended.

"We got to go," Josh said. "I'm sure someone will be here soon. We'll talk later."

With that, they both stood up and left the library before being seen by anyone. Josh went outside to sit and pray by the broken statue, despite what Father Gerald had said. Unbeknown to him, the entire neglected garden had hundreds of black hideous demons continuously circling overhead. With every pass, they were ready to pounce on Josh at any moment, had it not been for Kapriel, who was ever anxious to slash any one of them into fiery ashes had they dared to come close to him.

Another set of evil eyes was staring at Josh through his office window. Father Gerald was not happy. Cursing and pacing back and forth, he decided he had enough of Josh's shit. No, he wasn't happy with him. Not happy at all. In fact, he was infuriated as he had never had this much trouble from anyone else before. He was sick of listening to the complaints of his staff and senior seminarians. It was time to take more drastic steps if he was ever going to succeed in getting Josh converted to his side. Yes, more drastic steps, he thought to himself. One way or another, he was determined to have his way with him.

REPARATION: A STORY OF HOPE

Josh had no idea where David had disappeared too. Realizing it was getting late, Josh walked to the rec-room where he got a soda and cheese crackers to satisfy his growling stomach. Coming out of the room, he noticed that the lights were still on in Father Gerald's office. Hearing voices as he passed and not thinking much of it, he headed for his room.

Still unfamiliar with the various dormitory halls and deep in thought about his and David's conversation, Josh again had trouble finding his room. With his mind preoccupied from his and David's conversation, he turned down a hall and quickly noticed it was not familiar to him.

Somehow, he had turned in the wrong direction and ended up where the seniors were housed. Just as he was about to turn around, two naked guys entered the hall from the opposite end. Briefly looking at Josh, they entered their room. Glancing back at Josh, one of the guys gestured with his hand for Josh to join them.

Startled, Josh immediately turned away hoping to avoid any more embarrassing incidents. Trying to find his way back as fast as possible, he realized that most of the doors to the rooms were open. Glancing to his right, just as he passed a room in the center of the hall, he saw two guys sleeping in the same bed and in the room directly across, two guys were engaged in oral sex while two others looked on.

It was then that he realized what was going on everywhere in the building. Thinking the only safe place was in his room, he picked up his pace to almost a run. Beads of sweat were forming on his face as panic set in.

The sounds of sex grew louder. His head was swirling, and his vision deformed by sweat and black trails of mist dodging in and out of every room and all around him. Hundreds of red bloodshot eyes were piercing through the darkness and that putrid smell of sulfur, whenever evil was

CHAPTER III

present, was overwhelming. Finally, he reached the end of the corridor skidding to a stop. Spike and Rex burst out of their room blocking his way.

"Where do you think you're going, pretty boy?"

Not waiting for an answer, they grabbed him by the arms and shoved him into the corner room. Holding him in a vice grip they forced him to look at the two guys in the bed fornicating. Struggling and squirming to get free, Josh closed his eyes to block out the sight, but the sound of the headboard knocking back and forth in a rhythmic sequence could not be extinguished.

"Take a good look," one of his captors said. "Tomorrow this will be you."

Laughing, they pulled him even closer to the two naked guys, but to his surprise they unexpectedly let him go, still laughing as they slammed the door behind him.

Finally, reaching his room, Josh quickly shut the door half expecting someone to be following him. Once inside, he could still feel his heart pounding remembering what had just taken place. After a few minutes, and regaining his composure, he hoped that he could finally rest and clear his head of all the confusion of the day. David was already in bed but to Josh's surprise was not asleep.

"Where the heck have you been?" David asked.

Looking up at him, still somewhat out of breath, Josh took a deep breath, expelled it out of his lungs and said,

"I can't talk now... I'll tell you all about it tomorrow."

"I went to see Father Gerald," David mumbled.

"You did what?"

"Yeah, he listened and said he would take care of everything…"

"For God's sake," Josh said, "I told you not to talk to him!"

"No, no you didn't. You just said that *you* had talked to him," David hastily replied.

"What did you tell him?"

"I told him everything you told me."

"Oh no…Oh no…" Josh mumbled in a disappointed voice. He just sat there with his head in his hands.

"You won't believe what happened to me tonight. I'll tell you all about it tomorrow, but I'm telling you right now that we gotta get out of here. And don't talk to anyone else, understand?" Silence. "Understand?" Josh repeated.

"Yeah…yeah," David mumbled.

Josh quickly undressed and turning toward the door, he remembered that there was no lock on it. Instead, he shoved a chair under the doorknob before getting into bed. Turning to face the wall, Josh closed his eyes. Just before he fell asleep, he thought to himself, "Is this place really evil or are there just a bunch of gay jerks that need to be exposed…?" Then after a few minutes, he fell asleep with his rosary beads still in his hand.

Josh was up early. Immediately going over to David's bed, he shook him, but David was apparently in a deep sleep…

"Wake up…Wake up!" But still no response except for a few grunts.

"David! Wake up man." It was useless. Waking up David was always difficult. So, Josh headed off to the men's locker room for a quick shave and shower. Splashing the last bit of shaving cream off his face, and looking in the mirror, he was sure he saw two sets of legs in the toilet stall directly behind him. Quickly packing up his toiletries, he headed for the showers. As he stepped out of the shower and began to dry himself, one of the stall doors opened. This time there was no doubt about it. Bull and another senior stepped out. Quickly ducking behind the wall, he was sure they did not see him.

CHAPTER III

Back in his room, he again tried to wake David. Pulling the covers off him and shaking him, David finally opened his eyes.

"What's…what's going on?" David managed to mumble through his dry, crusty lips.

"Look, I don't have time to explain everything but stay in this room until I get back. We're getting out of here today. Do you hear me? Stay in this room until I get back!"

"OK... OK... I got it," David said while yawning.

"And get dressed," Josh said as he left the room.

Josh headed directly to Father Gerald's office. He would make one last attempt to get answers, or he and David were out of here. Unfortunately, no one was there except some senior seminarian taking phone calls and making appointments.

"Can I help you?" he said.

"I want to see Father Gerald. When will he be back?"

"Not sure. But I'll leave him a message that you want to see him."

"Fine," Josh blurted out and stormed out of the office.

Thinking Father Gerald and the others might be at breakfast, Josh decided to look for them there. It was worth a try. Entering the cafeteria, Josh spotted Spike and Rex who confronted him last night. They were purposely staring at him with sinister smiles on their faces. Rex pointed directly to Josh and began to communicate with him through hand gestures.

With his left hand he cupped his fingers together forming a circle or a hole. With the other hand he thrusted his index finger in and out of the hole, clearly indicating what was in store for him later that night. Paying little attention to it, Josh continued to look around for Father Gerald. Noticing that he, nor Father Jim were there, he walked over to the nearest table and asked,

"Do you know where Father Gerald and Father Jim are?"

"Damned if I know," some kid responded. "But if I were to guess they are in town, visiting various places and trying to solicit recruits."

"That's it," Josh said to himself, "we're out of here. I'm not waiting any longer." Returning to his room, he immediately noticed that the chair in the room was upside down and all of David's papers and books were spilled across the floor. More importantly, David was gone.

Confusion and panic set in. Where could he be? What happened? Did they take him? A million questions passed through his mind, but one thing was for sure, David would not have left unless he was forced to. Because Josh had only been at the seminary for a month, he was not aware of all the hidden tunnels or rooms in the place. He had to find his roommate, but where to start?

Looking quickly in the restroom, recreation room, and library with no results, he decided to check out the little chapel, although he knew it was off limits. Nevertheless, he decided to take the chance. Approaching the winding staircase, he slowly descended, step by step, making sure not to make a sound. Reaching the chapel entrance, he poked his head in. It was empty but the cross that David had described, was not upside down, but hanging correctly.

Hearing voices coming from behind him, Josh panicked. Quickly looking to his right, he saw nothing but a stone wall. Then turning he noticed what looked like a large storage closet.

Dashing to it, he barely had time to close the door. Searching for a light he pulled on a string hanging from the ceiling. The light revealed a large storage room containing various church items. Chalices, unconsecrated hosts, wine, altar cloths, candles, flashlights, and the like.

CHAPTER III

Looking further he discovered a hidden exit behind a false wall. Not wasting any time, with a flashlight in his hand, Josh stepped behind the wall. Three steps down and he was into a maze of tunnels, all constructed out of stone with rounded ceilings.

Trying to get figure out where exactly he was in the maze of it all, he walked forward passing a tunnel on his left. Continuing forward he eventually came to a huge room on his right. Slowly opening one of the huge double doors, he was met with total blackness and the damp smell of a cellar that reeked of musty and stale air. Thankful that he had taken the flashlight, he began to scan the room. Almost immediately as the light revealed the contour of the room, two shinny green eyes came into view, not more than three feet away from his face. Falling backwards in fright and dropping the light, he closed his eyes, huddling on the floor waiting for attack. Nothing. No attack. No noise. No movement. Nothing. Retrieving the light, he stood up and continued his search.

Again, two shiny green eyes. They were the eyes of the statue of Saint Joseph. Then another saint came into view, then another and another. Here were all the statues that had been removed from the church, and they certainly were not being restored. "That son of a B," Josh thought to himself. All lies. As the light illuminated the front of the room, he saw four upside-down figures of the crucified Christ. It was then that Josh remembered that all the crucifixes in the buildings were missing the figure of Christ.

Trying to figure out where he was in perspective to the above buildings, Josh figured this area was the basement under the church. Stepping back into the tunnel, after a few feet forward the tunnel turned right. All along its outside wall was a series of what Josh thought were individual altars with arched ceilings. In fact, they were ancient catacombs.

Turning around, he retraced his steps back to the hall that he had just passed. Slowly moving forward, he reached a fork. To his right a short tunnel led to a dark unlit descending staircase. The left fork emptied into a long hall lit every five or six feet with dim light bulbs hanging from exposed wires. Pausing for a moment, Josh contemplated which direction to take.

Suddenly, he heard a weak cry. The sound was coming from the dark unlit staircase. Again, he heard it, this time a little louder. Cautiously he poked his head down the steps listening for another sound. Perhaps it was just his imagination or perhaps the sound came from another tunnel, or perhaps it wasn't even human.

Just as he began to lean over the steps, the light hanging above his head burst into a thousand pieces, not only making the area darker but frightening him enough to cause him to fall down several steps. Desperately trying to regain his footing and his composure, he finally got to his feet, not sure of what had just happened. Feeling his heart pound and somewhat shaken, he was about to scramble back up, when once again he heard sounds, ever so faint.

Blessing himself, he continued down the staircase, ever mindful that he might not be alone. Reaching the bottom of the steps, he moved cautiously, expecting to be attacked anytime. Now he could clearly see a light coming from a single room that was located at the end of the tunnel. Yes, something was behind him, something he had never experienced before. Kapriel knew exactly what was coming his way. Josh entered the room as Kapriel stood guard at the door, sword in hand ready for the approaching attack.

"Oh, my Dear God," Josh said out loud as he entered the room, horrified at what he saw. Jay, who had just

CHAPTER III

arrived yesterday, was naked with his hands bound, held above his head by a chain attached to the ceiling. His back was blistered with whipping scars of dry crusted black blood and puss. Evidently, besides being abused, he was taught the lesson that he was told he would never forget. Josh didn't know exactly what to do. How could he release him? How could he release him from the chains with no key? Panic. Confusion. Then the lights went out, literally. And suddenly, just as fast as the lights went out, Josh was held from behind with a chloroform rag held over his face.

Kapriel did all he could to fight off the demonic attack happening in the shadows. Dozens of Warrior Demons along with nine Attack Demons were dispatched by Azazal. The Attack Demons were tall and thin but extremely strong. Their heads looked like a football with pointed faces... large, yellow slanted eyes. Teeth jagged and sharp, nostrils protruding far out from their skull.

Unlike ordinary warriors, their black wings followed the length of their bodies, jagged feathers sharp enough to cut a human in half with one swipe. One thing that made these Attack Demons so dangerous was their speed and long fingered claws that could sink in, hold on, or rip just about anything apart. Additionally, what bothered Kapriel so much was these attack creatures did not always abide by the heavenly laws forbidding them not to physically interfere or touch any human person. However, Kapriel knew full well that throughout the course of time, some had been seen to take part in various religious wars.

The attack came quickly and continuously, just as Kapriel expected. The first wave of attackers were small warrior demons that Kapriel had no trouble slashing to bits as fast as they attacked. Then came what he was dreading. Could he alone be able to fight off these attack creatures single handed, without attending to Josh?

The first shot past him barely missing his mark. Kapriel pulled back just in time to avoid its slashing wings, but not quick enough to make a strike with his massive sword. Before the first Attack Demon could slow down, it realized that the tunnel was far too short and narrow for him to maneuver or stop before smashing into the stone wall directly in front of him. Quickly stretching out his wings, they scraped along the tunnel walls, sparks flying, stopping him just short of slamming into the wall. Then a second and a third flew past, but not quick enough to avoid Kapriel's sword, slashing both simultaneously into fiery bits. By that time, the first Attack Demon had recovered and was approaching to continue his attack.

One could smell hatred and anger in the air. Screeching attack sounds accompanied by the smell of sulfur and slime emitted with each breath, as the demons continued their assault. Kapriel was even more frustrated as he was aware that Josh had been chloroformed and taken somewhere. Yet he had no choice but to stay until all these hideous creatures were eliminated.

Two more Attack Demons attacked so fast, but also not being able to maneuver, one flew directly into the first demon that had returned to attack Kapriel. The impact was with such force that both disintegrated instantly, while the second, not being able to stop, was obliterated into fiery ashes as it slammed into the wall at the end of the tunnel.

Hoping that the attack was over, Kapriel turned only to see two more Attack Demons getting ready to strike. Unlike the previous attacks, they realized that their speed and long bodies were useless in such tight quarters. Now both began to slowly move forward for a simultaneous attack.

However, Kapriel, not letting them initiate the attack, rushed so quickly toward them that they were taken

CHAPTER III

completely off guard. Before either one could move, one of the demon's wings were slashed off, not fatal, but enough to slow him down. The other never knew what hit him. Ten long sharp claws, sunk into Kapriel's back and shoulders. The demon hung on as Kapriel twisted and turned, reaching desperately to free himself from the claws that were about to rip him apart.

Out of the corner of Kapriel's eyes, he spotted an old iron torch holder, still attached to the wall. The torch holder was shaped in the form of two praying hands, folded together and pointing straight out. Without wasting a second, Kapriel lunged backwards with such force that the pointed fingers sunk deep into the demon's back, instantly crushing him into smoke and fiery ashes. The wounds on Kapriel's back were already beginning to heal as he brushed off the burnt ashes and began his search for Josh.

David had been locked in another tunnel room but was not harmed or molested. Kirt Williamson, the senior seminarian, who had warned Josh about the pills the first day he arrived, was sick to his stomach when he found out what had happened to Jay. He had always dreamed of the priesthood but was now so disillusioned after coming to this seminary that he had just about given up on the idea.

Realizing what was really going on, there was no way he was going to be a part of their sick plan to kidnap and brainwash guys into their way of thinking. "They must be really desperate," he thought to himself as he unlocked the door where David was being held.

"David! I don't know if you know me…I'm Kirt. No time to explain as Father Gerald and the 'priests' will be back soon. Go to the chapel and help Josh. I think they have taken him there. I'm going to free Jay and get him back to my room… once you get Josh, turn left at the fork of the tunnel, and keep going straight, then up the steps to the parking garage. I will meet you there." David stood frozen not understanding exactly what Kirt had just said nor what was going on.

"Get going, now!"Kirt yelled as he ran to free Jay.

Jolted free of his temporary trance, David headed for the secret staircase that led to the chapel. Spike and Rex stood over Josh's naked body, as he lay strapped to the altar table in the chapel. Just coming out of his chloroformed sleep, the first thing Josh noticed was the cross, hanging upside down.

"Remember us?" Spike said with a sadistic smile on his face.

Rex gestured with his index finger moving it in and out of his other hand, as he had done in the cafeteria. Six other seminarians were seated on the benches. They had been there previously waiting for Father Gerald to return. The room was filled with lit candles of all sizes and some sort of chanting music was softly playing.

"Let's get on with it," Rex said as he began to unbuckle his jeans.

"Not yet!" Spike insisted. "I wanna wait till he's fully awake. Don't worry, it won't be long," as he leaned over and started to caress Josh's thigh.

"Who the hell turned up the damn music?" someone yelled out as it got louder and louder. Yet, to their bewilderment, no one was near the player. Lights began to flicker, then they went out. The air began to swirl, causing some of the candles to go out while others burned even brighter. Smoke was everywhere, and of course, so was that sick putrid smell of slime and sulfur.

Suddenly, David burst into the room, smashing Spike across his head. Watching his buddy crash to the floor but before he could move, Rex also went flying across the room as a broomstick smashed across his face. Both were not going anywhere and would be knocked out for some

CHAPTER III

time. In the confusion, the six seminarians, half scared out of their wits, were scrambling out and up the staircase as fast as they could.

While David was releasing Josh and telling him that Kirt Williamson was in the process of rescuing Jay, they heard the shrill sound of something horrifying coming their way. Getting louder and louder, it was almost upon them.

"What's that?" David asked.

"I have no idea… but we gotta get out of here."

The putrid smell of sulfur was now even more present. Realizing that the chapel must be full of demons, Josh quickly told David to go to their room and get his wallet and the keys to his car. He in turn, would quickly get dressed and help Kirt. Then they would all meet in the garage and leave this place forever.

No sooner was David up the stairs and out of sight when the naked body of Josh was propelled across the room and slammed into the stone wall. Almost immediately, ten long sharp claws dug into his tender flesh and tossed him head over heels to the other side of the room. Bleeding and unconscious, Josh laid on the floor as the attack continued.

Again, the creature's claws began to sink into Josh's back, but before they were fully in, the demon burst into flames. Kapriel would have been there sooner, had he not been held up destroying yet another Attack Demon, who was on its way to the chapel.

Kapriel was now fully engaged in destroying all the other Warrior Demons that were still brave enough to hang around. Once the threats were gone, the music and wind suddenly stopped.

Leaving Josh on the floor, Kapriel rushed off quickly to get David.

For some strange reason, David had the urge to return to the chapel instead of going to the garage as Josh had told him. Seeing the condition that Josh was in, he immediately wrapped his wounds in altar cloths. Picking him up, he carried Josh down the hidden staircase, left at the fork, down the long tunnel until they were safe in the garage. Kirt was already waiting for them.

"Get in the car," David said without taking time to explain Josh's condition.

"No… I'm staying here. I got Jay safely back to my room. Pretty sure he'll be OK, but I gotta stay…no one suspects me of anything and besides, someone has to look out for Jay and the rosary group until you can come back and get all of us out of here."

"OK," David said. "We'll be back. Don't know when, but we'll be back!" yelling out the window as he drove off toward town. Speeding down the narrow drive but before reaching the main road, he spotted Father Gerald approaching in a van ahead of him. Swerving to his right to avoid hitting him, the wheels of Josh's car sunk into the muddy grass, skidding to a stop. Father Gerald was just pulling up beside them.

"Shit! Oh, shit," David instinctively blurted out.

Flooring the gas pedal, mud and grass flew back everywhere, sinking the car even deeper into the mud. Father Gerald, clearly infuriated, was just opening his car door and stepping out. With all the noise that the spinning wheels were making, David could just about make out what Father was screaming.

"What in the hell are you doing out here???"

David put the car in reverse, then forward, then reverse, then forward, rocking it back and forth, and then suddenly, it lurched forward, spitting mud and grass all over Father Gerald.

CHAPTER III

Turning on to the main highway, he raced toward the main area of Clarksville. Not seeing any hospital and not knowing where to stop, he saw what looked like a church.

Its sign read: *Welcome to Saint Andrews Catholic Church*. Stopping the car, he thought to himself, "Is this another one of those supposed to be 'Catholic' places?"

However, Josh was bleeding and needed immediate help. Taking the chance, he picked up Josh and headed up the steps. Once inside he spotted Father O'Malley who was just finishing confessions.

"Father, please! We need help! We need help! We need help!"

It took close to two months before Josh was well enough to get out of bed, and another couple of weeks to regain his strength. He had suffered six broken ribs, a broken collar bone, a dislocated elbow, multiple bruises, cuts and gashes to his face and body and of course those deep ripping puncture wounds to his shoulders and back. Father O'Malley had rushed him to the hospital where his wounds were stitched up, elbow reset, and his collarbone repaired with a pin. The doctors said it was a miracle that he survived, as he had lost a tremendous amount of blood.

After two weeks in the hospital, he was back at Father O'Malley's home where he and David cared for him. During the weeks he was healing, David had told Father everything that had transpired at the seminary. It was hard for him to believe everything David told him. Nevertheless, he vowed to find out exactly what was going on at that 'seminary' as soon as Josh was well and back on his feet.

On a Monday morning, eleven weeks after Josh's recovery, sure enough, Father O'Malley was on his way to confront Father Gerald and all that was going on at the

Sacred Heart Seminary. Pulling up to park his car, he passed by a beautiful small circular garden, with a statue of the Sacred Heart of Jesus in its center, surrounded by beautiful flowers. Strange, he thought to himself. Josh had described it as being totally in disrepair. Reaching the top of the steps, he turned around to make sure…Yes, the statue had both hands. Hum! Josh had described the statue with its hand broken off.

"Come on in, Father O'Malley. Please have a seat. I'm so glad we could make these arrangements to see you. I understand you have some questions." Without waiting for a response, he continued,

"Can I get you something to drink…water… coffee?"

"No thank you," Father O'Malley said. "You know, I've been caring for Josh Donovan ever since he left here. He was badly hurt while under your care."

"No, I didn't know that. I was under the impression that he just decided to leave. I think his roommate David Dexter also left. I have no idea how he was hurt, but I told him over and over not to go out after dinner, as there are often drunks and drug dealers on our grounds. Unfortunately, we can't afford full time security guards, but we do our best to keep our boys safe and especially insist that they remain inside after hours."

"Evidently, you failed with Josh."

"Well Father O'Malley, as I said, Josh chose to venture out after dinner hours and for all I know he was off the premises when he was hurt. You know, I immediately called the police when I was informed that he was not at dinner or in his room. We looked everywhere. You can check that out if you like but no one knew what happened to him until your call recently.

"By the way, how is he doing? I hope he's fine…you know he was such a good student. Perhaps he will choose to return at some later time."

CHAPTER III

"I doubt that very much." Father O'Malley continued his questions. "I understand that there are all sorts of tunnels under this place with various rooms to detain unruly kids. And I also understand that the images of Christ have been removed from all your crucifixes throughout the place. I was also told that all statues and religious paintings have also been removed. I wonder why in such a religious place as this, things like this would occur."

Taking a deep breath and exhaling loud enough to make an impression, Father Gerald stood up.

"I think the best way to answer all your questions is to let you see for yourself. Come, I'll show you everything."

First, he was shown the library. Two or three students were reading scripture and the cross that long ago had been removed, was hanging exactly where it should have been, with the crucified Jesus attached to it, not to mention a beautiful portrait of Jesus as the Good Shepherd hanging on the east wall.

Next came the church. To the far left was a group of seminarians practicing hymns to be sung at Sunday's Mass. Father Gerald made a point to show Father O'Malley all the statues that were in place, and to bring to his attention the large cross at the front of the church, also displaying a lifelike image of Christ. Of course, all of the stone carvings on the walls were there but now were separated by large portraits of various saints. Just before leaving, the lit sanctuary lamp was also pointed out.

Walking out of the church they stopped in front of the winding staircase leading down to the chapel.

"Now you asked about hidden tunnels. The only thing resembling a tunnel is our quaint little chapel. Please follow me." Slowly, they descended the tunnel staircase into the chapel. Two lit candles were on the small altar, with a beautiful Crucifix of Jesus hanging above it. A lit sanctuary lamp was also on display, a beautiful woven ancient looking rug tapestry, was hanging on the far-left wall, covering up the closet and hidden staircase, and to top it off, two seminarians were reverently kneeling, as they silently pretended to say the rosary.

Father O'Malley didn't know what to say. Turning toward the tapestry, he moved closer as if he was going to touch it. Father Gerald quickly yelled out,

"Please don't touch it! It's hundreds of years old and priceless." Satisfied, they returned to the lobby.

"Guess I owe you an apology," Father O'Malley reluctantly said.

"No, no Father. It was my pleasure. I don't blame you at all. I'm just surprised you were told such things. But quite frankly, if David had anything to do with these tails, well…"

"Well, what?" Father O'Malley said.

"Well… David was heavily addicted to drugs when I found him on the streets. It took us many months to get him sober. Don't think he really appreciated it. You know, I hate to say it, but I caught him several times trying to buy drugs from some slugs that were trespassing on the property. Maybe he was pissed at us… excuse my expression, and then again, perhaps he just made up these things to get back at me. Who knows?"

Reaching his office, Father Gerald said while shaking hands, "So glad I was able to clear up these discrepancies. Please feel free to call if there is anything else I can help you with."

Then calling Kirt Williamson over, he asked him to escort Father O'Malley out. As soon as they were outside, Kirt slipped O'Malley a neatly folded note.

"Don't read it until you're out of sight."

Father O'Malley waited until his car could no longer be seen before he stopped and proceeded to read the message:

CHAPTER III

TELL JOSH AND DAVID I'M OK. LOOKING AFTER THE GANG. EVERYTHING YOU SAW AND HEARD TODAY WAS A LIE...DON'T COME BACK FOR US...I HAVE A PLAN.

Sitting at the dinner table, Father O'Malley discussed everything he had seen at the seminary.

"Must have taken them weeks to bring all those statues up from the tunnels, not to mention all the paintings and crucifixes."

David added to Josh's comment, "Yeah... and don't forget how much time it took to hang and place everything back to their original place."

Father O'Malley had already called the Archdiocese and was told that the seminary was sold years ago to Anthony C. Wadsworth and was now in private hands. Bishop Nelson said that it was possibly being used as a secular seminary of some sort, but it was definitely not Catholic, and therefore the church had no jurisdiction over it.

"I just don't get it," Father O'Malley said.

"Why in the world would they strip the place of religious icons and then suddenly replace them? And why would they pretend to be a Seminary of any sort, and supposedly allow sexual activity and/or abuse to go on?"

"Not supposedly," Josh said.

Maggie Sunders, Father O'Malley's housekeeper and devoted cook, had prepared a wonderful meal for them. Sitting down, Father said the blessing and they all began to eat.

"Delicious!" Josh called out to Maggie, as she stepped back into the kitchen. Reaching for the salt, Josh let out a painful groan.

"Still hurting?" Father O'Malley asked.

"Yeah, my shoulder aches all the time."

David grabbed the salt for Josh.

"Father," Josh said as he seasoned his dinner, "all I know is a couple things for sure."

"There is a lot of sex going on there and Father Gerald knows about it, and I know that Jay was abused and whipped until his back was raw. What's more, I know that every month or two, Father Gerald and his group of his so-called 'priests and seminarians' go into town or who knows where else…"

"New York City," David interjected.

"And I can't tell you why except Father Gerald said they help the needy."

"Ha, 'needy'," David laughed.

"And they often come back with a recruit or two."

"'Recruit.' You mean *abducted*," David continued and added a few more of his thoughts. "I think they want everyone to be gay…gay and pedophiles."

"Gay pedophiles?" Josh said with a look on his face that meant "don't be stupid."

"Why would they want that?" he questioned.

Frustrated, David continued,

"Let me finish… maybe they are trying to get more guys posing as priests, legitimate or not, involved in scandals to hurt the Church. What better way to attack the Church and religious institutions than to discredit them? Create scandals of all sorts. Impure ministers and priests, gay ministers, and priests that abuse children or who engage in sex with each other.

"Crap, I mean it's still going on today! Who knows? This seminary could be an attempt to exploit it even more. Perhaps that's why the place is non-religious, with no formal prayers, no daily masses, no statues, and no paintings anywhere. And don't forget the upside cross and all that weird chanting. If you ask me, it's downright demonic."

CHAPTER III

"I think that's pretty far-fetched," Father O'Malley said. "But in any case, we know the Church is not involved and there's no proof that anyone has ever been abducted."

"Except for asking Jay," David said.

"Yeah…good luck with that."

"Come on Josh! Maybe we can get Kirt to help."

"Maybe… He did say he had a plan."

Letting the conversation rest, they continued eating their meal, although none of them had much of an appetite. After dinner the three sat down in Father O'Malley's living room. No one said much… just small talk. Weather, poor church attendance, work needed on Josh's car, future plans.

"Future plans... Glad you brought that up," David said. "This is going to blow your mind." Josh and Father O'Malley sat waiting for what he was about to say.

"Well, what's up?" Josh eagerly said.

"I think…I think I want to be a priest."

Josh laughed at his friend's words.

"No, really I want to be… I mean a real priest."

"I thought you weren't religious and…"

Father interrupted, "Let him finish," he said almost in a scolding voice.

"Well, being here with you guys, especially you Father, now I know what a real priest is… I mean it's so different from that seminary crap. I never had any motivation in my life except for drugs. Then I met you guys and I think it's what I want to do."

"I think that's great. You're a little young, but you have plenty of time to decide," Father O'Malley said. "I have friends at Holy Apostles College and Seminary in Cromwell, Connecticut. I'm sure we can get you into Cromwell High School to finish your degree and then on to the College and Seminary, if that's what you still want to do."

Excited and with one of the few smiles David had shown in quite some time, he stood up, hugged, and thanked Father.

"I'm really happy for you," Josh said. "I know you will make a really great priest." And he meant it.

"And what about you Josh?" Father O'Malley asked.

"I don't know. I know I always wanted to be a priest and always thought God wanted me to be one…but…but now I just don't know. So much has happened to me over the past five or six months. My experience at the seminary, not to mention Becky. She's been on my mind a lot. Guess I'm just confused. I thought I was sure. But now... I really don't know."

Josh sat staring out into space. The expression on his face clearly showed he was unhappy.

"Well, you have all the time in the world to sort it out. I'm sure the good Lord has a plan for you."

"I hope your right Father," Josh said. "In the meantime, I gotta get a job and a permanent place to stay."

Father smiled as he looked at Josh.

"Looks like the good Lord is already working in that regard."

Josh looked at him with a questioned face.

"I'm good friends with Buzzy Nevill. He owns a gas station right on Main Street, opposite the little strip of stores. I think Bogan's Coffee Shop is right on the corner. I'll call him tomorrow. He just may need some help. Of course, if that's alright with you, Josh?"

"Sure. Thanks! Sounds good to me."

"Now for housing. I have an empty apartment above me and would love it if you would stay there."

"Father, I appreciate it, but…"

"But nothing," Father said. "You would be doing me a favor. It's just going to be a waste of space. Besides, no one has responded to my advertisement in over a year.

CHAPTER III

Guess no one wants to live in an apartment above a Rectory..." All three began to laugh.

"But I don't even have a job yet."

"Don't worry about money. You can help me with the church. Who knows, maybe I will make a priest out of you yet. Besides, it will give you plenty of time to decide what your calling in life is."

Sure enough, Josh got the job at Buzzy's and David was accepted into Cromwell High. David was scheduled to be admitted after winter break, just a few months away. Father O'Malley planned for him to stay with an elderly couple he had known from childhood in the meantime.

Azazal was furious when he received word that not only were his Warrior Demons slaughtered, but all nine of his best Attack Warriors as well. Making him even more furious was the fact that they all were destroyed by one... *one* heavenly angel. The only solace he had was thinking that Kapriel was gone, and as far as he knew, would never have to deal with him again. However, to be sure, he surrounded the seminary with twenty of his finest sentinels and twenty Attack Warriors. Father Gerald constructed a huge electronic iron gate keeping any unwanted person out... or more likely anyone from leaving.

On a Wednesday morning, early in November, a familiar school bus drove up to Buzzy's Gas Station. As Josh walked up to the pumps, his heart began to race. Kirt was in the driver's seat and alone.

"Fill her up," Kirt said with a huge smile on his face. Both were ecstatic to see each other.

"I overheard that you were working here. Listen, I don't have much time."

Then he laid out his plan of rescue, step by step. Friday, all the so-called 'priests' would be leaving for New York

City. No doubt to acquire more willing or unwilling candidates. His plan was to pile the rosary group and Jay into the bus and escape soon after the priests had left. He was given the code to the gate, as he was well trusted. In fact, it was his trust that enabled him to look after and protect Jay. Unfortunately, in order to gain trust and protection for Jay, he often had to pleasure Father Gerald and partake in some of the dorm orgies. A small price to pay, if he ever was going to be able to fulfill his plan of escape.

Friday morning could not have come sooner. Father O'Malley had packed food and drinks for everyone. Knowing that the bus would quickly be spotted and apprehended, he had acquired two RV's. Once the bus arrived, the gang would transfer to the RV's and hopefully be quickly on their way to Cromwell.

Kirk would drive one vehicle while David would drive the other. David had made arrangements to arrive at his foster home earlier than originally planned and Kirt would take any of the older guys who were still interested to Holy Apostles Seminary. As for Jay, Father O'Malley told David to take him with him. He also planned for Jay to stay with David and to attend Cromwell High.

Sitting in the gas station's office, Father O'Malley, Josh, and David waited, with nerves on edge. Buzzy stood behind the counter with his trusty old double gauge shotgun, just in case something might go wrong. Just past 6:00am, Father Gerald and his band of fake 'priests' passed by the station. David immediately recognized the car. Now, how long before Kirt would show up?

Dozens of demons flew after the bus as it left the gates of the seminary. Simultaneously, several sentinels flew directly to Azazal to report what was occurring.

"Was Kapriel with them?" Azazal asked in haste.

"No master, only his guardian."

CHAPTER III

Summoning his top general, Azazal instructed him to dispatch four Attack Warriors and ordered them to stop the bus by any means necessary. Now smiling and quite proud of himself, Azazal boasted of the victory that would never come.

Exactly at 6:30am, Kirt was pulling up to the station. Josh and the others were getting ready to greet them and facilitate the transfer. But before they had a chance to move, Kapriel was already in front of the station with a sword in his hand. Dozens of demons and four Attack Warrior Demons were approaching with tremendous speed.

Kirt finally pulled up, turned off the engine, the door opened, and everyone piled out. Simultaneously, twelve massive angelic warriors slowly descended, standing side by side in front of Kapriel. They ranged in size from six feet to seven feet tall, and like Kapriel, had the strength of twenty. Each was covered in brilliant shining armor, and each carried two massive swords. The little demons had no chance. They were incinerated into fiery bits in seconds. The cocky, overconfident four Attack Demons flew in so fast that they hardly had time to realize they had just been cut in half before ever reaching Kapriel, who simply stood watching the ongoing slaughter.

Once out of the bus, Father O'Malley led everyone to the RV's. Quick goodbyes followed, except for Kirt and David. Josh warmly shook Kirt's hand and thanked him for all he had done and for the personal sacrifices he had to make in order for his plan to work.

"I'll never be able to thank you enough Kirt...God Bless you."

"We'll stay in touch," Kirt said as he opened the door to his RV.

Josh and David hugged each other. Not being able to hold back his tears, Josh said to his friend,

"I will miss you so much and never will forget…"

David interrupted, "Me too. Now look, it's not like we're never going to ever see each other again. Right?"

"Right" Josh said, remembering the same words Becky said when he left Jinksville. After one last goodbye, they all drove off to a new life.

"I'm going back to the church to pray for them," Father said.

"OK," Josh replied.

"I'll see you in a bit after I drop off this bus at the old, abandoned warehouse."

Things remained relatively the same in the town of Clarksville over the next couple of months, except Father Gerald and his crew were never seen in town again. Evidently, there was no one left to recruit. However, activity was still going on at the seminary, as delivery trucks were always seen going and coming from their campus.

Josh and Father O'Malley had a wonderful Thanksgiving dinner prepared for them, thanks to Maggie. They had become close friends over the past months. Josh helped as much as he could in the church and in maintaining the rectory. Josh's anxiety about the priesthood had faded, putting him back on the track. Father O'Malley spent considerable time teaching Josh much of what he should have learned in the seminary. Josh had picked up Latin easily and in fact, knew every prayer necessary to celebrate a Mass. Had he already been ordained, Father O'Malley thought he would have made a wonderful priest.

Sitting in Father's small living room, and enjoying Maggie's homemade pumpkin pie, they talked about so many things, including the condition of the town and the small attendance at Mass.

CHAPTER III

"The town is a mess," Father O'Malley said. "Public areas and buildings neglected, streetlights broken, businesses closed... The town appears totally neglected, and in my opinion, something is not right with the people. Many are nasty and those that used to come to church, are not attending any more. I can't put my finger on it, but it's not what it used to be."

"You know Father," Josh said, "I wonder if that evil 'seminary' has anything to do with this? Father Gerald told me that they came to town to help the needy. That was just a lot of bull. We know that they did nothing for the needy."

"So, what did they do?"

"They certainly did not recruit every time they were here. There aren't enough kids in town. Maybe they just went around bad mouthing the Church and religion. Who knows, but I think David was right on. In any case, it's something to think about."

Father O'Malley just sat and listened. He listened very carefully. Josh turned in early that night, as he had a lot on his mind. To his disappointment, he had not heard from Becky, nor did he know how to reach her. They did however hear from Kirt and David. Amazedly, all the rosary group guys still wanted to be a priest, including Kirt. The big joke was the only good thing about Father Gerald's so-called 'seminary' was they *had* received an excellent education... as how NOT to be a priest!

Unfortunately, after all that happened to Jay, he wanted nothing to do with the priesthood. He would go on to complete his high school and college degrees. As for David, he completed his high school refresher courses and then entered Holy Apostles College and Seminary.

If all went well, he planned to visit Josh in July. That put a smile on Josh's face as he missed his friend. Yet, as he sat in his room, he wondered again about the priesthood. What would he end up doing and what did

Jesus have in store for him? Unbeknownst to him, his life was about to change drastically. Not succumbing to depression, he picked up his rosary and began to pray. Falling asleep several times, he finally finished and headed for bed.

It was shortly after Christmas. The weather was mild for December and by now Josh was physically back to his old self. He worked out every day with the weights that he had kept in the trunk of his car all the time he was at the seminary. Every day he attended Mass with Father O'Malley and a few faithful parishioners.

Work at Buzzy's garage didn't start until 9:00am, giving him time to stop by Bogan's Coffee Shop each morning. Frank and Claudia were always happy to see him. They were some of the few who still attended church and would always bring a dozen delicious vanilla cream-filled donuts to church with them for their small social afterwards. After he walked into their coffee shop, and said his hellos, Josh ordered the usual, two cups of coffee and two vanilla-filled. One for him and one for Buzzy who always was anxious to receive his treat. Business was slow, so Buzzy took off early and told Josh to do the same. He could close at 5:00pm instead of the usual 6:00pm.

***

Josh walked slower than his usual pace, almost as if he were carrying a thousand pounds on his shoulders. Although it had been only six months since the attack had taken place at the seminary, he still couldn't get it out of

CHAPTER III

his mind... not so much as to what happened to him but more to what was going on in that place.

As Josh passed the steps of St. Andrew's, something was not quite right, he thought to himself. Yet all he could detect was a slight scent of sulfur in the air. The same scent he had so often smelled at the seminary.

"Who's there?" Josh yelled, turning around to see if someone was behind him. Then, out of the corner of his eye he thought he saw something black whizzing through the bushes on the empty lot across the street.

"Hey...who's there?"

Nothing, absolutely nothing. Perhaps it was just the wind he thought. Yet an eerie feeling crept along his spine. His house was only a few yards away and he was anxious to get home.

Despite his eerie feeling, Josh was not too concerned, as he often felt uneasy whenever night fell upon the city. Still the smell of sulfur was present, more present than before. Josh was sure that evil was nearby. "What's going on?" he thought. No sooner than the thought passed his mind when another flash of black whizzed past him. Then it was gone and so was the smell of sulfur.

The demon who had been assigned to spy on Josh rushed back to Azazal.

"He's going straight home tonight," the demon reported in a high-pitched voice.

"He didn't go to Church?" asked Azazal.

"No master, directly home."

"Hum..." Azazal mumbled as he scratched his head.

"Maybe we're finally getting to him!" as a slight smile emerged across his face. "Get back to him and don't let him out of your sight. Keep attacking...Keep attacking."

"I will, master, but I can't get too close. His guardian is powerful."

"So are we," Azazal screamed. "NOW, GO!"

As Josh reached his place he used the outside stairs, as he most often did, so as not to disturb Father O'Malley. Josh was breathing heavily, steam emitting from each breath as he reached the top of the steps. He was still shaking from what he had just experienced. Catching his breath, he quickly looked around before entering his kitchen door. Tears welled up in his eyes. "Oh Jesus," he said in a low prayerful voice.

"What's happening? What's happened to our world? To our country? There is so much evil, so much immorality in this city. Where have all the good people gone? Oh Dear Jesus, please help us…please help us…"

Josh unlocked the door, entered the kitchen, and went directly to the sink for a drink of water. After taking off his jacket, throwing it toward the hooks on the wall and missing them, he continued into his small, cramped living room. Looking up, he froze in place with an astonished and frightened expression on his face. Instantly falling back, flipping over a chair behind him, he huddled in the corner of the room, stunned by the light emitting from the figure standing in the room.

"Joshua, don't be afraid," the Lord said.

At the same exact time the Lord spoke, a tremendous light burst from every window.

***

There were no dreams, no nightmares, as he usually had, no worries, no anxiety, nothing except peaceful sleep. With that, the great light was gone

CHAPTER IV

HIS MISSION BEGINS

Early before sunrise, as soon as the great light disappeared, Azazal dispatched another several sentinels to identify where the light had originated from and if there was anything different in the city. By this time, Azazal had already been reinforced with a thousand warriors and had deployed over a dozen more to guard the seminary.

The sentinels soon reported that everything in the city looked exactly the same as it was before the great light. But why, then? Why did the Lord of Hosts visit the city, and who was visited? Azazal knew he would eventually find out. In the meantime, he would reinforce all those warriors who had survived the light with dozens more. No one was going to stop him from carrying out the plan they had worked on so hard to achieve. Little did he know that it would be a 23-year-old who could be the cause of his demise...

Josh's eyes were just opening and adjusting to the light. It was a bright, sunny day. Was it a dream or was it real? What happened to him last night? Then, realizing he was still on the couch where he had fallen asleep with his head on the Lord's lap. Everything came back, and with that, a certain amount of anxiety. Or at the very least some uncertainty, but one thing was for sure: he was going to carry out the Lord's message.

Josh knew that his mission would be difficult, and it would be a cross he would have to carry. He also remembered that Jesus had told him that he would be attacked by many, perhaps even Satan himself. However, he remembered the promise of Jesus. He would be protected and surrounded by two Angelic Guardians that would be with him constantly and provide a spiritual shield around him that nothing could penetrate. Most importantly, he remembered that Jesus said He would always be with him. Taking a deep breath, a smile of confidence came across Josh's face.

Now it all made sense; what Father Gerald was up to, what the seminary was being used for, why so many of the guys thought of nothing but sex. Then he remembered Jesus's exact words, "Satan is using all those in the 'seminary' to launch his attack against my Church." No wonder why the 'seminarians' came into town so often. Yes, David was right. What better way to deceive and turn people against Christian churches, Catholic priests, as well as the Church at large, than to discredit them through their deviant actions, their foul language, and through their lustful behavior.

Josh could hardly wait to tell Father O'Malley all that had transpired last night. Quickly getting dressed, he rushed down the inside staircase. Father O'Malley was sitting at his breakfast table having his daily cup of tea.

"Come on in," he said to Josh. "Sit down and join me for a cup. We have forty-five minutes before morning Mass."

CHAPTER IV

"I have a lot to tell you, but I hardly know where to begin!" After starting, stopping, and stammering a bit, Josh struggled with exactly what to say. Finally, he began.

"Father, what I'm about to tell you will be hard for you to believe. Actually, it would be hard for anyone to believe. But please trust me, I'm going to tell you exactly what happened to me last night. I'll probably sound like a fool or a total idiot, but it's the absolute truth."

"I trust you," O'Malley said. "You've never lied, and I have no reason to think differently now. So, what's on your mind son?"

Realizing that Josh was still having difficulty getting his words out, Father O'Malley said, "Slow down. Take a breath and just take your time and tell me what's on your mind." Again, not knowing exactly where to start, Father said,

"Let's start with a little prayer."

"Good idea," Josh said. "Dear Jesus, please help me to explain what happened last night and give me the strength to complete the mission You asked me to undertake…"

Taking a deep breath, Josh revealed word for word, detail after detail, exactly what transpired between him and the Lord, including the great light. Once he had finished, Father O'Malley sat perfectly still and never said a word. Checking his watch, he finally said,

"Oh my, it's almost time for Mass. As soon as it's over, let's sit down again. I have a million questions."

The same devoted group attended Mass, about a dozen, mostly women. Father O'Malley appeared distant throughout Mass and instead of giving his four-to-five-minute homily, he simply asked everyone to sit in silence and reflect on the day's Gospel. Mrs. Johnson, now widowed for ten years, was confined to a wheelchair for the past six years due to Degenerative Heart Disease. Her ankles and feet had swollen to the size of a softball due to

REPARATION: A STORY OF HOPE

poor circulation. Nevertheless, she never missed Mass, was always willing to help anyone, and had such a pleasant disposition about her that it always was a pleasure just to talk to her.

"Hi Josh," as she waved and called out to him after Mass had ended. "You look a little stressed this morning! What's the matter, is Father picking on you today?"

Father O'Malley, who was cleaning the chalice and tidying up the altar, turned and joked. "Are you kidding me?" he said with a smile. "He's the one always picking on me!"

All three responded with a little chuckle. Suddenly, Mrs. Johnson became very serious.

"I was wondering if you two would pray over me if you have time? Went to the doctors yesterday and things aren't good. Evidently my condition has worsened, and they think they will have to amputate my leg… perhaps both if I'm going to live another year." Tears were now running down her face. "And I think I'll let the good Lord take me… I don't want to…" stopping in the middle of her sentence as she was now crying uncontrollably.

Father O'Malley hugged her, and after calming her down, both he and Josh began to pray. Father asked the good Lord for His mercy and healing and to shower her with His grace. The prayers went on for quite a while. Josh simply prayed very quietly, mostly in tongues, a gift he had just received last night after the Lord's appearance to him

When they had finished, Mrs. Johnson thanked both for their prayers and assured them that she was perfectly alright to get home by herself. Turning her wheelchair around, she headed down the aisle toward the front entrance. About halfway down, Josh called out to her to stop.

"Mrs. Johnson! Mrs. Johnson!"

CHAPTER IV

As she stopped, Josh walked over to her while Father O'Malley looked on. Taking her hands, Josh knelt down beside her.

"Mrs. Johnson, Jesus loves you with all His heart and is so thankful for your faithfulness to Him. He has told me that there are so many sinners in this world. So many have abandoned Him. He's asking us all to repent before it's too late. He has empowered me with the gift of healing so that many will believe in His message, and His healing is for you this morning. Let your healing be an inspiration and lesson to all that His mercy is unending and that He is giving us one last chance for reparation for our sins. Therefore, in the Name of Jesus, I ask that you be healed."

As Josh stood up Mrs. Johnson sat dumbfounded.

"What are you waiting for?" Josh said. "Don't you believe that Jesus can heal you?"

"Yes… I do believe."

"Then stand up and be an inspiration to all so that many will also believe."

Standing up and looking down at her feet, she couldn't believe her eyes. Her feet were normal! She was totally healed.

"Oh, my Lord… Praise Jesus," she said repeatedly.

"Praise Jesus, Praise Jesus. Oh, my good and gracious Lord, thank you, thank you!"

While hugging Josh, she called out to Father O'Malley to witness her healing. Smiling, crying, and not sure exactly what had just happened, she turned and left the church, leaving her wheelchair behind, continuing to praise Jesus all the way home.

Back at the kitchen table Father O'Malley didn't hesitate to ask Josh to repeat all that had occurred to him.

Josh went on and on, giving every detail, while Father O'Malley once again listened intently.

"You're right Josh. It's hard to believe. Had I not witnessed what just happened, that is. God has blessed you enormously. You know, Josh, this healing is going to cause quite the commotion in this little town of ours."

"I hope it does," Josh said. "I hope it helps to spread the message of reparation, not only in this town but everywhere."

"I'm afraid it may do far more than that..."

"What do you mean, Father?"

"Well... you may be inundated with people who *just* want to be healed, if you know what I mean."

"Yeah Father, that's one thing that concerns me, but I'll just have to deal with it. Besides, I'm sure Jesus will lead me only to those who He wants healed."

Father O'Malley often heard reports of the 'seminarians' from Sacred Heart, getting drunk, using foul language, and even visiting some of the less reputable areas around town. Time and time again he refused to believe these reports. Unfortunately, as time went by, many of his close friends and parishioners had stopped attending Mass, no doubt influenced by Father Gerald's so-called 'priests and seminarians,' not to mention all the demonic spirits infiltrated throughout the town.

"You know Josh, people have been telling me for some time now about the unscrupulous actions of the 'seminarians' at Sacred Heart and I've dismissed them as highly improbable... talk about being a fool!"

"Don't blame yourself. Who would ever believe such things? It took me over a month living with them, day, and night, before I realized what was going on, and then, I didn't even fully understand it. Only because Jesus explained it to me in detail do I now fully understand.

CHAPTER IV

That's why we can't waste any time. We need to get people praying again and recognizing their sinfulness."

Unbeknown to Josh and Father O'Malley, Mrs. Johnson did not go straight home after church. She went running through town praising Jesus and telling everyone that she had been healed. Poking her head in shop after shop, proclaiming her healing and assuring everyone that Jesus loves us and wants us all to repent. Ending up in Bogan's Coffee Shop, she didn't waste any time telling Claudia and Frank all about her experience with Josh. And just as Josh had hoped, the snowball of reparation began.

Of course, others also heard about the healing… others with breath of sulfur and bloodshot eyes glistening with hatred. Azazal was enraged when news reached him that Mrs. Johnson had been miraculously healed. The fact that she had been healed didn't bother Azazal as much as knowing that her healing was a direct result of Josh Donovan.

Pacing back and forth, no demon dared to come close to Azazal while he was in this raging state. Now it was clear; the Lord of Hosts had come to the city to empower the Donovan kid. Azazal knew he should have eliminated him long ago and knew that he would pay heavily for this mistake. Soon there would be an army of warriors and higher-ranking generals who would, more than likely, take over his command, not to mention the severe punishment he would surely receive if he could not rectify this situation quickly and quietly.

Not more than two hours had gone by since Mrs. Johnson had been healed when a half a dozen people came knocking on Father O'Malley's door.

"What did I tell you Josh?" as Father stood up to answer the door.

"Good morning, Father, we hate to bother you, but would Josh happen to be here?"

Father O'Malley didn't know what to say, as he didn't want to put Josh on the spot. Before he could say anything, Josh stepped in front of Father.

"Yes, I'm here, what can I do for you, ladies?"

Not knowing exactly how to respond, they just stood staring at Josh. Realizing how uncomfortable they were, Josh invited them in. Father and Josh stepped aside as all six entered and were invited to sit down.

"Well," Josh said without wasting any time, "I suppose you're here because of Mrs. Johnson's healing."

"Yes! Yes, we are!" was an immediate response. But before they had a chance to utter another word, Josh asked them,

"What did Mrs. Johnson say to you?"

One brave woman quickly spoke up, "she said she was healed! Miraculously healed by YOU."

"What else did she say?"

Ellen chimed in, "She said that Jesus loves us and wants to heal all of us."

Another said, "Don't forget she reminded us that Jesus is asking us all to repent."

Josh continued his questions. Father O'Malley sat listening to their answers, wondering why Josh was asking so much of them.

"Was there anything else Mrs. Johnson said?"

"Not that we can recall… you know, Mrs. Johnson was so excited, and so are we."

"Why?"

"Well…" Sophia said,

"We all need healing! So… so we came here!"

Father O'Malley just sat, saying nothing as he waited for Josh's response. Josh sat for a few minutes without saying a word. Finally, breaking the silence, he began,

CHAPTER IV

"It's true Jesus loves all of us. Each one of us. Every one of *you*. And He's so pleased you have the faith to come here this morning. However, the most important thing you need to remember is that Jesus, *and only Jesus*, heals. Not me. I'm only His minister and have absolutely no healing power without Him. So, you see, it's not me who you should be asking for healing, but Jesus.

"Second, the real healing that Jesus wants is for all of us to be healed *within* ourselves. Within our souls. He wants us to repent for all our wrong doings. You are right in that Jesus wants all of us to be healed, but I don't believe He was simply referring to physical healing.

"Remember, when Jesus walked this earth, He did not heal everyone. Nevertheless, my mission is to show everyone who will see with both their eyes and their hearts that Jesus lives. That He loves all of us and wants all to repent before time runs out. Please believe me when I say that Jesus told me that the end is near, and all those who refuse to repent will not see the glory of God.

"You all have come in faith to be healed. It is my hope that people with faith, like you, will help spread His message of reparation. Jesus once said to many, 'Your faith has saved you'; now, He is saying 'Your faith has healed you.' Therefore, go and help me deliver His message to everyone you can."

Everyone continued to sit, not sure what to do or say next. Josh stood up and walked to the window. After what seemed like forever, he turned and said,

"Do you all believe that what I have just said is true?

"Yes," was the response from all six.

Josh looked at all of them, smiled and said, "If only more had faith like each of you." He then went to each, asking their name and what healing they were asking for. Sophie had severe cataracts, Amelia had painful arthritis in her hips, Ellen asked for healing of her kidneys as she was on daily dialysis, Vickie suffered from arthritis of the fingers, Hanna was about to have a knee replaced, and Alyson simply asked for her husband to be spiritually healed, as he had not been to Mass or confession in twenty-five years.

Everyone, except Alyson experienced their healing immediately. Praising Jesus with tears in their eyes, they left rejoicing in what Jesus had done for them and assuring Josh that the Lord's message would be told. Alyson, who was still inside with Father and Josh, watched her friends head home. Turning to face Alyson, Josh held her hand.

"Don't look so sad. Your request has saved not only your husband's soul, but yours as well."

Josh spent the rest of the day in prayer and seclusion. Father O'Malley responded multiple times to various requests for healing, telling each that Josh would be available after tomorrow's Sunday Mass. After dinner, Father sat down with Josh for what he called a serious talk.

"Josh, I want to go to Bishop Timothy and ask him if he would give me permission to personally instruct you in becoming a priest. I realize that you do not have a college degree but considering all that I have already taught you and especially what the Lord has revealed to you, I believe you know more now than any clergy on earth, and that it is The Lord's Will that you be ordained as soon as possible.

"And tomorrow, after Mass, I think you should talk to everyone. I'm sure the church will be full, and extremely anxious to hear directly from you everything that you have experienced. I believe you should explain your mission and what Jesus is asking people to do."

"You know Father, I don't have much experience in talking to large crowds."

"Well, you better get used to it. I'm sure the Holy Spirit will guide you."

CHAPTER IV

The next morning found the church not only full, but mobbed. People arrived hours before the 10:00am service. Mrs. Johnson, along with the other six ladies who were healed, arrived in plenty of time to have front-row seats. Although the church was overflowing with people, sitting, and standing everywhere, the crowd was well controlled although extremely noisy, and as expected, all were talking about yesterday's healings.

Before Mass started, Father O'Malley welcomed everyone, and in a way, jokingly expressed such surprise to see so many in attendance. Of course, he knew exactly why they all were there after so many years of absence. And not surprisingly, he took the opportunity to remind everyone when confessions would be available.

During Mass, Josh had a good opportunity to observe the crowd. Some were reverently participating in the Mass. Others just went through the motions of standing, kneeling, sitting, and the like. Still others, especially most of those who were standing, appeared to be quite impatient for Mass to end, anxiously waiting for what Josh had to say.

Unfortunately, as Josh scanned the church, a sick feeling came across him as he noticed several people standing in the far back corner of the church who had a red glow radiating from their heads.

Immediately after the final blessing, Father invited all those who were interested in hearing Josh share some of his recent experiences with the Lord to remain in their pews. Not surprisingly, no one left. Not a single person. Josh stepped up to the pulpit and began what would soon become the message delivered to the world.

"Let's begin with a short prayer. Dear Lord, please bless all of us here today, forgive us our sins, and open our hearts and minds to hear and accept all that is said today.

REPARATION: A STORY OF HOPE

Amen." Everyone immediately responded with a roaring "AMEN".

"Most of you by now have seen or heard about the healings Jesus performed yesterday and possibly have some idea of what I have personally experienced. In any case, I would like to tell you a little about it and to pass on to you exactly what the Lord has told me."

That comment brought a quiet mumble of confusion throughout the crowd. As Josh started to speak, someone yelled out,

"Will we be healed?"

Someone else yelled, "Will you heal *me*?"

"Me too," another said.

"What about me?"

"And me!" And soon the place erupted with calls for healing. People began to get up and rush forward. Father O'Malley stood up with a frightened and concerned look on his face, when suddenly Josh grabbed the microphone and in a very stern voice, yelled, "STOP! STOP THIS. SIT DOWN. PLEASE, SIT DOWN!"

Getting their attention, suddenly the chaos stopped. It only took a few minutes before everyone was seated again. This time, one could hear a pin drop. Josh, still holding the microphone, walked down the center aisle and began to talk.

"What is wrong with you people?"

No one dared to answer. There was nothing but silence and embarrassment from most.

"If Jesus himself was standing here, would you scream out to Him, demanding healing?"

Again, there was complete silence. No one dared to even try to answer that question.

"Although you cannot see Him, Jesus is here, just as you and I are. This is *His* house and I ask you to be

CHAPTER IV

respectful of that or else you are welcome to leave." No one left and no one said anything in response.

"Now I'm sure many are here for healing, but any healing is totally up to the Lord. More importantly, I'm going to tell you why I'm here, and what Jesus wants everyone to know. You can believe me or not. It's your choice! However, what I'm about to tell you is exactly what Jesus has told me. It is *His* message for all of us to hear."

"Oh, come off it, Josh!" someone in the back who had a red glow around their head yelled out. "Do you really expect us to believe that Jesus spoke to *you*?"

"Yes, I do expect you to believe. Why wouldn't you? Jesus speaks to all of us. You, me, everyone. Even sinners. The problem is most of us don't take the time to listen or we simply don't want to listen." Josh continued,

"Most of us are too busy in our daily lives to hear Him, but I assure you, just as He speaks to me, He also speaks to you. Of course, Jesus speaks to us in various ways. Most of the time, it's that inner voice that is guiding us. Sometimes He speaks to us through other people, like I'm doing now. Other times, it's through Scripture, or through someone's example…

"The point is, He *does* speak to us, He's always speaking to us, just as Satan and his evil spirits are always tempting us. If you have faith, you will surely hear His voice. My mission is to deliver His message. Again, you can accept it or not, it's up to you."

Josh did not expand on all the details of his vision to the crowd, as he had done with Father O'Malley. Rather, he condensed the Lord's message into its most important parts. He emphasized that Jesus loves us all and His mercy is unending. That He is asking us to repent for all our sins. That we need to accept Him into our lives and that we need to pray and pray, especially for the reparation of our sins and for the sins of the world. Most importantly, Josh stressed the point that Jesus is giving *one last chance* to repent, or the world will suffer the consequences. There was only a short period of silence after he had finished speaking. Then the questions and comments began.

"I don't really know how to pray," one middle aged man yelled out. "And it's been so long that I can't remember any of the prayers."

Josh continued to walk through the aisles, stopping each time to answer the concerns.

"Prayer is really just talking to God. Talk to Him in your own words. You don't necessarily need to pray formal prayers. However, the rosary, as some of you know, is a wonderful and powerful way to pray.

"The simple truth is that Jesus wants us to talk to Him. And He, in turn, will talk to us. Not necessarily in an audible voice, but in the depths of our minds. Like I said before, we just need to listen. And when you pray, pray consistently, not just occasionally, pray reverently, try not to be distracted, find a quiet place, and finally, remember to pray whenever possible."

"Doesn't Jesus get tired of us asking for something every time we pray?" another person asked.

"Actually no, I don't think He ever gets tired of us asking. But sometimes, as I'm sure you know, we may not be asking for the right thing. Remember," Josh continued, "prayer does not always have to be asking for something. We can praise Him with prayer, we can adore Him, we can give thanks for all He has done for us. All of that is prayer."

Another man standing next to a woman with a red glow asked, "But you're holy and I'm a sinner. Why would Jesus listen to a sinner?"

"That's a great question," Josh said. "But before I answer it, I want to go back to the previous question about prayer. I forgot to mention something very important. We

CHAPTER IV

also can intercede for others. That's another form of prayer. You can intercede for family or friends. Jesus has given all of us that gift and we need to remember that it is a powerful form of prayer.

"Now, back to your question. First, I'm a sinner just like everyone else. I'm sure you've heard it before…we are all sinners. All of us." As Josh said this, standing close to the person with the red glow, he looked directly at her.

"You, me, Father, all of us. But the good news is Jesus is *always* willing to forgive us, and to forgive you." At that moment, he was staring directly into the eyes of the woman. Then turning away, he continued, "That's why Jesus died for us. He knew our weakness and our sins. And because He knew our human nature, He also knew we would sin again and again. That's why His mercy is unending."

"But doesn't that make us hypocrites when we sin over and over, go to confession, and then sin again and again, especially if it's the same sin?"

Josh thought for a few seconds before answering.

"That depends. Unless we are *genuinely* sorry for our sins and make a sincere effort not to sin again, our confession would not be valid. So hypocrisy wouldn't even be an issue. On the other hand," he continued, "the reason Jesus forgives time and time again, is because of His endless love for us. So, when we sin again and again, even if it's the same sin, so long as we are sincerely sorry and are trying our very best not to sin again, then His forgiveness is always there.

"This is a little story Jesus shared with me. He said that millions and millions of people sin every day, which causes Him and his Blessed Mother much sadness. However, what makes Him most happy is when sinners repent, when they pick themselves up time and time again, day after day, and when they are always willing to start over.

REPARATION: A STORY OF HOPE

"Jesus said that so many people despair, so many are not sincere, so many pick themselves up and then after time, give up. And some don't even care at all. Some never repent. Jesus said what makes Him so happy, what makes Heaven rejoice and the angels sing, is when a sinner repents, realizing that they have done wrong, and tries their very best not to sin again. Picking themselves up and starting again. Picking themselves up and starting again. *That's* when Heaven rejoices.

"And that's why, my friends, His mercy is unending. It's like walking a narrow, steep path to Heaven. Sometimes we trip, and His hand is there to steady us. Sometimes we fall, but He's always helping us back to our feet. Sometimes we just can't take another step, and that's when He picks us up and carries us. Unfortunately, sometimes we *really* mess up. We fall so hard that we actually slip off that narrow road. But no matter how far we fall, Jesus is always chasing after us, reaching, and grabbing hold and pulling us back to Him. That's why it's so important to stay connected to Him. To pray and to always ask for His divine help. To never despair or give up if we sin. Just keep trying your best."

After a minute or so, there were no more questions. Josh, now returned to the front of the church, standing close to Father O'Malley, ended his talk.

"The most important thing to remember today is that the world is sinning. Much of this country has fallen away from God. People everywhere are sinning... many of us here are sinful! And although Jesus' mercy is unending, He has told me that time is running out. Time is running out for us to repent and to accept His love, to amend our lives and to pray. As I said at the beginning of this talk, pray for the reparation of our sins and for the sins of the world.

"If you put everything in perspective, the physical healing you may have come here for today is not as

CHAPTER IV

important as the healing of our souls. Let's pray a little and ask Jesus and Mary to shower us with their grace and to heal our inner selves. To heal our selfishness. To heal our pride. To heal our hatreds, our jealousies, our resentments, and to forgive every sin we have ever committed."

Josh and Father O'Malley knelt and were joined by many as they began to pray the rosary. When they had, there were only about fifty people remaining in the church out of two hundred. Those who remained were what Josh considered the faithful that had been touched by the Lord's message. Standing up Josh turned to face the group.

Just as he was about to speak, five people with red glowing mists around their heads entered the church. Evidently, they were waiting outside while the prayers were going on. Josh invited everyone who wanted healing to come forward, including the five standing in the back. As people in the pews started to get up and proceed forward, something strange appeared to be happening with the five in the back of the church.

As the five began to step forward, it was as if an invisible barrier was blocking their way. No matter how hard they tried to move forward, they were unable to do so. In fact, they were not able to move at all. Noticing their predicament, Josh calmly walked to the back of the church while asking those in the aisle to step aside allowing him to pass. Reaching them, he spoke very softly.

"I know you are not here for healing, and I know that you all have troubled hearts. I can tell you that *no matter what* you have done in the past, Jesus loves you and is hoping for you to ask for His forgiveness."

It was apparent after Josh spoke these words, they all wanted to leave, but all they could do was just stand there and listen. "Jesus has given you a great blessing today. I know you want to get out of here as quickly as possible. I know that you do not love Him just now, but be assured,

He loves you. And be assured that because He is holding you here for a moment, it will hopefully prove to each of you His desire for you to repent and to return to Him. You may not understand it now, but hopefully in time you will."

Returning to the front of the church, the five were instantly released and scrambled out as fast as they could. However, two of them had been touched by Josh's testimony. Walking down the steps, John Arron and his wife Nancy had tears in their eyes. Turning back to the church, they blessed themselves for the first time in many, many years, and asked for Jesus' forgiveness.

The other three looked on disgusted and horrified to think that John and Nancy had so easily been converted back to the Lord. Cursing and calling out obscenities to the two of them, they walked away without looking back.

Inside the church, only a few asked for physical healing. Because everyone had opened up their heart to the Lord, they were all healed, not only in spirit, but all those with any sort of ailment or disease were healed. Not a single person who left the church that night was not praising and thanking God for all that they had experienced. They were on fire with the love of God in their hearts and were anxious to share their conversion with everyone they met.

After all of this, Josh retreated to the sacristy. Waiting for Father O'Malley to finish hearing confessions, he prayed for all those who were healed. Not long after he began praying, he was interrupted with the noise of multiple footsteps behind him. Turning around, John and Nancy Arron were standing at the door. Immediately he recognized them; however, to his absolute delight, they no longer had the red glowing mist around their heads.

CHAPTER IV

John spoke first. "We just wanted to personally thank you for helping us to… repent." Nancy continued, "Yes, we've been so deceived and unfaithful to God these past few years. We just went to confession with Father O'Malley, and it's like a thousand pounds have been lifted off our shoulders."

"A million!" John added.

Just then, Father O'Malley entered the sacristy. "I see you found him."

John quickly responded. "Yes, Father we did, and again we are so thankful to you both."

"You don't have to be thankful to us. Just remember to thank Jesus," Josh reminded them. "*He's* the one who has blessed and forgiven you. And please don't forget to help spread the message of reparation."

"Absolutely, we certainly will," Nancy said, on behalf of both her and her husband.

After hugs and a few more thanks, Josh offered to walk them to the door. Outside of the church, a hundred furious demons were randomly circling overhead, dashing in and out, up and down, without any clear direction, while Belzar looked on. All of the demons who were attached to the people that were just healed, including John and Nancy, were hissing and screaming loud shrill sounds, eyes pooping and fangs ready to grab hold of anything in sight.

Those demons, who previously were in control of those who were just healed, were even more angered, as they now no longer had influence over them. Several of these foolish and desperate demons tried to reattach themselves but were instantly obliterated by Angels that were guarding them once again.

When Belzar saw Josh and the Arron's exit the church, his temper flared so high that even his two most trusted Attack Warriors, who were standing next him, quickly stepped away to avoid his slashing claws.

"Attack him!" he commanded, screaming at the top of his lungs. His breath was heavy and frequent, spewing out sulfur, slime, spit, and yellow mist. "Attack him NOW!" he screamed again.

Instantly, the two Attack Warriors shot forward. They attacked with tremendous speed and with the anticipation of cutting Josh in half. Of course, none of them, including Belzar, knew that Josh's guardians were surrounding him with their protective shield. The two Attack Warriors approached with lighting-like speed, but instantly burst into balls of fire as soon as they hit the protective shield of Kapriel and Lancer's wings.

Belzar couldn't believe his eyes. Furious as he was, he was no fool. Cautiously, he approached Josh, and his two guardians, stopping only a few feet from them. Kapriel and Lancer calmly drew out their massive swords. That in itself signaled to Belzar that it was useless for him to attack, especially remembering what had just happened to his two Attack Warriors. With no other choice, all he could do was to scream out obscenities and curse Josh.

"If it's the last thing I do, I will destroy you and all that you believe in!" he screamed as he and his band of demons flew away.

Josh just stood still for a few minutes gathering his thoughts. Although he could not see or hear what had just transpired, he clearly recognized the smell of evil all around him. Feeling the warmth of his protectors, a confident smile came across his face. Thanking Kapriel and Lancer for their protection, he praised Jesus as he re-entered the church.

Father O'Malley had made several announcements that healing services would only be held after Sunday's Masses. Josh and Father hoped that would satisfy the dozens and

CHAPTER IV

dozens of people who were constantly hanging around, but more so, it would hopefully protect Josh from being mobbed and constantly inundated with healing requests.

After breakfast the following week, Josh and Father O'Malley were off to see Bishop Timothy, who had agreed to talk to Josh. The purpose of the visit was to ask permission for Father O'Malley to train and prepare Josh for the priesthood, bypassing normal seminary preparation.

"Come on in," Bishop Timothy said, after his secretary announced their arrival. "Please, have a seat." After the usual hellos, coffee, tea and the like, they got directly to the subject.

"Father O'Malley tells me you want to be a priest."

"Yes, I do, your Excellency."

Taking a deep breath, Bishop Timothy began.

"As I am sure you aware, preparation for the priesthood is a very long and serious process and is most usually done through seminary preparation and only after formal schooling. However, I have been paying close attention to what has been occurring in Clarksville and have been deeply touched regarding what the Lord is doing through you. As Father has told me, you have been greatly blessed and I sincerely believe in all that you have revealed to us about reparation and how little time we have left to honor God's Will.

"That is why, after much prayer, believing that God has prompted me, I will agree that Father O'Malley may proceed with your training. And Josh, I would like you to know that I would be happy to personally ordain you as soon as Father O'Malley says you are ready."

Josh, along with Father O'Malley, were so surprised and excited that they didn't know what to say. In fact, they were speechless.

"Well…"Bishop Timothy said in a drawn-out voice. "Don't just sit there! You both have a lot of work to do."

Bishop Timothy shook Father O'Malley's hand and then reached for Josh's. As both clasped hands, Josh looked deeply into Bishop Timothy's eyes. Still holding his hand, he said,

"Your Excellency, as you know, and as Jesus has revealed to me, you have stage four pancreatic cancer. Because Jesus has great love for you and for your faithfulness to Him, as of this moment, Jesus has freed you of this illness." Releasing his hand, Father and Josh turned toward the door. Only the faint sound of weeping could be heard as they left the office.

Returning home, they set up a daily study schedule so that Josh could complete his training as soon as possible. But to Father O'Malley's surprise, it was Josh who did most of the teaching, or at least most of the talking. Evidently, Jesus had revealed much to Josh, especially about the Church, insights regarding the saints and Bible, various prayers, priestly duties, and other responsibilities he eventually would need to know.

Because Josh was now officially a seminarian, he dressed in the traditional cassock when in the church and the clerical white shirt with black pants all other times. He had not worn the cassock since he had left Father Gerald's so-called 'seminary', but now he wore it knowing that he was officially working for God.

Each day brought more and more people to repentance. Many from town were returning to the Church. One TV station was reporting the healings that were taking place, albeit with much skepticism. Not surprising, Josh remembered that Jesus told him not to be discouraged. *"Men will resist because of their hardened hearts… The entire world is in sin and so many are*

CHAPTER IV

under the influence of evil...and reparation will be difficult for many to accept..."

Josh figured that if people would not repent and turn back to the Lord, even after witnessing miracles, then most likely, nothing would persuade them to repent. In any case, Josh's mission was simple. Spread the Lord's message to as many who will listen. Tell them that judgement is near...very near...and Jesus is giving the world one last chance, pleading one last time for men to change their evil ways.

Although Josh knew that the Lord's message was being heard by many in the town of Clarksville, the herds of people that he expected to be flocking into town were not occurring. Time was running out as he had so much more to do. Josh knew that something more effective had to be done if he was to complete his mission quickly in Clarksville. But what? And then there was the seminary that had to be dealt with. Not to mention the illegitimate Father Hugh at St. Ann's in Jinksville. "Oh Jesus, please help me...show me the way..." was his constant prayer.

Back in his room after dinner one night, Josh knelt in prayer for guidance as he did every night. The shrill ring of the telephone broke the silence of his prayers. Picking up the phone, he hesitated just for a second.

"Hello?" Silence. "Hello...?" he said again.

"Hi Josh... this is Becky."

"Becky! Is that really you? How are you? Where are you? I have so much to tell you!"

"Me too," she said. "Me too." Neither one knew exactly where to begin, and after a little stammering and joking around, Becky spoke first.

"Josh, I'm back in Jinksville. We need you here. Could you possibly get away for a few days or so? I have so much to tell you."

Josh sat with a surprised look on his face.

"Sure…I'm sure I can get away. Is it urgent?"

"Yes…" Becky said. "It's the church…"

Josh, detecting the seriousness in her voice, said, "I'll be there as soon as I can. I'll leave immediately."

"Meet me at Costello's Coffee Shop," Becky said. "You remember? Billy and Michael's parents' shop."

"Yeah, Becks. I remember."

"Great." Becky said. "See you tomorrow."

After informing Father O'Malley and packing a small travel bag, he was on his way. Father O'Malley made sure everyone knew he was out of town, hopefully to reduce the crowds that were just looking for a miracle.

CHAPTER V

RETURN TO JINKSVILLE

Josh traveled all night arriving at Costello's Coffee Shop just a little after 10:00am. Twelve hours with two quick stops. "Not bad," he thought to himself as he walked into Costello's. Seeing Josh, Becky could not stand up fast enough as she greeted him with hugs and tears. Josh was wearing the traditional white clerical shirt and black pants.

Becky was taken back a little when she realized what he was wearing.

"Something wrong?" Josh politely asked. "What's the matter?"

"I thought you didn't go to the seminary...?" she said.

"What gave you that idea?"

"Well, I called Sacred Heart and was told that they've never heard of you."

"Not surprising," Josh said. "I'll tell you all about it later. So, what's going on here that's so important that you not only called me, but made me come down here?"

Before Becky could answer, she was interrupted by Mrs. Costello.

"Hi Josh! It's wonderful to see you in here," serving him and Becky coffee and homemade donuts. "On the house." Her smile helped him to ease the tension he was feeling.

Josh looked at Becky waiting for her response.

"Well???"

"I'll tell you all that I know when T.J. and Billy get here. They're supposed to meet us here around noon."

"T.J. and Billy?" Josh said with a surprised voice. "How are they?"

"They're doing great," Becky said, "but I'm dying to hear all about what you've been doing these past four years!"

Josh took his time, telling Becky that was caring for his mother for the first few years after high school, and that she had passed in December 2041. He related all that had happened to him over the past six months. His experience at the Sacred Heart Seminary, his attack, his friendship with Father O'Malley, how he is preparing for the priesthood, his spiritual experiences, the miracles in Clarksville, and most especially the message of reparation given to him by the Lord.

Becky was shocked but listened intently and marveled at how wonderful it was how much the Lord was working in his life. After Josh had finished, Becky smiled and said,

"Do you remember that you promised to tell me someday why you were late for graduation?"

"Yeah, I remember…"

"Well, is today a good day?"

"If you really want to know, then I suppose now is as good a time as ever."

Becky listened with sincere interest and never said a word, but Josh could see the sadness on her face. When Josh had finished, he said,

"But do me a favor? Don't say anything to T.J., or Billy, as that is history. And besides, I forgave them long ago."

CHAPTER V

"I won't say a word," promised Becky.

Changing the subject, she told Josh that word had spread quickly about how God was performing miracles through a kid named Josh Donovan. Josh looked stunned, yet so thrilled that word was beginning to spread.

"Do T.J. and Billy know?"

"Of course!" she said. "Everyone knows. I always knew that you were special in the Lord's eyes... and in mine too."

"Oh, cut it out," Josh said smiling at her. "You'll give me a big head."

"No, I really mean it."

Josh, not waiting for anything else Becky might say, quickly said, "What about you? What have you been up to these past four years? Did you graduate from South Carolina?"

"Yes, but several times I thought about quitting. Just got depressed a few times but it all worked out."

Becky told him that she had received her B. A. degree in Education and was currently teaching elementary school in Cloverville, just ten miles away. In almost an embarrassed tone, she said that she was single and rented an apartment there.

"Single? I thought you'd be married with kids by now!" Both responded with a little chuckle.

"No... I came close though. But I guess we both realized that the match wasn't right."

"Sorry about that. But that guy doesn't know what he missed out on. You've got plenty of time, and I'm sure the right guy will come along before you know it." Josh detected something wasn't quite right as he studied Becky's expression, but he knew that now was not the right time to pursue it.

No sooner had he finished speaking when T.J. and Billy arrived. Everyone greeted each other with hugs and smiles.

Josh had long ago forgiven them, and he knew that God was working in their lives.

"Hey, bro," T.J. said. "How 'bout giving me a little miracle?"

"Don't be such an..." Not finishing his own response, Josh jokingly said, "See! You almost made me use foul language!" Everyone laughed as they all sat down.

Becky did most of the talking, bringing Josh up to speed about T.J., Billy, and Michael. T.J. converted to Catholicism almost immediately after graduation. He also went to South Carolina University and received a B.S. degree in Kinesiology. Amazingly, Coach Patterson retired last spring and after applying for the position, T.J. was hired to teach physical education and coach football.

TJ added, "Not only did I become a Catholic, but I'm pretty successful in getting my father to come along with me to church every Sunday."

Becky chimed in, "Yeah, and he talked his dad into not serving alcohol to anyone underage anymore! He's also gone to other bars asking them to do the same."

"And I'm enforcing it," Billy said.

Turns out, Billy works for the Clarksville Police Department. He spent two years at Preston's College and his last two years majoring in law enforcement at South Carolina U.

"There's no doubt about it," Billy said. "Jesus had His hand in helping all three of us get jobs immediately after college."

"What about your brother?" Josh asked.

"Oh, Michael is another miracle. He's living in Wisconsin, married with twin girls and you won't believe it... he's a pastor of Saint John's Evangelical Community Church. Happy as a lark and is constantly preaching the message of love and repentance to everyone he meets, even me. Tell you the truth, he drives me crazy when he

CHAPTER V

visits my wife and me practicing his sermons over and over. Not really, though. We like to listen to him as he's a great inspiration to our faith."

"Wow!" Josh blurted out. "Who would have ever guessed? Looks like Jesus is alive in all our lives."

Everyone agreed as more coffee and donuts were served. Mrs. Costello greeted her son Billy with a kiss, then taking Josh's hand and looking deeply into his eyes, said, "We are praying for you. We are all praying for your success here."

Josh reacted with a bewildered expression. Recognizing his confusion, Becky finally began to explain why they asked him to return to Jinksville.

"Josh, this town is in trouble. More so now than ever before. We think this town is under a demonic attack."

"We *know* it's under demonic attack," T.J. added.

"We believe that Father Hugh…" Billy immediately chimed in.

"You mean Hugh the fraud?" Josh contributed.

"Yeah, that's exactly what we mean! Anyway he's been molesting kids… but we can't prove it. Everyone we have spoken to is too afraid to say anything. And poor Father Dennis… He was kicked out of the parish! Don't know all the details, but one day he was happily here and the next day, gone. No goodbyes. Nothing. Just gone. We asked Father Hugh, but he just said the Archdiocese transferred him."

"That's not the worst of it," Becky said. "Last week I went to see Bishop Angela to ask if he would be willing to consider reopening St. Ann's Grammar School. We are inundated with children from Jinksville simply because they closed the school. Quite frankly, Cloverville Elementary can't handle any more students. We are already beyond capacity…

In any case, while I was waiting in the outer office, another man was sitting across from me, also waiting to see the Bishop. After a few minutes, the bishop's secretary announced over their intercom that Anthony Wadsworth had arrived!

"Apparently," Becky continued, "they are good friends and Bishop Angela *personally* greeted him, shaking his hand, and putting his arm over his shoulder. 'So good to see you again, I've been expecting you!' Bishop Angela said. Then they walked into his office."

"Did you say Anthony C. Wadsworth?" Josh anxiously asked Becky.

"I don't know if he said Anthony C. Wadsworth, but he did say Anthony Wadsworth. Anyway, let me finish. So, I was sitting right next to his office door. Had my hands in my pocket and realized that I still had my recorder. Sounds crazy, but I record all my appointments and meetings I have with parents at school, just to make sure there are no misunderstandings as to what is said. Anyway, for some strange reason, I turned it on. The door hadn't shut all the way, so I heard and recorded most everything that was said.

"To make a long story short, it turns out that Wadsworth offered to buy St. Ann's Church, the school, rectory, convent, and all its properties for a whopping ten million dollars. He wanted to convert the properties into a seminary like the one in Clarksville.

"Now, here's the part that I'm absolutely shocked and upset about. I clearly heard Wadsworth say that this purchase will further help them *destroy* Christianity, the Church, and the Pope himself! And if that wasn't enough, here's the real kicker... if the bishop agreed to Wadsworth's plan, he would deposit into his personal bank account $1,000,000.00 and would continue to pay him $10,000.00 for every guy who graduated from the

CHAPTER V

seminary that he placed in a parish under his jurisdiction. I didn't see it, but I heard Wadsworth say, 'Here's a check for $10,000 dollars... a bonus of good faith.'

"The last thing I heard was Bishop Angela telling Wadsworth that they indeed have a deal and that he is just too generous. Wadsworth said he would draw up the papers tomorrow. 'Fantastic,' Angela said. They were joking and shaking hands as he left the office."

Becky and the others had no idea what was going on, but Josh knew exactly what was being proposed and was shaken to find out that Bishop Angela was a part of their demonic plan.

"Look guys, it's already two-thirty. I'm getting a room at the Holiday Inn down the street. I need to get some sleep. I've been up all night. Let's meet in my hotel room tomorrow morning, around 9:00am? That will give us time to think about how we can handle all of this."

"Sounds good to me," T.J. said, followed by Billy and Becky.

With the usual goodbyes and hugs, they all left. Before leaving, Josh went over to Mrs. Costello to thank her and to express his appreciation for the free food and prayers. Once outside the shop, Josh asked Becky if she wanted to have dinner together.

"I'd love to, but I have to get back home and let my dog out. But I'd love to take a rain check!"

"Great, no problem," Josh replied. "I'll see you tomorrow morning then." This was just as well, as he could hardly keep his eyes open at this point.

Other eyes, however, were wide open. Slanted, yellowish-bloodshot eyes. Denzil and Jarell were aware of Josh's presence. They had already received reports as to what was going on in Clarksville and the healing power that was given to him. However, when they saw Josh step out of his car, they were shaken with fear. Not only was

Kapriel standing guard next to Josh, but so was Lancer, another Angelic Warrior who was now constantly with him as Jesus had promised. Two massive powerful warriors now protected Josh. Kapriel alone was far too powerful for any of them to handle, but now two of equal size and strength? No way were they going to even get close to them.

Denzil and Jarell agreed. If Belzar wanted to engage, then he could do it himself. They were no fools; it was suicide to attack unless they had an army behind them. No wonder why there were so many of their kind arriving in Clarksville. It would take an army of massive size to defeat warriors like Kapriel and Lancer… and that was exactly what was being planned…

As agreed, everyone met in Josh's hotel room the next morning. Becky was the only one late in arriving. Making some excuse about her dog, Josh noticed that she looked tired and pale. Chills ran down his spine, remembering what his mother looked like when she was sick with cancer.

"You OK?" Josh asked as she gave her apologies and took a seat.

"Sure, I'm fine. Just had a rough night thinking about all this stuff."

"Me too," Billy said.

"Yup. Guess that makes three of us," T.J. chimed in.

Josh took the lead. He told them all about the 'seminary' in Clarksville, their plan to bring down the Church and all Christians, all about the fake Father Hugh and how he was the first to be falsely ordained and assigned to St Ann's. Additionally, he filled them in about Anthony C Wadsworth.

"I understand fully what their plans are," Josh said. "There's no way we can let them take over St. Ann's and no way is Hugh going to touch another person. I've been

CHAPTER V

thinking about it a lot and have some ideas. How 'bout you guys? Has anyone come up with a plan?"

T.J. and Billy immediately laid out their plan to catch Father Hugh in the act of molestation, while Josh explained in detail what he could do regarding Bishop Angela.

The next morning Josh arrived at St. Ann's Rectory a little after 10:00am. Father Hugh was busy conducting choir practice in the church, as he usually did on Tuesday and Thursdays.

Josh entered the iron gates to the garden a little after 10:15, giving himself plenty of time so he would not be detected by Father Hugh. Upon entering the garden, Josh instantly stopped, upset, and horrified at what he was seeing. The once beautiful garden had totally been neglected, evidently after Father Dennis was forced out. Weeds were everywhere. The flowers were gone along with the huge rose bushes surrounding the cross. Bricks were popping up in various places along the paths, most likely caused by neglect and by ice on the ground during the winter months.

Josh walked slowly until he approached the cross of Jesus. The same cross where he was healed with the blood of Christ so many years ago. "Oh, dear Lord," Josh said to himself as he knelt. "I'm so sorry for this offense against You, but I promise that I will return, and once again restore Your beautiful garden."

Standing up, he hurriedly entered the side door of the rectory, placing hidden cameras in various rooms where he thought Father Hugh might choose to abuse and molest someone.

Realizing that the church sacristy might be another place where molestation could occur, Josh decided to take the chance of not being seen and placed his last camera in a secure and hidden spot in the sacristy. No sooner had he finished securing the camera when Father Hugh entered. Josh ducked behind the inside sacristy door, hoping not to be detected.

Stopping just in front of the door, Father Hugh reached for the doorknob but surprisingly he released it, walking away mumbling how he was sick and tired of teaching these little brats how to sing. Once it was clear, Josh exited through the front of the church completely unnoticed.

T.J., being the new football coach and quite popular with everyone on his team, had a long talk with Shawn Justin, one of his best and most trusted players, and his parents. Shawn was only fifteen, young for a sophomore, but extremely bright and a very devoted Catholic. Not to mention a key member in the drama club.

Wednesday after school, at approximately 3:30pm, Father Hugh answered the rectory door.

"Yes…can I help you?"

"Hi Father, my name is Shawn. I was wondering if you need any help around the church or grounds?"

Father Hugh was just about to say no when Shawn interrupted him.

"I'm willing to do anything. My parents split and I'm currently living practically on the streets. I stay with my brother some of the time, but his girlfriend hates me being around. Please Father… I could really use the money, and I'll do anything you want."

Shawn was somewhat enjoying himself. His acting skills from drama club were now paying off.

Father Huge hesitated for a few minutes as he took a closer look at Shawn. Muscular, blue eyes, blond hair…

CHAPTER V

the typical hunk. Shawn was wearing worn jeans, holes in the knees with a sleeveless white tank shirt that he had sprayed with a little water to exaggerate his muscular build.

"Come on in, son. Please step into my office."

Sitting down at his desk while Shawn stood in front of him, Hugh began his inquiry. "So, you need work. What kind of work can you do?"

"Oh! I can do whatever you want. Clean, wash dishes, cut grass, anything. Anything at all. Please, Father… I'm really desperate."

As Father Hugh looked him over more closely, he was practically drooling. "Well, we certainly don't want you living on the streets, now do we?" Continuing with more questions, he asked, "You look like you're an athlete. Are you on a team?"

"No. Most of those guys hate my guts… I just work out after school by myself and stay away from most of them."

"And why's that?" Father Hugh eagerly asked.

"Don't really know… but I guess it's because I've had a couple of sexual encounters with a few guys. I'm not gay or anything, just messed around a little to see what it's like with a guy. Of course, they never say anything about the sex I've had with girls. Bunch of assholes. Excuse my expression Father, but it really pisses me off."

"Are you Catholic?" Father Hugh now asked.

"Hell no, none of my family go to church. Matter of fact, I don't really believe in anything, you know… anything spiritual. Shit… I hope that doesn't change your mind about giving me a job?"

Father was ecstatic. This young man was absolutely perfect. Just perfect.

"No, not at all," he said, "everyone is free to believe what they want. But, my boy, you're dripping wet!"

REPARATION: A STORY OF HOPE

Shawn indeed looked drenched, just as he had planned. "I'm alright, just sweating. Sorry, I finished my daily run before coming here."

"Take off your shirt," Father insisted. "I'll throw it in the dryer for you, it'll just be quick." Before Shawn could resist, Father Hugh had it off him in seconds.

"You know Shawn, contrary to popular belief, sex is not evil. Sometimes one just has to release tension from their body. You know what I mean?" Shawn nodded his head in agreement.

"Now, don't get me wrong, I'm not saying that people should just go out and have sex all the time, but sometimes it's OK. Even between one man and another. And believe it or not, even priests have needs occasionally."

Shawn stood perfectly still, waiting for Father Hugh's next move.

"You said you would be willing to do anything, right?"

"I suppose so," Shawn said quietly.

Father Hugh was already placing his hands on Shawn's bare chest, exploring his muscular body. Shawn pulled back ever so slightly.

"I thought you said you would be willing to do *anything*."

"Yeah, I guess so… if it means getting a job."

"Don't worry about a job... we can find you a *job* immediately."

With that, Father Hugh unbuckled Shawn's jeans. Now, real sweat was forming on Shawn's forehead, but he knew that to catch Father Hugh in the act, he had to wait just a little longer. Pulling down his shorts, Father Hugh gloated like the animal he was.

Shawn pulled back again but this time clearly saying, "No, stop. No I don't want you to do this…"

"Too bad, my boy. I'm going to do this whether you want it or not."

CHAPTER V

Surprisingly, there were no demons present, not even the one who was always clinging to Father Hugh. Evidently there were too many angelic Guardians present and waiting patiently in the next room. Not surprising how quickly evil abandons you when their cause is hopeless.

The instant Father Hugh touched Shawn, Billy and another officer burst into the room. They had been waiting for the exact moment to make their arrest.

"What the hell is going on?" Father Hugh yelled.

"Don't you know, you pervert?" Billy said as he placed the cuffs on Hugh and read him his rights.

"I'm a Catholic Priest, damnit! You have no right to arrest me. I'm under the protection of the Church!"

"You're under no such protection, and you most certainly are *not* a priest."

"That's a load of crap, you can't do this to me!" Father Hugh shouted out as he was placed in the squad car.

"Tell that to the judge! And don't forget to tell him that you just molested a fifteen-year-old *child*… and I'm sure there will be lots more coming forward after this one goes public."

"How did I do?" Shawn asked T.J. with a broad smile on his face

"What do you think?" T.J. asked, giving him a pat on the shoulders.

Shawn just smiled, as they both walked out of the rectory. Once outside, Shawn joined his parents who were waiting for him, while T.J. thanked them once again for allowing Shawn to help put away this predator, once and for all.

"We're so glad to have helped," Mrs. Justin said. "We love the Church very much and are so happy this monster is out of here."

Elsewhere in town, at exactly 3:30pm, just as Shawn was knocking on the rectory door, Josh was entering Bishop Angela's office.

"What can I do for you?" the bishop said, as he sat behind his huge desk with a huge red glow all around his head.

"You can call Archbishop Fernando and resign from your office. Better yet, you can tell him yourself in person."

Outraged, Bishop Angela stood up and demanded that Josh leave. Red-faced, he exploded with a few obscenities threatening Josh if he did not get out immediately. No sooner had he finished yelling than Archbishop Fernando and Becky entered the room.

"Your Excellency...!" Bishop Angela stuttered with a startled look on his face. "I was just about to call the police on this intruder."

"SIT!" the archbishop commanded, as he pointed to the desk chair. Astonished, Angela slowly sat down, not knowing what to expect next.

Earlier that morning, Josh and Becky managed to have an emergency meeting with the archbishop, thanks to several calls from Father O'Malley and Bishop Timothy. Josh explained all that was going on in Clarksville's fraudulent 'seminary,' the abuse at St. Ann's, the theft and mishandling of Church funds, and how Bishop Angela and Anthony C. Wadsworth were conspiring to purchase the church and church properties in hopes of establishing another fake seminary. Archbishop Fernando had difficulty believing everything until Becky played the recording she had made.

"Go on Josh, tell him why we are here."

With that introduction, Josh began, "I'll make this short. You've knowingly appointed 'Father Hugh,' a fraudulent priest, to St., Ann's Parish, where he has not only committed sacrilegious offenses pretending to

CHAPTER V

administer priestly duties but has been molesting children for years."

"Oh, come on! This is preposterous," Bishop Angela said.

"Preposterous?" Josh repeated. "Tell that to the court. Father Hugh is already in police custody."

"Now, you just sit there and listen!" Archbishop Fernando shouted, clearly upset and holding back his temper.

Josh continued. "You've also been stealing from the Church, pocketing most of the monies from St. Ann's and then closing the church and school, telling the parish that there was not sufficient money to justify keeping the parish open. You also receive $10,000 for every illegitimate priest you place in parishes under your jurisdiction. Not to mention accepting bribes, such as the $10,000 check that Wadsworth gave you and the $1,000,000 that he deposited in your personal bank account yesterday."

"You have no proof of this," Bishop Angela stammered out. "No proof at all!"

"We have all the proof we need. I suspect that the $10,000 check is still in your desk drawer and most of the church monies in your wall safe? Not to mention a recording of your entire conversations with Wadsworth."

Bishop Angela sat there trying to figure out what to say. As angry as he was, he said nothing. He just stared into empty space.

Archbishop Fernando stood up and stepped directly in front of Bishop Angela's desk. Looking at him square in his face, he said as calmly as he could manage, "You are released of all your duties, and I can assure you, you will be defrocked by his Holiness as soon as my report reaches him. Normally these matters would be handled by the Church. However, you have not only committed atrocities against God and the Church, but have committed felonies that will be handled by the proper authorities."

Without saying another word, Josh, Becky, and the Archbishop left the office, passing several police officers who were waiting to take Bishop Angela into their custody. Suddenly, the Archbishop stopped, turned around and politely asked one of the officers to remove the disgraced bishop's cassock.

"He's no longer a bishop and does not deserve to wear that sacred garment."

A burst of strong wind, flying leaves, and swirling dust greeted the three of them as soon as they exited the building. Just a few minutes ago, it was a clear beautiful sunny day, now the weather had changed so suddenly that it looked like all hell had broken loose, and so it did.

"Where did this storm come from?" Archbishop Fernando asked as he tried to hold down his own cassock.

"This is no ordinary storm," Josh said. "Stay very close to me."

Standing perfectly still, the three huddled as close together as they could. Debris of trash were flying everywhere. The wind and howling noise were deafening and increasing with intensity minute by minute. Branches from trees began to break loose and were propelled, not surprisingly, directly toward them. People were scrambling for cover, while several cars collided with horns sounding unceasingly.

Archbishop Fernando's black Cadillac was just pulling up in front of the steps, nearly missing the accident it had just passed.

"That's my driver," the Archbishop said.

Lunging forward, breaking out of the huddle, he approached the car. Just as he was about to open the door, Josh pulled him back, as a circle of whirling wind and what looked like black mist surrounded the vehicle, lifting it,

CHAPTER V

spinning it and eventually flipping it over and over until it finally came to a rest against a tree.

Archbishop Fernando blessed himself seeing what was happening while Josh reminded everyone to stay perfectly still and close to him. What they couldn't see was the battle that was taking place all around them. Shrill screeches were sounding from the dozens of demons that Belzar dispatched. Fights were breaking out everywhere. Angelic Warriors were rapidly descending to assist in the battle, no doubt because of all the many prayers that were being said for their success. Fiery bursts of yellow-red flames and ashes erupted everywhere as dozens upon dozens of demons were destroyed.

Filthy little demons were fluttering close to Josh, dodging in and out, trying their best to disrupt and distract Kapriel and Lancer from protecting the three huddled close together. They were more of a nuisance than a threat. Occasionally, Kapriel or Lancer would grab one or two of these little creatures who dared to get too close, crushing them with one hand, while swiping others away with their shields.

The attack plans that Belzar laid out was to concentrate on freeing Bishop Angela. His participation was essential if their plan was to succeed. However, as Belzar looked on, he could not keep his eyes off Josh. Steaming with hatred and revenge for all the times his attacks on Josh were unsuccessful, he was determined not to fail this time. Temporarily forgetting about Angela, Belzar became even more furious as he observed his warriors cut to pieces along with dozens of the little black creatures being crushed one after the other. Not being able to stand it any longer, Belzar let out such a loud scream that it set off numerous car horns, as well as blasting in several large glass windows.

Kapriel and Lancer were waiting for his attack with swords drawn. Because of his arrogance and conceitedness, he considered himself more powerful than the two Angelic Warriors waiting for him. Without thinking, he along with the two powerful Attack Demons, one on each side of him, shot forward, heading straight for Josh.

Lancer cut down one Attack Demon on his left while Kapriel demolished the one on his right, simultaneously slicing off Belzar's wings. Because of the speed and force of Belzar smashing into them, he burst into flames and ashes upon impact.

The sound and sight of the explosion of Belzar was of such magnitude, that it only took seconds for the other demons to realize that they were defeated. Instinctively they abandoned the battle and flew off as fast as they could.

Denzil and Jarell had been watching from a distance. Smart enough to realize that the battle was lost before it even started, they remained alive to fight another day. Flying off to join the rest of their retreating, crippled army, they never looked back to witness the slaughter of the other demons who weren't lucky enough to escape.

Just as quickly as the storm had started, it ended. The news reported that a small, unexpected tornado had touched down, causing little damage. Archbishop Fernando was so relieved to find out that his driver had suffered only a few scrapes and bruises.

Amazedly, their entire plan to save the town and parish had been successful. Hugh was in custody along with the defrocked Angela, and according to the reports they received, the two would most likely be put away for quite a long time. It didn't take long for Father Dennis to be returned to St. Ann's and plans were already in the works to restart the school and open back up the convent.

CHAPTER V

Prior to Father Dennis' arriving, Josh was true to his word. He, along with Becky, T.J., and Billy completely refurbished the garden. By the time Father Dennis arrived, it looked as beautiful as ever.

Josh remained in Jinksville for a little over a week, spending a lot of time at the church. He also spent time with Becky, taking her up several times on the dinner raincheck she asked for. Their talks were easier than before. Less…emotional. And both promised to stay in touch as much as they could.

The day Josh left, they all met at Costello's Coffee Shop to say their goodbyes. A special surprise was waiting for him. Michael Costello, Billy's brother, had flown in from Wisconsin. Josh was thrilled to see him. After introducing him to his wife and two children, Michael told Josh how his church, as well as several other large prayer groups, had been praying for their success.

"Don't forget the two hundred parishioners we gathered in the church to also pray," added Mrs. Costello.

Josh's heart was filled with happiness. Once again, he found it difficult to say goodbye. After hugging everyone, he waited to hug Becky last.

Whispering in her ear, he said, "You will always be in my prayers and thoughts. If you ever need anything, please don't hesitate. Friends. Forever."

Getting into his car, rolling down the window, he said, "God is good. Remember, prayer is so powerful. I will never forget you guys. Pray for me…" Then, waving to everyone, he blew Becky a kiss and drove back to Clarksville.

CHAPTER VI

A DREAM COMES TRUE

It didn't take long for people to realize that Josh was back in Clarksville. Only there a few hours, he was inundated with requests for healing. Noticing that there were dozens and dozens of people with red, glowing halos around their heads, he concluded that their only purpose was to deceive and cause confusion and doubt to the faithful. Somehow the entire crowd was able to squeeze into the church. Josh reminded everyone that his mission was not to heal, but to sound the warning that time was running out and people needed to repent before it was too late.

"Tell us when the end is coming!" someone with a red glow surrounding their head yelled out with an arrogant voice.

"I have no idea," Josh replied. "As Scripture says, only the Father knows the time and day but Jesus told me it was coming soon. Again, as I've said before, you can believe it or not. The choice is yours. But I can assure you, once I leave Clarksville, you" he said pointing to the person who has just asked the question, "you will not be given the message again."

Looking at the same person, Josh said, "Please allow me to ask you a question." Without waiting for a reply Josh asked, "Why do you hate Jesus so much?"

There was a moment of silence, but then, the response came.

"What makes you think I hate Jesus?"

"If you don't, then can I conclude that you love him?" Josh waited for a response, but again there was nothing but silence. "Well, do you love him?" Josh asked a second time.

The man's face turned bright red, and he was sweating profusely. This guy was clearly angry, and without answering, he and a handful of other red-glowing sinners walked out.

Another question emerged from another red-glowing sinner who remained in the church.

"Some are saying you are the 'Messiah returned,' while others are saying you are the antichrist? What do you say to all of this?"

This time there was silence throughout the entire church. So much so that you could hear a pin drop. All eyes were now on Josh, as he responded, "And who are all these people that are saying this?" But once again there was no response. The person who asked just shrugged their shoulders.

"Guess these people are not here today. In any case, I will answer your question. First, if I were the antichrist, I would not be praising and giving glory to Jesus every day, nor would any miracle that has been performed be done by invoking His name. Yes, I can assure you, if I were the antichrist, I would not be invoking the Will of Jesus for healing. Nor would I be spreading the message of reparation and asking people to repent and to return to the Lord.

CHAPTER VI

"As for being the 'Messiah returned,' you need to read Scripture. It is written in Thessalonians, 'For the Lord himself will descend from Heaven with a cry of command, with the voice of an archangel, and with the sound of the trumpet of God.' It is also written in Revelations that, 'He is coming with the clouds and every eye will see Him.' As you can see, none of this has occurred yet, and certainly can't be applied to me.

"Besides," Josh jokingly said, "I was born in *Jinksville*, had loving human parents, had a wonderful childhood, got into trouble occasionally, and you can check all that out with Father Dennis if you like. I graduated from high school. So, I can assure you, I did not descend from the clouds, nor did I come into this world with the sound of a trumpet." Laughter erupted everywhere and with that another handful of sinners left the church.

Then Josh said the following to the surprise of everyone, especially those who had the red glowing mists around their heads.

"I have said this before, and I will say it over and over again if I have to. Jesus, and *only* Jesus, is the one who heals. So, if He wants you to be physically healed, go home, and ask him to confirm it. When you return next Sunday, I will also ask Him. And if it is His will, then you will receive his healing."

Josh knew that there were many skeptics in the church, many who had absolutely no interest in true healing, spiritual or otherwise, but were there only out of curiosity. He also realized that the people belonging to Satan, who had remained in the church, would not return. They had absolutely no desire to be healed. However, the faithful that would return to the church would certainly receive God's blessing and healing.

Bishop Timothy was aware of the large number of people that had returned to St. Andrew's Church over the past several months. Father O'Malley was simply overwhelmed. Josh was a great help, but could not perform any priestly duties just yet. Recognizing the seriousness of the situation, Father Samar Sakaham, a newly ordained priest from India, was assigned to St. Andrew's. Father O'Malley and Josh were thrilled with this appointment and wasted no time bringing Father Samar up to date with all that was going on in the parish.

Father Samar was 32 years old and spoke several languages, in addition to several local dialects spoken in India. Father Samar had a wonderful devotion to the Blessed Virgin Mary and was delighted to coordinate the rosary group that Josh started just over a year ago.

Bishop Timothy had already filled Father Samar in regarding Josh's gifts and mission, so it was no surprise to him when Josh attempted to tell him about it.

"I can clearly see what is going on here," Father Samar said. "We also had several violent attacks on our seminary while I was training in India. It appears that there are quite a lot of people that don't want priests to be ordained. Luckily, no one was seriously hurt, but the fire they set caused my ordination to be delayed for over a year."

"I can't say it's hard to believe," Father O'Malley said. "The things going on in this world are so bad. No wonder Jesus is so sad."

"Yeah, and it's truly a miracle that He has given us one more chance."

"I couldn't agree with you more," Father O'Malley said to Josh.

"Well," Father Samar added, "I will do my best to help in any way I can, especially in helping to spread the message of reparation."

CHAPTER VI

"We really appreciate that," Father O'Malley said, "and we are so thankful and blessed to have you with us."

By the time mid-summer arrived, Josh's training and preparation for the priesthood was finally complete. Over the past months, he had spent considerable time secluded in the rectory and church preparing for the special event. Most of the time that Josh was present at Sunday Mass, only occasional healings took place. And most of them were related to family problems, loss of faith, or other psychological difficulties.

The call finally came from Bishop Timothy. Father O'Malley knocked on Josh's door, waking him up out of a sound sleep.

"Josh, get up. Bishop Timothy wants to see you today. Hurry up, we don't have much time and we don't want to keep him waiting. He's scheduled you for 10:00am."

Josh and Father were soon on the road. Father Samar said morning Mass and would take care of any business that might come up while they were away. During the drive, Father O'Malley questioned Josh on a variety of topics that he thought the bishop might ask. Josh was sweating, quite nervous, and had to remind himself that Jesus was in charge. Arriving just a little after 9:30am, they remained in the car for fifteen minutes of prayer.

After an extensive two hour written exam, Bishop Timothy not only quizzed Josh on all that Father O'Malley had reviewed in the car, but on so much more. More than a seminarian would have to know had he been trained under the normal process. To Bishop Timothy's delight, Josh answered all questions correctly and without hesitation, not to mention earning a 100% on his written test.

However, the celebration was short-lived. Early the next morning, Bishop Timothy called Father O'Malley informing him that the Archbishop wanted to see Josh immediately. He told Father that he did not know exactly what the meeting was about but the Archbishop sounded very angry and if he was to guess, it didn't look like the Archbishop would approve the ordination. Josh was in a panic. What would ever possess the Archbishop not to approve the ordination?

"All we can do is to trust the Lord," Father O'Malley said, as he, Josh, and Father Samar joined hands in prayer.

Father O'Malley waited in the outer office during the meeting.

"Come in," Archbishop Nelson said. Josh no sooner walked into the office than he stopped immediately, staring at what looked like a broken, angry old man. "Come in," he shouted again. "I have much to do, so I will make this short."

Josh sat down with no time to say hello before the archbishop began.

"Let me get right to the point. Bishop Timothy has informed me that Father O'Malley has personally trained you for preparation for ordination. This is highly unusual and quite frankly, I do not agree. There is no way I can approve such an arrangement, even though you have supposedly done an outstanding job on all tests given. I'm sorry, but you're just going to have to start over and prepare through the approved and standard route."

Josh sat for some time speechless. Saying nothing, he prayed to Jesus for help. "Dear Jesus," Josh said to himself, "please give me guidance and knowledge as to what to say. Please, send me your Holy Spirit. Enlighten me. Give me insight and guidance as to what to do…"

CHAPTER VI

Breaking the awkward silence, Archbishop Nelson said, "Well…I don't think there is anything more to be said here, thank you for coming in."

Josh slowly stood up and then after a few seconds, sat back down, looking the archbishop directly in the eyes.

"Your Excellency, I see a holy man, drowning in the sea. He's being pulled down deeper and deeper with each breath he tries to take. He struggles to free himself from the weight of sin that keeps pulling him under. He's struggling for life. Life that only Jesus can give him.

"Jesus is standing on the banks of the water, reaching out for him but with each effort to grab hold of the man, he sinks deeper, choking, spitting, coughing, and gasping for breath, for the breath of life. Yet he knows all he must do is to lift his arm up out of the water and Jesus will gladly pull him the rest of the way to safety. Jesus is in the water, rushing toward him, panicking, as he splashes and pushes water aside, trying desperately to get to him before he drowns. Yet, all the man has to do is to reach for Jesus's help…

"You, your Excellency, are the man drowning… drowning in a sea of envy, jealousy, and despair. Yet, Jesus loves you. He loves you even in your sins. Will you reach out to him? He's waiting. He's waiting for you. He has so much for you to do. Yet because of your self-pity, and the anger you have for so many above, you are blinded by truth. Take His hand and reach out to Him."

The archbishop sat motionless, staring with an astonished look on his face. To Josh's surprise, he said absolutely nothing. Detecting tears in the Archbishop's eyes, Josh stood up, and left the office without saying another word.

Returning home, Fr. O'Malley and Fr. Samar couldn't wait to find out what had transpired.

REPARATION: A STORY OF HOPE

"Well, tell us! Did the archbishop give his permission or not?"

Josh simply shrugged his shoulders, indicating he didn't know and headed directly to the church where he spent most of the night in prayer. It was a little after 3:00am when Father O'Malley interrupted him.

"Josh… Jesus has heard your prayer. You know as well as I do that if it is His Will for you to be a priest, it will happen. You need to get some sleep. Looks like you're going to have a busy day tomorrow, as there were dozens of people waiting for you today."

"Thanks, Father. Yes, I know Jesus wants me to be a priest…but right now, I'm more concerned about Archbishop Nelson."

"Why's that?" Father O'Malley asked.

Josh told him about the terrible anger the Archbishop had and the story the Holy Spirit had revealed to him.

"You know Father, I stepped out in faith sharing that story… I only hope the archbishop heard it in the same light."

Although he did not get much sleep, Josh was up bright and early, fully awake, and ready to face whatever the day brought. As he always did, Josh started his day with a little prayer. "Dear Lord, this is a new day, a new beginning, and a new commitment, bless me and all that I do for You today. Amen"

Josh was so pleased to see so many people at Mass and so many who were going to confession. Both Fr. O'Malley and Fr. Samar had long lines of people waiting for the grace, blessings, and forgiveness they would receive from the Lord. What a difference, Josh thought to himself, as he remembered how few attended Mass when he first arrived in Clarksville.

Not only were more and more people attending Mass, but many more believers were praying and attending religious services throughout the town. Josh couldn't help but smile, realizing that people of all faiths were listening to the Lord's message and reacting to it. However, he knew full well that there was so much more to be done.

After mass, Father Samar and Josh prayed the rosary along with about two-dozen others. Immediately after finishing the prayers, Josh left the church followed by quite a few people. Walking along the side streets, he came across several homeless men huddled against the side of Clarksville Diner. Reaching over to help a man up, he led the men into the diner and paid for whatever they wanted to eat. Several of the people who were walking with him just looked on, taking in all that was happening.

Continuing on his walk, he spotted more homeless living in tents under a small patch of trees across from one of the many bars in town. Poking his head into a tent, he saw a grubby old man half asleep in a dirty old sleeping bag. Josh told the man that there was a soup kitchen and food available at St. Andrew's Church and he and his companions were always welcome there.

In the meantime, he handed him $20.00 saying that he hoped this would help. The old guy, immediately stood up, took the money and practically tripped, as he rushed out across the street, into the bar.

One of the people who was following Josh, came up to him saying, "I can't believe you just gave that guy money. You see where he went! He's just going to get drunk again." Josh sadly looked at the person.

"I don't know if he's going to get drunk and neither do you. Besides, who are we to judge? And even if he does use it for drinking, perhaps he will remember this kind deed, which just might help him to find his way."

"Oh, Josh, you're living in a make-believe world, people don't just give money to bums."

"You're right, I am living in a world where people don't care about each other anymore, where kindness and compassion have been forgotten, where sin and immorality is rampant and where God has been forgotten." Without saying another word, he turned away.

Reaching into his pocket, he gave the other two men and one woman $20.00 each. They all took the money without hesitation, and with sincere smiles they thanked him and slipped it into their pockets as quickly as they could.

As the last man was taking the money, the old man who had run off into the bar was just coming out with his arms full of two bags of food. Crossing the street, he gave each of his companion's hamburgers, fries, and coffee that he must have just bought with the money Josh gave him.

That act of kindness brought Josh and some other onlookers to tears, and it secured the old man a place in Heaven. No one said anything, but the person who was so judgmental of the old man, and who had ostracized Josh, stood dumbfounded, hopefully learning a lesson that would most likely never be forgotten.

Two days later, the phone rang while Josh, Father O'Malley, and Father Samar were eating breakfast.

"I'll get it," Josh said. "Hello? Hello… Yes. Your Excellency, I can hear you. Yes, this is Josh. Will you repeat that? Yes, I'll tell them. Thank You. Thank you, your Excellency. Thank you."

Josh hung up the phone. A smile broke across his face. He even did a little two-step, although he had no idea what he was doing. Looking at them he said, "God is good. That's all I can say! God is good and answers prayers."

By now both Father O'Malley and Father Samar were practically off their seats waiting to hear what the call was all about.

CHAPTER VI

"Well...don't keep us waiting!" Father Samar blurted out.

"Yes, Josh, please! What's up?" Father O'Malley asked.

"That was Archbishop Nelson... It seems he has had a change of heart."

"Oh, my dear Jesus," O'Malley yelled out.

"Evidently he was deeply touched by what I said to him. He just got off the phone with Bishop Timothy and wants me to know that he has agreed to sanction my ordination as soon as possible."

"Praise the Lord," Father O'Malley said. "Praise the Lord."

"Did he say anything else?" Father Samar asked.

"Actually, he did. He said he lifted his arm out of the water and Jesus pulled him out."

Both priests looked at Josh with a confused look.

"Don't worry, I'll tell you all about it later."

The two demons, who were previously clinging to the Archbishop, quickly reported all of this to Azazal, who was resting peacefully in his cave.

"Master... we're no longer in control. The Archbishop is back in good graces with the King of Hosts."

Azazal turned slowly, as he looked at the two petrified demons. "You are no longer in control???" he screamed out with his eyes bulging. "Did the *Donovan* brat have anything to do with this?" he asked, trying ever so hard to control himself.

"We don't know Master...but he was there."

"Of course he was!" Azazal said with a scowl on his face. "What did he say? What did he *do*?" he asked as his voice grew angrier.

"It was all so confusing, master. The Archbishop said he would not approve the ordination of the Donovan kid and then the kid said something about the Archbishop drowning in the water..."

"...in the sea..." the other Demon interjected.

"Didn't make sense to us."

As soon as they finished their report, Azazal grabbed them by their necks. Lifting them up, he slowly crushed the life out of them as he screamed, "Didn't make any sense to *you*? Well it does to *me*, you fools!"

Still holding their dead, mutilated bodies, Azazal threw them against the cave wall. Circling and screaming, he tried to grab anything in his reach. Demons scattered in all directions as if he had just disturbed a nest of bats. Flying out of the cave to avoid his clutching claws, Azazal was left alone by himself. Finally, calming down, he sat still for a long time thinking of how he would now have to deal with the future "Father Donovan."

Preparations had to be made for the ordination, including inviting friends and planning the other church events. Josh was a little overwhelmed. It was almost like planning a wedding. In fact, it was! He was marrying Christ and the Church, and he couldn't wait.

Father O'Malley had never seen him so happy. A few days later, preparations were in place. The Archbishop and Bishop Timothy wanted the ordination to take place in St. Patrick's Cathedral in New York City but receded when Josh asked it to be held in Clarksville, at St. Andrew's Church. He wanted to keep the ceremony small and as low-key as possible.

It was Saturday, July 6th when the event took place. Josh invited Father Dennis, all his friends from Jinksville, David, Jay, Kirk Williamson, and of course Becky Flowers

The church was full of parishioners who had heard about the ordination and wanted to witness a little history,

CHAPTER VI

as Josh, 23 years old, was thought to be the youngest priest ordained since the early times of the Popes. In addition, there were several other priests present, personal friends of Bishop Timothy, Father Dennis, Father O'Malley, and Father Samar.

The Rite of Josh's Ordination took place during the Rite of The Mass, upholding centuries of sacred traditions of the Church. The ceremony began with the usual procession, commencing from the enclosed breezeway connecting the rectory to the church. Josh led the procession, followed by all the priests and finally Bishop Timothy. The Liturgy of the Word included special readings for Holy Orders.

Bishop Timothy read the Gospel, which preceded the beginning of the Rite of Ordination. Josh, who was sitting with his friends and among the community of parishioners, came forward as he was called by Bishop Timothy. The Church firmly believes that those who are called to ministry, such as Josh, answer the call from the Lord and are called from the midst of the community of the faithful. That's why Josh sat with his family of friends as soon as he entered the church.

Next, he was presented to the community. Josh was thrilled and could not hold back his smile as Bishop Timothy presented him to the congregation, asking them to approve his election of Josh to the priesthood by their applause. The rest of the ceremonial Mass continued as customary. Bishop Timothy gave a wonderful homily, including traditional priestly instructions, followed by a shortened period of questions, and the ancient custom of prostration, symbolizing Josh's submission to the Will of God.

One of the most moving parts of the ceremony was the laying of hands on Josh's head by Bishop Timothy, followed by all the priests doing the same. You could see the joy in Father Dennis', Father Samar's, and especially on Father O'Malley's faces as they prayed over him. The Rite of Ordination concluded with Bishop Timothy praying the prayer of consecration.

Josh, now a newly ordained priest, was vested with the traditional priest stole and chasuble, had his palms and hands anointed with Sacred Chrism. After so many obstacles and prayers, he was finally able to celebrate his first Eucharist along with Bishop Timothy and all the invited priests.

The widow, Mrs. Johnson, who was previously healed from Degenerative Heart Disease, lived by herself in a beautiful old house, on the corner of Elm Street, just two blocks from the church. She had graciously offered her house for a reception after the ordination. Once again, it was very low-key.

Josh had an opportunity to talk to each one of his friends and to catch up on the latest news. He spent considerable time with David and Kirk, filling them in on all that had occurred over the past seven months. To say that they were shocked when Josh told them about the Lord's visit to him would be an understatement. Both, however, were thrilled that they also would be ordained and be a part of the message of reparation. However, it was apparent they wished that they were already in that position.

"Don't get too anxious," Josh said. "Jesus has a plan for you. You'll be ordained in good time. Until then, please spread the message of reparation and pray for me."

"You know we will," David said, "and if we can help in any other way, please, please don't hesitate to ask."

T.J., Billy, and Michael were just about to leave as they had been awake for hours. Saying their goodbyes, Josh

CHAPTER VI

thanked them for attending and for traveling such a distance.

T.J. immediately said, "Think nothing of it... 'Bro,' ...I mean *Father* Donovan." Laughing, Josh assured him that "Bro" would always be OK with him.

"So, when are you going to hear my confession?" T.J. asked with a huge grin on his face.

"I'm not." Josh simply replied.

"Why not?"

"Because, I don't have three hours to listen to you…"

More laughs and joking around. After hugs and more goodbyes, they headed for the door.

"Don't forget tomorrow's 10o'clock Mass! I'm celebrating it by myself."

"Don't worry, we wouldn't think of missing it."

When the guys left, Becky was found sitting by herself. Sitting down next to her, now had an opportunity to talk to her more privately than he had earlier in the reception.

"OK, tell me what's going on," he said to her as he held her hand.

"Nothing…nothing really."

"You know you're now lying to a priest, right?" They both laughed a little.

"I really didn't want to bother you with this, but…"
Trying to find the words, she finally mumbled, "Josh, I have Multiple Myeloma."

"What!!!" Josh said confused. "Oh, no Becks, I'm so sorry. Are you sure? When did you know? Are you being treated?" So many quick questions were flowing from Josh.

"Calm down. And yes, I'm under treatment and am getting blood transfusions weekly."

"Weekly…" Josh repeated. "Oh, my Dear Lord…"

Becky, now crying, told Josh not to worry. She knew that she was in God's hands and… she was fine with whatever happened, no matter what the outcome was.

"I can heal you."

"No, you can't," Becky choked back. "Only Jesus can."

"Well, yes, of course I mean Jesus can," Josh said with somewhat of an irritated tone.

"I know you can ask Him, but I don't want you to. Don't you think that would be misusing your gift? Didn't you tell me that Jesus told you to use the gift of healing only to help the unbeliever to repent? To use it only for the purpose of showing sinners the urgency of reparation…to save souls…? Well," Becky continued, "I know I'm a sinner like we all are, but I don't need conversion and don't think I fit the criteria. Besides, I don't want you to. It would be too selfish."

Josh, with tears running down his cheeks, held Becky tight. All the priests, noticing what was going on, circled around both. Being informed of Becky's condition, they all laid hands over her and prayed for healing.

"Remember Josh, Jesus is in control." A needed reminder from Father O'Malley.

Sunday Mass was filled with friends and parishioners alike. Becky, T.J., Billy, Michael, and David managed to squeeze into one of the front pews. Josh's other close friends sat directly behind them.

Josh celebrated Mass without flaw and gave a wonderful homily on intercessory prayer. As Josh began, there was complete silence in the church. Not even a sound of a child or baby crying. His homily was brief, but down to earth, something that the average Christian could understand and apply to their everyday prayer life.

CHAPTER VI

"First, I would like to thank all of you for your support, prayers, and for honoring me by attending my first Mass. I can't tell you how much I appreciate it.

"This morning I would like to talk just a little about how important prayer is, specifically Intercessory Prayer... and I promise not to go over an hour." Almost everyone broke out into laughter.

"Just kidding…" More laughs.

"We all pray whenever we want something, or when we experience a crisis in our lives, or when we have a death in the family, and of course when we are in church… But prayer is not just *asking* for something. We can pray for others who are in need, who can't pray for themselves, or who won't pray for themselves." Josh hesitated just for a few seconds and then continued.

"Now, I know that you and I pray for others. However, Intercessory Prayer is somewhat different… it's what one might call a higher level of prayer. Prayer is like the fuel we need for a car to run, or the ammunition we need to fight Satan. Without fuel, the car is useless and without spiritual ammunition we're unable to fight evil.

"On the other hand, Intercessory Prayer is when we actually stand-in for another person. Whether the person we are praying for is present or not. It is as if the person themselves were praying, we are just interceding for them on their behalf. Sometimes one cannot pray for themselves. Perhaps they are deep in depression, or perhaps they have been so saddened by some tragedy in their life that they just can't find the strength to pray at that moment. I know many of us have experienced this in our lives," Josh continued.

"More importantly, we can intercede for sinners. Sinners who, without our prayers, would surely be lost. We can intercede for the reparation of sinners throughout the world. In fact, that is exactly what the Lord is, in part, asking us to do." Trying to be a little more personable, he said,

"This is a wonderful gift Jesus has given us. It really is if you think about it. The ability to actually pray for someone as if they were doing the praying themselves. What a blessing for us and what a blessing for them.

"There is one more aspect of Intercessory Prayer that I would like to touch on today. Intercessory prayer for those loved ones that have passed. Now I know that we all have been taught that once we die, well, that's it. There is nothing more we can do to help ourselves. And that's true. Once we di there is nothing more we can do for ourselves. But! There is something the living can do. We can intercede and pray for loved ones while they are living and continue to pray for them after their death. That is why the Church prays for the deceased, and why we offer Masses up for them. So, how does this work?

"We believe there's no real time limits in the Lord's world, as there is in ours. What may be a year for us could be a second for God, or less. In addition, God knows what will occur in the future. Therefore, He knows all future prayers, masses that will be offered up, and sacrifices that will be made on behalf of a particular person, even prior to their death. Because there is no time-limit in God's world, all those prayers we pray will be applied to souls upon their deaths. Consequently, we can be assured that our intercessory prayers, now or in the future, will be applied to needed souls upon their death. Even though we may think that someone has died in sin, those future prayers may be the cause of someone's salvation.

"Now, here's the real kicker," Josh said with a smile. "When we pray for the deceased souls, the souls in Purgatory, they in turn will pray for us. It's like a double whammy. So, my friends, prayer is so important in our lives. We need to constantly talk to God, and He, in turn,

CHAPTER VI

will talk to us. And remember that Intercessory Prayer, for the living and for the deceased, is such a wonderful gift that we should always use. In Jesus' name, Amen."

Immediately after Mass, the unexpected happened. Josh expected to talk to Becky and his other friends that attended Mass; however, he was caught a little off guard when multiple people approached him asking if he would hear their confessions. What started out to be four or five people ended up with dozens in line. Josh, being new to it, did not want to refuse anyone, nor was he prepared for the many different sins that were confessed.

It was well past 1:00pm when the newly ordained Father Donovan left the confessional. His friends had left, and he was completely exhausted. Rushing to his refrigerator for a sorely needed drink of water, he found himself in a state of depression. As he usually did when he was feeling down, he walked down the steps looking for his friend, Father O'Malley.

"I'm in here," Father called. "What's on your mind?" But when he saw the sad, depressed look on Josh's face, he knew not to ask anything else. Yes, he knew just what Josh had just experienced in hearing his first confessions.

Josh was teary-eyed, trying to hide his emotions as he explained how sad he was listening to all the many sins that people commit. Father simply stood up and hugged Josh until he regained his composure.

"So, you wanted to be a priest, did you?" Father O'Malley said jokingly. Both chuckled a little as they began to talk.

"I never expected it to be like this. I mean, yes, I know what goes on in confession and know we all sin, and I remembered all that you taught me how to react and handle certain sins, but… now it's the real thing. I guess I was naive to think that I would be able to separate my personal feelings about it all."

"You can't take their sins personally, Josh. Be glad that Jesus has empowered you to forgive them. That in and of itself, should make you happy. And another thing, you can't stay in confession for hours on end or you will never get anything done!

"This is what the priesthood is all about. You know this. Helping people, leading them to God, encouraging them to repent, forgiving them through the sacrament of reconciliation and, of course, constantly praying for them and for the sins of the world. Now, wipe those tears away and get back doing exactly what Jesus asked you to do."

"Thanks Father, I will."

That evening Josh called Becky. He was surprised to hear that she was going to remain in Clarksville. Evidently, Mrs. Johnson, and Becky were talking after Mass while Josh was hearing confessions. Mrs. Johnson invited Becky to stay with her, as she had plenty of room in her house and because the hospital was close, allowing Becky to easily receive her treatments instead of her having to travel 22 miles to a hospital in Cloverville every week. She had already resigned her teaching position, knowing that her health would not be getting any better. After about an hour of talking, praying, some laughs and tears, they said their goodbyes.

Putting down the phone, Josh was smiling and thrilled, knowing he could visit her often and be close in the event she needed any help.

CHAPTER VII

THE WAR BEGINS

War was raging everywhere throughout the country. Throughout the world. Spiritual warfare, that is. A war some did not believe in. A war that we could not see. A war that was taking the souls of missions and missions of deceived people. Satan and his army of demons were winning many battles.

Immorality was one of the strongest weapons. Deception and lies were close behind. Millions of babies had been slaughtered. Open sex, self sex and pleasuring, prostitution, sex slave trading, pornography, sexual abuse, adultery, and fornication were just some of the demons that the Prince of Darkness has loosed on the world, and especially on the children.

Now another attack strategy was set in motion. The attack on religious institutions, and the churches throughout the world, with specific aim toward Christian churches, and the Catholic Church, and the Pope himself. This attack strategy was initiated to discredit any person of God, Ministers, Clergy, Priests, Bishops, and Cardinals that would lead to confusion, loss of faith, and the massive exodus of believers.

Josh was aware that the war was coming to Clarksville, and that the Lord wanted the evil activity at the 'seminary' to end. No person could see it, but nevertheless, it was coming.

Azazal was gathering hundreds of warriors. Generals of all ranks were joining the fight. They were aware of the damage caused by the conversion of so many who had returned to the Lord, and whose prayers were helping to convert many more who had previously been under the influence of sin. The protection of the 'seminary' and the elimination of Josh was paramount if their evil plans were to succeed.

Azazal and his army were on edge. There was considerable division as to who was in charge. Arguments were breaking out everywhere, especially as to what attack strategy would be most effective. However, all agreed that the first thing that had to be done was to stop the thousands of prayers that were now occurring throughout the city. Consequently, the joint decision was made to send out many more Warriors to recapture the souls of those who were previously under their control.

In the meantime, Azazal continued to argue his point that he should be the one in charge. Although he was not the highest ranking General, he was the one most familiar with the 'seminary,' with the town, and especially with dealing with Joshua Donovan.

Because Belzar had been defeated in Jinksville, most of the demons under his command had broken rank and fled. Denzil and Jarell were no exception. However, to avoid punishment, they gladly joined the ranks of Azazal's army and were most eager to support his position.

To gain Azazal's favor, they quickly joined his side and told everyone that he was the right one to be in charge. Of

CHAPTER VII

course, they failed to mention that they had been unsuccessful numerous times with their own attacks against Josh. After much argument and dissension, Azazal finally won out and would be in charge, at least for the time being.

As time passed, the days grew darker, not by the clouds or time of day, but by the black swirls of evil mist forming, ever so thick, in the sky above.

It was several weeks after the Ordination, late in the day, when Josh was inspired to visit one of the most frequented bars in the town, located in the seedy east-section of Clarksville.

Walking into a smoke-filled room, all noise stopped as everyone looked at the young priest. Laughter and cheers broke out.

"This is no place for you, Father! Get the hell outta here," someone yelled out.

Others started to curse at him, some demanded that the bartender throw the 'bum' out. However, most just continued drinking, paying little attention to him.

Josh, ignoring what was being said, walked over to a lone man sitting at a table, slumped halfway over in his chair. On the table was an empty bottle of Jack Daniels, an ashtray filled with cigarette butts, and a folded-up newspaper, with red circles around the "Help Wanted" section. Next to him was a wheelchair. Missing one leg from the war in Iraq, he paid little attention to the man dressed as a priest who was now standing next to him.

"Gunna buy me a drink, Father?" the intoxicated man said sarcastically.

"No. I think you've had enough. But I'll tell you what I will do for you." Josh sat down, took the man's hand, holding it tight so that he could not pull it away. "I know all about you. Jesus knows all about you. He loves you so much. He knows all the hardships you have endured. He knows all the sufferings you are having and the great sacrifices you've made in the war. Because of His great love and mercy, He wants to heal you. To once again make you whole."

Josh, now realizing that the entire bar was intently listening to every word he said, looked back into the man's eyes and said,

"Let your healing be a sign for others to see the love of Jesus, the mercy of Jesus, and how much He wants us all to repent."

Josh prayed silently for a few minutes. Then, breaking his own silence, he said,

"In the Name of Jesus, King of Kings and Lord of Lords, I ask Him to heal you."

Instantly, all the windows in the bar burst into pieces, shattering glass with thundering noise everywhere. Men ducked for cover. One man fell off his stool. Beers spilled, and tear was on the faces of even the toughest looking men.

Before anyone could say anything, Josh stood up and assured them that everything was OK. "Don't be afraid, brothers and sisters. Satan is not happy whenever someone is healed."

In all the noise and confusion, no one noticed that the man's missing leg was completely restored. Just before leaving, Josh walked up to the man standing behind the bar and said, "Joey says not to worry. He's so happy. He's with Jesus." With that, Josh turned and left.

It was only a few seconds later when screams of joy and excitement rang out from the bar. Grown men ran out crying and praising Jesus. Men, who just a few minutes ago, were cursing and angry and full of sin, were now touched by what they had just witnessed.

CHAPTER VII

Zachary Jones, the vet who Jesus healed, now had two legs again and would never be the same. He would devote the rest of his life to God and spreading the Gospel and would be instrumental in the war that was approaching.

However, not everyone in the bar was so touched. Nevertheless, Josh knew that many would hear of the healing and that was enough to begin another snowball effect of reparation.

Sam Douglas, who owned the bar, was the man Josh spoke to. He was so bitter toward the Lord because of the loss of his three-year-old son, who died from a rare kind of leukemia. He, nor his wife, had gone to church for years. In fact, they lost their faith and did not hesitate to blame God for being so cruel. "God is dead," he would often say. "God is dead!"

It wasn't long before everyone left the bar. Sam couldn't remember if anyone had paid for their drinks. But it didn't matter. He simply stood still, not moving until everyone in the bar was gone. Locking the door behind him, he was in a daze. Leaving his car behind, he headed home on foot, a hefty one-and-a-half mile hike. Arriving home sometime later, sweaty, and exhausted, he entered the kitchen as his wife was preparing dinner.

"Oh my god," Clair shouted out. "What on earth happened to you?" Without waiting for an answer, she continued, "You alright, hun?"

Sam hugged her as tight as he could. Crying uncontrollably, he just held her, shaking and sobbing.

"Please tell me honey! Please tell me what's wrong,"

Still holding her close to him, he finally managed to choke out the name, "Joey… it's Joey," he said.

"Oh my god. What about him?"

Regaining some composure, they sat down as she listened to the entire event that had just transpired in the bar.

"Clair…we've been wrong. We've been so wrong. God is *alive*. I've seen it with my own eyes. That guy's leg was healed. One minute he didn't have it, the next minute, poof, it was there."

"Oh, Sam. What's going on?" Clair asked, with an unbelieving voice.

"I'm telling you his leg miraculously appeared as if it was always there. The guy stood up, and the damn leg was there! And then that priest…"

"What priest?" Clair asked.

"I don't know his name…some young priest. I think someone said from St. Andrew's? Anyway, he walked right up to me and said, 'Joey says…not to worry. He's so happy… he's with Jesus.'"

Stunned, and sobbing, they held each other as they hadn't done in such a long time. As the minutes passed, each felt as if the whole world had been lifted off them. Their anger was gone and so was their hatred for God. They too, had been healed and finally were at peace knowing that their son, Joey, was in Heaven.

Still sobbing, Sam reiterated, "God is alive…Yes, He is…God is alive."

Clair immediately added, "And I will tell that to every person I meet for the rest of my life."

Throughout the course of history, whenever miracles have occurred, herds of people have flocked to the area, hopefully to receive healing, or at the very least, a blessing from the Lord. Word spread that a priest in Clarksville could work miracles. Caravans started to arrive and migrate to the town of Clarksville.

CHAPTER VII

Stores and restaurants that had been closed reopened, and as expected, there was a boom in the demand for hotel and motel accommodations. Many of the townspeople took advantage of the situation and opened their homes into bed-and-breakfast establishments. St. Andrew's was no exception. It was overwhelmed with people seeking healing by the young priest.

Josh was frustrated that people considered him a miracle maker. He kept telling them that Jesus is the one who works the miracles, not him. Nevertheless, many didn't care who was doing the healing, just so long as they were healed.

Talking to Father O'Malley and to Father Samar about this concern helped relieve his frustration. Father O'Malley didn't quite know how to react. He remembered telling Josh that the healings would not only cause quite a commotion but that he would be inundated with people who just wanted to be healed.

"You know," Father O'Malley said, "most people of faith realize that Jesus is the healer. Sometimes they get caught up in the moment so just keep reminding them that Jesus is in charge."

Bishop Timothy, aware of the large numbers of people that were arriving in Clarksville, assigned two more priests to St. Andrews. He also told Josh that his responsibilities as a priest would not be the same as the other priests under his dioceses. His responsibilities would be independent of others. He was, as the Lord had asked him, to continue to proclaim the message of reparation to all the world.

The church acquired a small house one block away from the rectory. A perfect place to house the new priests. Father Scott and Father Gordon arrived one week after Josh's ordination. Father Scott attended the ordination, as he was invited personally by his friend Bishop Timothy. With the four priests now in the parish, it gave Josh time to continue to evangelize the message of reparation and in addition it gave Father O'Malley the extra help he so desperately needed.

The miracle of Zachary Jones' restored leg was, as the expression goes, 'the straw that broke the camel's back'. That miracle sparked the first wave of demonic attacks. Azazal had enough. He understood attacking Josh directly was useless. He also was totally aware of the strength of Kapriel and Lancer and the damage they had inflicted on the many demons that fought against him. All of this, however, was of little concern to Azazal.

Evidently the Prince of Darkness had revealed to him a completely new plan of attack. All that had to be done was to deceive and influence someone in town, who would be willing to carry out an attack on someone who Josh loved.

After all, if Josh could not be harmed, what better way to stop him than to attack those most dear to him? If he cared at all for the ones he loved, he surely would leave Clarksville. For the first time in ages, Azazal was smiling, as he sent out Denzil and Jarell to find the right person who would carry out his plan.

Mayor Robert Taylon was the perfect candidate. He was already under the influence of the evil one, with quite a large, red mist around his head. As Mayor, he had done a tremendous amount of harm to the city, all to help Father Gerald gain control. His plan was to intimidate and to create so much hysteria, confusion, and mistrust in the city that people eventually would be willing to listen to and cooperate with anyone who Father Gerald put in charge. In that way, there would be no interference from anyone in town, including law enforcement, allowing the 'seminary' to operate freely. In short, the 'Father' Gerald would be completely in charge of the city.

CHAPTER VII

The Mayor had cut back on many of the city's public services, influenced many police to look the other way when crime was committed, and blackmailed Judge Wallace, who was having an affair, not to prosecute anyone involved in the "Red Light Area" of the city or anyone involved in petty crimes. Not to mention all the stores and businesses that closed as a direct result the high taxes imposed on them. Taylon was getting rich with the payments Father Gerald was giving him and gloated at his accomplishments. He had managed to do all of this without anyone suspecting him.

Saturday night dinner at the rectory was always special. Meatballs and spaghetti, one of Josh's favorites. All the priests were so fortunate to have Maggie cook for them, as all of them could barely handle cooking an egg. When dinner was finished, Maggie said that she had strawberry shortcake for dessert.

While waiting for dessert, Father O'Malley said that he was going to look for more wine, as they were running low due to all the extra Masses that were being said on weekdays and Sundays. He thought that there was still a case somewhere in the church basement.

"I'll be right back. Don't start dessert without me."

Entering the sacristy through the enclosed breezeway, he walked across the room directly to the cellar steps. Turning on the light switch to the cellar, he realized that the light did not go on. Moving the switch back and forth several times, either the light was blown, or the switch was bad. In any case, he lit a candle and slowly descended the steps.

With barely enough light to see, he proceeded to the area where he thought the extra case of wine was. Reaching down to pick it up, a sharp painful stab penetrated his back. Then another stab, entered just under his shoulder. The last thing he remembered hearing was the heavy sound of footsteps racing up the steps.

Five minutes, ten minutes, then after fifteen minutes, Josh said, "Where the heck is he? Can't imagine he can't find the wine. I just saw it a few days ago."

"Josh," Father Scott said, "Why don't you go and see what's keeping him so long. Besides, that shortcake smells so good... I can hardly wait."

"Sure, I'll be right back. Go ahead and eat if you want."

"No, we'll wait...a good penance for us!"

Josh also found the light not working. Finding an old flashlight, he started down the steps. The cellar was cold and dark, reminding him of the tunnels at the 'seminary.'

"You OK, Father?" Not hearing anything, he yelled out again, "Father, you OK?... Are you there?"

A million thoughts were running through his mind. Perhaps he couldn't find the wine and left, perhaps he tripped and hit his head, what if he had a stroke? Slowly searching he could hardly see anything. The flashlight was dimming quickly. "Damn flashlight," he thought, shaking it several times to see if that would help. "Next time I'll buy a good one." Moving the dim light to where he thought the wine was, he suddenly stopped.

Horrified at what he saw, he rushed over to Father O'Malley. Josh couldn't believe what he was seeing. Father O'Malley, his dear friend, was lying dead, covered with blood, on the cold cement floor.

"Oh, my Dear God, no! NO!" he cried out. Not Father O'Malley. "This is all my fault," he sobbed.

"HELP! SOMEONE HELP US!"

Sobbing uncontrollably, Josh pulled Father O'Malley's lifeless body close to himself. He began to shake him, desperately hoping that he might be alive. Again, he called

CHAPTER VII

out in a choking voice, "HELP! Please help us…" But there was no answer.

Useless as it was, he continued his efforts to revive him, yelling out over and over for help. No one heard his call. Looking at the amount of blood loss and the lifeless body he was holding in his arms, Josh realized that there was nothing he could do for his dear friend. There was almost no light in the room, as the flashlight was dimming with every minute. Choking back his tears, he continued to hold him close to his chest.

Finally, after calming down, he began to talk to the Lord.

"Why Jesus? Why? This man is so good… he has so much more to give… so much more to do for You and for others. Oh, dear Jesus, I need him. I need him so much." But again, there was no answer.

As Josh continued to sit in the dark in tearful silence, he remembered Jesus's words of warning. *"Nothing will be able to penetrate the protective shield… this will infuriate them, and cause them to attack you with other strategies."*

His mind was racing. He realized that the attack on Father O'Malley was an effort to stop him. To end his ministry. And more so, to get him to leave Clarksville. But who? Who wanted him to leave so bad that they would kill? No one else came to his mind but Father Gerald and his evil followers.

Never for a moment did Josh think that the gift of miracles he was given would ever include bringing a person back to life. Only Jesus can do that. Sitting, still holding his dear friend, Josh's mind became clear. He remembered what he always said to people who referred to him as the healer. "Jesus is the one that performs all the miracles, He's the one that heals, not me."

Regaining confidence, he began to pray.

"Oh, dear Jesus, I need Father O'Malley. His ministry can save so many souls. He's so needed. Please, dear Jesus, I'm asking you, if it is Your Will, to heal him, please bring him back to us."

By this time, Josh could hear footsteps entering the sacristy. Father Scott yelled out, "Where are you guys? What's holding you up?"

The cellar was completely dark as the flashlight had gone out. There was nothing but silence. Deafening silence. Still waiting for an answer, Father Scott was about to call out again, when Father O'Malley responded, "We'll be right up. Hope you didn't eat my dessert!"

There were only three people who would know about this miracle, Father O'Malley, Josh, and the person who committed the crime. Bringing Father O'Malley back to life was never meant to be public. Rather, it was hoped that the magnitude of this miracle would be instrumental in causing reparation for the one who committed the crime, and whatever followed would be up to the Lord.

Father O'Malley and Josh spent most of the night in prayer, thanking Jesus for His miracle and asking for guidance as to how to best handle the miracle once the perpetrator realized that he was still alive. Of course, their concerns were in vain, as Jesus knew exactly what would happen.

The next day found Sunday's 10:00am Mass full. The choir sang a beautiful rendition of 'Ave Maria,' prior to Mass starting. As the entrance bell rang, everyone stood. Josh followed two altar boys holding candles up the aisle to the altar. Mayor Taylon and his wife, Patricia, were sitting at the end of a pew just about in the middle of the church. When Mayor Taylon caught sight of Josh walking up the aisle by himself, the smile on his face exploded, but his exhilaration would be short-lived.

CHAPTER VII

No sooner did Josh reach the altar, then Father O'Malley stepped out of the sacristy, joining him. Both kissed the altar, turned, and faced the congregation. Neither priest had time to start the Mass with the usual 'sign of the cross', when Mayor Taylon spring to his feet yelling.

"No! No...It can't be! Oh my God..." he said, with a startled voice and petrified face. "No, it's impossible, it's just not possible."

Everyone immediately turned and was staring at him, but Josh was the only one who could see the brilliant red glow surrendering his head.

"What's the matter, Robert? What's wrong?" his wife Patricia asked.

Still standing, Mayor Robert Taylon simply stared at Father O'Malley for what seemed an eternity. Suddenly, as if hit by a lightning strike, his demeanor changed and so did the red glow. It was gone as soon as he felt remorse.

"Oh my God, I am so sorry. I'm so sorry. I'm such a sinner. Please... forgive me," he prayed out loud.

None of the parishioners knew what was happening except how upset he apparently was. With tears in his eyes and paying no attention to anyone, he ran up the side aisle until he reached Father O'Malley. Falling at Father's knees, he cried out, "Please forgive me... please, please forgive me. I've sinned and I'm so sorry."

All eyes were now on both. Patricia just sat with her mouth open. She appeared stunned, with a bewildered expression on her face.

Father O'Malley helped Mayor Taylon up and led him to the sacristy. Josh broke the tension by saying,

"We are all sinners, but you don't have to be *that* dramatic for Jesus to forgive you." Everyone broke out with a little nervous laugh, while Josh continued to say the Mass by himself.

REPARATION: A STORY OF HOPE

Once in the sacristy, the Mayor pleaded for forgiveness from Jesus and from Father O'Malley. After a formal confession, he revealed all he had done to suppress the city and how helpless he felt over the past few years due to the influence of sin and Satan in his life.

"As far as last night, I can't explain it to you," he said. "It was as if my will had been completely taken over. I was home in my study when three seminarians knocked on the door. Although I did not know them by name, I had seen them many times before in town, stirring up trouble and hatred against God and the Church. I was sure Father Gerald had sent them, so I invited them in.

"Almost instantly the room became cold. I could see their breath as they talked, and I could smell sulfur as I always did whenever I was at the 'seminary' or had a private meeting with Father Gerald. Anyway, as they were talking to me it was as if I went into a trance. In any case, I can't remember much, other than opening my eyes and heading directly for the church."

Still pretty shaken, the Mayor continued.

"I know you probably can't believe me when I say I was helpless, but..." Father O'Malley stopped him at that point.

"Robert," he said, "I know exactly what you experienced, and I know you are telling the truth. Jesus forgives you and so do I. I'm here today because Jesus never gave up on you. It may have taken this miracle to make you realize how sinful you were but, I can assure you, His mercy is real, and that He has given you another chance."

"I know that Father. I realize that now. I've been extremely blessed, and I never will stop thanking Him or serving Him as long as I live."

The Mayor began that very day with his promise. He made things right with his wife, he fired the cops that were

CHAPTER VII

corrupt, he made amends with Judge Wallace, and over time he did all he could to restore the city by supporting new businesses, closing the red-light areas, improving all public work services, as well as returning to the church and evangelizing to all who he met.

No one ever knew about the miracle except the three who experienced it. But it was obvious that the Mayor was a new person. All those who had associated with him knew it immediately, and when asked about his apparent new disposition, he never hesitated to say it was a gift from God.

Azazal's demonic army was growing, yet there was more confusion and chaos developing within its ranks. Denzil and Jarell had eagerly reported back that the Mayor had murdered Father O'Malley, yet somehow he was seen to be alive and well.

Azazal had a reputation of ripping his demon sentinels and warriors apart whenever they failed in accomplishing the task given to them. However, Azazal vowed to be more cautious this time, as he wanted to be exactly sure what had occurred. Summoning both Denzil and Jarell, he began to question the frightened little demons.

"Yes, master... we are sure he killed the priest. We saw him stabbed twice in the back and he was dead before we left."

"Was anyone else there?" asked Azazal.

"Not at the time of the stabbing, but we did see the Donovan priest crossing the breezeway that leads into the church, as we were leaving."

"Father Donovan. Father Donovan..." Azazal slowly and sarcastically repeated, growing angrier and angrier the more he thought about yet another failed mission. Letting out a scream that summoned his Generals to his side and shook the two little demons off their feet, he began to pace back and forth. Finally stopping, he turned to the two petrified demons.

"Come here," he commanded, but the two creatures froze in place. Azazal slowly stepped closer to them. Bending down to reach their level, he calmly said, "Well done. You did exactly what I asked. Now go and keep me updated."

The two demons were so thrilled, they didn't actually know what to say. However, not waiting for Azazal to change his mood, they flew off and did exactly what was commanded.

One of the higher-ranking Generals stepped forward, brazenly criticizing Azazal in his latest plan of attack toward Josh.

"I told you I should be in charge," shouted the General. "You think your plans are so good and yet all you do is fail! Over and over, you screw up. Let someone else who knows what they're doing be in charge!"

By now Azazal was fuming, but somehow able to control himself. Slowly turning toward the brazen General, he calmly replied, "So, you think you're smarter than Lucifer himself?"

Immediate confusion came across the General's face. "Lucifer?"

"Yes, you insubordinate fool! Lucifer himself laid out the plan." Although not even Lucifer knew the kid priest would be given the power to raise the dead.

Still quite contemptuous, the general continued his protest. "How do we know O'Malley was really dead? I for one don't believe it."

"I'll be glad to show you," Azazal said.

Moving close to the General, as fast as lightning, with one swipe of his wing, he cut off the General's head.

CHAPTER VII

"Now that's how I know he was dead, just as you are dead!" Azazal mockingly said. "But you don't have a miracle to bring you back."

There wasn't confusion, but fear. Now there was no doubt who was in charge. Azazal looked at all his Warriors and Generals gathered around him.

"Now, is there anyone else who dares to question my authority?"

It wasn't long before Denzil and Jarell returned with their report.

"Master…the sentinels that you sent out to reclaim the souls of those who were once ours are being slaughtered. Their Angelic Guardians are too strong. They have turned away from us and their prayers are very powerful."

Azazal immediately flew to the highest point where he could observe the city. To his dismay, it looked like fireworks going off everywhere. Unfortunately for him, it was dozens of his army being cut down into fiery ashes. And he knew exactly why they were being defeated.

"Those fools! Those damn stupid fools! No wonder why they're being slaughtered. They are attacking the souls of believers! Get them back here," he screamed. "Recall all of them before I kill them myself! They should know better not to attack or to deceive unless they are invited."

Looking directly at Denzel and Jarell, he screamed once again. "Get them back to me as fast as possible!"

Deep down in the pit of the cave was the largest cavern where his army and Generals could all assemble at one time. Once all his sentinels had returned and he had calmed down enough to address them, Azazal began by sternly reminding them that they cannot force themselves on souls that have not opened themselves up to them.

Beginning to lose his temper again, he blasted out, "You fools! How many of us have to be destroyed before you realize that the angels of the righteous have the authority to obliterate you if you even dare to attack them when you are not invited?"

Then turning his attention to his plan of attack, he instructed several Generals to take charge of the 'seminary'.

"Gather up all our people in town and assign them to various posts around and inside the 'seminary'. They will be able to find arms at the old warehouse."

Next, he assigned his top ranking General to gather another group of followers and instructed them to attack the church. "I want it destroyed. Use fire or any means necessary, but I want that building destroyed."

Josh and Father O'Malley noticed, as they greeted people on the steps of the church after Saturday Mass, many men standing in the distance with angry, hateful expressions. Some looked as if they were about to pounce on both priests. However, they simply stood still, as if waiting for instructions. One thing was for sure, they all were glowing "red'.

Josh informed all his fellow priests that he was sure something bad was about to happen. Consequently, Father's Samai, Scott, and Gordon decided to stay the night in the rectory with Josh and Father O'Malley. They would be there if something happened.

It would be another sleepless night for all the priests. While everyone was having a cup of coffee and discussing all that had occurred over the past couple of days, Josh excused himself, retiring to his room for a few hours of isolated prayer. This was Josh's usual habit, so no one thought anything of it on this particular night.

Once in his room, Josh knelt next to his bed and began his usual rosary prayers, asking the Blessed Mother and Jesus to give them all guidance. Immediately after finishing

CHAPTER VII

his rosary and his usual intercessory prayers, he sat down with his hands on his face, head held down. All he was aware of was the deafening silence in the room.

For some strange reason he suddenly looked up and there standing in front of him was Kapriel and Lancer. Startled and frightened, he pushed back on his bed as if trying to distance himself from the two seven-foot men standing in front of him. One would think by now that Josh would be used to such spiritual occurrences.

"Do not be afraid," Kapriel said, in a calming voice. "We are your Guardians that Jesus told you about at the time of His visitation. I am Kapriel and this is Lancer."

As soon as Josh heard their names, he was completely at ease, as he was familiar with their names and had often spoken to them in the quiet of his mind. However, never in a million years did he think he would ever see them in person.

Both stood before him as ordinary men if you could call seven feet tall 'ordinary'. Kapriel had light brown hair, deep glowing blue eyes, and a light tan complexion, with a scar across his cheek. Lancer was just a bit shorter with black eyes, black hair, and his skin was a deep bronze color. Both were bare chested but had some sort of leather covering over their waist attached by a single leather strap over their shoulder. Their massive muscles were impressive. Each carried brilliant shields, and each had two massive swords crisscrossed over their backs. However, despite their size and intimidating muscular strength, they were quite meek and easy to talk to. Kapriel began to tell Josh why Jesus had sent them.

"The Lord is angry that Satan has gone beyond the boundaries and authority given to him. He is preparing to attack and destroy this church tomorrow, and to release evil men from the 'seminary' to infiltrate Christian churches. He not only has gathered many men who are under his influence but has instructed them to kill anyone not faithful to him.

"More importantly, Satan has authorized his most powerful Attack Warriors to engage in the battle, and to use any means necessary to destroy the church and all within it. This is a direct violation of Heavenly law."

Upon hearing all of this, Josh was visibly shaken and was sweating with a certain amount of anxiety. Kapriel, noticing his demeanor, quickly assured him not to worry.

"It's not me I'm worried about," Josh said. "It's everyone else who doesn't have the protective shield that I have."

However, Kapriel assured him they all have angelic guardians that will protect them, and the Lord of Hosts will send other warriors that will assist them throughout this battle.

"But...their most powerful weapon is prayer and trust. You need to summon as many people as possible, before dawn, to pray for success so that this evil army will be defeated. Remember, no demon, not even Satan, can overcome the power of prayer."

Kapriel reminded Josh of one more important thing. "Remember the church is only a secondary target. The demon's main mission is to defend the 'seminary', as they are about to send out six deceivers who plan to infiltrate parishes everywhere and many more are scheduled to be released next month."

Lancer continued with a very concerned voice. "It is imperative that this plan is stopped."

"But how can I accomplish such a task?" Josh asked.

"You can't by yourself, but prayer can. That is why it is so important to get as many as possible to pray. Remember, don't be anxious. Jesus is in control."

When Kapriel said that to Josh, he remembered one of his favorite verses from scripture, Philippians 4-6:

CHAPTER VII

'Do not be anxious about anything, but in every situation, by prayer and petition, with thanksgiving, present your request to God.'

"You know Josh," Kapriel added, "Jesus will never force His will on anyone. That's why prayers are so important, otherwise, Satan will have his way... There's one more gift that Jesus will give you during this battle. You will be able to see beyond the veil of human eyes, you will be able to see the spiritual world of evil as they attack you and this town. As frightened as you may be, this will help you in many ways. For one, it will give you insight as to the power of prayer. The more prayers offered up, the more successful the righteous will be.

"You will also be able to see the strategies that Satan and his armies use for future insight in fighting him, and it will also help to show you their weaknesses. Most people have no true idea that evil is constantly around them. If they knew, as you will see tomorrow, there certainly would be less sin and more prayer. However, therefore Jesus has given everyone the gift of faith. Those who believe, will be able to recognize evil and destroy it through prayer and reparation.

"Lastly, remember to remain within our shield. No harm will come to you so long as you remain close to us. You will be frightened, as no man has witnessed what you will see tomorrow. But trust in us, remain calm, and pray constantly."

Josh related all that he was told to the other priests. They, in turn, began to carry out their assigned tasks.
Father O'Malley called Becky and Mrs. Johnson, relating the entire scenario to them, and asking them to contact as many as possible for prayers. Father Samar contacted all those in his rosary prayer group to do the same.

Father Scott asked Sam Douglas, the owner of the bar, if he would send out the alarm to all his patrons that the church was going to be attacked by a mob of hateful men tomorrow. Sam assured him that all those who had witnessed the miracle at the bar, as well as those who were told about it, could be counted on for any help needed, and in addition all their families would be in prayer.

Father Gordon had a hard time getting off the phone with Maggie, who wanted to know every detail. In any case, she assured him that she would summon up a large group of women who would be at morning Mass for prayer.

"No one is going to burn down our church, if I have anything to do with it," she said, as she hung up the phone. Likewise, Josh had called Zachary Jones to see if he knew of any Christian fellow Vets that might be willing to assist if needed.

"You bet I do," Zachary said. "Now that I have two legs, I, along with my buddies, will be standing at the door of the church as needed."

The last call Josh made was to Mayor Taylon. After explaining the imminent threat and violence that was expected, both spiritually and physically, Robert Taylon assured him that he would call as many people as possible and in addition would contact the Chief of Police, who he was good friends with. The Chief promised his help and his department and could be counted on to arrest anyone breaking the law.

After a restless night, Sunday morning finally arrived. By 6:00am, the church was packed with prayerful believers. Everyone had been true to their word. Those who did not come to church remained home in prayer. Just as expected, Zachary and a large group of Marine Vets were already standing inside the church by the doors when people started arriving.

CHAPTER VII

After a brief explanation by Josh and Father O'Malley, people were made aware of the severity of the situation and had no difficulty believing in a supernatural world of evil, especially after witnessing so many of the miracles that had been performed in their town. With that, people began to pray collectively. Josh couldn't help smiling as he remembered how powerful prayer can be when people join seeking the help of the Lord.

Walking with Kapriel and Lancer to the entrance of the church, Zachary opened the doors as they stepped out. Instantly, Josh froze as he witnessed what no man should ever see. Hundreds of red, bloodshot eyed demons were flying and circling everywhere. Rows and rows of attack warriors lined up, ready for battle. The sky was streaked with black and red-looking clouds. It was a picture of evil.

Then, for the first time, he saw Azazal standing off in the distance. Kapriel pointed him out to Josh. A smug look was on his face. Evidently, he was pleased that there were no Angelic Warriors in sight. Unfortunately, neither Josh nor his two Guardians could see any sign of Angelic help either. Josh, still quite shaken from viewing the spiritual world that he was now witnessing, asked, "Where is everyone? I mean, Jesus's Warriors?"

"Be patient," Lancer said, "There is still a possibility that the demons will not attack." That possibility was short-lived. After Lancer had just said those words, all hell broke loose, literally.

Thunder and streaks of lighting appeared out of nowhere. Rain began to pour down and along with the howling wind, one would swear they were standing amid a hurricane. Inside the church, people screamed and were shaken with fear. However, Father O'Malley quickly calmed them and urged them to continue to pray.

Now the screeches of demons could be heard everywhere, as they prepared for battle. Josh was trembling but was reassured by Kapriel that he was safe. Both Kapriel and Lancer simply stood perfectly still on the steps of the church, calm and patient, as if they didn't have a care in the world. Their demeanor was comforting to Josh. Nevertheless, his rosary was quite visible, shaking in his hands, as he tried to repeat the 'Hail Marys' out loud.

Suddenly, a huge explosion was heard coming from the east end of town. Mayor Taylon remembered early that same morning that the old, abandoned warehouse was full of guns and ammunition. Somehow, he had felt the urge, a compelling urge, to destroy it. Not hesitating, he set charges to blow early in the morning, well before Father Gerald's men could get to them.

Josh was looking directly at Azazal when the blast occurred. The expression on Azazal's face changed from a smirk to fury; yet, he still had not given the order to attack. "What was he waiting for?" Josh wondered, although he was in no hurry for the battle to begin.

Not long after that thought, the red glowing band of men approached the church, armed and ready to fight. Several were holding bottles filled with liquid.

"Get away from those doors," someone yelled, but his voice was hardly heard through the rain and thunder. With one throw of a lit bottle, the war began. Bottles, bursting into flames, smashed on all sides of the doors, including one directly in front of Josh.

Josh instinctively threw up his hands to cover his face, forgetting that he was within the Lord's protection, surrounded by the shield of his Angels. Had it not been for them, it would have engulfed him in deadly flames. To the shock of the throwers, Josh simply stood unharmed. However, some of those who threw the bottles, turned, and ran away as fast as they could, in total disbelief.

At the moment the bottles were thrown, Azazal gave the command. Demons rushed forward and began their

CHAPTER VII

attack. Josh stood perfectly still and continued his prayers. Several Attack Warrior demons headed directly toward him, while most headed for the steeple and large crucifix on top of the church. Before Josh had a chance to finish one 'Hail Mary,' heavenly Angelic Warriors descended by the hundreds.

Kapriel slashed and demolished both Attack demons as they approached. Those who were attacking the steeple never reached it, being cut down by dozens of the Lord's Angels. Likewise, the fires on the church doors from the explosive bottles that missed Josh were immediately distinguished by the torrential rain splashing against them.

Throughout all of this, men were breaking into the church through the front doors. As the doors burst open, the armed Vets waiting inside were met with gunfire. The fight lasted only a few minutes, but unfortunately, several were killed. One Vet was immediately hit in his side while another fell hard to the floor after being shot in the leg. Both were superficial wounds and were immediately bandaged by several of the women. Two of the six intruders were killed, one was detained and immobilized by Zachary.

The other three quickly retreated and were joined by several others who were determined to break in. Several firebombs were thrown through windows. Anticipating this type of attack, the priests were prepared with multiple fire extinguishers that quickly put out the fires. Unfortunately, several parishioners were cut from flying glass and one woman received burns on the back of her neck. Thankfully, these injuries were superficial.

Maggie, who happened to be standing close to the back door in the sacristy, realized someone was opening it. Letting the intruder get one step inside, she quickly smashed him over his head with her trusty frying pan. Falling back and tumbling down the steps, he never knew what hit him as she said cried out, "No one is going to burn down my church!" Then reflecting on what she had just done, she locked the door and blessed herself.

By this time, there were hundreds of demons and Angelic Warriors battling. Fiery flames of ashes were bursting everywhere. Kapriel and Lancer remained on the steps but were constantly under attack. Azazal, still at his distant advantage point, ordered a hundred of his Attack Warriors to simultaneously strike Josh, Kapriel, and Lancer. Azazal figured that no matter how powerful they are, they couldn't possibly fight one hundred of his finest at once. What he didn't realize or even contemplate was that besides Kapriel and Lancer, there were five hundred Angelic Warriors descending directly in front of Josh and his two Guardians.

The Attack Demons never had a chance. They flew blindly into the five hundred patiently waiting for them. Azazal wanted to call them back, but he realized it was once again too late.

Gun fire continued to ring out from all over the church grounds. Bullets simply exploded, as they struck the shield surrounding Josh. Zachary and a few of his marine friends were having a difficult time controlling Father Gerald's mob. Fortunately, once the police arrived, the tide began to change.

Throughout all this chaos, the rain, thunder and lightning never let up. Although lightning struck the church several times, no real damage occurred except for a few loose shingles and several broken windows. More importantly, although they were frightened, the people never stopped praying. Finally, the thunder and lightning stopped, but the rain continued. More police sirens were heard, and true to the Mayor's word, the police helped to round up and arrest anyone who took part in the assault.

CHAPTER VII

When Azazal saw his recruits being arrested, he finally lost control. Realizing that the destruction of the church was futile, he went crazy. Screeching, foaming at the mouth, eyes bulging, and cursing the Lord of Hosts, as well as at Josh and his Guardians.

Then, out of nowhere, he suddenly stopped. The doors of the church were slowly opening. Becky was exiting and looking for Josh. As she looked at Josh, he was simply standing, by himself praying his rosary at the foot of the steps.

Azazal, quickly realizing that she did not have the protection that Josh did, picked up his huge spear and propelled it directly toward her, yelling out, "If I can't kill Josh, then I'll kill YOU!"

Josh, seeing and hearing all of this, panicked and broke out from his protection, trying to grab Becky before the spear struck her. However, Lancer instantly pulled him back, while Kapriel lunged in front of Becky.

Then a most unexpected thing occurred. Before the spear struck Becky, Kapriel grabbed it in mid-flight, stopping it before it struck her. With a flip of his hand, he repositioned the spear and with the speed of lightning, threw it toward Azazal. It all happened so quickly. Azazal didn't even have a chance to blink as the spear passed through his neck. It created such an immense explosion, that many in his army were so full of fear, they immediately defected, flying off never to be seen again. Others, more loyal to Azazal's cause, flew directly to the 'seminary' to fight with those who were waiting there.

Josh was mesmerized by all that he had just observed. It all had happened so quickly. Kapriel, being concerned that Josh might leave the shield again, sternly reminded him never to leave the Lord's protection.

"I wasn't thinking, not about myself, that is. Sorry…it won't happen again."

Then turning to see if Becky was alright, to his horror, two men with unmistakable red mists around their heads had abducted her. Searching through the rain, he could barely hear her screams, as they drove off with her toward the 'seminary'.

Josh rushed into the church panicking.

"What's wrong?" Father Gordon asked.

"They've taken her!" Josh yelled out in a frantic voice."

"They've taken who?"

By this time all the other priests had gathered around.

"They took Becky... they took her to the 'seminary'."

"Calm down, son," Father O'Malley said, as he tried to get Josh to relax.

"Yes, Josh, calm down," Kapriel said, as Josh realized they were still visible to him.

"This war is not over yet," Lancer reminded him. "Remember to trust and to continue to pray."

"Please, I will continue to pray, but let's get going. We need to go before something happens to her!"

"We're going with you," Zachary said as he motioned to his fellow Marines to follow. Zachary was out in front of the church in no time at all, waiting in his off-road jeep. The others followed in several vans.

Father O'Malley called Ken Blanchard, the Chief of Police, to report the abduction and once again to ask for his help. The other priests remained behind, reminding those in the church to continue to pray. To pray continuously as their prayers were essential.

Inside the 'seminary,' Father Gerald was conducting an ordination service for six of his senior 'seminarians'. Father Gerald had once again removed all the crucifixes from the church but had left all the statues and artwork in place. Evidently, he still wanted to give the impression that the place was an authentic seminary, in the event someone else might question its authenticity.

CHAPTER VII

Hideous demons were clinging to those who were scheduled to be ordained. Others were flying everywhere and attaching themselves to the walls, hanging objects or anything they could grab hold of all to get a better view of the festivities.

When Becky was dragged into the seminary, everyone, especially Father Gerald, was overjoyed.

"Nothing can stop us now that we have Donovan's pathetic little girlfriend. Just let him try and stop us, and I will cut her throat without blinking an eye!"

With that comment, she was taken to a storage room, and locked inside. Soon after that, the faux ordination continued with various satanic chants and rituals. In addition, instructions were given to each 'seminarian' about their assignments, as well as reminders to their mission to destroy the credibility of the Church in any possible way.

By now, the army of demons had reassembled under the command of Valafar, another top ranked demon, sometimes referred to as the 'Duke of Hell'. Additionally, there were numerous guards surrounding the 'seminary'. However, because of the warehouse explosion caused by Mayor Taylon, guns and ammunition were scarce.

As Zachary's jeep approached the seminary, stopping a few hundred feet away from the entrance gates, Josh could see all that awaited him. Every guard was accompanied by a half dozen demon sentinels. Hundreds more were clinging to every conceivable part of the buildings. Thousands more, many more than had been at the church, were assembled and ready to strike. In front of every division of demons were twenty huge Attack Warriors, exactly like the ones that attacked Kapriel in the tunnels. Their sleek, black, steel-like wings waiting to cut down any Angelic Warrior that dared cross their path.

The sky was still red, covered with black clouds. Yet, it was still morning. Only an hour and a half had passed since the first attack on the church. The rain continued and severe thunder and lightning erupted once again. It erupted so loud this time that the entire ground shook.

The demons were startled with fear. They knew it was not caused by the Prince of Darkness. The thunder and lightning continued and intensified. More fear came across the demons. Dozens fell off their perches while several hundred flew off in fright. Those who retreated were mysteriously destroyed before getting very far. A good lesson for those who wanted to join them.

Inside the 'seminary', one could hear the thunder and brilliant cracks of lightning striking over the building. Streaks of sparks and fire also had its desired effect. Confusion everywhere. With the ceremony temporarily interrupted, Father Gerald and Anthony C. Wadsworth retreated to Father Gerald's office for a brief conference. Evidently, Wadsworth was there, not only to observe the ordination, but to help coordinate each person's assignment to specific parishes. And of course, there were the usual payments given to Gerald and his associates.

Without waiting any longer, Zachary floored the jeep. Its wheels began to spin, throwing out dust and stones. Gunshots were fired as the jeep crashed through the gates. Two more vans pulled up with men piling out, shooting, and taking cover. A few of Zachary's people were immediately wounded while getting out of the van.

Additionally, several guards on the wall were shot, falling to their deaths, while at the same time the Lord's angels were attacking everywhere. While the gunfire continued, Josh quickly followed Kapriel and Lancer out of the jeep and up the steps of the 'seminary'. Multiple bullets hit, but instantly bounced off them. Foolish

CHAPTER VII

demons attacked, only to be struck down as soon as they reached the length of Kapriel and Lancer's swords.

Once Valafar saw Josh and his Guardians approach the 'seminary', he released his army. All his Attack Warriors, who were waiting in front of every division of demons, shot forward simultaneously. They had hardly flown a hundred feet when they smashed directly into a wall of huge Angelic Warriors.

At the moment of impact, they were annihilated instantly. Subsequently, they were followed by each division of demons, after Valafar gave the signal for them to attack. Division after division charged forward. Thousands of black creatures, screaming with bulging, bloodshot eyes, filled the sky.

As they approached the 'seminary', the wind and rain increased in intensity so severely that hundreds of demons were tossed and thrown in all directions. They looked like a massive flock of birds caught in a whirlwind storm. Having no sense of direction, many fell to their demise while others were mercilessly slaughtered by waves of Angels.

Although Josh was not as frightened as before, he remained frozen inside the confines of his protectors, praying constantly while observing all that was going on before him.

Suddenly, a scream louder than thunder was heard. Almost instantly, all fighting temporarily stopped, as thousands of warriors listened to the approaching sound. Off in the distance in the sky were thousands of demons that were approaching with tremendous speed, and the Prince of Darkness was leading them.

Although Kapriel, Lancer, and the other Angelic Warriors were not worried, they were confused since they had not been informed of this happening in the battle. As the massive cloud of demons approached the seminary, the Prince of Darkness flew aside, giving the command to the others to attack.

With that command, a streak of lighting, massive in size and cracking louder than any noise ever heard before, exploded into the sky. The light was so bright that it was seen over thirty miles away. Valafar, his entire army, and the thousands of demonic beings that just arrived, were destroyed in a split second. Gunfire was still heard here and there, but with the approaching police, their fight was essentially over.

Josh slowly followed Kapriel and Lancer into the 'seminary'. No sooner did they enter the lobby than The Prince of Darkness came crashing through the circular skylight above them. As the glass settled, Satan found himself surrounded by dozens of the largest and most powerful Angelic Warriors that God had created. Saint Michael, of course, was among them.

Slowly, he turned toward Josh. Stepping close to him and without saying a word, Satan stared intently. All the Angelic Warriors knew that he would not dare attack. Consequently, Kapriel and Lancer allowed him to approach.

As Josh stared back, Kapriel and Lancer held Josh close to them. Although he was completely under their protection, they simply wanted to assure Josh of his safety and to help calm his fears. After all, no matter what protection he had, experiencing the Prince of Darkness in such proximity would petrify anyone in that situation.

The hideous body, that was once the most beautiful Angel God had ever created, now had the appearance of death. His face, if you could call it a normal face, was crusted, and wrinkled. His lips were the color of black blood, and his eyes were sunken, bloodshot, and oozing with something that looked like slime.

CHAPTER VII

A closer look revealed that his once beautiful white wings were now dark black, stained with blood. They were long and covered with distorted looking torn, ruffled feathers. His hands resembled something like claws, and his fingernails were pointed, sharp, and filthy. And of course, the odor of putrid sulfur was everywhere. Yes, all in all, he looked like death. Pitiful death.

Suddenly, The Prince of Darkness realized that Josh could see him. Immediately, he lunged forward trying desperately to grab and crush Josh. Kapriel and Lancer could not help but smile as his hands bounced off the shield of their wings.

Again and again, he tried and failed. His anger was increasing by the second. His eyes began to bulge, and his temper rose to a rage. Now he was boiling over with fury and anger.

Determined to prevail, he tried another approach. He attempted to pry open Kapriel and Lancer's wings, but to his dismay, his bloody hands kept slipping and sliding with every attempt made. Furious, and somewhat embarrassed, as he had never experienced this lack of power, he turned to the Angelic Warriors that were watching his every move.

Then he turned back at Josh, then again to the Warriors, all the time cursing and screaming out obscenities. Realizing the protection Josh was receiving from God, he knew it was useless to attack, especially with Michael present. Rather, turning toward Josh and with all the hate he could muster, he screeched out, "THIS IS NOT OVER! NOT OVER AT ALL!"

Josh immediately spoke back before Satan had time to turn away. "You are absolutely correct. It's not over at all. The war is just beginning. And you can be sure that we will not lose." As quickly as he arrived, Satan now vanished from the seminary.

From a human perspective, Josh was standing completely by himself. The crack of thunder and lightning that destroyed the army of demons had petrified Father Gerald and all that were assembled in the church. Several large windows crashed in on them and a few huge stone statues crumbled into bits.

Thinking that an earthquake or perhaps a tornado was occurring, Father Gerald led Wadsworth and all his 'seminarians' down the curved staircase, through the small chapel under the church and into the tunnels. Once inside, they decided to head for the 'punishment room,' where Jay had been so mercilessly tortured. They would be safe there until the storm passed, and then, they would resume their service.

No sooner had they reached the room when the walls began to shake. Bricks and stones fell from the ceiling while the floor began to sink in. In an instant, all the tunnels throughout the complex caved in. It would later be reported as an unexplainable earthquake, yet Josh and his guardians knew better.

Josh, still standing in the lobby, yelled out for Becky, hoping she was somewhere in the building. Father Gerald, in his rush to get to safety, had forgotten about her. Josh continued to yell out for her as Kapriel and Lancer directed him forward. Finally, a faint voice was heard.

Continuing to call her name, he finally located her. Rushing to her side, he picked her up, but he knew immediately that something wasn't right. Through all the trauma she had experienced over the past few hours, her condition had deteriorated. In fact, her cancer was far more advanced than she revealed to anyone.

As Josh walked out of the room with Becky in his arms, he was met by Zachary, Father O'Malley, and Father Scott.

"Let me have her," Father O'Malley said. "We'll rush her to the hospital. Our car is just outside."

CHAPTER VII

"No. I will do it," Josh said, holding back his tears.

"Josh, you are far too upset. Besides, Ken, the Police Chief wants to talk to you regarding what was going on here. You can catch up to us in a while."

Not waiting for an answer, Father's O'Malley and Scott left with Becky in their arms.

While explanations were given to Blanchard, several yells were heard coming from the dormitory. Four young guys, in their early teens, had been locked up while the fake ordination was going on. They had not yet been indoctrinated to the evil ways of Father Gerald. In fact, they had just arrived less than a week ago, under the cover of night.

They were sold to him, taken from a sex slave group, who were selling young kids for money. Father Gerald always preached that he was doing these kids a favor, but they were simply moving from one slave group to another.

It was the perfect opportunity to explain to Chief Blanchard that young boys and men were being held against their will at this fake 'seminary' to be indoctrinated to attack and discredit churches and Christians throughout the country. That's all Ken Blanchard needed to know. Being told that Gerald and his entire group had been crushed in the tunnels, he looked at Josh, trying his best to hold back a smile.

"God works in mysterious ways, doesn't He?" Not waiting for an answer, Ken Blanchard turned and left, bringing the four young men with him in hopes of reuniting them with their families.

Becky's condition was deteriorating as they approached the hospital. Immediately they rushed her to Intensive Care, but there wasn't much they could do for her except make her comfortable. Father O'Malley and Father Scott knelt next to her bed and prayed.

Zachary had returned to the church, informing every one of the success at the seminary, but sadly had to relate Becky's condition to everyone. The entire congregation decided to remain in the church and continue to pray, this time specifically for her.

Mrs. Johnson reluctantly called Becky's parents in California, informing them of their daughter's deteriorating condition and assured them that she would keep them updated.

"No... I don't think it's necessary for you to come now," Mrs. Johnson said, "besides I don't think you will be able to get a flight until tomorrow. I'll keep you posted...You're welcome... yes, we are praying, all of us. Thanks," She sadly hung up the phone.

On the way to the hospital, everything that could go wrong did go wrong, or so it seemed. Josh was speeding. Rounding a curve, his car skidded off the slippery wet road and slid to a stop in the muddy wet grass. Desperately trying to rock the car out of the ditch, with each attempt, the wheels only dug deeper and deeper into the mud. Frustrated, he called out to his two Guardians, as if he expected them to move his car.

"Where *are* you??" but Kapriel and Lancer were nowhere to be seen or heard for the first time since they first made themselves visible to him.

In desperation, Josh had no choice but to walk and hope for a ride to the hospital. Multiple cars passed without even slowing down. "Why won't anyone stop and give me a ride? Can't they see I'm a Priest?" he thought to himself. Half running and half walking, he continued toward the hospital.

Any other time, especially mid-day, there would be dozens of cars passing this way, but today, there was hardly any. After what felt like hours, a car approached but kept

CHAPTER VII

moving slowly forward. Just before Josh was about to lose his mind, the car stopped. Running, Josh jumped in.

"Can you take me to the hospital?" he asked, somewhat out of breath.

"Oh, yes, Father. I most certainly can," the old man said with a slow, very drawn-out voice. Still speaking slowly, as if he didn't have a care in the world, he continued, "Beautiful day isn't it, Father? What parish are you from? Don't think I've seen you before... but then again, I don't get around much."

Josh was leaning forward in his seat, as if that would help get the car moving. Still the car hadn't moved an inch. In fact, he just realized it wasn't running at all. Impatiently, Josh asked, "Could we get going? I'm kind of in a hurry."

"Oh, of course, Father. I'm sorry, where are you needing to get to again?"

"To the hospital! Please, can't you go any faster?"

"Sure Father, but I don't want to get a ticket. You know, I never had a ticket in my entire life."

Josh kept thinking that he probably could run faster than the car was moving. To the old man, thirty-five was speeding. To Josh, they were practically crawling. Finally, they arrived. Thanking the man, Josh jumped out of the car ready to dash to the entrance.

"Father, Father... wait a minute," the man called out.

Josh stopped, turned around and asked, "What's the matter?"

"Father, will you give me your blessing?"

Holding back his emotions, but also realizing how kind the old man had been to him, he responded, "Yes, of course I will."

Blessing him and again thanking him for the lift, Josh headed for the emergency doors. No one knew where Becky was. Panicking, he rushed to the main floor where they finally located her. As he raced down the hall, he caught sight of Father O'Malley and Father Scott standing in front of Becky's room. Slowing to a walk, he wondered why they were not inside her room praying. Continuing his slow walk, he finally reached them.

"Becky? How's Becky?" Josh waited for an answer he was dreading.

"You're too late," Father O'Malley said.

Immediately, Josh fell to his knees and burst into tears. Father's Scott and O'Malley reached down and pulled him to his feet.

"I didn't say she was *dead*. I said you're too late. Too late to heal her, that is. Evidently, you're not the only one who can heal."

Breaking from them and rushing into her room, he was greeted by a smiling Becky, alive and completely healed.

"Oh Becky!" he said as he hugged her. "I don't know what I would have done if anything had happened to you. One thing I do know, I would have asked Jesus to heal you. You have so much more to do for Him."

"Josh, I told you that I didn't want to live... that I didn't think I could live without you. But I now realize that even though we will never be together in the way that I had hoped for, we will always be together in other ways. Good ways, helping others and leading people to the Lord".

"I love you so much Beck...you will always be a part of my life. Thank you, Jesus...thank you for healing her."

While they sat and talked, Father's O'Malley and Scott came back in.

"Thank you both for your prayers and for healing me."

"Not us," replied Father O'Malley. "Jesus is the one who heals."

As Josh looked up, Kapriel and Lancer were also standing in the room, visible once again. "Now you show up," Josh said in a loud voice. But before he could finish, Father Scott interrupted.

CHAPTER VII

"Who? Us?"

"No, no. Not you… never mind," Josh said in an embarrassed tone.

Kapriel leaned over to Josh and whispered, even though no one else could hear him.

"We never left you. We were there all the time. You must get used to the little trials that the Lord will give you. It's all a test of faith."

Josh simply nodded his head in agreement while everyone looked at him a little bewildered.

After everyone else left the room, Becky asked, "When will I see you again?"

"Not sure when, but you certainly will see and hear of me. I'll be leaving tomorrow. Don't know exactly where I'll be going, but you'll know when I'm there." Josh continued to talk to her, thinking for the second time in his life that there was a possibility he might never see her again.

"Listen Beck don't worry about me. You will always be in my heart and prayers. I'll try to stay in touch as best I can. Just pray for me, that's all I'm asking. Just remember, wherever I am, you will always be with me in my heart. 'Friends Forever,' remember?"

Smiling, she responded, "Friends Forever."

As they all left the hospital, Josh was touched and saddened by all the many sick people he saw, especially all the young children with cancer and missing limbs. It was a sight that would be hard for him to forget, nor would he ever want to.

Becky returned home with Mrs. Johnson and immediately called her parents telling them the good news. She also told them that she would be returning to Jinksville, to teach at the restored St. Ann's Catholic Grammar School. All the priests went directly back to the church. They wasted no time thanking the Lord for all that he had done that day.

Satan had been defeated, Father Gerald and his band of 'priests' were gone, and the sadistic plan to use the 'seminary' to indoctrinate young men into destroying the Church had been crushed. However, as Josh had said, the war that he and so many others would face was just beginning. This battle was won, but he knew there would be many more.

Maggie had once again prepared a wonderful meal for all the priests. After the meal, Father O'Malley returned to the table after hanging up the phone.

"That was Bishop Timothy. You'll never guess what he just told me. It seems that the Church once again owns the seminary!"

Evidently, Wadsworth after purchasing the place, secretly signed the deed over to the Archdiocese without them knowing it. In the event that something went wrong, he would be protected by saying he never owned the place. In any event, all the land and buildings once again belonged to the Church. Bishop Timothy said that he is planning to restore it to a legitimate seminary as it once was so many years ago.

After dinner, Maggie kept asking Father O'Malley for absolution.

"Absolution for what?" Father asked

"For smashing that guy over the head with my frying pan during the fight!"

Trying his best not to laugh, he assured her that the Lord understood, especially under the circumstances. Nevertheless, it took three absolutions for her to finally accept forgiveness and to give Father O'Malley a well-deserved rest.

CHAPTER VII

Josh retired early to his room. Exhausted by the day's activities, his mind kept racing and remembering all that had occurred that day. He especially could not get the sight of the spiritual world and Satan out of his mind. Oh, how evil he was. He kept thanking Jesus for the blessings he had received throughout the day, for Becky's healing, and especially for the defeat of all the evils that he had seen. He was happy that so many people had responded to prayer and had returned to the Church. He thought to himself that Clarksville was well on its way to becoming a place where people of all faiths would want to live.

Josh was not alone in his thoughts or in his room. His faithful companions, Kapriel and Lancer were with him.

"Will this be the last time I will see you?"

Kapriel smiled, "As you said, the war is just beginning. We will be with you to the very end. Whether you see us or not, it is up to the Lord, but be assured we will always be with you, protecting and guiding you as Jesus directs. As for seeing beyond the veil of human eyes, I'm sure at times that gift will be again given to you. But once again, it is not for us to say."

"What's next?" Josh asked.

"Don't you know?" Lancer said. "You were asked to spread reparation throughout the world. You were to start in this city, and now that your mission is completed here, you must move on as the Lord directs you."

Josh stood up and the three embraced. As the seconds passed, his two Guardians slowly evaporated out of sight. "I know you're there," Josh yelled out as he slipped under the covers for a well-deserved sleep.

The next morning, he was up bright and early. After Mass and breakfast, he said his goodbyes to everyone. Father O'Malley began to tear up as the goodbyes were said. Josh took him by the arm and pulled him aside from everyone else.

"Please don't be sad. You will always be with me in my thoughts and prayers. Besides, you have a tremendous job that awaits you here. Many will be visiting, converts made and the Lord's message to be proclaimed by you and all the priests."

Father O'Malley perked up somewhat. "Don't know if I can handle all of that."

"You can, along with the Lord. Remember, Jesus is in control."

A few more hugs, and Josh was on his way.

"Oh, by the way," Josh yelled back after taking a few steps, "Don't forget to call Archbishop Florentino to tell him I will be arriving tomorrow."

Josh made two stops before he departed Clarksville. He first visited the seminary. Standing in the lobby, he visualized its transformation back into a legitimate training school for future priests. He visualized numerous Catholic priests being trained and eventually ordained into the service of the Lord. He also visualized the town's people once again returning to its beautiful church to celebrate Mass every Sunday. Exiting the massive doors, he glanced at the garden with the statue of the Sacred Heart of Jesus in its center. After a smile and a prayer, he headed for the hospital. Josh never entered its doors. Rather he simply knelt, bowed his head, and prayed silently.

As he flew toward his next destination, he looked out of the plane's window. The hospital was directly beneath, and he thought he could hear the cries of joy and thanksgiving, as everyone in it was completely healed. Clarksville and St. Andrew's church would forever be a place where caravans of the faithful would come to pray and hope for the healings that the Lord gave to so many.

CHAPTER VIII

HIS MISSION CONTINUES

Sitting back in his seat, Josh closed his eyes trying to recall all that had occurred over the past several months. Unexpectantly, the woman sitting next to him poked him, trying to get his attention to the news that was just breaking. On the monitor in front of her, news was being reported nationally that miraculous healings had taken place, just about two hours ago, in a small hospital located in the town of Clarksville, N.Y.

There were less than one hundred patients in the hospital at the time of the healings, and all had been cured. People with cancer, heart disease, kidney disorders, and every other category of sickness were suddenly healed. Two amputees who were undergoing physical therapy and prosthetics fittings for missing legs were completely healed, as witnessed by both doctors and nurses. In addition, several small children with cancer and one paraplegic walked out of the hospital as if they had never been sick or injured.

Needless to say, it was chaotic, as patients came running out of the place. Some were crying, others were waving

CHAPTER VIII

their arms back and forth, proclaiming that they had been cured by the Lord. Others simply ran out saying nothing.

Several nurses fainted as they witnessed the events. Doctors stood bewildered, dumbfounded, and simply amazed. It didn't take long for the news to reach town, nor to reach national news. Parents, friends, brothers and sisters, relatives and many curious onlookers were arriving by the minute. Soon the entire parking lot of the hospital, as well as nearby streets, were totally packed with people and news reporters.

Eventually the questions started. "Who did this miracle and why?"

Of course, there were many theories and unfounded explanations, especially from a few men who still wore the red halo around their heads. However, no one could explain it or knew exactly what and why it had occurred, except Father O'Malley, and all those who knew Josh and had been touched by him.

When the reporters finally arrived at the church with their numerous questions, Father O'Malley assured them that Jesus had performed the miracles.

"But why did He do it?" asked a curious and skeptical news reporter.

Father looked directly at the reporter and said, "Because Jesus is reaching out to all of us to repent. He is desperately trying to get our attention. He is pleading with us to pray for the reparation of our sins and the sins throughout the world. He is giving us one last chance to repent before it's too late. Every miracle that has taken place in this town, in our hospital, and every miracle you will see in the future, are all for this purpose."

"What do you mean, 'before it's too late,' and how do you know all of this?" asked another reporter.

"How do I know all of this? One only has to look at the miracles to realize that God is real. One only has to look at the world and the times we are living in to realize that the end is approaching. I don't expect everyone to believe me. Jesus could be standing right in front of some people, and they still wouldn't believe.

"As for you, you can believe it or not, it's totally up to you. When we say, 'repent before it's too late,' it means God's Judgement is coming soon, unless we change our sinful ways. Again, one only must look at the events throughout the world to realize that the signs of the end times, so clearly explained in the Bible, are upon us."

Pushing and shoving to better position themselves to ask another question, a tall dark-haired man pushed forward.

"Father, you referred to future miracles. Can you explain what you were referring to?"

"Sure, I would be glad to," continued Father O'Malley. "As many Christians realize, there's a spiritual war going on all around us. Many are being deceived by Satan and his evil spirits. Men and women, and unfortunately even children are sinning and have fallen prey to Satan's deceptions. As this war continues, I'm sure there will be other unexplained events and miracles that occur, all to help the unbelievers change their evil ways. I can't tell you for sure when and where they will occur, but when they do happen, remember what you have heard here today. Now if you will excuse me…"

"Father! Father! One more question, please." The reporter who had asked the first question asked another without waiting for Father's response.

"Where is that young priest? I think his name is Donovan. Didn't he have something to do with all these miracles?"

"Father Donovan is not here. He has left Clarksville and I don't know where his future will take him. As far as whether he had anything to do with these miracles, I can

CHAPTER VIII

assure you he did. You may not be aware of it, but Jesus appeared to him in this very church months ago, giving him many gifts and asking him to spread the Lord's message of reparation.

"Father Donovan is a very holy man, and the Lord uses him as he uses all of us in different ways. Even you, my friend. That's why I hope you will report to the world the urgency for reparation."

By now, Josh had turned on his own monitor, just in time to watch another report. Evidently, after checking the hospital's surveillance cameras, a young priest was shown kneeling on the grass in front of the main entrance, approximately two hours before the miracles occurred, just enough time for Josh to drive to LaGuardia Airport, check-in and depart for Washington National. It didn't take long before Father Donovan was identified.

Turning off his monitor, Josh turned toward the window, closed his eyes and prayed. He knew that questions about the healings would eventually be directed to St. Andrews Church and that Father O'Malley, the other priests, and all those who had previously been healed, would explain the reason for the miracles. And that is exactly what happened.

Newspapers all over the country, although some less than others, were reporting the events of the day, and repeating the message given to Josh. The astonishing event was even reported throughout Europe, with the Vatican paying close attention to it.

Josh was wearing a lightweight jacket over his black shirt with his white tab collar open. To look at him quickly, one most likely would not recognize him as a priest. This was exactly what he was hoping for, as he preferred not to be recognized until he reached his destination at the Cathedral of St. Matthew The Apostle in Washington, DC.

His face had been displayed all over the news while the report of the miracles was being broadcasted. Obviously, he did not want to be surrounded by mobs of people so quickly, especially in a strange city.

After the plane landed, Josh remained in his seat until everyone was out, except for one young couple who were sitting in the very first row. He had observed them throughout the flight. They were carrying their newly born infant twins, who cried almost continuously throughout the plane ride.

After retrieving his small travel bag from the overhead compartment, he walked down the aisle to where they were sitting. As he reached them, he stopped and said hello. Both parents looked up at him with a surprise look.

"Are you a priest?" the mother asked.

But without waiting for an answer, she scornfully said, as she uncovered the blanket from her twins.

"This is what God has done," revealing that her twin boys were attached together by the hips, and each had only one arm.

Josh was taken back, but despite this, he thought they were beautiful. Smiling and looking directly at both parents, he lifted the blanket back over both twins saying, "No, this… this, is what God has done." Without saying another word, he left the plane, quickly walking up the ramp, losing himself in the crowd. The two parents looked bewildered at each other until they saw that each boy was now separated and had been totally healed.

To Josh's surprise, a limousine from Saint Mathews was waiting for him. "Get in, Father," a young driver said as he opened the door for Josh. "Father O'Malley called and said when you would be arriving."

"Great, I'm looking forward to the visit. I've never seen St. Mathew's, or D.C. for that matter."

CHAPTER VIII

"Well Father, it's beautiful. Actually magnificent. I'm sure you'll like the Cathedral. How long will you be visiting?"

"Not sure, that all depends on the Lord's plans."

Not knowing exactly how to react to that comment, the driver simply said nothing. As they continued toward the Cathedral, the driver helped pass the time with more questions; however, it was evident that he had absolutely no idea who Josh was, until he asked the jackpot question. Just before arriving at the rectory at St. Matthews, he asked, "So, Father, you never told me where you're from."

Josh hesitated for a few seconds and then answered, "I just left St. Andrew's in Clarksville, N.Y."

"Oh...Clarksville...CLARKSVILLE!" he repeated in a loud, surprised voice. "Isn't that where all the miracles have occurred?"

"Yes, it is," replied Josh.

For the next few minutes, as the limousine approached the rectory, nothing more was said. It was obvious from the driver's expression that he realized who he had just picked up from the airport.

"It's been an honor driving you," he said, as he held the door open for Josh to exit.

Archbishop Florentino warmly greeted Josh on the steps of the rectory. He was somewhat surprised at how young he looked, but remembered he was not quite twenty-four yet. Josh greeted the Archbishop with respect as he kissed his ring.

"It's my pleasure to meet you, your Eminence. Thank you for putting me up for a while."

Smiling in acknowledgement, the Archbishop led him into the rectory. A young deacon took Josh's luggage to his room while the Archbishop introduced him to the facility's Pastor, Rev. Msgr. John Moore, the two Resident

REPARATION: A STORY OF HOPE

Priests, Rev. Thomas Vitali and Rev. T.W. Bishop. In addition, several deacons were introduced.

After the brief introductions, Archbishop Florentino and Josh headed for a cozy room to talk and discuss Josh's upcoming plans. Coffee was served with sandwiches and fruit. The Archbishop expectedly had many questions to ask, but being polite, he did not want to offend Josh by rushing into them. Instead, they chatted, discussing the flight, the traffic during the ride, the D.C. weather, and of course the beautiful Cathedral itself, that Josh was anxious to see.

"Would you like to see the Cathedral now, or perhaps later?" the Archbishop asked.

"I'd love to see it now. I've heard so much about it and have only seen pictures."

"Wonderful, I'll have someone show you around."

Deacon Vincent Denison, the same person who picked Josh up at the airport, was thrilled to accept that assignment. As they headed to the Cathedral, Vince, as he wanted to be called, apologized to Josh for not recognizing him sooner.

"No need for any apology. I'm just another person, like you, trying to do God's good work."

Entering the Cathedral, Josh was mesmerized at its beauty. Vince was thrilled to give him a personal tour. He pointed out its Renaissance Revival Architecture, including its high vaulted ceilings and beautiful stained-glass windows, its various statues and altars, its magnificent paintings, and portraits, as well as giving an extended version of the various highlights of the Cathedral that are not usually mentioned in public tours.

When the tour was over, Josh invited Vince to join him in saying the rosary.

"I would absolutely love too," replied Deacon Vince. "Let me light a candle before we start."

CHAPTER VIII

It was his habit of lighting a candle every day for his special intention. Both knelt and prayed quietly together, without anyone paying attention to them.

When their prayers were over, Josh walked over to the candle and blew it out.

"Why did you do that?" Vince asked, somewhat bewildered.

Josh put his hand on Vince's shoulder, smiled and calmly said, "I blew it out because you don't need it anymore. Let your nephew's healing be confirmation to all those in your family that Jesus loves them, even though many in your family have abandoned Him and blamed Him for the deformity. And let his healing be a reminder that He is calling all of us to reparation."

Vince just stood there, not knowing what to say as Josh returned to the rectory. Immediately calling his sister, Vince did not have to ask anything, as he could hear the cries of joy and excitement going on over the phone.

Archbishop Florentino invited Josh and a few other Archbishops, some Bishops from other dioceses, a few influential priests, and a few of his most beloved permanent deacons to dinner. The dinner was held at the Archbishop's Residence. Josh was somewhat nervous as he had never been around so many high ranking and influential church hierarchy. Nevertheless, he remained calm and soon felt the warmth of his welcome. After dinner, everyone wanted to know all about him and his experiences with Jesus.

Josh began by giving a brief description of his youth and upbringing, leaving out most of the spiritual occurrences that had happened to him during those young years. He talked about his Ordination and how that came about so quickly.

When he began to talk about his visitation with Jesus, everyone sat and intently listened to every word. Josh concentrated on the Lord's message, emphasizing the Lord's anger for all the sinfulness in the world, for the lack of reparation by everyone, for the immorality taking place throughout the world, especially in His Church, and for all the abortions that are so frequently performed. Josh told them that Jesus is giving mankind one last chance to repent and to change their sinful ways.

As Josh spoke, he emphasized the part of the message that time is running out. That the end is near and therefore, it is imperative that reparation occurs soon. Josh asked that this message be told in every church throughout this country and throughout the world.

"It must be preached with conviction and at every Mass."

Archbishop Florentino interrupted at this point and said that many churches were already including this message in their sermons.

"That's wonderful, your Eminence, but it needs to be a priority and proclaimed in *every* church."

Another Archbishop took that opportunity to express his concern. "Josh, we all believe in the message and in the importance of delivering it as quickly as possible, but The Holy Father has not approved it yet. In fact, does he even know about it? After all, we all are subject to him, aren't we?"

Josh did not want to get into a confrontation, so he took a minute to respond.

"Your Eminence, if the Holy Father has not heard about this message and all the miracles that have been occurring, he soon will. And in all due respect to the Holy Father, I have been asked to spread this message to the entire world by Jesus Himself, so I'm sure the Holy Father will not be opposed to delivering it through the ministers of the Church."

CHAPTER VIII

There was a moment of silence but was quickly followed by a unanimous consent.

Another asked, "We have heard all kinds of reports about what occurred at the seminary in Clarksville. Can you fill us in as to what actually went on there?"

Josh was more than happy to discuss the major events that occurred and emphasized the plan to infiltrate the Church with fake priests. He told them about the spiritual battles that took place, the power of prayer, and how that led to the fake Father Gerald's defeat.

Last, he discussed how the Lord has given him insight into many things, his vision of spiritual warfare occurring constantly around them, his encounter with Satan, and how he is protected by Kapriel and Lancer. That statement initiated another round of questions.

Eventually, everyone had depleted their concerns and questions. Time was getting late, so Archbishop Florentino thanked everyone for attending and especially thanked Josh for answering so many questions, and assured him that the Lord's message would be proclaimed in every church.

The next morning there was a knock at Josh's door. Opening it, Deacon Vince rushed in. Without saying a word, he grabbed Josh's hand and kissed it.

"You healed him! Praise God. Father, I don't know how you knew all about our family nor how we will ever be able to repay you."

Josh pulled his hand away and immediately said, "You know as well as I do, Jesus did the healing. And as far as repayment, you owe me nothing. It's God that you should thank. As far as knowing what I knew, Jesus often gives me the gift of insight. In any case, again, He is the one you should thank, not me."

"We have," Vince said. "Our entire family has thanked Him. More so, they all have asked for forgiveness."

REPARATION: A STORY OF HOPE

By this time, Vince had calmed down. As they both sat, Vince explained, "My sister's son was born deformed. They had trouble having children, but after six years of trying, she finally got pregnant. The entire family was thrilled as the doctors told her she would never be able to conceive.

"We all thought it was a miracle until her son was actually born. One side of his face was sunken in. He was missing an ear and only had three fingers...total. To make a long story short, she and her husband and most of the family blamed God. They kept asking why He would allow her to conceive and then 'reward' her with such a deformed child. I tried my best to explain that this wasn't God's fault, nor was it any kind of a sick reward. Nevertheless, my words were useless."

Vince continued with his story.

"Of course, as time went on, they loved him, and accepted him exactly as he was. We all did. However, no matter how much I tried to explain and show them that God was not to blame, that hundreds of people are born every day with deformities or problems, they were deaf to the truth. In fact, they stopped going to church, along with many others in our family. When the miracle occurred, my sister's son was sleeping. When he woke up, he was completely healed."

Josh could see that Vince was clearly upset. With tearful eyes, he asked Josh, "Why did it take something like this for my family to believe, to return to the Church and to admit that they had unjustly judged God?"

"Vince don't be too hard on them. Jesus knew that they were hurting. He knew that inwardly they loved Him. He also knew that because they were hurting so much, they were not able or even willing to express their love. You know, Vince, the great thing about Jesus is He truly loves us and knows exactly the type of person we are. Deep

CHAPTER VIII

down inside all of us, He knows our true self. Despite His efforts to pull us back, sometimes it takes a nudge or even a kick, to get our attention.

"In this case, well, it took a healing for them to recognize their mistakes... their sins. I believe with all my heart that the gift of healing and miracles Jesus has blessed us with, will lead people of all faiths to Him," Josh continued.

"There are so many reasons why certain things happen, why Jesus allows good and evil to occur. Why, as an example, was your nephew so deformed? Perhaps his deformity and subsequently his healing will lead thousands of people to Jesus. Had this miracle not occurred, or you might say, had her son not been born with a deformity, thousands of people may not have been saved. So, you see Vince, we need to live a life of faith, trusting in the Lord in all things even though we may not understand them."

Vince listened with sincere appreciation and promised to relate everything that Josh told him to his entire family.

Josh remained in the rectory for about a week, secluded, resting, and conversing with the Lord as to his mission in the Washington and Baltimore areas. True to their word, the reparation message was told in every church throughout the surrounding Washington Diocese, although a lot of parishioners were skeptical of what they heard.

In fact, many people and even some priests were not aware of the various miracles that had occurred. Recognizing this, Archbishop Florentino asked Josh if he would give a healing service to the parishioners of St. Matthew's Cathedral. The Archbishop was well aware that there would be large numbers of people who would rush to the Cathedral if miracles and healings might occur.

Knowing that this event would help non-believers and sinners to repent and would get national attention that would most certainly help spread the message of reparation, Josh agreed, but insisted on there being security present as this could involve hundreds and hundreds of people.

Sunday, November 11th at 2:00pm, the service began. As expected, the Cathedral was full, seating over twelve hundred people. About another two hundred were outside, not being able to get in. The service began with a Benediction of the Blessed Sacrament, followed by a brief talk by Archbishop Florentino. Josh was then introduced, and without wasting any time, he explained the message of reparation exactly as it had been given to him by Jesus

Just before he began to pray for healings, he reminded everyone that Jesus does the healing and that it may not be the Lord's will for everyone to be healed. He asked everyone to pray for their intentions, and to confess their sins to the Lord.

"I know there are some here that do not love Jesus. There are some here that are disciples of Satan. Therefore, it's important that we pray for the Lord's protection and that any evil here will be rebuked."

Many in the congregation turned and looked, as if they would be able to see the evil that Josh had just described. Josh reminded them that nothing can prevail against the power of prayer. He told them that the Cathedral was surrounded by demons trying to deceive, but there were far more Angelic Warriors also surrounding us with their heavenly protection.

With that, Josh began to pray. "Jesus, I ask you to heal all those faithful who are blind, heal those who cannot hear, heal those who have cancer or other internal ailments, heal those who are cripple, or for any reason are wheelchair bound. Lord, I ask for healing for all those faithful who are missing limbs, those who were born with any sort of problem, whether it be physical, psychological,

CHAPTER VIII

or emotional. Please heal those with addictions, alcoholic, drug, or sexual, and finally Jesus, I ask you to heal, to forgive and bring back to you, all those who have lost their faith."

After Josh had asked all of this from the Lord, there was complete silence. No one spoke a word. No one at this point had been healed. Then, Josh turned and knelt beginning to pray. Still, not a word was spoken. After a few minutes, he stood up, and turned to face the faithful.

"I have asked Jesus for these healings. I have asked Him so that you and the world will recognize the urgency of repentance. I have prayed that all those, throughout the world, who commit the horrendous sins of immorality, abortion, murder, hatred, and abuse, will be led to repentance. You can amend your life, or not. You can respond to the message of reparation, or not. And you can help others believe, or not. The choice is yours. With all my heart, I hope and pray that you will respond to all that Jesus is asking. For all of you with a repenting heart, and willing to respond to his message, I humbly ask Him to heal you in the NAME OF THE FATHER, THE SON AND THE HOLY SPIRIT... AMEN."

It would be a mistake to try to accurately describe the joy, excitement, the tears, and of course the chaos that occurred immediately after the word 'AMEN' was spoken. People with every possible illness were healed. Wheelchairs were left behind, people regained their sight, the lame walked, and limbs were restored. Others cried, prayed, praised, and fell to their knees worshiping HIM.

Archbishop Florentino, and the other Archbishops, Bishops, and Clergy were astounded. Some fell to their knees. Others broke out in tears while some ran to assist in helping the chaotic crowd exiting the Cathedral. Outside, all those who were standing unable to get in, were also cured. Car horns blasted, people prostrated themselves on the lawn, many knelt and prayed while the majority hugged their loved ones and thanked Jesus for all He had done. Those unrepentant stood with their mouths open in amazement, wishing with all their heart's that they had responded to the Lord's call. Those with that evil red mist radiating from their heads, cursed the Lord with anger and hate plastered all over their pathetic faces.

News reporters were not invited nor were they aware that such a healing service was being held. However, it didn't take long for news to reach most reporters and stations. They were all there within a half hour, asking questions, interviewing, and filming all that was happening at St. Matthew's Cathedral.

The headlines made the front page of major newspaper:
'MIRACLES OCCUR AT SAINT MATTHEW'S CATHEDRAL.'... 'HUNDREDS MIRACULOUSLY HEALED BY YOUNG PRIEST AT CATHEDRAL.'

Still another heading on the front page of a major newspaper read:
'A CALL TO REPENTANCE…VERIFIED BY MIRACLES.'

As Josh slowly walked back to the rectory, he couldn't help smiling as he knew he had won another victory against Satan, and that these miracles would be instrumental in assuring that the message was well on its way to be heard worldwide.

When the Archbishop reached his residence, several reporters were waiting for him. Although he was exhausted, he took the time to respond.

"The miracles that have occurred is a testimony as to the existence of God and His call for worldwide repentance."

CHAPTER VIII

Dozens of questions were shouted out to him, but he simply turned and entered his residence. Perhaps he was tired, perhaps he didn't know what else to say now. Perhaps he just could not comprehend for himself what has just occurred. One thing was for sure, he was visibly shaken.

Just before retiring to bed each night, and after his usual nightly prayers, the Archbishop would take several strong pills for the severe arthritis in his hands. As he reached for the bottle of pills, his swollen knuckles and the severe pain were gone. Unbeknownst to him, he also had received the Lord's healing blessing.

John R. Fitzpatrick's daughter was one of the many that was healed. Caroline Fitzpatrick had been crippled for the past nine years after a head-on collision on the Baltimore Beltway. Another drunk driver had changed her life forever.

Fitzpatrick was reluctant to take her to the healing service, but after considerable pressure from his daughter and her mother, he relented, although he had absolutely no faith that she would be healed. However, that all changed when she stood up from her wheelchair and embraced him and her mother.

It was several days later that Fitzpatrick requested a meeting with Josh. Josh had been in relative seclusion since the healing service and was not taking interviews or questions from anyone. However, something led him to meet with this one man. They met in the same room where Josh first met with the Archbishop. As soon as Fitzpatrick sat down, to Josh's surprise, he burst into tears. It took several minutes for him to calm down before one word was spoken.

REPARATION: A STORY OF HOPE

Fitzpatrick finally told Josh how appreciative he and his entire family were for his daughter's healing. He described how badly their marriage had been affected due to the accident, blaming himself for allowing her to use the car even though it was the drunk driver's fault. He went on to describe how bitter he had become toward everyone, especially toward the Lord. How he refused to go to Mass and would not even agree to take his daughter to church. He left all that up to his wife. Again, Fitzpatrick began to cry as he asked for forgiveness for all his anger, hatred and sins committed over these past years.

"Is this a formal confession?" Josh asked.

"I suppose it is," he responded. "Father, I'm here, not only to thank you and the Lord but, well...if there is anything I can do for you, or the Church, please tell me."

It was then that he revealed he was extremely wealthy. "For the first time in my life, I realize that all the money in the world is worthless without love, without family, without friends and of course, now I realize, it's worthless without God in my life. In fact, when I saw my daughter's healing, I finally realized how blessed I have been and how selfish I've been in not sharing my wealth and love with those in need."

Josh smiled at the man and his words. "There is nothing that I need from you in return. The gift of miracles is a free gift from God. As for the Church, they can always use financial help, but no compensation is certainly needed. After scratching his head and thinking a little more, Josh continued, "However, if you are sincere about sharing your wealth with others in need, I have some wonderful ideas. But they will be quite expensive."

Fitzpatrick leaned forward and eagerly asked what he could do.

"Well... once again," Josh said, "it's going to take a lot of money."

CHAPTER VIII

"That's no problem…"

"I'm talking about *a lot* of money."

"I'm listening, Father. Tell me all about your idea." A smile of sincere appreciation broke across Josh's face.

Several weeks later, the plan was underway, although it would take years to complete. The plan involved the revitalization of slum and dilapidated areas in our major cities, starting with Washington D.C. and Baltimore.

Josh hoped that many of the millionaires and billionaires would join Fitzpatrick in donating some of their wealth to help in the construction of low-income housing, cafeteria facilities to feed the hungry, and shelters that were clean, had private sleeping areas, and open to all those in need.

Fitzpatrick was quick to purchase several blocks of abandoned row houses, with many more scheduled. They would be demolished and replaced with dozens of low rent facilities and shelters. The project began in Washington and would quickly be expanded to Baltimore. Thousands of locals would be put to work, with many permanent jobs created. Construction companies would be employed, and millions of dollars donated.

In one of the many conversations Josh had with Jesus, he was told that this revitalization plan would become one of the largest humanitarian projects ever created. City after city would eventually follow suit. Other billionaires, companies, and people of various skills would be inspired to contribute their wealth and talent to support this humanitarian effort. All because of the miracle that cured one young girl.

The snowball effect of reparation was working. Many more people, of all faiths, were touched by the miracles and by the message given to them by Josh and through the many sermons of Ministers, Rabbis, Priests and other leaders of faith organizations.

Unfortunately, many of those in higher places of government had not responded. Still consumed by power, influenced by big-tech and lobbyists, and personal wealth, they continued to disregard the Lord's message, remained blind to truth and to the message of reparation.

Josh had been given insight to the cause of this. Satan and his evil spirits were well at work throughout the halls of Congress. Many were deceived by the demons of deception. Others by the demons of deaf and dumbness, greed, confusion, immorality, and lies. These demons were everywhere, throughout every room, office, closet and hall of the House and Senate Chambers.

Of course, no one other than Josh knew this. Satan was quite happy with his achievements, as he had long ago infiltrated not only the United States Congress, but many Courts, Governors, Mayors and Political positions throughout the world.

It had been less than a month that Josh had arrived in D.C., and his mission was just about complete. The President of the United States, Thomas W. Jacobs, invited Josh to the White House. The President was a very devoted Christian and had been paying close attention to all that was occurring over the past three weeks. He was aware that there was a Christian movement taking place throughout the States and wanted to 'pick' Josh's brain as to his thoughts on the matter.

People were protesting over many concerns that Congress had not fully addressed. They called for better and less expensive health benefits, for more jobs with

CHAPTER VIII

higher wages, for environmental reforms and of course for less taxes.

Although these types of demonstrations had been going on for years, the amazing change that was occurring was that thousands of people in many cities across the country were calling for the return of Christian beliefs that the country was founded on. Citizens were writing to their senators and representatives to support the majority opinion that changes needed to be made and to return to the belief that this is indeed 'One Nation Under God.' Unfortunately, nothing much had been done except hollow promises.

A presidential limousine picked Josh up and it wasn't long after that he was sitting in the Oval Office with the President. Josh declined the coffee and tea offered him but did accept a bottle of water. Little time was wasted before the President's questions began.

Josh answered all his questions about the miracles and their meanings. He made sure that the President understood the Lord's message and the urgency of it. Morality, or, the lack of morality, was a major concern of the President. He told Josh that he felt helpless to do much about it, as so many in Congress had little or no concern about the subject, not to mention how difficult it was to deal with all the lobbyists.

Many in congress believed that morality or sin was not a subject that should be discussed in the Halls of Congress. The President confessed that he had supported abortion and other bad decisions, giving the excuse that he had little choice as he was obligated to his party supporters and lobbyists.

Josh listened to all that the President said, and when asked to give his opinion, he finally responded.

"Mr. President, I don't think you or the members of Congress realize the urgency of Jesus's call for reparation.

It's not a question of what congress believes, or what pressure various lobbyists place on them. It is a question of life or death. Salvation or damnation. The truth is, time is running out, and unless people change, laws and injustices are corrected and repentance is made, there will be severe consequences.

"As for you, Mr. President, you're either with the Lord, or you're not. You're either going to support Christian beliefs, or not. You're either going to accept Jesus into your life and all that it means, or not… the choice is yours.

"But, Mr. President, if you accept these things, you can make such a difference in this world. You can help millions of people with the right legislation, you can show millions what Christian love truly is, and you can help influence many to accept the Lord's message. Again, the choice is yours."

President Jacobs thanked Josh for his time and his comments. From the expression on his face, it appeared that the President was deeply moved. As Josh shook his hand to say goodbye, President Jacobs unexpectedly said, "Wait, Father. Please sit down again, I want to ask you something."

Josh had no idea what he was about to be asked but was overjoyed, and somewhat terrified, at the President's request.

"Father Donovan," the President said, "Would you be willing to join me in addressing a joint meeting of Congress? Many in Congress are perplexed as to the current miracles that have been occurring and are being overwhelmed with calls regarding the current outcry for the country to return to the Judeo-Christian Beliefs.

"I have to say that I believe most people believe that this country still operates under the official motto, 'IN GOD WE TRUST.' Unfortunately, Congress continues to legislate as if this Nation was not founded under this

CHAPTER VIII

motto... In fact, we have gone so far the other way that many want to ban religion altogether. I believe it's gone too far. That's why I hope you will agree to address Congress, if for nothing else, to wake them up. Make them realize how important and urgent it is for all of us to remember that this is a Nation founded under Judeo-Christian ideals."

"Mr. President, I believe that I was called to this city for a purpose, and I believe you have just verified it. Yes, of course, I would be happy and most honored to address the United States Congress. But I do believe it will be a very hostile audience.

President Jacobs laughed. "So? That's nothing new," he said.

It took a couple of days for Congress to rearrange their schedules to accommodate such a rushed meeting. As one might expect, there were complaints and concerns whether this type of address should even take place, but in the end, it was decided that the joint meeting would occur on Friday at 1:00pm considering such a meeting had no legal or political ramifications, nor did it require making any decisions.

Josh was escorted into the Capitol Building, along with the President, the Secretary of State, other Officials, and numerous Secret Service Personnel. He appeared to be quite nervous. His nervousness was not due to what he would say, but rather because the address would be televised to millions and millions of people throughout the world of all faiths, religions, and non-believers. He was also aware of all the evil that would be present, verified by the strong scent of sulfur that lingered throughout the halls, and the attacks he would have to endure. Not to mention that he would be speaking to an extremely hostile congressional audience.

The President's entourage and Josh entered the Hall at exactly 1:00pm and immediately were seated. Next, the President was announced. President Jacobs explained that the meeting was being held in part to address the overwhelming concerns that the Country, and Congress, were moving further and further away from the Judeo-Christian ideals that the country was founded on, and in part to explain the significance and reasons for all the supernatural miracles that have been occurring over the past several months.

The President reported that he, along with Congress, had received thousands of letters, phone calls, and signed petitions to address this concern. He believed that these letters and petitions had been sparked by the numerous healings and miracles occurring. When he had finished his short explanation, he introduced Josh.

"I have invited the one person who is capable of explaining the purpose for all the supernatural phenomena that has been occurring. Please don't let his good looks and youth fool you. God works with the young and old alike."

That comment brought a little laughter, exactly what the President was hoping for, to help relieve some of the tension in the room.

"Members of Congress, it is my pleasure to introduce to you Father Joshua Donovan."

After a brief applause, the hall was deafeningly silent as Josh took the podium. Before he said one word, he could see smirks, doubtful smiles, expressions of concern, looks that questioned his youth and many indignant expressions, most likely because they were being addressed by a kid of twenty-three years. Nevertheless, Josh put all this aside, said a little prayer to himself, and began his address.

CHAPTER VIII

"Mr. President, Mr. Speaker, and members of Congress. I am honored to have been invited to speak with you today regarding the message that I have been delivering over the past year and a half, and to explain the miracles taking place, associated with this message of reparation.

"I stand before you not as a Catholic Priest, not representing any religion, and certainly not with any political agenda in mind. Rather, I stand in front of you and all those who are watching, as a simple servant of God, who has been asked by the Lord to deliver a message of reparation to the world. What I'm about to tell you is the absolute truth. As I have said to many others, you can believe it or not... the choice is yours. It is not my purpose to convince, but only to deliver what the Lord has told me."

Josh continued to talk about the message of reparation and the urgency of repentance. He was sure to exemplify the fact that the Lord was upset and saddened by all the sin, immorality, and hatred throughout the world. That He was giving all of us one last chance to repent or His Judgement would soon be upon us. Josh didn't pull any punches. He told his story exactly as it was revealed to him, even though he knew it was upsetting to some, especially to those who did not believe. As for the miracles, Josh said their main purpose, in short, is to help the unbelievers to believe and to show the glory and mercy of God.

"God is hoping, beyond hope, that when people witness these miracles, it will soften their hardened hearts, it will open their eyes to Him, and to impress on all the urgent calls for reparation."

As Josh paused, some of those ugly and indignant expressions were gone. Others were even more hateful. After taking a sip of water, he continued.

"I realize my appearance today is upsetting to some and the question has arisen as to why I am addressing you. The United States Congress is more important than perhaps you realize. You can change the world. You can pass legislation that will help the poor and homeless. You can end abortion by providing alternatives for pregnant women and less restrictive adoption rules and regulations. You can lead the world in moral legislation. You can pass laws that benefit the people rather than big-tech companies, lobbyists, or the millionaires you are indebted to. And you can revert back to the Nation's motto, 'IN GOD WE TRUST.' You can do all of this or not. You can believe in all that I have told you, or not. Again, the choice is yours. But I would be remiss if I did not emphasize that the wrong choice will lead to severe consequences."

Before ending his address, he said, "There is one more thing. Three people in this assembly have asked the Lord for healings. Two are wheelchair bound and one is missing an eye. For you to see the glory of God and believe in every word spoken today, I have asked Jesus to heal these three."

With that, Josh blessed the entire assembly. "May the Lord Jesus love you; may the Lord Jesus forgive you and may the Lord Jesus open your hearts and bless you, in the Name of the Father, and of the Son and of the Holy Spirit...Amen."

The instant Josh said 'Amen,' as in other healings, the three were healed. However, by the time everyone had realized that the healings had occurred, Josh was already gone, heading for the limousine to take him back to the rectory of St. Matthews.

CHAPTER VIII

He took no interviews or answered any questions. Rather, he went directly to his room, skipping dinner as he was mentally and physically exhausted. As he began to pray, there was a knock on his door. Opening it, Deacon Vince told him he had a phone call.

"Please tell them I'll call back tomorrow", he tiredly said.

"But... Father Donovan, it's urgent. It's, well... it's Rome on the phone."

CHAPTER IX

ROME

The Vatican provided the Pope's private plane to fly Josh directly to Rome. Although he did not want to leave Washington so soon after his address to Congress, the call from the Vatican was urgent. The Pope's private jet arrived at Washington International in the early hours of the morning.

After clearing all the required inspections, Josh was on board just a little after 4:00am. Monsignor Angelino, the Pope's personal attendant, greeted him at the foot of the boarding steps.

"So glad to meet you, Father Donovan. My name is Monsignor Angelino. I'm sorry for such a rushed invitation, but Pope Nicholas is gravely ill. We have been hearing wonderful things about you, and His Holiness has personally asked for your presence."

"The pleasure is all mine, Monsignor. How long is the flight back to Rome?"

"Approximately, a little over eight hours, but by the time we depart, which should be any minute now, we should be back inside the Vatican hopefully in about nine and a half hours."

By now, they were both seated in the plane, and the pilot had already been given approval for takeoff.

"Once we are airborne and the seat belts are off, please make yourself at home. And please, if you would like anything to eat or drink, just ask one of the attendants. Sleeping areas are in the rear of the plane if you prefer to rest before eating."

"Thank you, yes, I think I would like to get a few hours rest and then perhaps have a little something to eat."

"Excellent," the Monsignor said, as the plane was lifting off the ground.

Back in Washington, there was a slew of reporters waiting outside of Archbishop Florentino's residence. Everyone wanted to interview Josh and question him on all that transpired during his address to Congress. No one had an opportunity to interview him as Josh immediately left the House Chamber once he was done and was unavailable for questions.

However, many others had already been interviewed as soon as the meeting was over. Some refused to say anything while others expanded on what Josh had said, expressing their personal beliefs of the importance of the message.

Crowds had gathered around Senator Jonathan Miller and Representative Ellen Kelly, marveling at their miraculous healings. After being wheelchair bound for most of their lives, each stood up and began to walk as soon as Josh ended his blessing with the word "AMEN."

Senator Justin Davidson was no exception. He had lost his right eye during the war in Iraq, and like the other two who had asked for healing, his missing eye was totally restored. Senator Davidson, cried out with joy the instant he realized he was healed. Falling to his knees, he praised

CHAPTER IX

Jesus over and over as the rest of Congress and the world looked on.

Just about every newspaper in the country was reporting the events, and now everyone wanted to talk to the young priest who Jesus had so wonderfully blessed. Unfortunately, to the disappointment of all the reporters, and TV News Vans waiting for their interviews, Father Donovan was already 32,000ft in the air, flying to Rome.

In the invisible world around all of us, Satan and his army of demons were furious at the recent healings and especially upset with the many conversions that took place as a direct result of Josh's address. Many people all around the world who witnessed the events in Congress were starting to believe in God once again.

In addition, Satan was still fuming over his inability to penetrate the shield surrounding Josh, and how mortified he felt in front of so many Archangels when he confronted Josh at the 'seminary' in Clarksville. Consequently, now, more than ever, Satan and his army of demons were even more determined to stop Josh in any way they could.

Unfortunately, Satan also had to deal with the surge of people returning to the Lord. Especially of concern was the influence Josh had on the members of Congress. Satan and his army of demons had worked for *centuries* to deceive politicians that the laws passed and the decisions handed down from the courts concerning abortion, morality, and religious freedom were in the best interest of mankind and upheld the rule of separation of Church and State.

For the first time in many years, Satan's deceptions and lies were now in question. And only after such a short period of time. As a result, he was spread very thin, having to deal with Josh as well as worldwide conversions.

The flight was quite comfortable. A custom Boeing 777, commonly known as Shepherd One, was built for the Papacy years ago due to the frequent distant flights required of popes. After sleeping for five hours, Josh, along with Monsignor Angelino, were served a wonderful meal, but neither had much of an appetite. Rather, they spoke of the condition of the Pope.

"No one knows exactly what illness he has." Monsignor Angelino said. "His physicians think it's some kind of virus, but every test taken comes back negative. This sickness came upon His Holiness quite quickly. Last week he was up and around doing his normal routine. Monday, he felt ill but managed to complete his appointments; however, he retired for the night quite early. Tuesday, he remained in bed all day. By early evening his physicians were called, and they have been treating him ever since. Blood work is inconclusive."

"Have they considered moving him to a hospital?"

Monsignor Angelino cracked a brief smile. "That was the first thing his physicians suggested. But our Pope is, how shall I say it…very stubborn."

"How long has he been in bed?"

"Let me see... today is Saturday. He's been in bed five days now and still refuses to leave the Vatican. Yesterday, he asked for you."

Time passed quickly while they talked for hours, mostly about Pope Nicholas, and about the Lord's message. Just as Monsignor Angelino was about to tell Josh that his message had been heard throughout Europe and especially by the Vatican, the pilot announced that they would be starting their descent soon and for seatbelts to be fastened. No sooner was the announcement made than a thundering noise was heard. The pilot reported that he thought birds had hit the plane. Yet, he knew that there could not be birds at 32,000ft.

CHAPTER IX

As the minutes passed, it was apparent to Josh that this was not a bird attack. Hundreds of black bird-like creatures were smashing into the plane on all sides, with their claws digging into the fuselage. Food carts were tossed around and smashed into the galley wall. Loose objects went flying everywhere. The plane was bouncing, rolling back and forth, dropping suddenly, desperately trying to recover.

Another loud, thundering noise jolted the plane as the far-left engine suddenly stopped and caught fire. Both right engines were now out and soon all the engines were on fire. The pilots tried desperately to activate the automatic fire-extinguishing system, but it only helped to reduce the flames a little.

By now the plane was descending rapidly. 'May Day' was radioed out.

"We're going down!" the pilot frantically announced, giving his position and the condition of the plane.

Fuel was released. All this happened in minutes. The plane was only 10 miles out from the airport, yet it really didn't matter how close they were, as there was no way the plane was going to land safely.

As the plane rapidly fell from 32,000ft to a little less than 1,000ft, it suddenly leveled off. Not a sound was heard except for the rush of the wind passing over the wings. All engines were off, the flames were extinguished, and there was no power. Steering was next to impossible, yet the plane was quietly descending, heading straight for the airport runway. Josh looked out his window and immediately sat back with a smile on his face.

"What did you see? Monsignor Angelino asked frantically. "I'll tell you when we land."

"LAND?" the Monsignor shouted out.

Both pilot and copilot just stared at each other as the Boeing 777 ever so gently descended. Although numerous calls were being transmitted by the radio tower, neither pilot nor copilot responded, being speechless and amazed, as the plane made a perfect landing.

Later inspection of the plane showed dents, scratches, and thousands of small holes throughout the plane's fuselage. The engine's turbine blades were completely bent, and most were totally gone. Black, feathery substance was scraped off the engine walls, and the putrid smell of sulfur was everywhere.

"How was it possible for us to land after incurring such damage from birds?" the Monsignor asked.

Josh continued to smile as they both got into the limousine waiting for them. "God works in mysterious ways... doesn't He? I'll tell you all about it after I see the Pope."

The Monsignor simply looked at Josh, not knowing exactly what to say.

Before long, they arrived at the Vatican. Entering a side door, Josh rushed to the Pope's residence. One of the Monsignors standing at the entrance of the Pope's bedroom, whispered, "He's not doing good."

Disregarding his comments and not paying attention to anyone in the room, Josh walked directly to the Pontiff's bed. Immediately kneeling, he began to pray. After a few minutes, he asked everyone to leave while he continued his prayers. Detecting a little resistance, Monsignor Angelino complied with Josh's wishes and ushered everyone out.

It wasn't long after the room was empty that all those waiting outside of the bedroom heard laughter. A jovial conversation was going on between the Pontiff and Josh. Within minutes, Pope Nicholas asked everyone to enter.

"I prefer to keep this as quiet as possible," the Pope said, "As I don't want to bring attention that Father Donovan is here."

The Pontiff thanked his physicians and attendants for all the care they had given him. Expectantly, he asked to

CHAPTER IX

be filled-in on his schedule that was interrupted during the week of his sickness. In the meantime, the Pontiff asked not to be disturbed, as he and Father Donovan had quite a lot to discuss. None of those who were present in the room said anything about the Pope's healing, no one had too, as they all were aware of the reason Josh had been summoned to the Vatican. Nor was his presence made public, as the Pope had requested.

However, it didn't take long for the news to spread within the Vatican that the Pope was healed by the young priest from America. The Vatican press reported that the Pope had been ill for a few days but was now fully recovered and would resume his schedule starting next week.

Pope Nicholas and Josh hit it off together beautifully. The Pope was thrilled that Josh was doing the Lord's work and kept praising Jesus for the miracle of his healing.

"I'm convinced that my illness is not the only reason you are here. I believe there is a far greater purpose for you being here which is yet to be known."

Josh and Pope Nicholas talked for hours, interrupted only occasionally by an attendant bringing a fresh cup of coffee, and a little something to eat.

Josh related all that he had experienced, including the miracle of the angels guiding the plan to safety.

"It appears that Satan didn't want me here," Josh said with a slight chuckle.

In addition, he related to the Pope all the miracles he had personally witnessed as a young boy, all that occurred in Jinksville and of course all his experiences in Clarksville, including the night Jesus appeared to him. Josh was also sure to tell the Pope of his encounters with Satan and his evil spirits but was also mindful not to mention that he was able to detect evil people by the red glow around their heads.

"That's such a powerful and inspiring account of your life," Pope Nicholas said as he sat back and appeared to be consumed in all he had just heard. He then quietly said to Josh, "Your account of Satan, his evil demons, and your report of the 'seminary' training fake priests, is of particular interest to me." Pope Nicholas hesitated for a minute and then continued.

"I do believe that the Church is being attacked and that there is evil even within these walls. I can't put my finger on it, but I feel it's here. I heard some of my Cardinals talk about planning some sort of event for the new seminarians, but never thought much about it. That is until last week when I overheard Cardinal Morelli talking to a few Deacons about a drunken orgy. I startled them when I walked into the room where they were talking.

"I asked them if I was correct in hearing them talk about a drunken orgy. They hesitated at first but assured me that the word 'orgy' was an exaggeration for what they were referring to as a drunken brawl that took place last week involving some of the young parishioners from one of the local parishes.

"They said it really was nothing to worry about other than it was a little embarrassing, as several Catholic young men were involved. In any case, they assured me it had nothing to do with anyone in the Vatican or Vatican City. Nevertheless, I felt very uneasy about his choice of words, and you know Josh," the Pope continued to say, "I am pretty good at reading faces… and they looked guilty as sin! Please excuse the pun."

Josh listened intently at every word the Pontiff said and agreed to remain at the Vatican for as long as he was needed. The Pope was delighted, and he immediately looked more at ease.

CHAPTER IX

"I think it might be best to keep your identity as low-key as possible for a while, although I'm sure your presence will soon be known throughout the country."

Josh was shown his room and later escorted throughout the Vatican by Deacon Kavinsky, another personal attendant for the Pope. Josh was also invited to pray in the Pope's private chapel, a privilege that very few had ever been given. Likewise, he was introduced to most everyone and given access to every room in the Vatican. Although he met most of the resident Deacons, Priests, and Cardinals, he did not meet everyone, as some were out of town while others, such as Cardinal Morelli, were at their private residences.

Additionally, Deacon Kavinsky offered to accompany Josh if he wanted to visit anywhere outside the Vatican. Josh gladly accepted this invitation. Josh grew accustomed to Vatican life sooner than expected. He quickly learned the ins and outs of the facility and became very familiar with the Pontiffs chapel and private library. He was often seen in the chapel, deep in prayer.

On one occasion, His Holiness and Monsignor Angelino were conversing as they passed the open door of the chapel. Josh was not aware that they were watching him, as he was apparently having a conversation with someone. After closer observation, Josh was clearly talking to someone on each side of him. He would turn to his right and then to his left, deep in dialogue.

Pope Nicholas and the Monsignor watched for several minutes. Eventually, Josh stood up, took a few steps forward, and knelt in front of the small altar. He held both of his hands out to his sides, as if he was holding hands with someone on each side of him and prayed.

"Who do you think he's talking to?" Monsignor Angelino asked.

"I have no idea, but I'm sure it's no one from this earth."

Angelino looked at the Pope and nodded his head in agreement as they continued on their way.

Christmas Mass was such a meaningful occasion for Josh. He had seen the ceremony many times on television but being present and sitting so close to the Pontiff was not only a thrill, but an honor that he never imagined. Although he was very close to the altar, he remained relatively out of sight from the congregation, again to keep his presence as low-key as possible.

As he looked around St. Peter's Basilica, he marveled at its beauty and magnificence. Looking at the statues, the many altars, the magnificent paintings, the beautiful stained-glass windows, and its spectacular ceilings, he couldn't help feeling humbled and so privileged to be present on such a joyful church occasion.

Listening to the songs of the choir prior to Mass starting, his eyes caught attention to the Cardinals sitting directly across from him. As Josh looked more intently at each Cardinal, his heart practically stopped. Feeling sick to his stomach, he asked the Deacon sitting next to him who was the Cardinal in the back row sitting on the end of the pew.

"Oh, that's Cardinal Morelli," the young Deacon said. "Haven't you been introduced to him?"

"No, I haven't. He wasn't around when I was introduced to everyone."

"Would you like me to introduce him to you?"

"Not at this time... it's not necessary but thank you anyway. I'm sure I will get to meet him soon enough."

Despite the beauty surrounding him, and the splendor of the Mass being celebrated, Josh's thoughts kept returning to the Cardinal, particularly because of the red glow surrounding his head.

CHAPTER IX

Pope Nicholas invited Josh to stay with him at his summer residence throughout their short Christmas break. They, along with several other close friends of the Pope, had a wonderful Christmas dinner. It reminded Josh of the wonderful dinners that Maggie often made. Despite the Pope's formal appearance, Josh realized that the Pontiff was down-to-earth. He could easily talk to him on just about any subject, and as time went on, they would spend hours together discussing various topics from world issues, politics, and of course spiritual and Church matters. This particular evening was no exception.

Once everyone left, Josh asked the Pope if they could talk before retiring for the evening. Sitting close to each other in two lounging chairs, facing a roaring fireplace, Josh began.

"Your Holiness, some weeks ago you told me that you thought there was evil within the walls of the Vatican and that you had concerns about Cardinal Morelli. Your Holiness, I cannot divulge how I know this, but you are correct. There *is* evil in the Vatican. I'm not exactly sure the extent of it, but I do know that Cardinal Morelli is not a holy man. In fact, he is under the influence of Satan himself. I would have told you this sooner, but this was just revealed to me at Christmas Mass."

The Pope looked stunned, almost like he was about to be sick. "I can hardly believe it. I know the Lord is working with you and therefore I have no doubt that what you have told me is true. Now the question is how to deal with it. I can't just defrock the man. I need proof, and he has many friends. In fact, he would very much like to be the next Pope if he had his way."

"That can never happen. We will have to pray about this and ask Jesus for guidance and insight as to how to handle this. In the meantime, may I suggest, Your Holiness, that you do not assign him any new duties, and if there is anything you can reassign to someone else without causing suspicion, it would be best to do so until we can eliminate this threat."

The Pope did exactly what Josh had suggested. He reassigned several critical duties to others and omitted inviting Cardinal Morelli to key meetings, all without thinking he had caused any suspicion.

December came and went. Josh celebrated his 24th birthday on January 12th with Pope Nicholas and several of his staff. Additionally, he received several calls from Becky, Father O'Malley, and his old roommate, David, wishing him their best and a happy birthday.

It had been a little over a month since Josh had arrived at the Vatican. He had not ventured outside of its walls, prayed for any miracles, or preached the message of reparation. However, the news reports from America were encouraging. Congress had promised to return to the motto, "IN GOD WE TRUST" and had passed legislation to help the homeless and to reduce the many unjust taxes that were initiated years ago.

The Fitzpatrick Plan, as it was now called, was so successful that other billionaires and cities were incorporating the plan in their cities as well. Unfortunately, there was still considerable debate on the abortion issue, with congress equally divided.

One week after Josh's birthday, while he was praying in the Pope's private chapel, a brilliant light emerged from under the door. A light so bright that one could not look directly at it. In fact, it was the same brilliant light that burst from the windows of the rectory when Jesus appeared to Josh in Clarksville.

Pope Nicholas and Cardinal Mancini happened to be close to the chapel when the light burst out from under

CHAPTER IX

the door. Both were stunned as they looked at each other and immediately fell to their knees. There was no doubt in their minds that Jesus was in the room with Josh.

Josh, less afraid this time, fell to his knees and kissed the feet of Jesus.

"Come sit with me, my son," as Jesus took Josh's hand and led him to a pew.

"I'm so pleased with you and your efforts to proclaim my message of reparation and to bring so many back to me."

Josh simply listened, with tears in his eyes, as he continued to hold the hand of the Lord.

"I have come to you tonight to prepare you for another great battle that is approaching. Satan and his evil angels are aware of your presence here and are planning an attack on you and the Pope. Kapriel and Lancer are with you. Once again you will be able to see beyond the veil of this world into the spiritual world of good and bad. Do not be afraid, no matter what happens, as my spirit will always be with you. Continue to trust me, as in the end, my will shall prevail."

Josh closed his eyes and when he opened them again, the Lord was gone. However, standing close to him were his guardians Kapriel and Lancer.

"Oh, I'm so happy to see you again!" exclaimed Josh as he stood up and rushed toward them. Although Josh had often conversed and prayed with them, he was overjoyed to be able to look at them once again. "I wanted to ask Jesus about the attack, but He left so quickly."

"Don't worry my friend. Just remember to stay close to us and no harm will come to you."

"What about His Holiness?" Josh asked with a concerned voice.

"He will be protected from any harm, as will you. Remember to trust in the Lord," Kapriel reminded him.

Lancer handed Josh a pencil. "Write this name down. Anthony Capetta…"

"Now, go tell Pope Nicholas all you have been told and especially remind him to gather his Cardinals to pray constantly for the defeat of the upcoming attack."

When Josh opened the door to the chapel, Pope Nicholas and Cardinal Mancini were still on their knees praying.

"You have witnessed the presence of the Lord," Josh said. "We must be in constant prayer as great trials are about to befall us."

Josh quickly related most of what had transpired. Cardinal Mancini immediately went to gather others to join him in prayer while Josh and the Pope returned to the chapel where Josh explained in more detail what was about to happen.

Cardinal Morelli and the sex orgy he was planning had to wait. There were now more important matters to contend with. Morelli was not as naive as the Pope had thought he was. He suspected that the Pope was on to him after being relieved of several key duties and meetings. Realizing if he was defrocked, he would have no chance at the Papacy. Consequently, Morelli initiated another plan that would eliminate both the Pope and Josh. Morelli's followers were ready to assist him. All they needed was for him to initiate the plan.

Satan and all his demons were also ready for the attack. Flying in circles above the Vatican, the bloodshot, red-eyed demons could hardly wait and were frothing at the mouth just thinking about killing the Pope and Josh.

Josh awoke early in the morning, and as he looked out his window, he could already see swarms of black demons gathering in the far distance. Pope Nicholas was in prayer in his chapel. Skipping breakfast, Josh and the Pope prayed

CHAPTER IX

for hours while dozens of others prayed in the Basilica. No one knew when the attack was coming, but Josh was sure it would be soon.

After a quick lunch, Pope Nicholas invited Josh to join him for a short visit to the little Sisters convent, ten miles outside Vatican City. Although Josh was hesitant to go, not knowing when the attack would take place, he agreed to accompany the Pontiff. Besides, he knew that Pope Nicholas was determined to keep his promise to visit the nuns at their convent, as the visit had been delayed for weeks.

As instructed, just prior to leaving, Josh handed Cardinal Mancini a brief note containing the name of Anthony Capetta, the name that Lancer commanded he write down. The note read:

'In the event of trouble, have the police question Anthony Capetta, Cardinal Morelli's personal attendant.'

Josh had no clue who Capetta was, but during his prayers, he was given that name and instructions on what to do with it. Preparations were made and the Pontiff, Josh, and several attendants were on their way just a little after 1:00pm. The motorcade, as usual, drew many well-wishers who waved as they saw the Pope's limousine approach. Paying closer attention to the driver, the Pope asked, "Where's Angelo? Isn't he supposed to be driving?"

"Your Holiness, Angelo called in sick today so I'm his replacement. My name is Dornato and this is Gino, an extra driver if needed. Please excuse me for not introducing ourselves sooner."

"Not to worry," replied the Pontiff as he sat back and waved to more well-wishers.

As the lead car in the Pontiffs Motorcade turned right to continue to the convent, the Pope's car, along with the rear car, continued straight and immediately picked up speed.

"What's going on?" the Pontiff asked in a concerned voice. However, Josh knew immediately. There were dozens of black hideous creatures surrounding the car as they followed it throughout the city streets. Again, the Pope asked what was going on. Gino quickly turned around holding a gun.

"Don't say another word, or it will be your last."

Josh tried to calm the Pontiff down, but he remained petrified as the cars increased speed. The Vatican Police were immediately notified as soon as the Pope's car left the motorcade. Motorcycles and police cars seemed to come out of nowhere as they raced throughout the streets, weaving in and out of traffic.

"Red light ahead of us!," Gino yelled out, "Red light! Slow down!" but Donato sped up even faster as they flew through the intersection, barely missing two cars. The rear car wasn't so lucky. It burst into flames as it crashed into the side of a huge truck. Unfortunately, it contained three of the Pontiff's personal staff.

Several other cars slammed into the back of the truck, causing a massive pileup, and blocking the police cars from further pursuit. Smoke, fire, debris, and people were everywhere. The police motorcycles swerved onto the sidewalk, causing pedestrians to scramble, as the cycles raced by, trying desperately to catch up to the Pontiffs' vehicle.

Two other black vehicles joined the chase. Gunfire was exchanged back and forth between the two black cars and the motorcycle police. Suddenly, the first black car slammed into one motorcycle. The cycle reared off the road, bursting into flames as it smashed into a stone wall. Bullets coming from the other black car hit the rear tire of the second cycle, causing the driver to lose control. Trying

CHAPTER IX

desperately to remain steady, it skidded off the road into a ditch, eventually coming to a rest in a deep gully.

By this time, the police cars were rerouted and were again in pursuit. Additionally, several Vatican helicopters were dispatched to join the chase, but unfortunately neither the police cars nor the helicopters were successful in catching up to the Pontiffs car. In fact, it was as if the Pontiffs car had suddenly disappeared. And indeed it did, along with the other two black cars.

Two eighteen-wheel trucks were waiting at a designated secluded spot with their cargo doors open and ramps ready to receive the approaching vehicles. As the Pope's car arrived, it was guided up the ramp into the truck. Once the doors were closed, it continued its way with the contents completely concealed within. The same procedure occurred with the other two black cars.

The search went on for hours, with dozens and dozens of buildings, warehouses, and farms to search, all potential places where the kidnapped Pope and Josh could have been taken. The police and helicopter pilots were dumbfounded as to where they had disappeared too. Dozens of Vatican Police swarmed all over the Vatican, interrogating everyone in residence. Cardinal Mancini was waiting at the front doors of the Vatican as soon as he got word of the kidnapping. Handing the note that Josh had given him to the head investigator, the Cardinal made it clear that Capetta most likely knew about the kidnapping.

As eight police cars pulled up to Cardinal's Morelli's residence, the young Anthony Capetta panicked, fearful that he would be accused of involvement in the kidnapping. It didn't take long for him to confess that he had overheard the Cardinal planning the attack.

"I didn't tell anyone about it as I was afraid for my life. All I do here is serve the Cardinal," the young man said.

"Mostly I just have sex with him… but I had nothing to do with the kidnapping!"

"Where did they take the Pontiff?" the head investigator impatiently asked.

"I honestly don't know."

"You don't know. You knew about the kidnapping, but you don't know where they have taken him," the officer shouted.

"I swear! I don't know. I don't know," the kid repeatedly said, as he burst into tears.

"Think," the officer blasted back. "Think!"

"All I remember is they were going to hide the cars in an eighteen-wheeler and then later transfer them to someplace, but I don't know where they were going. You must believe me... I swear I don't know anything else."

Finally, after further questioning with no results, the young kid was taken away in handcuffs and the premises were searched. It turns out that the basement floor of the residence was a secret sex dungeon where the Cardinal and his boys held their orgies.

After rehashing all that the kid had told them, they quickly realized that there were only a few routes that an eighteen-wheel truck could take and less than a half dozen truck stops along those routes. It took less than five minutes to initiate a massive search.

Unfortunately, by time the search began, the Pope and Josh had already been transferred to a Van and were now prisoners inside an old rundown warehouse located close to the Tiber River.

One by one the truck stops were identified and searched. Two eighteen-wheelers were parked outside of the last truck stop to be searched. One truck contained two black cars, full of bullet holes and the other contained the empty Vatican limousine.

CHAPTER IX

Five minutes later, the place was surrounded by the Vatican and Polizia Police. Four officers entered the front door. Two others came in through the rear, while another two entered through the kitchen. There were only a dozen people in the restaurant, so it didn't take long before the drivers were apprehended. Although it took a little persuasion with a few zaps from a stun gun, they reluctantly revealed where the Pope and Josh were taken.

The Pontiff and Josh had their hands tied behind their backs and were sitting on the cold cement floor about twenty feet from each other. Josh could see numerous demons flying around, screeching and emitting slime from their mouths. Their hideous features and shrill screams sent chills up Josh's spine.

There were also dozens of men guarding the place, armed with all sorts of automatic rifles and guns. Kapriel and Lancer were standing close to Josh while the Pope's huge Guardian stood next to him. No demonic fighting had occurred, but by their sounds and movements, it was apparent that something soon was about to happen.

A metal door slammed shut as Cardinal Morelli stepped out of the office. Walking up to the Holy Father, the Cardinal smiled and sarcastically said, "So glad you could make it Your Holiness. This day is such a special occasion. Your reign will end is about to end and mine will begin."

Then he walked over to Josh.

"I'm afraid your days are numbered too, young man. In fact, I do believe this will be your last day alive, so enjoy the few minutes you have left."

Josh looked at Kapriel and Lancer, but neither one said or did a thing.

Returning to the Pope, the Cardinal grabbed one of his guards and gave the order to kill the Pope. The guard looked stunned, but before he had a chance to even point the gun, one of the guards ran in shouting.

"Police! The police are here!"

Gunfire rang out and within seconds the place looked like a battlefield. Simultaneously, the demons began their attack. Swarms rushed toward Josh completely unaware of his protection or the strength of Kapriel and Lancer. Within seconds, demons were bursting into flames of ashes as dozens more joined in only to be slaughtered.

The Pope's Guardian, as huge as he was, was having trouble fighting off so many demons who were attacking in swarms.

Josh called out to Kapriel and Lancer. "He's having trouble fighting off so many at one time! He needs help. Go to him... Please! Save the Pope."

The demons quickly realized it was useless to attack Josh. Consequently, they joined in with the attack on the Pope. Josh's guardians knew exactly what Josh was saying and as reluctant as they were, left him to assist in protecting the Pontiff.

Gunfire was still going on. Several on each side were wounded and killed. Sirens were blasting and police were scrambling everywhere in hopes of breaching the warehouse doors.

As the demonic fighting continued, Josh suddenly turned pale with fright. In the distance a red figure was approaching. A very large, red, glowing, evil, and ugly figure. Josh realized he had seen it before.

Satan appeared and went unnoticed with all the fighting going on. There were so many fiery ashes surrounding the Pontiff, that Kapriel and Lancer didn't see the figure that was now staring at them. Satan began to walk toward the Pope but suddenly stopped when he noticed Kapriel and Lancer fighting alongside the Pope's Guardian.

CHAPTER IX

Turning slowly toward Josh, Satan smiled, revealing his blackish teeth. Realizing that Josh was not shielded, he quickly advanced up to him.

"Well now, look what we have here. I finally get to meet you up close without the protection of your pals."

Grabbing Josh with one hand around his neck, he lifted him off his feet. Kicking desperately to free himself and struggling for air, Satan gloated at his prize.

"I've been waiting for this moment for quite some time." As he squeezed tighter, Josh's face turned blue while he struggled helplessly to free himself. Before another second went by, a brilliant flash of light smashed into Satan, propelling him across the entire length of the warehouse, smashing him into and through the cement brick wall.

Kapriel and Lancer had just returned to Josh as Satan smashed through the wall.

"What took you so long?" Josh asked his two Guardians as he rubbed his sore neck.

"That wasn't us..." Kapriel and Lancer answered. "That was the Hand of God that saved you."

By now, the gun fight was over. The doors were breached and the few remaining surrendered to the police without any resistance. Cardinal Morelli was also apprehended when he tried to escape through the rear door.

There was quite a commotion worldwide. News stations reported that the Pope and the young priest with him had successfully been rescued, completely unharmed except for a few scrapes and bruises. The details that were reported were sketchy, but all reported that it was the mastermind of Cardinal Morelli, who had plotted to kill the Pontiff and then to replace him, as he was the most senior and qualified Cardinal to assume that position.

All in all, fourteen of Cardinal Morelli's inner circle were involved. Eight were thugs that he recruited, and all had criminal records. Six of the eight were killed during the skirmish. The other six were young Deacons that evidently were a part of his sex orgy parties. Two of the six were also killed during the fight. In addition, two police were also killed. The car and truck drivers that assisted in the kidnapping were also taken into custody.

Thankfully it didn't take long for things to return to normal. Pope Nicholas gave strict orders not to discuss the event with anyone, especially news reporters. He wanted to protect the integrity of the Church as much as possible and was adamant about his privacy.

Josh's identity was soon known to the public. The pictures in the newspapers and magazines revealed to the world that he indeed was the young priest from Clarksville visiting Rome and the Vatican. As expected, it didn't take long for herds of people to gather in St. Peter's Square, seeking all kinds of healing. However, to their disappointment, it wasn't the Lord's will to heal the righteous who already had a relationship with Him. After saying his goodbye to the Pontiff and staff, Josh promised to return.

Josh was already flying back to the USA by time the entire square was full of believers. Recognizing the situation, Pope Nicholas addressed the crowd from his balcony window.

"You have come here for healing and with all my heart I know that the Lord, Jesus Christ, will bless each of you abundantly. However, Father Donovan has left the Vatican and is currently flying to his next destination."

CHAPTER IX

Hearing this, the crowd began to mumble with disappointment. After regaining the attention of the crowd, the Pontiff continued.

"Father Donovan has asked you to pray for the reparation of sinners throughout the world. This is what Jesus has asked of him and what he is asking from us. You have just witnessed the terrible, evil events that have just taken place here in the Vatican. Therefore, we implore you to pray. Pray for yourselves and for the sinners of the world."

With that the Pope blessed the crowd and ended his address. Returning to his chapel, he thought to himself, "I fear Josh will be back sooner that he expects…"

CHAPTER X

COMPASSION

It was a quick decision, but Josh had the strong feeling that he should make a brief stop in Clarksville before heading onto his next destination. After landing in LaGuardia, Josh flagged down one of the dozens of yellow cabs and was soon on his way to St. Andrew's. It was a good feeling, as he was once again back in the town that meant so much to him.

He had kept in touch with Father O'Malley and was aware that they had acquired another priest at the church and that the Seminary was once again operating as a Catholic Institution. The amazing thing was that it was almost at full capacity. The seminary had a total of twenty-five rooms and were now converted back to one person per room. Twenty candidates had applied and eighteen were accepted.

Father Patrick O'Neil was the new priest at St. Andrew's and Monsignor John Ribson has been assigned as the Pastor and Head Administrator of Sacred Heart Seminary. Josh was eager to meet them and most excited to reunite with his dear friend, Father O'Malley and all the other priests. Passing Buzzy's Gas Station, Josh smiled remembering the events that took place there.

Passing the Church, the taxi stopped directly in front of the rectory. Father Scott let out a loud hello as soon as Josh opened the door. Father Gordon and Father Samar came running out before Josh had time to enter the rectory. Smiles, laughter, and hugs were exchanged. They all gathered in the kitchen.

As soon as Maggie realized that Josh was there, she came rushing into the Kitchen to greet him. "You're just in time for dinner," she said as she hugged Josh.

"Can't wait", Josh replied. "Where's Father O'Malley and Father Scott?"

"Oh, they should be just finishing up confessions."

Sure enough, both walked in a few minutes later. Father O'Malley broke down into tears as he saw Josh, which of course caused several others to wipe their teary eyes.

Several hours while catching up on all that occurred since Josh left town. The Seminary was a big part of their conversations. Father O'Malley promised to personally introduce Josh to Monsignor Ribson just as Maggie was calling everyone to dinner. Josh insisted that Maggie set another plate and join them.

"I want to hear everything about these guys," he said to Maggie. "You're the only one here that will give me a straight scoop on what's been going on!" Laughter broke out with a few friendly groans. All in all, it was such a happy reunion.

Josh and Father O'Malley were off to the seminary first thing after morning Mass. Josh remained out of sight, watching Mass through the open sacristy door. Arriving at the seminary, Josh immediately noticed how beautiful the buildings and grounds looked. It brought a tear to his eye

293

CHAPTER X

as it now looked as he had imagined it would when he first arrived years ago.

Getting out of the car, Father O'Malley headed directly for the main entrance steps but stopped when he realized Josh was not with him. Turning around, he noticed Josh heading for the small circular garden with the statue of the Sacred Heart of Jesus in its center. Quickly joining Josh, they stood together, as they marveled at its restored beauty. Unlike before, it now had white marble benches surrounding the statue, with flowers and evergreens everywhere. After a few prayers of thanksgiving, they headed up the staircase toward the massive wood doors depicting the carvings of Christ and His Apostles.

Monsignor Ribson, warmly greeted Josh and after a brief conversation, the Monsignor was anxious to show Josh around the seminary and show how it had been renovated and beautified since Josh had last been there.

All the beautiful statues, paintings and crucifixes had been returned to their original places. The entire building had been painted, and the kitchen, cafeteria and dorm rooms had all been redone and modernized. The small chapel beneath the church was converted into an Adoration Chapel. As for the tunnels, only the tunnel from the chapel leading to the church basement and the old catacombs remained. All the others were gone.

It was just a little after 11:00am when Josh and Father O'Malley were ready to leave. However, Monsignor Ribson insisted that Josh meet all the seminarians and asked that he bless each before he left. Gladly accepting the invitation, they headed for the cafeteria where all the seminarians were eagerly awaiting him. All except one.

As Josh entered the room, everyone stood to greet him. After asking the seminarians to sit, Josh explained how proud he was of everyone and how happy he was that the Seminary had been so beautifully restored. He was about to continue when he suddenly stopped. Looking at a young man sitting in the far corner of the room, that sick feeling came over him again. Regaining his composure, Josh continued giving a brief account of the spiritual battle that took place years ago and how Satan and his evil demons were defeated within these very walls. Finally, wishing them well and hoping that they all would accept the call to the priesthood, he gave his blessing.

As he walked back to the circular lobby, he asked the Monsignor if he could meet with the blond-headed young man who was sitting by himself in the corner of the room.

"Oh, you must mean Andy Jackson. He's quite a loner here. Can't figure him out and he is angry most of the time. I've talked to him, but nothing really resolved."

Five minutes later, Andy entered the library. Josh greeted him warmly, despite a faint red glow surrounding his head. There was something about this kid that prompted Josh to explore, rather than to immediately have him expelled from the seminary.

"Please have a seat. I noticed you sitting by yourself. Is anything bothering you? Perhaps some problems with some of the other guys?"

"Nope. Nothing's wrong," Andy said.

"Well, normally it wouldn't make any difference to me, but in your case, I really think something is not right. Perhaps you can tell me about it?"

The kid just looked down, fidgeting with his fingers, but again said that nothing was bothering him. Josh persisted.

"Andy, do you really want to be a Catholic Priest?"

"Yes, Father, I do."

"Tell me about your upbringing, especially about your religious education."

Andy looked directly at Josh. "I really don't know why this is of interest to you. In all due respect, you are not

CHAPTER X

even connected to this seminary," he said with an indigent voice.

"Son, I am more connected than you think. Now what about your upbringing?"

Andy realized that he was not going to win out with this conversation, so reluctantly he answered.

"If you must know, I went to Catholic grammar school and then public high school. Then two years at Sussex Community College. I never knew my father. He left when I was two. My mother said he beat her and was a drunk. Mom died when I was in seventh grade. Aunt Ruth and Uncle Bill raised me and paid for my education, including this place. I have no brothers or sisters. Now, does that answer all your questions?"

Ignoring that question, Josh asked, "Why are you so angry??

"I'm not!" Andy shouted back.

"Then why do you look so angry and why are you shouting?"

"I just get upset when people try to control me."

"I'm not trying to control you, Andy. I'm trying to help. I'm trying to find out what's really bothering you."

"Why are you so interested?"

"Why do *you* hate Jesus?" Josh asked in reply.

Andy looked shocked. Immediately he stood up and headed for the door, but Josh yelled out before he reached it, "What are you so afraid of?"

Andy stopped and quickly swung around.

"YOU! I'm afraid of you and all like you," he tearfully said.

Josh stood up and embraced him. Andy tried to pull away, but Josh held him even closer. Eventually the struggle lessened and soon the kid was crying like a baby, holding ever so tight to him. Josh held Andy until his crying ended, letting him get it out of his system. Sitting down, Andy began to open up. He told Josh that he was abused by a priest when he was in seventh grade. He had just become an altar boy when the incident occurred.

"From then on, I was forced to do various sex acts until I graduated from eighth grade. With my parents dead, I never told anyone. Once in high school, I got mixed up with a rough group of kids and eventually got into drugs. As time went on, I became bitter and bitter about the church and priests.

"Then one day, shortly before I entered the seminary, I was in a bar, drinking and feeling no pain. As I sat there, a stranger sat next to me and before long we were in a heavy conversation. Turns out this guy was a defrocked priest who also was abused and angry at the Church. This guy hated the Church for its hypocrisy and for its position on sex. He told me that the best way to get back at the Church was to attack it from within. Then he told me I should become a priest, like him, and cause scandals... lots of scandals."

"At that point," Andy continued, "I was totally shocked and got up to leave. Before I had a chance to get off my seat, he pulled me back saying that he would explain what he meant.

"The worst part? I sat and actually listened... I don't know why, but there was something about this guy that almost compelled me to stay. Can't really explain it but it felt as if something or someone was on top of me holding me there. Now, here comes the weird part. He said there was a lot of sex going on in all churches of all faiths. Homosexual sex, straight sex, pedophile sex, you name it.

"Then he blasted the churches, telling me that they have been covering up these scandals for years. He said that he believes the cover-ups make the churches just as guilty as the person doing the abuse. Putting his arm on my shoulder, looks me square in my eye and says,

CHAPTER X

'Churches need to be destroyed and exposed to their hypocrisy. So, what better way to expose these cover ups, than to bring disgrace on them?'

"The stranger had a deviant smile on his face. I have to say that I wasn't very comfortable, but again, I felt I had to listen. And what better way to do this than to have the disgrace performed by priests and religious. Doing the unthinkable! Priest, ministers and religious having sex with each other, with children, with whoever. 'Disgrace religious institutions from within. Eventually the church will be exposed and its downfall certain, and people like you and me will be avenged!'

"Then the bartender asked me if I wanted another drink. When I turned back to the stranger, he was gone. I sat there for some time. At first it didn't make sense to me, but the more I thought about it, the more I began to think that destroying the Church from within was a pretty damn good idea, even if some abuse had to occur to bring it down.

"So that's how I got here. I guess that was my plan. But here's the crazy thing... Since I've been here, I don't feel that way anymore. Every night I have nightmares. I'm surrounded by all sorts of men holding me down, telling me to hate Jesus and the Church. When I wake up, I'm sweating and feel like the dream was real. Yet after being here for six months, I really am beginning to like it here and I'm starting to believe that although there are some bad priests, not everyone is bad. Yet, every morning, after that same dream, I'm again full of hate."

"What do these men look like in your dream?"

"Like normal men. Some are dressed in black; others have regular clothes on, some are women, I think. But the funny thing is they all have some kind of a red glow around their heads."

Josh took hold of Andy's hand. "I'm so sorry you had that bad experience with that stranger and even more sorry that you were abused, especially by a priest. And I'm sorry that no one has been able to help you. But Jesus *does* love you, so very much, and wants you to be a part of His church. I'm sure I have returned to this place specifically for you. Placing his hands on the top of Andy's head, Josh began praying for him to receive an outpouring of the Holy Spirit, and for the exorcism of any demons that might be clinging to him.

After a few minutes of Josh praying in tongues, Andy began to shake. Then he twisted and bent over still shaking. This continued for some time, all the while the prayers continued. Andy collapsed to the floor as Josh continued to pray over him. Suddenly, there were loud screeching screams, as several demons gave up their hold on the young kid who had been so violently abused as a child. Andy remained perfectly still on the floor for a while. Realizing that the heaviness and anger he had felt for so long was gone, he began to cry as Josh helped him to his feet.

"You're a child of God now," Josh said, "and will make an absolutely wonderful priest."

Both walked out of the library with smiles on their faces. Andy was glowing; not with a red glow, but with a glow of happiness, love, and peace.

The flight to Los Angeles International took a little less than five hours. After flagging down a taxi, he was on his way to St. Martin's, a small Catholic Church about five miles from the airport. As the taxi got off the freeway, and onto the smaller side streets, Josh was amazed and heartbroken to see so many homeless living in tents, cardboard boxes, and any other kind of makeshift

CHAPTER X

coverings imaginable. Although federal legislation was passed years ago providing funds for the homeless, for shelters, and for low-income housing, it was apparent that these funds had not reached this area of the country.

Driving along the block where St. Martin's Church was located, Josh caught sight of St. Martin's Elementary school. It had long ago been closed. Remembering St. Ann's Elementary in Jinksville, Josh wondered how many of these Catholic Schools had succumbed to the lack of funds and the lack of religious necessary to run them.

Josh knocked on the door of the rectory several times before Father Henry opened it.

"Hi, I'm Father Donovan."

A blank stare greeted him.

"I called you an hour ago." Still no response.

"Father Donovan…" he repeated.

"Oh, yes," Father Henry finally said as he recalled their conversation. "You asked to stay for a while?"

"Yes, that's right. Just until I'm on to my next assignment."

"No problem at all," the elderly priest said.

After a few seconds of staring at him, Josh finally said, "So, may I come in?"

"Oh, yes, yes...please excuse me. I can't hear as well as I used to."

Father Henry was well into his eighties and had been retired for years. A visiting priest would say Mass every Sunday at St. Martin's, and other than his housekeeper and cook, Father Henry lived alone.

Mrs. Vivian, as she wanted to be called, finally arrived at the door. "Please excuse me Father, as I was out back putting out the trash when you knocked. Please let me show you to your room."

Mrs. Vivian was as friendly as Maggie and was very devoted to Father Henry, being his housekeeper for the past twenty-some years.

"If there is anything I can get you, please don't hesitate to ask. Dinner is at 5:00pm. It's a little early, but Father Henry goes to bed around 7:30pm every night."

"Absolutely no problem."

Josh was quite impressed at her spryness, being elderly, well into her seventies.

Neither Father Henry or she had a clue as to who Josh was, nor had they heard of any miracles that had occurred over the past months. Of course, both were isolated from, shall we say, the *world*, as neither ventured out much, not even for groceries, which were delivered each week. Josh had been led to this parish for a reason, and although he had no idea what it was, he knew he would soon find out.

Dinner was delicious. Pot roast, mashed potatoes, gravy, and stewed carrots were a favorite of Father Henry, who went to bed exactly at 7:30pm, just as Mrs. Vivian said. In the evening, Josh decided to take a brisk walk around the block. As he walked, he could not help but notice all the homeless and rundown homes, many of which were boarded up. Returning to the rectory, he immediately went to his room. Getting into his lounging pants and loose shirt, he knelt and said the rosary as he has done since childhood. He especially prayed for all the unfortunate and how he could be a help to those in need.

After his prayers, he started to reflect on Andy back at the seminary and wondered how many defrocked or fake priests there were trying to destroy the integrity of the Church. Opening his eyes, Kapriel and Lancer were once again visible.

CHAPTER X

"Another battle?" Josh asked, hoping that he was wrong.

"Not yet," answered Kapriel. "We will be visible for most of the time from now on, and the Lord will grant you sight of the spiritual world whenever necessary. As time goes by, your mission will get more difficult. Our presence will help you to cope and to remember that no matter what happens, we along with the Lord, will be with you. "

Josh thought for a few minutes. "What do you mean, things will get more difficult for me?

"Not to worry," Lancer said. "You must be aware that Satan is not happy with you and all that you have achieved. His fury is directed directly toward you. Remember always what Jesus said. *This will be no easy task...it will be a heavy cross you will have to carry...you will be attacked by many, by evil spirits and by Satan himself.*'

Josh remembered everything and was once again ready to meet any obstacle placed in front of him. "I can't say that I'm not a little worried, but I trust in Jesus and in your protection." With that, Josh took a quick shower, and was soon fast asleep, knowing that his Guardians were watching over him.

Father Henry was a friendly and compassionate person. During his younger years, he served as Chaplain in the US Army and then later was assigned to various parishes in Colorado, New Mexico, and California. He served as Assistant Pastor and eventually Pastor of St Martin's, where he has remained for the past 22 years. During the early years at St. Martin's, he taught religion at the now closed elementary school.

One of his proudest accomplishments was the influence he had in convincing the Diocese that such a school was needed. Mrs. Vivian said that he was thrilled when asked by the Archbishop to oversee the construction of the school, and to serve as its head administrator. She told Josh that his heart was broken when, after eighteen years of successful operation, the decision was made to permanently close the school due to lack of funds, the lack of religious, and the general decline of parishioners from the area.

Josh got to know him quite well. He reminisced about his early years and the many happy times he had. Josh was happy to listen and over time they became quite friendly. Unfortunately, Father Henry was not in the best of health, as he often either forgot or repeated himself frequently. Nevertheless, he was quite aware of what was going on and seemed content to live out the rest of his days at St. Martin's. However, despite his relative alertness, he had never heard of Father Donovan or of the miracles that had taken place over the past several years. And that was absolutely fine with Josh.

During breakfast, about a month later, Josh said that he had an idea to reopen the school.

"Father Henry," he said. "What do you think about converting the school into a first-class homeless facility? We could convert the classrooms into dorms for men and women and update the cafeteria to feed the needy."

Father Henry looked at Josh with a downcast face. "Don't think I haven't thought of that. You know the place is just deteriorating more and more every year. But let's be realistic, that will take a lot of money, and quite frankly, the Diocese won't be any help to us with any kind of funding."

Josh just smiled. "You get permission from the Archbishop, and I will take care of the money."

Father Henry looked at Josh with skepticism but agreed to the proposal. Three days later, John Fitzpatrick was on his way to Los Angeles. Before arriving at St. Martin's, he

CHAPTER X

met with a few of his wealthy associates and secured their participation in helping to fund the shelter. Once the Archbishop was assured that this project would be completely covered by private funds, he agreed. Architects were hired, and the project was soon underway.

Luckily, the school had not deteriorated too much over the past eight years. The classrooms on the first floor would be converted into dorms for women, while the rooms on the second floor would specifically be for men. In addition to the classrooms, there were several offices on the first floor slated for administrative personnel. Half of the gymnasium would be converted into men's and women's, recreation, and TV areas.

The other half of the gym would be converted into a first aid/emergency-care facility. Additionally, the cafeteria and kitchen would be updated, and open 24/7 to feed the needy. Not only was this project successful, but it inspired other cities to do the same. The Fitzpatrick Plan was now national and, as Jesus had said, would become one the largest humanitarian projects ever created.

While the renovations were taking place, Josh visited many of the homeless living in tents and cardboard shelters. He brought them food and often attended to their medical needs. Many healings occurred, yet no one knew that it was Josh's prayers that caused their cures. By the time the shelter was complete, Josh had become quite popular, not only with the homeless, but with the locals as well. He was affectionately known in Spanish as "REGALO de DIOS" meaning, "A Gift from God."

The project took a little over five months to complete. By the time its doors opened, it was practically full. Word had spread and the homeless and needy were coming from all sections of the state, with the 24/7 cafeteria feeding hundreds weekly. Father Henry was never happier. He supervised the construction every day, or at least in his mind he did.

Sadly, just one month after the shelter opened, Father Henry passed from this earth to his Heavenly reward awaiting him. The funeral service was small. His only brother flew in from Ohio for the service and the Archbishop celebrated Mass and gave a wonderful homily about his life and service to the church. Mrs. Vivian could not stop crying as she had lost a dear friend.

During the next few weeks, Josh consoled her as much as he could. Although she tried to be as cheerful as possible, she just couldn't shake her depression. In fact, she was determined to pack up and leave, as she believed her service was over. That was until the new Pastor arrived. Father Riley was a stout man in his late fifties. Direct from Ireland, he had an accent that was hard to understand, yet was so intriguing to listen to. He had a wonderful personality and always had a joke or two to tell. Mrs. Vivian took a liking to him immediately, especially after he raved about her cooking As it happened, Mrs. Vivian's Grandparents also came from Ireland which assured her that they would have many wonderful tales to tell in the years to come.

Josh had been at St. Martin's for a little over seven months and had just finished celebrating his 25th birthday. Finally, the time came when he was led to move on. Kapriel and Lancer had directed him to head to San Diego where his mission would be revealed to him.

It was difficult for Mrs. Vivian to say goodbye, as she had come to love him as a son. "I was hoping that you would be here when I had my cataract surgery next month."

CHAPTER X

"You won't need the surgery," Josh said as he touched her eyes and asked the Lord for healing. As Josh drove away, she waved goodbye with tears in her eyes, although she could see perfectly clear for the first time in such a long while.

Unlike his previous stays, Josh got a room at the Wyndham San Diego Bayside. It was late in the night when he arrived and finally settled in for a good night's sleep. Early in the morning, he looked out of the window, and well understood why Kapriel and Lanced were visible. Although it was a sunny day, swirls of black mist, looking like dark clouds, were everywhere, as were dozens and dozens of men gathering, all with that evil, red glow radiating from their heads. Josh couldn't believe his eyes. He had no idea what was going on, although he soon would find out.

Located in the heart of Downtown San Diego, Josh was in the center of so much activity. From a tourist perspective, everything appeared to be normal. The weather was perfect. The sun was out, people were walking, laughing, and having a wonderful time. Kids were eating ice cream, while other children played in Waterfront Park. There were boats and plenty of activity going on in North San Diego Bay. From all perspectives, it was a perfect day.

From Josh's perspective, it was far from perfect. Evil was all around. Hundreds of hideous demons were everywhere, especially congregating around the men with red-glowing mists around their heads. After eating his breakfast, Josh ventured outside and was appalled at what he saw. Young boys and some young girls were apparently being loaded into the back of a canvas covered truck. The kids were quiet and from all appearances, everything looked fine.

The men were laughing, smoking, and cracking jokes. Just as Josh was about a half block away, the truck, along with about four cars drove away heading south on North Harbor Drive. Dozens of demons followed the caravan while simultaneously, swarms of small black hideous demons flew toward Josh and his Guardians. Circling them like an angry bunch of bees, they apparently did not want to engage in a confrontation, but merely wanted to block Josh's view as the truck sped away.

One week later, the same exact scenario occurred. However, this time it appeared to be all young girls. Josh had rented a car and was following them as soon as the truck took off. Exiting Harbor Drive, the truck headed for the pier areas, eventually pulling into what looked like an old run-down warehouse.

Although Josh was very concerned and suspicious of what he thought was going on, he had no proof that anything illegal occurred. He had seen no fighting, no weapons, no arguments, and most importantly, none of the children seemed to be in trouble. The only thing he knew for sure was evil was present and that in and of itself, was enough for him to be worried. Sitting in his car across from the warehouse, Josh was perplexed.

"I really don't know what to do," Josh said to Kapriel. "I know something is not right, but what?"

"Be patient," Kapriel said with a reassuring voice.

Five minutes later, a young girl burst from the side door of the warehouse screaming for help. Immediately Josh ran to help her. Just as he reached her, three men ran up to her grabbing the girl by the arms and dragging her back to the warehouse.

"What do you think you're doing?" asked one of the men looking directly at Josh.

"Look!" another blurted out. "He's a priest!"

"Can't be a priest," another said. "He's too young."

CHAPTER X

"He could be a damn undercover cop," the first man angrily said.

By now all three had moved very close to Josh, so close that they were touching him. Before another word was spoken, everything went dark. When Josh came-to, he was in some kind of holding cell, deep below the warehouse.

Kapriel and Lancer were with him and immediately reminded him to trust in the Lord. Although it took a few minutes for him to calm down, they reassured him that everything was alright, and as time passed in his cell, they explained the purpose of his visit to San Diego.

Josh had stumbled onto one of the largest child slave trafficking organizations in the United States. Marcus Lorenzen ran the operation along with some thugs in Mexico. Children were groomed and recruited from Mexico and Venezuela through any means available. Sometimes they would buy them from the Cartel, other times they were bought directly from their parents for the promise of safe passage into the U.S., but mostly by kidnapping.

Once the children were secured, they would either be smuggled or walked across the border, as if seeking citizenship, and then later brought to a central location. Or, they would be loaded onto a boat and smuggled into the country through the Tijuana River or directly via the San Diego Bay and unloaded somewhere along North Harbor Drive, close to downtown San Diego.

The lower level of the warehouse had numerous holding cells, none equipped with water, toilet, or beds. One would consider themselves lucky to have a blanket. Buckets were provided as a toilet and once a day they were given a flimsy meal to eat. As time went on, Josh realized that the kids would do just about anything for a little extra food or water.

Josh was more than appalled at what he saw. He was heartbroken to see so many helpless and abused children. Many would be sold and used as prostitutes. Others, especially the young boys, would be used to pleasure wealthy men and women. Some would be used as personal slaves for whatever purpose their owner wanted.

"How could this happen in America?" he asked Kapriel and Lancer.

"There is much evil in this world," Lancer said, "and you are just beginning to see it."

"Now you have a little better understanding why the Lord is so angry and ready to pass Judgement on this world," added Kapriel.

It wasn't long before two men, along with Marcus, descended the steps and entered the cell area. Walking directly up to Josh, they began to laugh and jeer at him.

"I hope you're comfortable Father, or whoever you are," Marcus sarcastically said. "Please give your *blessing* to everyone here."

"I will," Josh said with a sincere voice, "including all of you as well."

That comment wiped the smile off their faces and only created an outburst of cursing.

"Please, let these children go," Josh pleaded. "They are just innocent children. What do you want them for? Please...for the love of God, let them go."

"I'll tell you what I want them for," Marcus blurted out in an angry voice. "Better yet, I'll show you."

With that, he opened the cell directly across from Josh, grabbed the nearest girl and raped her, all the while laughing and repeating, "This is what they are here for."

Josh turned away with tears streaming down his face and did the only thing he could do… he prayed. He prayed

CHAPTER X

for the girl, for all the children, and somehow, he prayed for Marcus and his gang of thugs.

Despite Marcus's occasional outbursts of lust, he had made it clear that none of the girls were to be sexually molested, as customers wanted their property untouched and to be virgins. This, however, did not exclude other forms of perverted sex acts that some of the captors would occasionally treat themselves too.

Unfortunately, this left the boys open to all kinds of abuse. Some guards forced the boys to perform sex acts on them or themselves. Others took pleasure in having anal intercourse, while some preferred oral sex.

One of the men who guarded the kids was extremely cruel and perverted. Before the kids were sold, he would force a teenage boy to have oral sex with him and then repeat this act with other boys throughout the night hours. As if that wasn't enough, he took great pleasure in beating them with his belt until their bare butts blistered. Fortunately, not every guard abused the kids.

One such guard recognized Josh the moment he saw him. He had heard of the miracles and had seen his picture in the papers. Nevertheless, he had kept quiet, as he was afraid of Marcus as much as the kids were.

About two weeks after Josh was kidnapped, Slick, as they called him, walked up to Josh during his guard duty. Whispering, he said, "I know who you are. I've seen your picture in newspapers and have heard of the miracles performed. I'm sorry you have to be here, but I can't do anything about it. I never wanted this job, nor did I know what it was about when I agreed to work for them. Once I found out, I wanted out, but they said they would kill my wife and kids if I dared to leave or even say one word about this operation. So here I am... stuck...but I treat the kids right. I give them extra food and water when I'm on duty and I would never, never abuse any of them."

Josh looked at him with compassion, but also with a certain amount of disappointment or even some anger.

"There are so many young lives you could save if you went to the police. I'm sure they would protect your family."

"You have no idea how deep this operation goes and how ruthless these guys can be. I've seen them cut off the heads of men who dared to question their orders. I can't imagine how they would torture my family if they even suspected me of disloyalty."

Just then, the next guard arrived. Slick quickly returned to his desk area and left. Another week went by. Sadly, a bunch of new children arrived almost just a few days after the others were shipped out and sold. Marcus unexpectedly made a surprise visit. Screaming at the guard to leave, he walked over to Josh. Staring at him for what seemed an eternity, he finally spoke.

"I've been having nightmares ever since you arrived. The nightmares are about you. Now, tell me why. Why am I having them when I don't give a shit about you?" Marcus spit on the ground in front of Josh, disgusted as his own perceived weakness.

Josh looked deeply into Marcus's eyes.

"It's not about me. It's about you. It's about how much Jesus loves you and how hopeful He is that you will repent and return to Him."

"You've got to be shitting me, I don't care about you or about Jesus."

"You may not care about Jesus, but He cares about you. He cares about your wife, Eleanor, your five children and your family. He loves you all but hates your sins. Please listen before it's too late." Josh was pleading with him. "Please... turn back to Jesus while you can."

CHAPTER X

"You son of a bitch! How did you know my wife's name and how many kids I have? Who told you?" He looked around wildly, as if to catch the person who had shared this personal information.

"Jesus has revealed many things to me about you, especially about your fate if you do not repent."

Marcus looked shocked. "What about my fate?"

"Come close, and I will show you."

Marcus didn't quite know what to do. On the one hand, he didn't want to appear afraid, yet on the other hand, he didn't want to comply with anything the priest said. However, after a few minutes, and remembering that he was completely alone with no other guards present, he slowly walked up to Josh.

Josh placed both his hands on Marcus's face. Immediately the vision of Hell came into Marcus's mind. He saw himself suffering in everlasting agony. All around him were cries and screeches from hideous demons everywhere, torturing and tormenting him. He felt loneliness and despair that was indescribable.

Marcus let out a scream of fear as he fell to his knees. His face was twisted with horror as he slid away from Josh. Standing up, he drew out his gun and fired directly at him. After the second shot bounced off his target, he continued to shoot until his gun was empty. With even more horror on his face, the petrified Marcus cried out.

"Who the fuck are you? Who are you? he repeated.

By this time, several guards had heard the gunshots and had run down the steps, immediately drawing their own weapons, and joining Marcus.

"Kill him, kill him!" he shouted.

Every bullet was aimed perfectly but simply bounced off their target. Now all the guards stood horrified with their mouths open. One collapsed, then trying to get to his feet as fast as he could, he half crawled and half tripped, as he rushed to get away. The other ran as fast as he could back up the stairs, practically tripping over the first guard. Marcus once again stood by himself.

"Who are you?" he said, this time with a much more terrified, almost humbled, voice.

"I am a priest. I am delivering God's message to you and to the world. I have been asked to spread the message of repentance, as I have asked you to repent. Please, turn away from all of this and back to Jesus. Please, before it's too late."

Marcus simply stood as tears began to flow. All he could think about was the vision of Hell and the torment awaiting him. Suddenly, he dropped to his knees and began to sob. For the first time in his life, he began to think about all the children he had abused and sold, and how many lives he had destroyed.

Demons came rushing toward him from all directions. They were furious that they were losing hold on him. The creature that was clinging to him was desperately trying to hold on, yet with each sorrowful tear that dropped, the demon's grip lessened and eventually it broke free from him.

Kapriel and Lancer were destroying other creatures as fast as they were attacking. Soon it was apparent that these little demons had no chance against two seven-foot powerful warriors from God. Within minutes, the place was quiet with only Angels present.

"God will never forgive me," he kept repeating. "I'm so sorry, but God will never forgive me"

Suddenly, the lock on Josh's cell door mysteriously opened. Kneeling next to Marcus, Josh assured him of the mercy of Jesus.

"So long that we are *truly* sorry, Jesus will always forgive us, no matter what sins we have committed. The Divine mercy of Jesus is Infinite."

CHAPTER X

Then Josh wrapped his arm around the still crying Marcus and said this prayer:

"ETERNAL FATHER, I OFFER YOU THE BODY AND BLOOD, SOUL AND DIVINITY, OF YOUR DEARLY BELOVED SON, OUR LORD, JESUS CHRIST, IN ATONEMENT FOR THE SINS OF MARCUS, FOR OUR SINS AND FOR THE SINS OF THE WHOLE WORLD... JESUS I TRUST IN YOU."

Marcus looked up at Josh.

"Father, forgive me for all my sins, I have been so unfaithful, but from this day forward, I will try my best to make things right." And that is, exactly what he did.

The children were fed, provided with new clothes, and released to the proper authorities. Marcus cut a deal with the local police and the FBI, by providing them with the names and contacts of his associates in Mexico. Additionally, he gave details of how the organization operated, including the drop-off facilities in New York, Chicago, Florida, and New Mexico.

Likewise, the locations where the children were sold were also provided. Many of the thousands were rescued, which basically ended one of the largest child trafficking operations in the country. Six weeks later, Marcus was found shot to death in one of the alleys in lower San Diego. Although his life was full of corruption and sin, it ended with love in his heart, and with sincere repentance. He did all this before it was too late for him.

After settling his account at the Wyndham Hotel, Josh was on his way to Mexico. Getting off the bus at Navajo, Josh was warmly welcomed at The Parish of The Sacred Heart Of Jesus. Josh explained he would only be visiting for a day or two as he was on his way to Mexico City. The next morning, Josh was up early ready to celebrate Mass.

Although he had never spoken Spanish before, he greeted the parishioners as they entered the church, speaking and understanding Spanish as if it was his native tongue.

While waiting for Mass to begin, still standing outside the church, Josh noticed a young boy. Bending down, he held the deformed hand of a young boy and prayed. Likewise, he prayed over two elderly women in wheelchairs.

During his homily, he repeated the message given to him from Jesus, and once again stressed the urgency of repentance. As Josh was delivering the message, he noticed three rough-looking men standing in the rear of the church. They appeared to be listening to every word spoken. After Mass, Josh stood outside, once again greeting the parishioners and wishing them well. Before leaving, the crowd, including the boy with the deformed hand and the two women in wheelchairs, asked for his blessing, and just as before, when the blessing ended with the word 'AMEN', the three were healed.

Immediately the rough looking men grabbed Josh and pulled him into a van.

"We're sorry to be so forceful with you Father, but we were afraid that you would not come with us. We all recognized who you are. We're asking you to meet with one of the biggest and most powerful Cartel leaders in the country, Jose Alejandro Hernandez."

"Why are you so interested in me visiting him?"

"Father," one of the men said, "we all have heard your message and have asked the Lord, and for that matter, our families for forgiveness. Although we did not work directly for Hernandez, we have been involved in the transportation of drugs. After your message, we realize how wrong we were and how wicked and harmful these Cartels are. We were hoping, perhaps beyond hope, that

CHAPTER X

you might be able to, well, convert Hernandez back to the Lord... or, at the very least, convince him to stop trafficking."

Josh took a deep breath.

"That's a tall order you are asking but... I will do my best to help. However, as I hope you know, I can't convert anyone by myself, but Jesus can. I can't promise you anything, but I can, at the very least, try and give him the Lord's message."

They drove for hours, eventually winding up on dirt roads and in jungle vegetation. About a quarter mile from the entrance of the estate, the van stopped.

"We can't come any closer as it's too dangerous. You will have to walk the rest of the way. We'll meet you here at dark."

Josh got out of the van feeling very uncomfortable, but with Kapriel and Lancer, he was not afraid. As he approached the Hernandez estate, he was abruptly met by multiple gunmen.

"Halt!" they shouted. "Stop! Or we will shoot."

Josh stopped and waited.

"It's a *gringo* priest," one of the guards said as they all laughed. "What do you want?" they shouted in his face.

"I'm here to see Jose Hernandez."

Surprised that he could fluently speak and understand Spanish, they took a moment to respond.

"Is he expecting you?" one of the guards blurted out.

"No, but I'm sure he will see me."

"Wait here," another guard commanded as he phoned Hernandez for permission.

"Who did you say you are?" asked the guard on the phone.

"I didn't say," replied Josh. "But if he must know, tell him I am "REGALO de DIOS".

Looking around the compound, there were dozens of small demons everywhere. Atop the roof, perched in various places, were what looked like gargoyles, but Josh knew they were large demon sentinels protecting the compound.

"He's a priest... a *gringo* priest," the guard said on the phone to Hernandez. "I have no idea. Yes, he's alone... Yes, sir...right away."

After hanging up the phone, Josh was frisked for weapons and then escorted up a winding staircase into a huge room full of plush leather furniture and exotic paintings. Two lightly clad young women were sitting close to Hernandez while a third was sitting on his lap.

Immediately, Hernandez whisked them away as he motioned Josh over to him.

"You *are* a gringo priest," he mocked.

"My name is Father Donovan."

"I have to say, you have some balls to come alone to see me. Don't just stand there, sit down, and tell me why you're here." Half laughing, Hernandez continued, "Actually, let me take a guess. You're here to tell me what a bad person I am, eh? To give me religion and then I will miraculously be converted and saved. Something like that?"

"I'm simply here to deliver a message. As for you being converted and saved, that's entirely up to you."

"A message from who?" he demanded.

"I'm here to tell you that you are loved more than you can imagine. I'm here to tell you that Jesus loves you with all His heart, and no matter what you have done in your life, He will always love and forgive you."

"Great," Hernandez said. "I didn't know that I was loved so much, nor did I know that I needed forgiveness. Since your Jesus loves me so much, I guess he likes what I'm doing," he sarcastically said.

CHAPTER X

The expression on Josh's face saddened. "Mr. Hernandez, I said Jesus loves you, but never said He likes what you are doing. Jesus is asking you to turn away from this lifestyle. To amend your life and to return to Him before it's too late."

"You've got to be F***ing crazy," Hernandez said. "You think I'm really going to believe that crap!"

"I'm not crazy, and what I have just said is true. Jesus loves you and forgives you. He is pleading with you and others to repent. The truth is that time for repentance is running out for all of us. The day is quickly coming for Judgement, and unless we change our ways, His judgement will not be kind."

Hernandez was furious.

"Who the hell do you think you are? Barging in here and telling me about my sins and that I better get my act together before it's 'too late'."

"That's exactly what I am telling you and to the entire world. You can believe me or not, the choice is yours."

"I don't care about time running out, nor do I give a damn about your Jesus. Now get the F* out of my house and off my property before I change my mind and kill you myself!!!"

"I'm sorry you feel that way Mr. Hernandez. I have simply told you what the Lord has told me. Again, I hope you will believe me and make the right choice."

Hernandez could hardly control himself. Standing up, he screamed, "GET OUT OF HERE! NOW! Get out you F***ing Gringo."

Sweat was pouring off his forehead and unfortunately the red glow around his head was still there, glowing even brighter. Josh stood up and left accompanied by a guard. Walking down the steps, Josh could still hear Hernandez screaming. The guard himself couldn't get out of there fast enough, for when Hernandez got that mad, there was no telling what he might do.

As Josh was halfway down the driveway, heading for the guarded gates, suddenly a woman yelled out.

"Wait! please wait for me, Father! Please wait."

Startled, Josh turned to see a young woman running toward him. Before anyone could react, she was in his embrace.

"Take me with you" she pleaded. "Take me with you. I have to get away from this place." Victoria Hernandez was pleading to escape the clutches of her papa and the restricted lifestyle she was forced to live.

"Stop her! Stop her, you idiots," Hernandez screamed from an opened window.

"Stay close to me," Josh said as he wrapped his arms around her.

Immediately the guards attempted to grab her, but it was useless. Confused, it was as if she was behind a sheet of glass, and in a sense she was. As they struggled to grab hold of her, their hands simply slid down the invisible shield that now was protecting Josh as well as her. Stupid demons flew directly into the shield, trying desperately to free her, only to end up bursting into flames and ashes. The large Gargoyle Demons perched on the roof apparently knew better than to attack such powerful Guardians as Kapriel and Lancer.

Hernandez continued to shout from the window.

"Stop her and kill the gringo priest!"

Frustrated and dumbfounded, the guards could not grab hold of her. Shots rang out as several guards fired directly at Josh. Still feeling helpless, one of the guards in desperation attempted to smash his rifle over Josh's head, only to have it break in half. Soon, all efforts to free Victoria and to kill Josh stopped.

CHAPTER X

Turning to the guards, Josh said, "Don't ever underestimate the power of God. Leave this place as fast as you can and amend your lives before God's Judgement comes upon you."

Immediately after warning the guards, Josh, Victoria, Kapriel, and Lancer turned and walked away. By this time, Hernandez had caught up to them, yet he, nor any of his guards, were able to pursue Josh or his daughter. They were essentially frozen in place. Something more powerful than they could have ever imagined was holding them back. After a few minutes of walking, the four finally reached the rendezvous point and as promised, the van was waiting for them.

Josh was on his way to Mexico City early the next morning and Victoria was off to the United States. She would be eventually placed in a protective witness program where her identity and location would be secure. Thanks to her cooperation and her concern, she would be instrumental in helping the FBI locate and destroy many of the secret processing drug locations her father created.

Mexico City was exactly as Josh visualized. A crowded, busy, metropolitan city with the largest population in Mexico. Josh's ultimate destination was the Metropolitan Cathedral of the Assumption of the Blessed Virgin Mary. However, he made arrangements to stay at St. Jose's, one of the local smaller churches in the city.

Father Ronaldo met him at the door. He was a short, cheerful man of only 5'2". However, despite his size, he was a 'no nonsense' person who was in command of everything occurring in his parish. He welcomed Josh with open arms and to Josh's surprise, he along with his fellow priests knew of him and the message he was delivering. Josh was amazed and so pleased as to how far the Lord's message had traveled into South America. Unfortunately, despite it being proclaimed in many churches, the people who really needed it were not hearing the message.

Father Ronaldo said it was like preaching to the choir. The people who really needed to hear the massage were, for the most part, non-church goers and most probably nonbelievers.

"You have your work cut out for yourself," Father Ronaldo said to Josh as they enjoyed a glass of wine.

Josh agreed and was committed to deliver the message to as many as possible. One thing he was sure of, Jesus was in charge.

Early the next morning, after Mass and a small breakfast, Josh was out and about, walking the city streets. No sooner had he walked a few blocks when he came upon a red-light area. Although Josh knew prostitution was legal in Mexico, with close to 300,000 prostitutes, he was surprised and saddened to see so many soliciting their service so publicly.

As he continued to walk, a young girl, who probably wasn't older than sixteen, came up to him.

"Can I make you happy today?" she asked with no hesitation, despite Josh being dressed in his priestly garb.

"No, thank you," he said as he smiled at her and continued walking.

Not far from her was an apparently homeless beggar sitting against a wall. Josh stopped, sat down next to the beggar, and began to talk. This caught the attention of several young ladies soliciting in the area. Although they could not hear the conversation, they remained focused on such an unusual sight.

As they approached closer, the beggar wrapped his arms around Josh. It was then that they realized that the beggar was a cripple, seeing his crutches lying on the

CHAPTER X

sidewalk next to him. Suddenly, Josh helped him up and through the power and will of God, the man could walk.

Crying and praising Jesus with his hands waving over his head, he yelled out with joy, "I can walk! I can walk! Praise Jesus! I can walk..."

Repeating it over and over, he ran down the street. All the girls stood watching perplexed and astonished at what they had just witnessed. Josh, now standing close to them, smiled and in a very kind and forgiving voice said, "Jesus loves each of you also, but He's so saddened by your sins. I know life is hard here, but you always have a choice."

With that, he turned and continued his morning walk. Unbeknownst to him, one of the girls followed him, most likely because of curiosity and also because she was touched by what he had said and what she had just seen. After a few more blocks, stopping periodically to talk to people, and to ask directions to the Cathedral, he came upon a bunch of boys playing football in one of the few open fields in the city.

As he was watching them, a wild throw flew close to his head. Immediately reaching up, he caught the ball and threw it back, a perfect spiral, just as he always did in high school.

"Nice catch", one of the boys yelled out.

"Nice pass", another said.

None of the kids could pass very well, so when they saw a perfect spiral, they were pretty impressed.

"Hey Father," another boy yelled out, "how about throwing a few to us?"

"Sure, it's been a while, but I'll do my best."

Before long, Josh was passing the ball to each as they lined up to wait their turn. Eventually he began to instruct them how to correctly hold, throw, catch and kick. Kicking was the icing on the cake. They were mesmerized at how far Josh could kick the ball and were so eager to learn his

REPARATION: A STORY OF HOPE

technique. Finally, after close to two hours, Josh said he had to leave.

"Please stay, Father, please stay." They cried out together. Josh smiled and assured them they would see him again.

It was then that Josh caught the eye of a young boy sitting on the grass watching as the other boys continue to play.

"Why don't you join them?" Josh asked.

However, as he stepped closer to him, he could have bit his tongue realizing that the boy was missing a leg. Josh sat down next to the boy.

"What's your name?"

"Anthony," the kid said, "but everyone calls me Tony".

"Well Tony, do you like football?"

"Sure," the boy replied but he didn't have to say another word as Josh could see that his heart was broken from not being able to play and join-in with the other boys.

As Josh hugged the boy, he silently prayed that the boy's leg be restored. "Let his healing be a sign for all to see that you are Lord, and your message of love and reparation is real."

Tony had no clue what was going on.

"Do you love Jesus?" Josh asked.

"Sure, I love Him very much. I go to church with my mom and dad every Sunday."

"Well Tony, Jesus loves you also, and because He loves you so much, he's going to give you your leg back."

Tony just stared at Josh.

"Now, I want you to close your eyes, and say one Hail Mary. When you're done, then open your eyes and you will have your new leg. Will you do that Tony?"

"Yes, Father I will."

"Great."

Josh stood up thanking Jesus and continued his way.

CHAPTER X

"Hail Mary, full of grace, the Lord is with thee...." Tony finished his prayer just as he promised Josh and opened his eyes. He screamed so loud that everyone in the neighborhood heard him. When Tony looked down, his missing leg was fully returned.

Pandemonium broke out as all the boys playing football ran home to tell their parents what had just occurred. The young prostitute who was watching all of this, fell to her knees and began to cry. Sister David Marie, as she would later be called after becoming a nun, would be instrumental in converting dozens of prostitutes back to the Lord.

Josh continued to visit various parts of the city and soon became quite friendly with the locals. Most of his days were spent with the sick and the poor, encouraging them and spreading the message of the Lord. Children would continuously gather around him listening to the many stories he would tell of Jesus and His disciples. Many healings occurred, although Josh was more focused on the spiritual healing of those who had lost their way.

Word had already spread that there was a young American priest in the city preaching and working miracles, and it didn't take long for Jose Hernandez to realize that his name was Father Joshua Donovan. Unfortunately, he soon got word of his location, thanks to his vast network of spies.

On a Sunday afternoon in late July, just as Josh approached the Cathedral of the Blessed Virgin Mary, a crowd of people gathered around him while he proclaimed the message of reparation and love. Eventually, he had a huge crowd of people listening to him, including many prostitutes. In addition, he noticed that Tony, his parents, and the boys who he had played football with were also present.

Josh continued delivering his message. Most listened intently. Others marveled at his youth while some were amazed at how fluent he was in speaking their language. Unfortunately, some gave him dirty looks and walked away. However, all those who did remain were touched and spiritually healed by the Lord.

Just as he was about to give his blessing to the crowd, Kapriel and Lancer surrounded Josh with their protective wings. Racing toward the Cathedral were four cars. As they turned the corner, they headed straight for Josh and gunfire soon erupted. Machine guns blasted from all the cars. People screamed and began to scatter in all directions. Many were mauled dawn by the cars, indiscriminately hoping that Josh was among their targets.

Kapriel and Lancer covered Josh as he, along with others, ran into the Cathedral for cover. "Please Jesus, spare the lives of all these people," was his prayer that he repeated while taking cover. Throughout the chaos, smoke and confusion, gunfire continued hoping that Josh was among the casualties.

By this time, the police had arrived. The square was ablaze with gunfire. Police were everywhere. Escape exits were blocked, barricaded off with police cars. However, Hernandez was well prepared. Using rocket launchers, he tried to escape by ramming through the barricades, all to no avail. Before long, a police helicopter arrived and within minutes it's heavy-duty guns and launchers eliminated one of the largest and most powerful Cartels in the country.

Inside the Cathedral, there was a lot of crying and panic. However, Josh assured them that all would be alright.

"Pray with me that Jesus will spare the lives of the faithful outside." Josh and those around him prayed for the Lord's mercy that no innocent person would be killed.

CHAPTER X

They prayed and prayed until no noise or gunfire was heard.

Newspapers reported that miraculously no bystander was killed, although many were wounded. Wounds that should have been fatal were not. Jesus had answered the prayers of His faithful. Instead of a day of mourning, the city celebrated a day of living. A miracle that not only saved the lives of many but caused thousands to repent and accept the message of Jesus.

Josh remained in the Cathedral until the wee hours of the morning. The Archbishop of the Cathedral personally drove him back to St. Jose's Church, which gave him a perfect opportunity to review with the Archbishop the entire message given to him. To Josh's joy and delight, he was promised that this message would be told throughout Mexico and that they would hold a weekly day of prayer for the reparation of sins in the world.

Just as Josh was getting into bed, a message from Rome appeared on his cellphone:

URGENT...A SECOND ATTEMPT ON THE POPE'S LIFE HAS OCCURRED...PLEASE COME QUICKLY...

CHAPTER XI

THE MAKING OF A CARDINAL

Josh looked at Kapriel and Lancer. "Do you know anything about this?"

"You need to get there as fast as you can."

"I'll call and make flight arrangements!"

"That will be too late..." Lancer said.

"The Pope has been poisoned and we need to leave...Now," Kapriel followed.

Josh looked at Kapriel with unbelieving eyes. "Poisoned?! But why? Who...?"

Kapriel didn't bother to answer, but simply instructed Josh on what to do. Without wasting any time, Josh rushed down the hall to Father Rolando's room. It was two o'clock in the morning, and Josh was sorry he had to wake his fellow priest up at such an early hour. His instructions were brief but thorough, and Father Rolando had no problem understanding them or complying with Josh's request.

Rushing back to his room, Kapriel and Lancer circled around Josh.

"Close your eyes," Kapriel said. With that command, Josh could feel a great light surrounding them. When he opened his eyes again, he was standing in front of the private entrance to the Papal palace in Rome.

"Oh, my dear Lord, how did that happen?" he blurted out, not expecting an answer.

He had experienced too many miracles to be shocked as to what Jesus could do, nevertheless, because this was a totally new experience to him, he was somewhat bewildered and shaken.

As Josh headed to the entrance, a huge demon sentinel, with its wings spread out, hissed and spitted out sulfur and slime as he guarded the entrance. It continued to hiss at Josh as he approached and raised its claw-like hands ready to strike, but immediately flew off as Kapriel and Lancer drew their swords. After knocking multiple times, Josh waited impatiently until the door finally opened. Looking up, Josh couldn't believe his eyes. Standing before him was *evil*. Cardinal Ferraro stood there with his mouth open and a brilliant red glow surrounding his head.

Cardinal Ferraro couldn't believe his eyes either. He knew Josh was supposed to be in Mexico.

"What are you doing here? How? How did you get here?

"Please step aside "Josh said, not waiting for another question.

"You're not welcome here," the Cardinal said, as he refused to move.

Without hesitating for a second, Josh reached up, grabbed him by his collar and pulled him down the steps. As he tumbled to the ground, Josh said in a stern voice, "You're a little mixed up. It's *you* that is not welcome here Now, get your things and leave."

"You're too late," Ferraro angrily said, "he's already dead."

Josh proceeded directly to the Pope's Apartment, passing another Priest with the same red haze around his head. More demons approached but scrambled away as fast as they could when they caught sight of Kapriel and

CHAPTER XI

Lancer. Reaching the top of the stairs, on the third floor, Josh turned left and headed down the hall where the Pontiff's apartment was located.

Standing in front of the closed door were two Guards. They were dressed as Swiss Vatican Guards and had been smuggled in by Cardinal Ferraro. They also were glowing red.

"Stand aside," Josh said, speaking perfect Italian.

"No one is allowed in here except Cardinal Ferraro."

Josh simply looked at them, and for some strange reason, they lowered their heads and stepped aside.

Deacon Rugato boarded Aero Mexico early in the morning and, before the sun came up, he was on his way to Rome. He was a young man studying for the priesthood in Mexico. He had blondish hair, similar to Josh. He was about the same height and age as Josh and had all the correct identification papers needed for him to identify himself as Father Joshua Donovan. The facade was created to give the impression that Father Donovan was aboard the plane, flying to Rome, when in fact, he had already been miraculously transported there.

Deacon Rugato would arrive late in the evening in Rome, be driven to the Vatican, and from the public's perspective, it would appear as if Father Donovan was entering the Papal Palace at approximately 11:00pm. In the meantime, Deacon Rugato would change into layman's clothes and be back on his way to Mexico City, without anyone knowing the better.

Cardinal Mancini and Monsignor Angelino quickly greeted Josh with open arms as he entered the Pontiff's bedroom, although they had no idea how Josh had arrived so quickly after Cardinal Mancini's phone message.

REPARATION: A STORY OF HOPE

"He's pretty bad," Cardinal Mancini said, wiping the tears from his eyes.

He told Josh how quickly the Pope had taken ill, and that Cardinal Ferraro had just about taken over the moment the Pontiff got sick. He insisted that he had seniority and that he was in charge. He refused to allow anyone into the room except his physicians, who were perplexed as to what was ailing the Pontiff. They all agreed it appeared he likely acquired some strange virus or perhaps had some kind of food poisoning, but they felt that was highly unlikely. However, no conclusions could be made until extensive tests were done. By then, they said, he most likely would be dead.

Josh told Cardinal Mancini and Monsignor Angelino that the Pontiff did not have a virus but was poisoned. They both looked at Josh with unbelieving eyes but were well aware that Jesus had often given Josh insight into various matters and had no reason to doubt him. Likewise, they were aware that the Pope had many enemies. Many were not in agreement with the Pontiff's philosophy and how the church was being governed. But to attempt murder on the Pope, especially after the kidnapping scandal when Josh was previously in Rome, was beyond their imagination.

"Come, kneel and pray with me."

All three laid hands on the Pontiff and asked for the Lord's healing. Cardinal Mancini continued to weep as he held the hand of his stricken friend. It wasn't long before the Pope opened his eyes and took a deep breath. Cardinal Mancini immediately kissed the hand of his dear friend while praising Jesus for the healing that just occurred.

Angelino kept his head on the bed as he prayed and thanked Jesus. Likewise, Josh thanked the Lord for his mercy and asked for His help in restoring the integrity of the Vatican and identifying all those who were involved in

CHAPTER XI

the attempted murder of the Pontiff. All three continued to pray until the Pope sat up and cheerfully greeted his most loyal friends.

Pope Nicholas was in his late seventies, but to Josh's disappointment, he looked like he had aged ten years since he had last seen him. The strain and heaviness of the last year had taken a heavy toll on the Pontiff.

Unknown to the Pope, there was far more corruption in the Vatican than previously believed. Additionally, there was a network of Vatican Priests and lay people that were also involved in the plot to destroy the Pope and the Church.

The four sat and talked for hours. Pope Nicholas told Josh that he believed there was an undercurrent of plots to oust him from office. Last Christmas, several Cardinals, including Cardinal Ferraro, seemed so concerned about the Pontiff's health that they practically insisted that he retire and allow someone younger to take over his office.

Cardinal Mancini said he was against the Pope's retirement, and thereafter was ostracized by many of his fellow Cardinals and Bishops, even those who he believed were acting in the best interest of the Pontiff. Monsignor Angelino related how many of the younger priests often came to him complaining about the Pope. 'Why can't he be a little more liberal?' they would ask, especially when it comes to morality, homosexuality, and their role in the Church. Several that 'the Pope has to go.'

"And who would replace him?" I asked. "Cardinal Ferraro was their reply."

"Cardinal Ferraro is evil, and so are those guards at your door," Josh said. "They are imposters and work for Ferraro. I don't know all those who are involved in this plot, but with the help of God, we will find out."

The two guards stationed at the bedroom were more than surprised when the Pontiff opened the doors and walked out along with the other three. Two legitimate Swiss Guards escorted the two intruders out of the building and immediately placed them into custody.

Sitting in his office, the Pontiff instructed Monsignor Angelino to give him a list of all guards and personnel that Cardinal Ferraro had recently hired. An order was immediately issued to dismiss all those on the list. It was soon discovered that a new cook was also hired by Cardinal Ferraro and coincidentally shortly after that, the Pope got ill.

Josh instructed several trusted Swiss Guards to search the personal belongings of the new cook. It didn't take long for them to discover the poison that was used in the attempted murder of the Pope. After extensive questioning, the cook admitted that he was promised a considerable sum of money by Cardinal Ferraro if he would carry out his plan to eliminate the Pontiff. Cardinal Ferraro, several young Vatican priests, the 'physician' that examined the Pope, and several other imposter Vatican guards that he recently hired, were nowhere to be found.

Josh was sure that the evil in the Vatican was far more extensive than the few that they were already aware of. Vatican authorities were called, including the City 'Polizia' and the 'Corps of Gendarmerie,' to conduct the investigation. However, it would take weeks for them to fully understand the extent of the conspiracy. Of course, the entire investigation was kept a strict secret to protect the integrity of the Pope and Church.

From the time Josh left the Vatican one year ago, Satan and his evil army were well at work, infiltrating both Rome and the Vatican. Abaddon, one of Satan's highest Generals, was placed charge of the campaign to remove the Pope by any means possible, and to replace him with Cardinal Ferraro, who was under his direct control.

CHAPTER XI

Abaddon gathered a legion of warriors and deceivers that entered the city shortly after Josh left.

Because of Cardinal Ferraro's envy and lust for power, he was especially vulnerable and had succumbed to the will of Abaddon. He soon was not only planning the murder of the Pope but was recruiting as many as he could from the Vatican to join his campaign. Abaddon was also aware of Josh and the miracles he had performed. Although he was not afraid of him, he knew he would be difficult to contend with.

Three days later the Holy Father called a meeting of the resident Vatican Cardinals, Monsignors, Priests, and Staff. After reviewing his conservative traditional philosophy on governing and his plans to rid the Church of all the corruption going on within it, he instructed all those who could not support his goals to immediately leave and to resign from their positions. Everyone sat completely stunned waiting for something to happen.

Finally, one newly ordained priest got up and left. Most of the permanent residents, Vatican Staff, Monsignors, Bishops and Cardinals remained in their seats. Several Monsignors, one Bishop and two Cardinals, along with seven newly ordained Vatican Priests also remained. They all sat there innocently hiding their loyalty to Satan. Although they looked innocent enough, they were unable to hide the red glows emanating around their heads from Josh.

Josh and Pope Nicholas meet immediately after the meeting. Josh took note of those who were under the control of Satan and gave their names to the Pontiff.

"Your Holiness, please trust me when I tell you these people are evil. They are trying to infiltrate and destroy you and the Church. Please, get rid of them immediately."

Holding his head, he continued in a frustrated voice, "I just can't understand how they all have rejected Jesus in such a short time since I saw them a year ago."

The next morning Josh had another private meeting with Pope Nicholas and was relieved to hear that the Pontiff had already taken action with all those on the list.

"Your Holiness, these people who you have ousted are more than evil, they are directly working for Satan and are under his control. I realize that you have already expelled them from the Vatican and have stripped them of their priestly duties. However, your Holiness…here comes the bad part…

"It's not these men so much we have to fear, but the evil forces that are at work here in the city. Satan and his army of demons are everywhere. They are infiltrating Rome and Vatican City by the thousands. By the *thousands*, your Holiness."

Because Josh could see beyond the veil of human sight, he could see that there was far more evil present than he had expected. Almost every building had demons perched on it, waiting to attack anyone susceptible to weakness.

"Their mission is to deceive as many as possible. They will try to deceive people to believe that you are changing the inherent integrity of the Church, and even that you are ruling under the influence of the evil one."

Josh continued to address the Pope. "I know what I have told you is difficult to comprehend and even harder to believe, but once again, I can only tell you what I have said is true, as Jesus has revealed it to me."

Pope Nicholas listened intently to every word Josh had said.

"What concerns me the most," the Pontiff said, "is the demonic attacks going on against God's people, and unfortunately the youth are easy prey. Schools, social gathering places, and clubs where kids and young adults

CHAPTER XI

hang out, are all places for demons to pull our young into their webs of deception and lies. I'm sure those responsible for the attempts on my life will be found and punished. However, the infiltration of evil in this city is another story."

"Your Holiness, I'm sure you know, as well as I do, that Jesus will show us exactly what needs to be done to defeat this attack."

"I know He will. He always does." However, as the meeting ended, the concerned expression on the Pontiff's face was still there.

Multiple Bishops and Cardinals, including the Pope and Josh, prayed for hours in one of the larger chapels within the Vatican. All agreed to fast and bypass dinner. Eventually evening came. Josh went to his room, and began his ritual of rosary prayer and intercession, joined with Kapriel and Lancer. Finishing his prayers, Josh sat perplexed and extremely concerned. Looking directly at his two Guardians, he said, "I just reminded Pope Nicholas that Jesus will help us, but look at me, I'm the one worried as what to do next."

Kapriel and Lancer smiled, reassuring him, as they always did, that Jesus was present and already very much engaged in all that was occurring.

No sooner had Josh gotten into bed, then he sprung up rushing for the phone. Picking it up, he called Monsignor Angelino. Answering the phone, Angelino immediately thought it was an emergency.

"No, I apologize, it's not an emergency," Josh said. "I'm wondering if you know the name of the young priest who walked out of Pope Nicholas's meeting yesterday?"

After several minutes of thought, Angelino said his name was Father Brice. "Shawn Brice," he repeated. "Just ordained last year. Very intelligent and speaks multilingual languages. His Holiness had high hopes for this young man... but I guess that's not going to work out."

"We'll see," Josh replied. "I'd like to contact him if I can find out his whereabouts."

Monsignor Angelino said he recalled him coming from a parish in the north part of Rome.

"Let me see now...Saint...St. Angela Merci. Yes, that's correct. St. Angela Merci. Is there something else I can help you with?"

"No, not at this time. Thanks, and please keep me in your prayers."

"I will," the Monsignor said, as he hung up the phone.

Josh looked at Kapriel and Lancer smiling. "I believe the Lord just told me where to begin."

Josh couldn't believe how spiritually dark Vatican City was, and for that matter, how dark most of Rome was. Being able to view the ugliness and the perpetual attacks of evil forces, Josh was frightened as his driver drove him through the city. Had it not been for Kapriel and Lancer constantly at his side, he knew he would be overcome with horror and trepidation. As Josh left the city, he could see demonic battles taking place everywhere. Fiery ashes were exploding like there was a celebration in town. Unfortunately, this was far from anything to celebrate.

After driving for some time, Josh was shocked to see a trail of demons following the car. These demons were nothing like he had seen before. They were extremely large, with long slender bodies, and bright yellow eyes, twice the size of humans. The most unusual features were their exceptionally long sweeping black wings. Josh estimated their wingspan to be at least twelve feet. Thinking to himself, these creatures looked more like birds of prey rather than attack demons. They had football

CHAPTER XI

shaped heads and displayed huge eight-fingered sharp claws that clearly could lift a car as easily as an eagle could catch a fish.

Just as Josh looked toward Kapriel and Lancer, one of these demons crashed through the front window, sinking his claws into the driver's chest, and carrying him off, easily ripping him in half. Instantly the car was airborne, carried off by another one of these creatures who, after violently shaking the car back and forth, as if it were a rag doll, finally tossed it away, watching it crash and flip down the hillside, eventually ending in a fiery crash. Circling the wreck, the demons were satisfied with their attack and eventually flew off boasting about their accomplishment.

Kapriel told Josh to remain still until he was sure the demons were gone. Evidently, the demons knew nothing about the shield that protected Josh. Exiting the engulfed car unharmed, Josh quickly flagged down a driver who kindly gave him a ride back to the Vatican. Thanking the driver, he began his walk back to the Pope's residence. Once he arrived, although he was exhausted, he related all that had just happened, including the tragic death of the driver, to the Pontiff and Cardinal Mancini. Pope Nicholas was visibly shaken and immediately retired to his chapel where he prayed for and mourned his driver.

Abaddon was not happy when the two demons reported their attack on Josh.

"You stupid fools!" he screamed. "Who gave you permission to attack him?"

Knowing that they made that decision themselves, they simply stood silent, quivering in place.

"Don't you know, you idiots, that Donovan can't be destroyed as long as his Guardians are with him???"

"But we saw the car explode into flames…" one of the demons reluctantly said.

Now screaming at the top of his lungs, Abaddon was furious. "Didn't you hear me? *He can't be destroyed.* Our mission is to destroy the Pope, and to assure that Ferraro replaces him, not to attack the Donovan priest! Now get out of here and back to your assigned duties before I really lose my temper and crush you with my own hands.

As it turned out, the young Father Brice was not at St. Angela Merci Church at all, but rather was still in Vatican City. Fortunately, Josh was told by a friend of the young priest that he could most likely be found at his favorite hangout, Luelli's Pizzeria and Bar, just outside the city walls. Exhausted as he was, Josh decided to look for him before the hour got too late.

Changing into regular lay clothes, so as not to be recognized and inundated with healing requests, Josh was on his way. Not sure where the Pizzeria was, he stopped to ask someone for directions. Continuing toward the Pizzeria, he spotted a small church and decided to make a quick stop for a prayer or two. Entering the church, two small evil sentinels were startled and immediately flew away. Josh prayed for guidance and asked the Holy Spirit to guide him in whatever needed to be said.

Opening the door to Luelli's, he was reminded of the smell of smoke and at the dingy bar in Clarksville, where Jesus had restored the missing leg of the Veteran, Zachary Jones. However, unlike the bar in Clarksville, Luelli's was an all-gay establishment. Realizing this, Josh quietly suggested to Kapriel and Lancer that they might want to remain outside. Both looked at Josh with a 'you've got to be kidding' look.

"OK," Josh said, as they entered the place.

Immediately the smell of sulfur was overwhelming and the many demons throughout the place scattered as far

CHAPTER XI

away from Kapriel and Lancer as soon as they caught sight of them. No sooner had Josh taken one step into the bar when he was met with friendly and suggestive looks and smiles. Some were dressed in tight black leather pants. Others simply wore tight jeans, while almost everyone was shirtless. Loud music was blasting. Most were dancing, some were making out and flirting with each other, while others were simply drinking and chatting.

"I'm looking for Shawn Brice," Josh asked as he walked up to the bar.

Before the bartender had a chance to answer, a shirtless young kid stepped behind Josh. Putting his arm around Josh's waist, he said, "What can I do to please you?"

A little startled, Josh turned and said, "Nothing, unless you can tell me where I can find Shawn Brice."

"Oh, that's too bad. I was hoping we could get together... you know...for a little fun," he said with a big grin on his face. "However, if it's Shawn you're looking for, he's downstairs," pointing to the direction of the dimly lit stairs. As Josh started to walk toward the steps, the kid yelled, "However, you won't have as much fun with him as you would have had with me." With that comment, he and a few others broke into laughter.

Reaching the bottom of the steps, Josh saw Shawn sitting by himself at another smaller bar located at the far end of the room. The music was also loud, the place reeked of beer, weed, and smoke, and the lights, as one might expect, were very dim. Unlike the general atmosphere upstairs, downstairs offered an opportunity for erotic dancing, touching, and even some nudity. Some guys walked around in leather jockstraps, as if this was normal dress.

Wasting no time, Josh sat down next to Shawn.

"What'll ya have?" the bartender asked.

REPARATION: A STORY OF HOPE

"Coors Light," Josh replied as he and Shawn greeted each other with a quick nod. Shawn did not recognize Josh and continued to drink his beer.

"Put it on my tab," Shawn told the bartender without looking up.

"Thanks," Josh replied looking directly at Shawn. Not getting a response, finally Josh turned and asked, "What are you doing in a place like this?"

A little bewildered and irritated, Shawn answered, "What the hell do you think I'm here for. This is a gay bar and I'm gay."

"You're also a priest."

"What!" Shawn blurted out, spitting some of his own drink, as he looked at Josh with confusion. As he continued to stare at Josh, he finally recognized him.

"What the hell are you here for?" he asked.

"I'm here for you."

"Look Father Donovan or whoever you are... I know you're a holy person but cut the crap. You need to get out of here. This is no place for you."

"It's no place for you either," Josh immediately replied.

Now quite annoyed and feeling the mood of the night getting ruined, Shawn threw back the last of his beer and stood up, ready to leave.

"Where are you going?"

"None of your business," Shawn answered without looking back at Josh.

"Won't you even take a minute to talk to me?"

"Look, I've come here to have a good time, to dance and to have some fun. Sex, to be exact. I came here to have sex."

Josh persisted. "Just give me a few minutes, that's all I'm asking. Just a couple of minutes of your time and then I'll be gone."

Shawn turned facing Josh and flipped him the finger.

CHAPTER XI

"What are you afraid of? Aren't you at all curious as to why I've taken time to find you and to talk?"

Shawn turned away from Josh once again, then suddenly stopped. Still with his back to Josh, he said, "Ok, Father, if you want to talk, come dance with me...if you dare".

Josh, somewhat shocked, contemplated the invitation for a minute. He thought to himself, "If that's what it takes to talk, then sure, why not."

"Don't worry," he said to Kapriel and Lancer. I won't take off my shirt."

"What did you say?" the bartender asked.

"Oh, nothing. I was just talking to my angels."

"What?" the bartender said over the noise, and without waiting for a response, he walked toward another customer at the far end of the bar, twirling a finger around his ear indicating that this guy is crazy. Kapriel and Lancer laughed.

"You know," Kapriel said, "I bet you probably can't even dance."

The music was fast and so was the dancing. Josh was considerably uncomfortable, but to his Guardians' surprise, was quite a good dancer. Shawn was having a blast, or at least he appeared to be. In fact, Shawn was quite surprised that Josh had agreed to dance with him at all.

"So, what do you want to talk about?"

"I want to talk about you and why you left the meeting."

"What?" Shawn shouted. "I can hardly hear you."

The smile on his face indicated that the comment was just a load of crap. In fact, Shawn was thoroughly enjoying himself, or at the very least, he was forcing Donovan to dance with him in a gay bar. After a few minutes, which seemed like an eternity to Josh, the music slowed. Without hesitating, Shawn stepped forward and embraced Josh.

Both said nothing as Shawn stepped closer and tightened his grip.

"That's better. Now I can hear you."

Josh stopped dancing.

"Look Shawn, let's stop this game. I really would like to talk to you if you would give me a few minutes."

Standing still facing each other, Shawn looked perplexed not knowing exactly what to say. Finally, as if Shawn broke out of a trance, he said, "OK, a deal's a deal…you've got ten minutes."

Luelli, the owner of the bar, was good friends with Shawn, and allowed them to meet in his private office on the top floor, secluded and away from everyone including the noise.

"Your ten minutes have officially started," Shawn said, as he sat down.

"I was pretty positive there was a good reason why you left the meeting, but to tell you the truth, I felt compelled to find you and to ask you directly why."

"Go ahead, ask."

"Well, why did you leave?"

"That should be obvious. I'm gay and the Pope hates homosexuality, or at least it appears that he does. He made it clear that unless we were on board with him and his policies, we were to resign and leave."

"That's not true, the Pope does not hate gays."

"Come on Father, if he doesn't hate gays, the Church he rules does, or at least their policies reflect it."

"That's also not true."

"True or not, that's the way it's often expressed and the way I perceive it. I knew when I became a priest that I could be true to my vows and wanted to set an example for other gay priests, as well as helping those in the gay communities to find the Lord. However, after working in the Vatican, I feel there's no way this could ever be

CHAPTER XI

possible, nor would I ever be accepted, not by my fellow priests, not by the Pope and probably, not even by my parents."

"Have you ever talked to anyone about it?" Josh asked.

"You've gotta be kidding... come on Father Donovan, give me a break. You know how people still feel about gays. Besides, no one except the people in this bar know that I'm gay, not even my parents."

"Why not?"

"For starters? Fear, I suppose. My parents are *very* Catholic. Besides, I suspect that I would have never been allowed to be a priest in the first place, if they knew I was gay."

"You're wrong," Josh said with conviction. "Times have changed."

"Open your eyes, Father. Times may have changed, but people have not... not really. And even if I am wrong, how do I minister to anyone when the Church says there are only right and wrong answers? I feel hypocritical when all I can offer is standard answers that represent a moral vs. immoral philosophy. How do I tell young kid who is struggling with their sexuality that they have to be celebrate the rest of their life in order to be loved by God and accepted by the Church? And yet, they are human, and therefore sexual beings like all of us. And then comes the sin part. They want to know if they were made in the image of God, like everyone else, if it is still a sin…How does one truly answer these kinds of questions?"

The expression on Shawn's face was rapidly changing and Josh could clearly see he was getting angry. "Times is ticking, Father. Your ten minutes is just about over."

Josh knew what he was about to say could be the difference in whether or not he would be successful in helping this troubled priest. Finally, after asking the Holy Spirit for guidance, Josh made one last attempt.

"Shawn, I know you are upset, but I hope you will be able to hear my perspective. You and I both know that morality is the same for everyone, single, gay, lesbian, or married. There aren't two sets of rules. Jesus asks all of us to live a moral life. It's the same for everyone, no matter what your sexual preference is.

"However, I believe the difficulty is the assessment of sin... what is sin? What is a serious sin? Or less serious? Here's where perhaps the Church has standard answers that may or may not necessarily be appropriate or even accurate. Of course, there must be standard rules to follow. People procrastinate and usually do what is easiest or most appealing to them. However, there are always exceptions. I truly don't know how you would counsel a person as to what is sin unless you know the circumstances and facts involved. It would depend on so many factors, and then I'm not sure one could make a hands-down judgement. I *do* know however, that Jesus can. I also know that I would not be quick to judge and act as to its sinfulness. Judgement is always up to the Lord, not us."

Looking intently into Shawn's eyes, Josh continued, "I know my time is running short but let me just say a few more things. First let me say you are not hated by me and I'm sure not by the Pope or any clergy in the Church. And I'm even more sure your parents will always love you, whether you are straight or gay. I'm sorry that you feel differently, but I hope as time goes by, you will come to realize just how much you are loved.

"As for how to counsel, only you can answer that question, according to what the Church teaches and to the specific situation as the Lord speaks to you. I, for one, believe sin can become a very complicated issue. As an example, some things that are traditionally considered sinful may not be as sinful as we were taught to believe. Depending on the age of the person, on the circumstances,

CHAPTER XI

and emotional stability and even the habitual addictiveness. Who am I to judge?

"Likewise, living together, same sex or not, is another difficult question to answer regarding its sinfulness. Two people who truly love each other, who have committed their lives to each other, who have remained faithful to each other, perhaps have raised children, and led a Christian life of love and sharing, may not be living in sin as we so often say they are. Again, only Jesus knows what's in their hearts and only He can truly judge them.

"Unfortunately, we as human beings are too quick to judge and label and condemn people based simply on what we see. As for me, I will always tell people what the Church teaches and hopefully lead them to the right decisions, but as far as sin and judgement, that's up to the Lord. My job is to love and to share my love and Jesus's love as much as I can. And I truly believe you can do the same. I believe Jesus has called you to His Church for a reason and that if you accept it, your ministry will be the very thing that helps people, especially gay people, to find the Lord."

Shawn sat still, not paying attention to the ten minutes that had long passed. Josh, still trying to get to the heart of the reason why he had left the meeting, continued and hoped to break through any barriers that still might be there.

"So, let's be truthful with one another, what's really bothering you?"

Shawn continued to sit, staring at the desk. Without looking up, and with a soft quivering voice, he confessed, "I hate being gay. I hate myself and I think people hate me and, believe me or not, I think Jesus hates me too."

Shawn continued to sit with his head held down. Tears and emotion were welling up inside him, and for the first time in his life, he revealed his innermost feelings and pain.

In a sense, he looked as if he was carrying the weight of the world.

After hearing what Shawn said, especially how wrong he was about how people viewed him, Josh could not hide his own emotion. He knew that Jesus loved Shawn more than he could ever imagine, but how would he ever relate that to him? Again, after asking the Holy Spirit for help, words began to flow.

"I don't know why someone is born cripple, or why another has deformities. I can't tell you why one person is born blind while others have perfect eyesight. Why are there people of different colors? Why was I born white, and my best friend born black? I can't tell you why some are born with all kinds of talents while others appear to have none. Why are some born with too few or too many chromosomes? Why are some gay while others are straight? Only God can answer these questions. I do know however, that we all have a purpose in life and that Jesus loves all of us exactly as we are. He loves me, and Shawn… He loves you, and He is calling you home. He loves you so much that if you were the only person in the world, He would go through his entire passion all over again just for you."

Josh took hold of Shawn's hands. "Close your eyes and let Jesus show you just how much He loves you."

Instantly, the vision of Jesus' passion unfolded. From the agony in the garden, the scourging, the crowning of thorns, the carrying of the heavy cross, to the crucifixion. Shawn was present, witnessing the entire event. No other witnesses were there.

Shawn realized that every painful lash of the whip, every painful fall, every nail that pierced His hands and feet, and every drop of blood, was shed for him. And as Jesus hung dying on the cross, taking His last breath, Shawn knew He did it just for him.

CHAPTER XI

Shawn never looked up at Josh but simply cried his heart out. For the first time in his life, he realized just how much he was loved and how much Jesus loved him. Loved him just as he was, and from that day on, he pledged himself to live a chaste life, loving the Lord and serving Him as His priest for the rest of his life.

Breakfast the next morning was a bit unusual, as it was rare that the Pope joined them for their morning meal. After the blessing and just as coffee was being served, all conversation suddenly came to an abrupt stop. Shawn was standing at the far end of the room. As soon as Pope Nicholas saw him, he rushed directly toward him and without hesitation, embraced him with love and acceptance.

Shawn fell to his knees and begged forgiveness from the Pope. Although no one could hear them, everyone knew that the Pope was showering him with love and mercy. Josh could not help smiling, as he recalled one of his favorite biblical verses in Luke's gospel:

'He was still a long way from home when his father saw him; his heart was filled with pity, and he ran, threw his arms around his son, and kissed him. Father, the son said, I have sinned against God and against you. I am no longer fit to be called your son. But the father called to his servants, Hurry! He said. Bring the best robe and put it on him. Put a ring on his finger and shoes on his feet. Then go and get the prize cafe and kill it and let us celebrate with a feast! For this son of mine was dead, but now he is alive; he was lost but now he has been found.'

REPARATION: A STORY OF HOPE

Inspector Roberto Vintani, who was heading up the investigation concerning the attempted attack on the Pope's life, received an anonymous call from someone deep inside Father Ferraro's organization late in the evening. Evidently, a young priest within his network was having second thoughts about joining Ferraro's efforts to replace the Pope. Initially, the young priest was under the impression that the Pope would be removed peacefully or forced to retire. However, when he realized that the Pontiff was poisoned, he wanted no part of the conspiracy.

Remorsefully, he called Inspector Vintani, revealing the whereabouts of Ferraro and his associates, who all were a part of the plot to kill the Pope. No sooner had he hung up when two strong guards of Ferraro grabbed him and dragged him back to the center room where they had been holding satanic rituals. The young priest's shirt was stripped off. Hung up with both arms stretched out, Ferraro had him beaten and whipped until he was dead with little to nothing left on his back except bloody bones. Demons were exhilarated. His blood was collected and placed on an altar for future veneration.

Abaddon sat on his perch high above the altar witnessing the entire event. Without wasting any time, he summoned the same two demons he reprimanded for attacking Josh.

"Make sure the Inspector never has a chance to report our location to anyone. Now go, and this time don't screw up."

Large, black shadows silhouetted the walls of buildings as they searched for the whereabouts of the inspector. Circling in the sky above and scanning the area with their large yellow-piercing eyes, they finally spotted him.

After receiving the phone call, Vintani made a U-turn and immediately headed back to his office. Although it was late in the evening and no one was there, he was ready to

CHAPTER XI

summon his team and initiate an immediate search. Getting out of his car, he sensed something in the air.

Walking beside the tall brick wall, heading for the steps to his office, he stopped and turned, thinking he saw shadows on the wall, yet nothing was there. He still felt uneasy, and cold sweat began to form on his brow. Something was not quite right, and he knew it.

Before he could take another step, multiple long, sharp fingerlike claws sunk into his shoulders as he was lifted into the air. Screaming with pain, he was immediately tossed to the other demon who caught him on the downfall. Tossed back and forth like a rag doll, it didn't matter; he was already dead with so many puncture wounds before they ripped him apart.

Just before noon the next day, the Vatican learned that the body of Roberto Vintani was found. Evidently, the consensus was that a rogue animal had attacked him. His body was found mutilated and in multiple pieces. Tragic as it was, the investigation of the attempted murder continued with his assistant now in charge.

Unknown to anyone, the young Father Brice knew the whereabouts of the compound. Shawn had attended a sex party at the location some months ago, and it didn't take long for him to put two and two together to figure out that it must be the same place where Ferraro was hiding. Shawn consulted with the investigators and concluded that the best time to approach the compound would be at night when everyone from all parts of town would most likely be there.

By evening, just as Shawn predicted, all were present at the compound located outside of the Vatican walls, toward the north section of Rome. A small army of police from the Vatican and the city were in the process of surrounding the compound. Unaware of the police activity, Ferraro continued planning his attack on the Vatican. His team was organized and ready. Weapons and ammunition were distributed.

A half-dozen of Ferraro's men wore Swiss Guard uniforms. They would lead two dozen of the attack team into the Vatican. Once inside, others loyal to Ferraro would follow, and before long, a new Pontiff would be in place. Later he planned a rigged election to give the appearance that he was legitimately voted into office. By that time, Satan would already oversee the Catholic Church.

Abaddon had recalled most of his army of demons who also were assembled within the compound. They, being so intent on the instructions that Ferraro was giving and on the scent of the bloody decaying mutilated body of the priest still hanging from the rafters, were oblivious as to what was going on outside. Rain was falling and the sky was alive with thunder and lightning.

People were in prayer from all parts of the world. Pope Nicholas had made an appeal to all churches to pray for the defeat of evil in the world and especially in Rome and the Vatican. Priests, Bishops, and Cardinals personally reached out to all the parishes in their dioceses for prayers. Likewise, Josh also contacted many of the churches he had visited in the United States and Mexico. Thousands were in prayer as the attack was about to begin

At approximately 11:00pm, an announcement blasted out from a bull horn asking all those inside to surrender.

"The compound is surrounded, come out now or we will open fire. You have five minutes to decide."

Pope Nicholas had remained at the Vatican surrounded by his Swiss Guard. However, Josh chose to join the brigade of police, in hopes that he might somehow be able to stop the shed of innocent blood. Five minutes passed,

CHAPTER XI

but no one had surrendered. A second appeal for surrender was made and still no response.

Suddenly, Josh looked up into the sky.

"Oh, my Dear Lord," he said out loud.

Several standing close to him were bewildered as to what he had just said. Still looking up, Josh continued to speak.

"Not even the powers of Hell will prevail against the Lord's Church."

No one knew exactly what he was saying or what he meant. Descending from the dark clouds, thousands of Angelic Warrior Angels, dressed in brilliant white robes, hovered above the compound, preventing any demon from escaping. Before the command was given to storm the compound, Josh was already approaching its heavy doors. Upon reaching them, the locked doors miraculously burst open, allowing Josh to enter. Demons scattered in all directions as Kapriel and Lancer surrounded Josh with their swords drawn. Gunfire broke out from everywhere inside. Nothing, of course, penetrated the shield surrounding Josh. When the bullets ended, Josh stood there totally unharmed. There was total silence and astonishment.

Josh calmly pleaded with everyone to surrender so that no harm would come to anyone. Demons hissed and cursed while not a person responded to Josh's appeal. Leaving the compound, the doors slammed shut. Thunder erupted, shaking the ground, as if an earthquake was occurring. Fear struck everyone, inside and outside, as horrendous rain and thunder continued.

The Angelic Warriors continued to remain in place while bolts of lightning lit up the sky. To say that everyone was afraid would be an understatement. Finally, a huge, crashing bolt of lightning struck the center of the compound. Instantly, it exploded into a brilliant flash of light as flames consumed everything and everyone inside. The ground shook and the compound began to sink into the depths of the earth.

When it was over, not a single person nor a single demon was alive. Nothing remained but smoke and a pile of ash where the compound once stood. No gun was fired from any person outside, and not a single police officer was harmed. Josh continued to gaze at the destruction, as he repeated what he had previously said.

"Not even the powers of Hell will prevail against the Lord's Church..."

During the next seven months, the prayer vigil continued. The plot to kill the Pope had been defeated, and the demonic attacks on the people of Rome and the Vatican were getting weaker and weaker by the day. Josh went from church to church, town to town, preaching and spreading the message of reparation of sins. Miracles were performed. As time went by, it became necessary for the Pope to assign an entourage of Swiss Guards and Priests to protect and assist Josh wherever he went, as people often flocked to him in groves when they heard he was visiting their town.

Father Brice joined Josh on many occasions, and both of them had a tremendous effect on the gay communities of the country. Although some people were still prejudice, many were realizing that we are all children of God and deserve all the love we can give each other. Josh made it a priority to visit as many towns as possible in Italy before he left to ensure that the message of reparation was heard.

Additionally, he often visited the sick. Most visits were unannounced because he did not want the herds of people to disrupt the communities and hospitals. Food facilities and housing for the needy were also established in many

CHAPTER XI

towns, as a direct result of the continuation of the John R. Fitzpatrick Foundation for the Needy.

November came and went. Christmas was once again approaching, and Josh was looking forward to spending it with Pope Nicholas for the second time. Preparations were made for Midnight Mass at the Vatican. As before, Josh was amazed at the number of preparations necessary for such an occasion. However, unlike the last time, Josh was on the altar as one of those honored to assist in the celebration of the Eucharist.

More people attended this Mass than ever before in the history of the Church. Thousands were present. Well over a thousand stood in the freezing cold outside of St. Peter's Square, thankful to be able to take part in this Christmas ceremony and hopeful to get a blessing from the Pope, and perhaps even a healing from Father Donovan.

The Pope gave a warm and emotional homily, stressing, love, forgiveness, and charity. Additionally, he spent considerable time repeating the message given to Josh for the reparation of our sins and the sins of the world. In his ending remarks, breaking traditional protocol, he personally thanked Father Donovan for the many blessings that were given to the people of Italy and throughout the world, and especially, for the many miracles that Jesus had performed through Josh and his ministry. Just after the Pope's final blessing, he unexpectedly asked everyone to be seated.

Then turning to Josh, he asked him to come forward. There was complete silence in the Basilica, as nothing like this had ever occurred at the end of a Christmas Mass before. Pope Nicholas signaled to several of his senior Cardinals to come forward. They were holding a red 'Zucchetto,' cap.

"It is my pleasure to announce today, I have appointed Father Joshua Donovan to Cardinal Priest. Do you accept appointment?"

Josh was clearly shaken. Tears began to run down his cheeks. Turning to the Pope he hesitated. Everyone waited to hear his response. Still, he hesitated. It was so quiet both inside and outside the church walls. Finally, turning to the Pontiff, Josh responded, "Yes, I accept."

With those words, he placed the cap on his head. Immediately, applause broke out as everyone stood and continued to applaud. Turning back to face the congregation, Josh hoped he made the right decision.

Looking down the long aisle of the Basilica, Josh could see what no other could. Angels were dancing and singing with joy. Brilliant light was streaming through every window, even though it was night, and far off in the distant light, Jesus was smiling at him.

News spread quickly that Father Donovan, a young priest from America, had been made a Cardinal by Pope Nicholas. The Pontiff announced the appointment at the end of Midnight Christmas Mass. News reporters all over the world wanted to get firsthand information. Not only was the timing of the appointment very unusual, but Josh was the youngest person appointed Cardinal in centuries, and even more unprecedented, had bypassed the traditional rise to this position without being appointed Bishop or Archbishop.

Josh remained secluded in the Vatican throughout Christmas day and into January, spending much of the time in prayer with Pope Nicholas and his resident Bishops and staff. The Pope spent considerable time reassuring Josh of his decision to appoint him, and why he bypassed the normal sequence of progression.

CHAPTER XI

Sitting in the Pontiff's apartment, Josh was very concerned about his appointment.

"Your holiness, you know how honored and humbled I am that Jesus has led you to choose me to be Cardinal Priest. But I must confess, I'm very concerned that it does not cause any disagreement or bitterness between the other Bishops. After all, your Holiness, who am I to be Cardinal at age 25? Besides, I may have been premature in accepting..."

"Stop." The Pontiff sternly said. "I have prayed, consulted, and made my decision, and I will hear no more of it. You are Cardinal Priest, and I, along with many others, give you my blessing. Besides, no one has contributed more to the Church, in recent years, than you. Do you realize just how many people your message has affected?"

Without waiting for an answer, the Pontiff continued. "Millions, yes, *millions* have repented and recommitted themselves to God and the Church. Now I want you to understand this," Pope Nicholas said. "Your ministry will not be interrupted by this appointment. I want you to be independent and to continue to proclaim the Lord's message. You will not be assigned to any particular church or diocese, but rather will officially be assigned to the Vatican to advise me in my duties in governing the Church whenever necessary. You will have your own apartment within these walls and will have at your disposal staff and personnel to assist whenever needed."

Josh was humbled but accepted the wishes of the Pope. Of course, he was extremely pleased that he would continue to deliver the Lord's message of reparation.

Christmas Day was bright, sunny, and cold. Numerous TV vans descended on the city once word got out about the appointment. Reporters, standing with microphones ready, stood in St. Peter's Square anxious to interview the young Cardinal. Men and women pushed and shoved to secure a better position for their interview. Unfortunately, their interview would have to wait.

Calling Josh to his private office later in the evening, they sat and talked for hours. The Pontiff was amazed that Josh was given insight on the proper protocol for his new position of Cardinal. Of course, Jesus had also enlightened him when he was ordained a priest, not to mention the various languages he could fluently speak and understand.

"I had no idea this was a gift from the Lord," the Pontiff said. "I knew you were multilingual but assumed that you achieved this through your studies."

Shifting in his chair and appearing a little embarrassed, Josh replied, "I can't tell you how blessed I am, but it's all been given to me for the sole purpose of evangelizing the message of reparation to the world."

Pope Nicholas smiled, nodding his head in agreement. "I'm sure it is, and I hope that your position as Cardinal will assist you throughout your ministry."

As the evening wore on, they talked, laughed, reminisced, and even shed a tear or two. The Pontiff knew that he might never see Josh again. When he said that, Josh knelt in front of him. Kissing his ring, he once again thanked the Pope for all his support, not only for him personally, but for helping to spread the message of reparation. He assured the Pontiff that Jesus was so pleased with his pontificate and that although they may never meet again in this life, they would in the next. With that, Josh hugged his dear friend for what he thought would be the last time and retired to his room.

CHAPTER XI

Time was late and the day had been busy. Josh had just finished showering when his phone rang. Picking it up, his expression changed to pure joy.

"Oh! It's so good to hear your voice. How are you?... I am wonderful! Thank you, but no congratulations are necessary... Yes, it was a shock to me also. You're... what?" Josh said. "Oh...Becky, I'm so very happy for you. Have you set a date yet? What's the lucky man's name? Barry Callaghan... Sounds like a good Catholic Irish name. Listen, tomorrow I will be flying back to the U.S... Yes...landing in JFK International, then I will be visiting Father O'Malley up in Clarksville...Most likely will be there for my birthday. Can you guys make it? I'd love to see you. Great...I can't wait...I'll see you soon."

Josh teared up. Not because he was sad that Becky was going to be married, but because she had asked him if he would marry them. In fact, he was thrilled that she had found someone who she could love for the rest of her life.

Pulling the covers up, he couldn't wait to see everyone, realizing just how much he had missed his friends. Morning came quickly but something very different had occurred while he was sleeping. No longer was he seeing beyond the veil of human sight, nor were Kapriel and Lancer visible. Shocked and somewhat disappointed, he knew his Guardians were with him and when the time was right, Jesus would reveal to him, once again, the spiritual world of good and evil.

The Vatican News had reported that Cardinal Donovan would be leaving for America early in the morning on December 26th. Many returned the next morning determined to get their interview. A black limousine pulled up just as Josh and a young priest, Father Robert Bell, who had been assigned to assist him, exited the Vatican.

Reporters surged forward, yelling out questions. More questions and more shoving. The Swiss Guard had trouble keeping them at bay. Josh stopped just short of getting into the limousine to take a few questions.

"Were you surprised about your appointment? Did you have any idea that you were going to be appointed Cardinal?" The first reporter yelled out as he struggled to get his microphone up to Josh.

"Yes... I certainly was surprised and no, I had no idea whatsoever."

"How do you feel about by-passing others and not following the set protocol of progression?"

Josh looked at the reporter with a surprised and somewhat annoyed expression. "The appointment of a Cardinal is totally up to the Pope, and although there is a usual progression, there is no set protocol for advancement. In fact, a lay person could be appointed to this position. I certainly hope that no one is upset as that would be undermining the Pope's integrity."

"What will you do now that you are a Cardinal?" a woman reporter asked.

"I will continue with my ministry of proclaiming the message of reparation."

She immediately followed up with another question. "How will you deal with all those who are against your message?"

"First, it's not *my* message, but the Lords and second, He will deal with those who will not listen, not me." Before another reporter had a chance to speak, she snuck in a quick question. "Where is your next stop?"

"The US and then...who knows? It will be where the Lord leads me."

"Your Eminence, have you been assigned to a particular Diocese or Church?"

CHAPTER XI

Josh continued to make his answers short and to the point. "No. I will officially be housed in the Vatican as one of the advisors to the Pope. Last question please," Josh said as he moved closer to the door of the limousine. "I have a flight to make."

Everyone surged forward trying to get their last question answered.

"Do you think you will be the next Pope?"

Josh looked stunned but held his composure. "Absolutely not. It would be a great honor but I believe the Lord has other plans for me. Besides, what a stressful job! I hear it's the quickest way to get gray hair."

Laughter broke out, as everyone yelled out more questions.

Father Robert held the door of the limo open. Josh quickly thanked everyone, waved and was on his way to Clarksville.

CHAPTER XII

THE FINAL PLEA

The flight was uneventful with Josh sleeping most of the time. Smiling to himself, he recalled how quick the trip was when Kapriel and Lancer wrapped their wings around him and instantly transported him to Rome.

"Wishing we could have done it like that again," he mumbled to his Guardians.

"Excuse me, your Eminence, what was that?" Father Robert asked.

"Oh, nothing. I was just talking my thoughts out loud."

Father Robert was assigned to assist Josh for as long as he needed him. Josh had told the Pope that he did not anyone to assist him, but finally agreed when the Pontiff insisted and agreed that Josh would only keep him for as long as he was needed.

Father Robert was born in the United States, went to The University of Notre Dame, and was ordained at St. Joseph's Seminary in Dunwoodie, N.Y. After a brief stay in the Bronx, he was recommended for further study in Rome. Unknown to Josh, Father Robert, along with three other priests, had petitioned the Pontiff to allow them to asisst Josh in his duties as Cardinal and in his ministry.

REPARATION: A STORY OF HOPE

All four had been deeply touched by the message of reparation and wanted to assist in spreading it throughout the world. Little did Josh know that the 'Holy Order of Reparation' was beginning to unfold.

Arriving at John F Kennedy Airport, cameras clicked as the media and crowds surged forward when Josh stepped out of the plane and descended the steps. Wearing a traditional Black Cassock with red piping, red buttons, and a red sash, not to forget the traditional Red Zucchetto Cap, Archbishop Nelson and a handful of Priests greeted Josh at the foot of the steps. Additionally, as expected, hundreds of enthusiastic well-wishers also cheered and waved as the event unfolded. Unexpectedly, mobs of protesters were also present. Evidently, many were not happy with the message of reparation, especially as it applied to morality and abortion. Printed signs of support were everywhere, but also were many ugly and hateful signs opposing his message and his visit back to the U.S.

"Go back to Rome," several screamed out.

"God bless you," a woman shouted in response.

"He's doing God's work, we love you," which only sparked more anger from the protesters.

Shouting erupted from both sides. Boos, cursing, and eventually a pushing match occurred between the two groups. Airport police had trouble separating them and restoring calm, while Josh was hurried into the Archbishop's limousine and rushed away. TV crews recorded the entire event. Unfortunately, it all happened so quickly, that the media lost their opportunity to interview Josh.

"I apologize for that," the Archbishop said. "We had no idea that so many protesters would be here. Unfortunately, not everyone is convinced that the Lord's

CHAPTER XII

message is real or urgent, not to mention the issue of abortion, which only infuriates those who feel it's none of the Church's business."

"God forgive us all," Josh said. "I hope to address this when I visit St. Patrick's in a few weeks."

Father O'Malley, and the rest of the priests at St. Andrews, as well as Bishop Timothy, were waiting anxiously on the steps of the church for their dear friend. Clarksville Police had erected barriers to hold back the media and crowds of well-wishers and protesters alike. Most of the residents of Clarksville were already sitting in the church, some since early morning hours, all waiting to see the new Cardinal and to attend his Mass.

Josh slowly exited the limousine and blessed the crowd with multiple signs of the cross. Cheers arose, far outnumbering the few protesters. Bishop Timothy was first to greet Josh by immediately greeting him formally as 'Your Eminence' and kissing his ring.

Josh accepted the greeting but immediately hugged the Bishop and was overheard saying, "I will always be Josh to you all."

Immediately, Father O'Malley and the other priests rushed forward with formal greetings and hugs. When Josh embraced Father O'Malley, he could not hide the tearful greeting seen by everyone. Father Robert and the rest of the Archbishop's entourage were introduced and warmly greeted by everyone.

Turning to the crowd, still being held back by the police, Josh shook hands with many, thanking them for their prayers and support. The media who had managed to push forward began to shout their questions. However, most of the questions were ignored, except for two questions from a local reporter representing the Clarksville Press.

"Your Eminence, how long do you plan to be here in Clarksville? and where will you be going after this?"

Waiting for the crowd to quiet down, Josh said, "I plan to be here most likely for a few weeks. I plan to celebrate my birthday here and then a quick visit to St. Patrick's Cathedral."

"And then what?" someone else yelled out.

"Wherever the Lord leads me."

On his way up the steps to the church, Josh slightly lost his footing and tripped, but was immediately caught by Father Robert. Looking at Robert, Josh jokingly said, "I guess I needed your help after all."

O'Malley quickly asked if he was alright. "Is there something wrong? Are you OK Josh?"

"Everything is fine, just a little lightheaded."

Once inside St. Andrew's, the parishioners stood as Josh and the other clergy proceeded up to the sacristy. Others packed in, including the media, but no filming or flash was allowed. Music and songs occurred for the fifteen minutes before Mass was scheduled to begin.

Finally, Josh entered the altar wearing his Red Cassock and Cap, one of the few times he would be seen in this attire. Father Robert, and Bishop Timothy, assisted him in all the correct protocol necessary when a Cardinal celebrates Mass, including removing his Zucchetto Cap, at the start of the Preface of the Mass and replacing it, at the conclusion of Communion, once the hosts were secure in the tabernacle.

His homily was brief, but to the point, stressing the urgency of repentance. One could tell from Josh's tone, that he was more serious and concerned than ever.

"I can't stress enough, that time is running short. Jesus is not happy because so many have refused to change their

CHAPTER XII

ways and because so many countries, including the United States, have continued to commit atrocities... atrocities such as fornication, adultery, slave trade, and abortion.

"We need to pray and do so fervently for the reparation of these sins and for all the atrocities that are so hurtful to the Lord. Otherwise, Judgement will come to all of us... all of us here...within our lifetime, unless we repent and change our ways.

"My dear friends... I can't be any clearer. Unless significant changes are made, we all will suffer the consequences. I have said it time and time again, you can believe what I have just said or not, the choice is yours. But know, this will be the last time I will be preaching this message in this church. Continue to be strong, continue to have faith and to trust in the Lord. And I humbly ask all of you to pray for me."

"Josh ended his homily by blessing the congregation. "May Jesus bless each of you and give all of us the strength to amend our ways."

After Mass, Maggie prepared a wonderful lunch for everyone. One could tell, by the subdued tone throughout the meal, that there was quite a concern for the reality of the message that Josh talked about.

"Listen," Josh said with an uplifting voice. "Jesus is merciful, and many are repenting and changing their ways. This message is being preached worldwide, so all is not lost.

"However," he continued, "we all must be more proactive in our efforts to show everyone just how serious repentance is."

Archbishop Nelson and his entourage returned to St. Patrick's, along with the media and a large number of the crowd, although a good many parishioners remained in the church and prayed. Josh, along with Father O'Malley, Fathers Scott, Samar, Gordon, O'Neil, and Monsignor

Ribson retired to the rectory living room, where they reminisced and caught up with one another.

Maggie was busy preparing an evening feast. Father Robert gave a brief history of his education and desire to be a Vatican Priest but confessed that after seeing and being so connected to Josh, his true desire was now to join Josh in his ministry.

"That's great," Father O'Malley said. "If I was a little younger, I'd join you."

"If you were a little younger," Father Scott chimed in, "you'd probably have gotten married, knowing what pressure you are under today." Everyone began to laugh.

Monsignor Ribson brought the room up to date as to how well the Seminary was doing, with a half dozen young Seminarians ready to be ordained.

"Your Eminence, would you do us the honor of ordaining these young men?"

"It would be an honor and I'd love to," replied Josh to Monsignor Ribson, "but I believe it would be more appropriate for Archbishop Nelson to do the honors."

Reluctantly all agreed. The other priests, including Father O'Malley, gave their account of the past months. Josh had the most to tell and related his experiences in LA, San Diego, Mexico, and Rome. He omitted his miraculous travel experience to Rome, and the attempt on the Pontiff's life, but emphasized how cunning and persistent Satan and his army of demons are.

For the next several days, Josh remained inside the rectory away from the media and crowds that had gathered daily, many looking for a cure or personal blessing. He, in fact, had appeared to be quite depressed, often remaining in his room for hours on end. Sensing his disposition,

CHAPTER XII

Father O'Malley knocked on Josh's door. Entering he found him on his knees praying his rosary.

"Oh Jamie, come on in."

"I was wondering when you would start calling me by my first name."

"I was waiting until I became Cardinal." Both looked at each other and smiled.

"So, what's bothering you?" Father O'Malley asked.

"To tell you the truth, I'm pretty depressed." Josh admitted. "I'm so concerned that too many have not yet responded. Maybe I'm not doing enough…?"

"Let's go downstairs and you can tell me all about it over a nice hot cup of tea."

"Sounds good."

Often Josh had sat at the kitchen table and poured out his soul to his friend and mentor. This time was no different. No sooner did he begin to talk when the kettle began to whistle. Father O'Malley rescued it from its screeching sound and poured the tea. After a few sips, Josh related how depressed he felt.

"You know Jamie, despite the many miracles that have been performed to help people believe that the message of reparation is real, and that Jesus is giving us another chance, many still have not changed in the least bit. In fact, so many are not concerned at all.

"Are they stupid? Or just not paying attention. Or what? I just can't understand why so many have not responded, despite being firsthand witnesses to the miracles and message. Don't they realize that Hell is very real? That this world is under spiritual attack and that thousands of souls are being lost every day?"

Jamie began to answer but was immediately interrupted by Josh.

"No need to try to answer… that was a rhetorical question." He continued. "It reminds me of the passage in

Luke 16, where the rich man, who had died and was in Hell, asked Abraham to send Lazarus to his brothers to warn them to change their ways before they also receive the same punishment."

Josh opened his bible and began to read:

'Then I beg you father Abraham, send Lazarus to my father's house, where I have five brothers. Let him go and warn them so that they, at least, will not come to this place of pain. Abraham said...your brothers have Moses and the prophets to warn them; your brothers should listen to what they say. The rich man answered, That is not enough, Father Abraham! But if someone would rise from death and go to them, then they would turn from their sins. But Abraham said, if they will not listen to Moses and the prophets, they will not be convinced even if someone would rise from death.'

"That's exactly how I feel...it's almost as if people and governments are so blind to the truth that nothing will change their ways, even if Jesus Himself was standing in front of them."

Josh knew full well that Satan was indeed on the rampage to keep people from accepting the message of the Lord. Although many battles had been won, there was so much more to be done and Josh had no idea how much time Jesus would allow before time ran out. He also knew that Satan had been unsuccessful in attacking him personally. Time and time again, no harm had come to him during these battles. Satan was no fool, and Josh was sure he would use still more severe strategies to stop the message.

Rather than attacking Josh personally, Satan would infiltrate the hearts of thousands of people to achieve his goals. Already hundreds of people were protesting, and he was confident that Satan and his army of demons would

CHAPTER XII

be deceiving and influencing many more to rise up, protest and create havoc.

Five young Seminarians were ordained at The Sacred Heart Seminary in Clarksville on Sunday, January 11th, 2046, one week after Josh had arrived and one day prior to his 27th birthday. Archbishop Nelson ordained the candidates, with Monsignor Ribson and Josh assisting. It was the first time since its official closing in 1972, that seminarians were *officially* ordained into the Catholic Church at that seminary. The occasion was especially joyous for Josh, considering his history with the facility.

January 12th was such a special day for Josh, not only because it was his 27th birthday, but because Becky and her fiancé, Barry Callaghan, would be there celebrating it with him. Of course, their conversations included catching up with each other but centered around her upcoming wedding.

Barry was a joy to meet. A good Irish Catholic, tall, light brown hair, and deep blue eyes. The type of eyes you can't help staring at. Their plans were to be married on Saturday, August 10th in Palm Springs, California, close to where Barry grew up. Becky's parents live a few miles away and they thought that they would like to settle there if all goes as planned.

As they were leaving, Josh reassured them that he would do his very best to marry them, although because it was so far in the future, he really had no idea where he would be or what he would be doing at that time.

While Barry was getting into the car, Becky turned to speak to Josh alone. Without saying anything, Josh could read her expression and understood the tears running down her cheeks.

"I'm happy for you Beck, I really am."

Becky threw her arms around her friend and cried. "If things were different…" she managed to say.

"Stop your blubbering, you hear me? We knew a long time ago that it would never work out for us. Jesus had other plans."

"I know, I know."

"Friends forever…remember?"

Becky nodded in agreement repeating, "friends forever."

As she walked away, Josh yelled after her, "Pray for me, Beck. I'm really going to need it."

Getting into the car, she turned, blew him a kiss, smiled and with that 'gesture of affection,' they drove off.

Josh remained at St. Andrews for about a week, mostly secluded and in prayer. On Sunday, prior to leaving for the Cathedral, while saying Mass at St. Andrew's, blood began to drip from his nose. Not realizing it, he began to distribute communion to the Eucharistic Ministers standing next to him.

"Your Eminence," a minister said just as Josh was giving him communion. "Your nose…it's bleeding."

Josh handed him the chalice while he quickly wiped his nose.

"Nothing more than a nosebleed," he later told Father O'Malley. "My blood pressure must be high. Guess I'm somewhat a little stressed thinking of my sermon next week at St. Patrick's".

"You need to get it checked out, if it continues."

"Don't worry, I will." but his expression was not reassuring.

"I mean it," O'Malley sternly said.

"Yeah, yeah, I promise if it continues."

CHAPTER XII

The next morning, Josh awoke finding blood on his pillow, but not enough to cause him to worry. After his shower, he prayed the rosary, asking Mary for her help and intersession as well as saying the Divine Mercy Chaplet, a prayer that he had started praying regularly, after Jesus had visited him in Rome.

Josh found Father O'Malley and Father Robert in the kitchen, apparently in deep conversation.

"Sorry to interrupt. May I join you?"

"Of course," Jamie said. "We were actually just talking about you."

"What about me?" he said as Robert poured him a cup of coffee.

"No tea?" Jamie sarcastically asked.

"Nope. I only drink tea when I'm upset."

"Very funny," Jamie said with humor in his tone.

"So, what were you all talking about?"

A few seconds of silence.

"Well... Robert hesitantly said, "I think…"

"*We* think," Father O'Malley interjected, "that you are stressed and need a rest. You have been going nonstop and quite frankly, we think you need to slow down before…"

"Before what?" Josh asked.

"Before you end up in the Hospital."

"Has Jamie been talking to you about my nose bleed?" Without waiting for an answer, he said, "Come on…give me a break." Standing up, he continued with a tone. "I appreciate your concern but I'm quite alright."

"Give him a cup of tea," Father O'Malley said.

"Oh, you think I'm upset now?"

Again, a few seconds of silence. Then laughter broke out as Josh sat down.

"I must admit I'm a little uptight, mostly about the many who appear to have so little concern about the

Lord's message of reparation and about all the protesters. I know Satan is behind it. But these people are good people... so deceived though. They actually think that abortion and all kinds of perversion is perfectly alright. I know Jesus is very patient, but I'm not. There is so much to do and so little time to do it."

"That's exactly why you need help," Father Robert said. "I want so much to help you."

"You are helping me.".

"I don't mean attending to you, assisting at Mass, holding the door open, and driving you places. Sure, I'm more than honored to do those things, but I mean helping you proclaim the message of reparation."

Josh looked at Robert. "You actually would help me do that?"

"Of course I would and so would others. I know two or three in Rome, dying to join you."

Father O'Malley interjected.

"That's answered prayer. I have been praying that you would find help, especially as you say, because time is running short."

Josh sat listening to every word. "You know Jamie, I have often said to you there are no coincidences...I'll pray about it."

"Sounds good to me," Robert said.

Just in time, Maggie's pancakes were ready.

The following Sunday, Josh was celebrating Mass at St. Patrick's Cathedral. Just as expected, the Cathedral was packed with hundreds of people, as well as dozens of the Media. There were hundreds of well-wishers standing outside accompanied by just as many protesters. Each held their appropriate signs.

CHAPTER XII

The NYPD were everywhere and erected barricades to hold back the crowds. Evidently, the Mayor had expected violence. He ordered two ambulances that were parked close by, waiting to transport any victim if necessary. The media had been given permission to film the entire events as they unfolded inside the Cathedral.

Archbishop Nelson and Father Robert assisted Josh throughout the Mass. In addition, Archbishop Nelson was thrilled to co-celebrate the Mass and also gave a brief, but wonderful, homily on the gospel of the day. He also said a few words about Josh, his accomplishments, his recent appointment to Cardinal, and of course, some brief words about the message and healings that Josh would be giving immediately after Mass for those who wanted to remain.

Not a single person left after Mass ended. All were anxious to hear from the new Cardinal and perhaps witness and receive a possible healing, evident by the large numbers of wheelchairs lined up one after the other along the aisles and the numerous people with crutches.

All eyes were of Josh as he approached the pulpit. As he took his first step up to the Pulpit, he stumbled and fell to one knee, catching himself by grabbing the rail. There was an immediate sound of concern, a hush sort of sound. Father Robert immediately rushed to his aid. Helping him to his feet, Josh continued up the few steps until he reached the top of the Pulpit.

"Sorry about that. Have you ever tried to climb steps in these long gowns? It's new to me."

Sighs of relief and laughter broke the deafening silence. When the congregation calmed down and Josh composed himself, he began one of his most difficult addresses.

"This will not be easy for me to say, nor will it be easy for some to accept, but as I have so often said before, I will speak the truth just as Jesus has asked me to. I pray that the Holy Spirit will open your ears, so that you will be able to hear the Lord speaking through me. So let us begin, in the Name of the Father, Son and Holy Spirit, Amen.

"I stand before you, simply as a messenger from God. Most of you know my story, but for those who do not, on December 27th, 2041, five years ago, Jesus appeared to me, and gave me a message to deliver to the world.

"He made it absolutely clear that unless people repent and change their evil ways, Judgement would fall upon all of us. In fact, He was ready to judge the world for all the atrocities committed, five years ago, had it not been for the vast number of prayers, in particular His Mother's intersession pleading for mercy and for more time before judgement on the world occurred.

"I have delivered this message over and over, yet many still do not believe or perhaps do not understand the urgency of it. Perhaps they just have not heard it. However, this morning, I will try, once again, to explain it, in clear, understandable simple language

"In short, sins and atrocities are still occurring at an alarming rate. The message is clear: either we change our evil ways or suffer the consequences. Most upsetting to Jesus is the atrocities that are committed by so many and by the legislation passed to justify them. Many miracles and healings have been performed to specifically prove the authenticity of His message, yet still after five years, these sins and atrocities are still occurring.

"So today, I will spell out exactly what these atrocities are, knowing full well that what I say will be rejected by many and justified as 'individual rights'. In this year of 2046, 72,310,000 babies have been aborted worldwide, and over 3,000,000 in the United States alone. I am here today to tell you that this is not a matter of a woman's right or a man's right. No, it is a matter of right or wrong, a matter of life or death.

CHAPTER XII

"The predominance of human biological research confirms that human life begins at conception, or if you will, at fertilization. The fact is that once life begins, no one has the right to take that life. Nowhere in scripture or even in society, does it give anyone the right to murder another person. Taking a life, aborting a baby, is murder and is no justification because we think it is our 'right' to do so, or because society believes that it is a perfectly acceptable form of birth control.

"We all know that there are certain rules in society that we have to follow. And if we don't follow them, there are consequences. Sometimes severe consequences. One cannot steal or rob a bank. One cannot falsely yell "fire" or "bomb" in a crowded public area, even though we are protected by the First Amendment. You cannot speed or ignore traffic lights or drink while driving, or carry a concealed weapon without a permit, all without consequences. And most obvious, one cannot murder without severe penalties.

"The same is true with God's laws. Yet, for so many, that law is unimportant or even nonexistent. Jesus asks each of us to live a life of love that negates sin, and sin is what he is asking us to stop. So, what is sin? What exactly am I talking about? Sin is the killing of the unborn, all kinds of immorality, such as pornography, rape, sex outside of marriage, orgies, fornication, adultery, human slave trading, and so on. All these are offenses against God, and are subject to consequences, some of which have severe consequences.

"Now, I realize that there are thousands that totally disagree with me and what Jesus is asking of us. Here lies the problem… Satan has been deceiving people for *centuries*. He has convinced mankind that these acts are not atrocities or sins. He has been so successful, that, as an example, such things as pornography, fornication, and abortion at any level of development, even after birth, are acceptable and are not sinful at all. His deception and his demons are everywhere, tempting us, deceiving us, lying to us, and convincing us that these acts are, not only alright, but are our individual rights, to do as we wish.

"Again, I am not here to debate, or to try to convince. The choice is yours. It has always been yours; but unfortunately, as I have just said, time is running out. I'm pleading with you to pray for the reparation of your sins, for these sins and the sins of the world. Pray especially for those who will not accept this message. There are hundreds outside this Cathedral, and perhaps within these walls, who do not believe and have been so deceived that they will do most anything to discredit these truths.

"Now, the good news is that Jesus is merciful and will always forgive us, no matter what our sins are, so long as we repent and are sincerely sorry. The bad news is, even though Jesus is merciful, once time runs out, it will be too late. Once again, I am here telling you that time is short. How short I do not know, but if Jesus has personally appeared and delivered this message and has verified it through many miraculous miracles, then we must conclude that, not only is He giving us one last chance, but He is desperate to save as many as possible. Time is short. Time, my friends, is running out. Please, *please*...pray for the reparation of all the wrongs of the world."

Throughout Josh's talk, the entire crowd was silent. In fact, so silent, that he probably didn't need a PA system. His entire speech was broadcasted live and many times throughout his speech, the sound of camera clicks were heard.

Father Robert noticed something very unusual throughout Josh's talk. Periodically he would appear to close his eyes, as he rubbed his forehead. At first, Father Robert thought it was simply because he was hesitating to

CHAPTER XII

collect his thoughts. However, after multiple times of repeating the same gesture, he wasn't sure. Was he disturbed? Was he thinking or confused? Was Jesus talking to him? Was there something going on that no one knew about? Whatever it was, he would soon find out.

After mass, Josh invited all those with ailments to come forward. One by one he prayed over each as the Lord healed them. Some came forward with red, glowing heads but were quickly turned away. The entire process took over two hours. The media went crazy, recording, reporting, and interviewing all those who were cured. It was later reported that more people worldwide watched the events at St. Patrick's Cathedral than any other event in history. Satan was furious as more and more believed and began to change their ways.

As Josh, Father Robert, and the Archbishop, exited the Cathedral, they were met by groups of supporters and protesters. Josh immediately noticed many dozens with that evil red glow emanating from their heads.

Immediately, one man yelled out, "Your Eminence, will you give us your blessing?"

Josh smiled, raised his hand, and began to make the sign of the cross, when a protester yelled,

"We don't want your blessing! Go back where you came from and stop ramming down our throats your religious crap."

Three gunshots rang out. Two seconds after the gun shots occurred, a tremendous bolt of lightning and horrendous thunder exploded as if a bomb went off.

The lighting was sharp and struck approximately where the gunman was standing, although no harm came to him or anyone else. The thunder was so loud, that the ground and buildings shook. People screamed and scattered in all directions, mostly in fear from the lightning and thunder as opposed from the three gunshots. Some, who were standing close to the doors of the Cathedral, including the Archbishop and several of his attendants, quickly ducked inside seeking cover.

Two police officers and three undercover police tackled the perpetrator. Confusion abounded everywhere, except for Josh, who simply stood in place as if nothing had happened. Once order was restored, both groups, as well as the millions watching, were mesmerized, as they stared at Josh who was completely unharmed. Media went wild, reporting the event. One news reporter was heard to say that it was a miracle that none of the shots hit the Cardinal.

Josh once again made the sign of the cross and gave his blessing to everyone. However, this time both groups stood silent and fell to their knees as the blessing was given, except for those devoted to Satan, who fled in all directions.

After his blessing, Josh said just a few words.

"Remember, repent and pray that society will change their ways. Let today be yet another warning. Jesus is merciful, but time is running short."

Getting into the limousine that had been parked at the foot of the steps of the Cathedral, and after saying his goodbye to the Archbishop, he and Father Robert drove off to JFK, where the Pope's plane was waiting for him.

"Are you all right?" Robert asked Josh.

"Sure, you know that my Guardians protect me."

"I'm not talking about the shots fired, I'm talking about you tripping and holding your head throughout your talk."

"Oh, I just had a migraine, but it's gone now. Nothing to worry about."

Millions of people were going ballistic over Josh's speech. Those representing women's rights, abortion advocates, as well as many of the LGBTQ communities

CHAPTER XII

were protesting and condemning Josh and his message of reparation before he even reached JFK airport. Every detail of his sermon was being scrutinized by the media and picked apart in every detail. Fortunately, there were also thousands who praised his speech and vowed to lobby congress and state governments until changes occurred.

Additionally, the message of reparation was broadcasted worldwide along with all the miracles that occurred. Thousands and thousands of people were touched and converted. And as Josh would later discover, the quiet majority were beginning to speak and unite against the atrocities that Josh had identified.

Surprisingly, of the hundreds who were at the Cathedral, no one condemned the message after witnessing all that had just occurred. People were shaken, some shaken to the roots of their faith, while others were strengthened to know that God is real and that the message of reparation is indeed valid, given to Josh from the lips of Jesus Himself.

For many, especially for those who witnessed the entire events of the day, it was hard not to believe in all that was said by Josh. When thunder causes the ground to shake like an earthquake, when lightning strikes on a beautiful sunny day, in the midst of people, and causes absolutely no harm to anyone, when dozens and dozens of healings are witnessed, cures that can only be attributed to miraculous events, and finally, when bullets strike and yet have no effect, one is hard pressed not to believe and accept the message given.

Some of the skeptics who initially doubted were perplexed when later, slow motion, frame by frame analysis, unequivocally revealed that all three bullets directly hit Josh, two in the chest and one in his neck. The recovery of the crushed slugs confirmed that the bullets did hit him, yet he stood unharmed. Nothing could be concluded other than it was indeed a miracle.

TWO DAYS PRIOR, Pope Nicholas was deep in prayer in his private chapel when three young Vatican priests interrupted him.

"Excuse us, Your Holiness, but if you could spare a minute or two, we would like to talk to you about Cardinal Donovan."

Pope Nicholas warmly greeted the priests and invited them to join him in his private office. Before they had a chance to say a word, the Pontiff said, "I have been in prayer all night and most of this day, waiting for you to arrive. You're here to ask my permission to join Cardinal Donovan in delivering the Lord's message of Reparation."

"Yes, Holy Father, that is exactly why we are here, but how…?"

The Pope interrupted. "I know because the Lord revealed to me last evening that you would be asking for this request, and that He wanted me to sanction it. Of course, you have my permission to join Cardinal Donovan. I'm sure he will be overjoyed to have additional help. As soon as possible, I want you to fly to JFK on my personal plane. When you meet Cardinal Donovan, hand him this package and this letter that explains everything and affirms my approval. I realize this procedure is most unusual, but because of the urgency of the message of reparation, and the fact that this request came directly from the Lord, I am sure he will fully understand and move forward with his mission."

Fathers Jason, Russel, and Christian were waiting for Josh as he and Father Robert arrived at JFK. Most reporters were still covering the events at St. Patrick's Cathedral. However, the landing of the Pontiff's plane

CHAPTER XII

aroused the curiosity of a few reporters who were waiting at the airport ready to report whatever events might occur.

Once Josh stepped out of the limo, he was immediately recognized and rushed by a mob of people. Security guards cleared the way as he and Father Robert made their way to a VIP room where the other priests were waiting.

Although Josh had been informed that the plane would be waiting for him, he had no idea why the other priests were there. Josh immediately recognized them from his visits at the Vatican and warmly greeted them. Father Jason spoke for the others.

"Your Eminence, this letter is for you from Pope Nicholas. But before you read it, we would like to explain our presence. We are here to help. To assist in whatever way we can and to join you together, or independently, to spread the message of reparation. We have asked His Holiness for permission, and he has agreed, of course pending your approval. Your Eminence, we all would be honored to join you in this endeavor."

Josh looked at each one intently.

"This is not an easy request you are asking. Satan is furious and is using any means he can to stop or discredit the Lord's message, and to attack those who dare to deliver it."

"We know…"

"Let me finish," Josh said. "As you know, I have been protected from all harm, but I can't promise you will be. You could end up giving your life for this cause."

"We realize that your Eminence and are more than willing to give our lives for the Lord."

Josh smiled as he sat down to read the letter. Finishing it, he looked up while all three waited for his answer.

"It looks like Satan will have to contend with more than just me."

"Do you know what is in this letter?"

All shook their heads indicating that they had no idea. Sitting down, Josh gathered them close and revealed what Pope Nicholas wrote.

"Besides giving you permission to join me, it appears that Jesus and his Holiness wants me to form an order of Priests, suggesting that it be called 'The Holy Order Of Reparation." All sat somewhat dumbfounded, including Josh.

"There's more… he has already sent word to Monsignor Ribson, that the Sacred Heart Seminary, in Clarksville, will now be called, 'The Holy Order of Reparation Seminary.' It will become a seminary for others to be ordained as Priests of Reparation, and it is there that we will be officially housed."

Josh had hardly finished when a cheer of joy erupted from the group.

"Wait, there's still more... Father Jason, I believe the Pontiff gave you a package to give me?"

"Yes, your Eminence, here it is."

"Now before we go any further, please call me Josh. I feel so much better being addressed by my first name".

"We will, your Eminence. Sorry, I mean…"

"Never mind," Josh said as he opened the package.

"It looks like the Pontiff wants you to be identified as Priests of The Holy Order of Reparation by wearing this thin red-roped belt. The color red represents the blood that Jesus shed for the Reparation of sins. I also will wear it when not wearing my official Cardinal attire."

When he had finished, another cheer of joy broke out.

"Don't be too quick to celebrate." Josh reminded them. "There is much to do and not much time left to do it." He emphasized that evil is everywhere.

"You will find Satanic cults, people in all fields of business and in all levels of society that are under the influence of Satan and drugs, unholy churches, and

CHAPTER XII

unfortunately even young kids that also have been influenced and misled. Please remember, that our mission is not so much to convert but to spread the message of reparation. If people will repent and change their ways and begin to pray more frequently, then Satan and his evil agenda will be defeated."

Josh continued, "Of course, if we can convert people to Jesus while proclaiming this message...all the better. Remember my brothers, time is short. Closer than I imagined. Stay true to your mission, pray the Rosary and the Divine Mercy daily and ask for guidance always. Last, remember that this message comes directly from Jesus. He is in control. Trust in Him and be assured that He will be with you always."

As the four sat and listened to every word spoken, Josh began to assign each where he believed the Lord wanted them. Jason was asked to go to the west coast, starting in California, to begin the message with the many homeless and immigrants. Russel would begin in Canada while Christian was sent to England and Ireland. Robert would begin in New York and work his way south. Josh was led to fly to South Korea. Thus, their ministry began. All were excited and yet very aware that it would be no easy task.

A reporter spotted Josh boarding the Pope's plane but had no idea where he was flying to. The confusion occurred as the media tried to decipher what the other priests were up to. Father Robert, who had been with Josh since Rome, was hailing a taxi and quickly disappeared in the busy streets of N.Y. The other three priests, all wearing their red roped belt sash around their black cassock, stood at different ticket counters, each apparently off to a different destination.

REPARATION: A STORY OF HOPE

Josh was quickly on his way to South Korea. Arriving many hours later, he went directly to the Diocese of Seoul, where he was met by Archbishop Yang. Although it was a surprise to the Archbishop, Josh was greeted as if expected, immediately housed in a private apartment and given the use of a parish car.

Archbishop Yang was a small man of stature and, as Josh would soon find out, had a heart of gold. No sooner was Josh settled in, than Archbishop Yang personally introduced him to his staff, his resident Deacons, and Priests. Josh briefly explained the purpose of his visit, but in fact, there really was no need to, as almost everyone in the Diocese had just seen him on television delivering his message at St. Patrick's Cathedral.

The Myeongdong Cathedral, (The Cathedral Church of the Virgin Mary of the Immaculate Conception) was magnificent. Archbishop Yang personally gave him a VIP tour. Josh remembered that Pope Francis visited the Cathedral and said Mass there in 2014. The Korean language was no problem for Josh. Once again, Jesus had blessed him with the gift of speaking and understanding various languages. In fact, Archbishop Yang could not believe how fluently Josh could speak it.

Josh wasted no time in getting to know the people. He often was seen walking throughout the city streets greeting people, visiting various shops, and admiring the beautiful, handcrafted objects that were so meticulously carved. It was his plan to eventually visit all fifteen Dioceses and proclaim the message of reparation. However, Jesus told him that first he was to touch the hearts of the people through love, kindness, and healings.

It wasn't long before the media caught wind of his presence and were following him almost everywhere he went. Word quickly spread of the message he was delivering in the many churches and places he visited.

CHAPTER XII

Likewise, people quickly began to realize that he was blessed with the gift of healing. Soon, many of all faiths were seeking his help.

Two months after his arrival, a young man approached Josh one afternoon asking for a healing for his mother. Upon entering the home, Josh quickly realized that he had entered the home of a Buddhist. Without hesitating, he entered her bedroom where her husband and other family members had gathered. To Josh's surprise, he had the feeling that he was expected, graciously greeted and without thinking, he returned the greeting speaking in their common dialect.

"Can you tell me what sickness she has?"

The son answered, "Cancer, stage four. The doctors give her days or at most weeks."

Josh took the woman's hand. Looking at the son and scanning the others who were watching intently, he said, "I will ask for healing. I'm sure you know that I pray to Jesus and if healing occurs, it is through Him, not I that heals."

Then without looking up, Josh prayed silently. After a minute of two, he paused. Again, he looked up at everyone and said, "Jesus is love and He loves all of you."

Briefly looking at the young son who had the courage to ask for healing, then looking directly back at the suffering women, he said, "In the Name of Jesus, I ask that you heal her from all afflictions and bless this family abundantly."

With those words, the woman opened her eyes. They were bright, alert and the color in her face returned. Immediately the family rushed to her side with tears of joy, and as expected, some confusion. Excitement, tears, hugs, happiness and almost a feeling of disbelief occurred over the next few minutes. No one realized that Josh had already left, except the young son. Rushing after Josh, he hugged him as he continuously thanked him for the miracle.

"Remember," Josh said, as he smiled and placed his hand on the shoulder of the boy, "it was Jesus Christ who healed your mother, and His love is for everyone, for you and for your family."

With those penetrating words, he drove off, back to his apartment. Before he was out of earshot, the boy yelled, "I'm going to tell everyone what Jesus did...everyone!"

Father Robert, Robbie as Josh now referred to him, had little trouble finding protesters as he spread the message. Although he had already visited several churches, he spent considerable time on the streets of N.Y. For the most part, people listened and always had questions that he gladly answered. Robbie spent a good amount of his time lobbying the N.Y. legislators to change the abortion laws. Soon, he was joined by many supporters and unfortunately protestors as well. The news reported the event daily and before long, dozens and dozens were gathering demanding change. Abortion was the news of the day and soon it became apparent that considerable pressure was being felt to change the legality of the law.

Josh heard from Fr. Christian that he had safely landed in England and was warmly welcomed. In fact, he had already had several meetings with leaders of the Church of England as well as with several Catholic Archbishops. He had not experienced as many protesters as Father Robert, but then again, he wasn't in N.Y.

Fr. Russel arrived in Montreal and began preaching the very next day. His enthusiasm as a young priest was electrifying and it wasn't before long that he had a following. In fact, three weeks after his arrival, two young men approached him requesting to become a priest of the

CHAPTER XII

Holy Order of Reparation. Russel gladly accepted their request and instructed them to go to Clarksville, N.Y. to attend the "Holy Order of Reparation Seminary."

Father Jason, on the other hand, was under attack from the moment he departed JFK. The entire flight was met with severe turbulence and heavy black clouds, although the weather reports indicated fair weather. As Jason's plane was landing at LAX, the engines stopped, causing the plane to smash into the runway. Its wheels collapsed as they smashed into the ground. The noise was horrendous. Hundreds of people helplessly watched the rear end break off from the rest of the plane, spinning out of control, and finally coming to a stop on a grassy slope. The rest of the plane burst into flames as the engines smashed into the runway. Flames and explosions followed before any fire fighting vehicle had arrived.

The demon called Raum and his associate, sat atop of the Air Traffic Control Tower, watching joyously as the entire event unfolded. Raum was dispatched to attack and stop Father Jason at any cost. Slime dribbled from his distorted, smiling mouth. He was elated at his accomplishment. Later it would be discovered that black birds hit the plane just before landing, causing its engines to fail. Black birds sent by Raum.

Within minutes, the trucks and ambulances arrived. At first it was thought that no one had survived, and sadly no one did in the main section that was now burning uncontrollably. Raum slowly stood up as he peered toward the rear section. Two stewardesses and four passengers miraculously staggered out from the wreckage.

Raum went ballistic as he recognized Father Jason as one of the survivors. Before he even thought about attacking, dozens of angelic warriors surrounded Jason, sending a clear message that he was under the protection of the Lord of Hosts and that it would be futile to attack him.

Sunday morning, the entire Buddhist family that Josh had visited, were waiting outside the Cathedral for Josh. Rushing to him, they greeted him with smiles and hugs.

"Thank you so much, thank you so much," the mother said in broken English.

"I've told everyone!" the young boy said.

And indeed, he was true to his word, as many more in the Buddhist community came to know and respect Josh. Soon word spread and hundreds lined up every Sunday for prayers and healings. Likewise, the message of reparation was taking hold. More people in the city of Seoul were praying and attending religious services than had in many years.

Unknown to Josh, his message and healings had also spread to North Korea. Pictures, news reports and personal healing accounts were smuggled across the border to relatives and loved one's separated from one another because of communist rule.

Monday morning found dozens of reporters and hundreds of Koreans waiting for Josh at his apartment. Josh was nowhere to be seen. His car, along with his personal possessions were gone. Even Archbishop Yang had no idea where he had gone, although he admitted that he was aware that he would be leaving.

Sunday evening, after dinner, Josh had thanked him for all his hospitality but did not indicate where or for how long he would be gone. However, the Archbishop was aware that Josh had indicated that he wanted to visit most, if not all, of the fifteen dioceses in the country.

Once again it became apparent that the message of reparation was being delivered in various churches,

CHAPTER XII

temples, and cathedrals throughout the country. The problem for the media was they never knew the location where Josh was until reports of his presence or healings were reported. By the time they arrived to investigate and report, he was already off to another location.

On a sunny day, two months after he had arrived in Korea, his car got stuck in a ditch along a country road separated by fields of rice patties. Unable to free the car, he began to walk, hoping to find help. Before long, he came across a poor farmer working in the patties. Graciously the man stopped working and agreed to help.

Before dark, Josh was eating a simple dinner provided by the farmer, and his wife. Their family consisted of five children, two daughters and three sons as well as the farmer's elderly mother. Realizing that they barely had food enough for themselves, Josh felt somewhat guilty eating their food but also felt blessed to experience such love.

"Do all of your children work the fields with you?" Josh asked.

"Yes" the farmer said, smiling and showing what little teeth he had.

"We all work. Mom helps as best she can. My wife cooks and also helps in the fields. We cannot afford help so we must all do our part."

As the wife was serving dinner, Josh noticed she had no fingers on her left hand, evidently due to an accident long ago. She tragically lost all five fingers when their wagon flipped over, severing them and crushing her youngest daughter.

As the elderly mother started to get up from her chair, one of the younger boys immediately got up to help her to the table. It was then that Josh realized she also was disabled.

The woman was blind. Although they were extremely poor and had experienced tragedies and hardships throughout their lives, they were happy and full of love. A love and kindness that they were glad to share with a stranger. A love and kindness that would soon bring them much happiness.

Morning came quickly and after a few bites to eat, Josh was once again on his way. The entire family stood outside their meager dwelling waving goodbye and wishing him well. Suddenly, the blind woman could see the car as it disappeared down the road and all five fingers on the wife's hand were restored as she waved goodbye.

Staring at each other and crying with joy, the youngest daughter handed her father an envelope that Josh had given her. Opening it, he found two five hundred American Dollar Bills and a note:

"Thank you for your help and love. May the Lord Jesus continue to heal you, bless you and keep you safe always. Cardinal Joshua Donovan."

Josh arrived in a small community in the South Gyeongsang Division of Korea. As always, he was warmly invited into the church's rectory, given food and a place to sleep. During the night, he was woken by his guardians Kapriel and Lancer who were visible once again. They sadly informed him that Father Robert had been attacked, and badly beaten. Beaten to the point of death. However, Kapriel assured Josh that he would recover and because of this attack, it would spark even more support for him and his appeal to change the abortion laws in New York.

Kapriel and Lancer tried their best to lift up Josh's spirit. Depressed would not be sufficient to describe how he felt. He simply collapsed on the floor next to his bed and cried, blaming himself for allowing Fr. Robert to assist him without the protection that he himself had.

CHAPTER XII

Sobbing uncontrollably, he hardly realized the brilliant light that illuminated the entire room. Wiping the tears from his eyes, he felt and recognized the warmth of Jesus in the room. Kapriel and Lancer knelt with their heads bowed low.

"Forgive me Lord for my despair, but I'm so saddened that my fellow priests are so vulnerable to the attacks of Satan. I'm protected but they are not."

Jesus took Josh by the hand, helped him up and sat down next to him on the bed. Looking deeply into Josh's eyes the Lord spoke softly.

"Sometimes suffering and martyrdom is the very thing that will change the course of history. Fr. Robert's suffering is for that purpose and will eventually be the stimulus needed for change and lead souls to salvation. Everything, my son, is for a purpose. There will be much suffering. Suffering from those who are faithful to me. Remember, as I have told you...this will not be an easy task to undertake. Keep faith and trust in me always, for in the end, my Will shall prevail."

Jesus continued to speak as they both stood up.

"Your task here is almost complete. Continue to proclaim my message throughout South Korea. Then you are to go to the North and deliver the message that I will reveal to you. Then China, and after your mission is complete there, travel to Russia as I will direct you. Your guardians will be visible to you from now on. Take refuge in them until the end."

Josh looked at Kapriel and Lancer who were still kneeling. When he looked back, Jesus was gone.

The media eventually caught up with Josh, reporting and documenting all healings that took place. Josh traveled throughout the country visiting all 15 dioceses, preaching the message of reparation in churches, temples, and towns. He had no trouble spreading the love of Jesus and proclaiming that Jesus is the way to eternal life. Hundreds and hundreds were converted, but the actual numbers were far more as indicated by the rise of Christians and Catholics throughout the country.

One of his last stops was returning to Seoul where he was mobbed by hundreds of well-wishers and converts. Archbishop Yang was thrilled to see him again. Josh returned the parish car and stated that he would be leaving South Korea permanently, but first he would visit the Yoido Mega Full Gospel Church (the biggest mega Pentecostal church in the world), where he would deliver his last appeal to the people of Korea.

Word quickly spread of his intentions. The next day, hundreds of Koreans gathered on the streets as he passed by on his way to the church. Media were everywhere. Upon arrival, Josh was surprised to see that the church was full of thousands of people representing many faiths.

His appeal was almost exactly the same as he had delivered in New York. He spoke slower than usual and was noted to have slurred several of his words. Something was not quite right with him, yet no one knew what, nor did he. After the address, to his amazement, the entire congregation of people broke into a rousing round of applause, so much so that it lasted for over two minutes. Josh did not have to invoke the Lord's healing as dozens of healings simultaneously occurred after his talk. The place was alive with excitement and with the Holy Spirit.

Just before leaving, when almost everyone had gone, a Korean man approached Josh.

"Your Eminence, I know this request is very unusual and dangerous, but many of us here have families and relatives in the North. Would you be willing to visit some

CHAPTER XII

of them, administer communion and perhaps ask Jesus for healing, as so many are sick and suffering?"

Josh remembered what Jesus had instructed him to do: *'After proclaiming your message, go to the North.'*

"Yes, of course I will go, but how will I be able to cross the border?"

"There is a secret tunnel that we use regularly. No one knows about it. We will be able to pass under the border and then will have others to escort you to relatives."

That evening, Josh was met by two men. They traveled far north into the Gyeonggi regions of South Korea, eventually ending up at a small, isolated farmhouse. Far under the barn floor was a tunnel that led to a bigger one that brought them out into an almost inaccessible rocky cliff area. Another quarter of a mile of hidden winding paths eventually led to the tunnel that had been so painstakingly hand dug so many years ago.

Once into North Korea, Josh hid under a tarp in a hand pulled wagon. After about a half hour the cart suddenly came to a stop as two police approached. Slipping unnoticed out of the rear of the wagon, into a thick mass of weeds and brush, the two police guards searched the wagon, reviewed the men's identification papers, and apparently satisfied, proceeded on their way. Another half hour passed until they reached their destination. Josh was appalled at the poor conditions of the homes, if you wanted to call them homes, and the terrible unhealthy conditions the people in the village were living under.

Entering the first hut, he was immediately embraced by at least eight elderly people. All were Catholics unable to worship or attend Mass. In fact, most Christians had either been executed or were in hiding. After distributing communion and giving them his blessing, he proceeded to ask Jesus for various healings, some of which included skin infections, blindness, cancer, and tumors.

REPARATION: A STORY OF HOPE

Josh went from hut to hut until everyone was attended to. When told that he had to leave to get back to the tunnel before dawn, Josh chose to remain in the North, explaining that he had greater business to attend to. Perplexed but conceding to his wishes, his guides departed and headed back to the tunnel. Josh on the other hand, left the village and found a perfect spot close to the riverbank where he, along with Kapriel and Lancer, prayed and waited for the Lord's instructions.

Dawn broke revealing a beautiful, warm sunny day. Josh had been in prayer most of the night and had a clear understanding as to his mission. Surrounded by Kapriel and Lancer, he closed his eyes and was instantly standing in the private bedroom of the Supreme Leader of North Korea. Upon awakening, there was confusion and disbelief as a man dressed in his Cardinal Cassock stood staring at him.

Within seconds, pandemonium broke out as the Leader shouted for his guards. Again, he shouted and shouted but to no avail. Although his guards were standing directly outside his room, they never heard a word. Now fear came over the Leader as he tried to get out of bed, yet despite his efforts, he was frozen in place. Josh continued to stand directly in front of his bed, remaining perfectly silent. Finally, after a few minutes, a sense of calm came over the Supreme Leader. Speaking in fluent Korean, Josh introduced himself.

"I know who you are!" shouted the Leader. "Guards! Guards!" But no one responded. "What's happening to me?" he demanded.

"Jesus, the Son of God, the King of Kings and the Lord of Lords has sent me here to deliver a message."

"Get out of here," the Leader demanded. Still struggling to get up, he finally gave into his captivity and began to listen.

CHAPTER XII

"No harm will come to you today. I am here to tell you to free your people. To allow freedom of religion, to unite with the South and to stop the executions, the torturing and the abuse of your people. Jesus also wants you, along with other countries, to dismantle all of your nuclear weaponry, and to live in love and peace."

The Supreme Leader looked shocked and yet confident that these requests will never happen.

"If you do these things, peace and prosperity will come upon you and your country. Your economy will flourish, and you will be held up as one of the greatest leaders of all time. Your people will love you and you will be blessed with happiness, and good health. Most important, if you give up your evil ways and repent, amending your life according to the love that Jesus gives, then salvation will be yours. If you do not, you will suffer eternal damnation."

With those words, Josh pointed to the far wall and immediately the Supreme Leader saw and experienced himself in the torments of Hell. Excruciating agony and torment came upon him. Fear, helplessness, and hopelessness were written across his face. Within seconds, it ended, yet he was shaking with fear and sweat over his entire body.

"You have been given a great blessing." Josh said. "Not many have been allowed to experience what you have to save their souls. Take heed before it's too late."

The Supreme leader began to scream. He screamed and screamed louder and louder as his guards rushed in. No one saw Kapriel and Lancer wrapping their wings around Josh as they disappeared.

It had been five and a half months that Josh had been in Korea. Newspapers and TV programs reported daily the events as they occurred, including the work of Fathers Robert, Jason, Christian and Russel, who also had been preaching the Lord's message and converting many.

REPARATION: A STORY OF HOPE

The last report of Josh in Korea was the day he preached in the Yoido Full Gospel Mega Church in Seoul. Of course, a few others knew he had entered the North, but all were perplexed when news reported him stepping off a plane in LAX. When Josh opened his eyes, he was disembarking from the steps of a 707-jet airliner that had just landed. Although there was no record of him booking this flight, it was assumed that some major booking mistakes had been made or lost. In any event, Josh was back in the United States, anxiously waiting to marry Becky.

A quick flight to Palm Springs, where Becky and Barry Callaghan would be married at Our Lady of Solitude Catholic Church. Becky was overjoyed to see Josh once again. And after the usual greetings and catch ups, the wedding plans were discussed and finalized. Saturday was a beautiful sunny day in Palm Springs. Becky looked beautiful in her white flowing dress which was accented against Josh's red Cardinal Cassock.

Their marriage vows were beautiful, spoken from their own words and touched the hearts of everyone present. When Josh pronounced them man and wife, a tear or two trickled down his eyes, although no one was aware of it, nor did anyone notice the small drop of blood dripping from his nose.

The reception was wonderful. Music, flowers, dancing, and food, more food than he had seen in months. Just the variety of hors d'oeuvres would have been enough for a full meal. He couldn't help thinking of the simple staple of food the Korean people lived on, and the hardships so many of them endure every day.

CHAPTER XII

Josh gave a beautiful blessing to the couple but left immediately after, as he was due back in Clarksville the next day. Becky walked him out to the waiting cab.
Reaching into his pocket, he handed her a small wooden carved crucifix he had picked up in Korea.

"Pray for me often," he said to her. "Friends Forever."

Happy, tearful goodbyes, as he drove off.

Father Robert who had spent so much time in NYC, was finally successful in getting the Legislators to change the abortion laws. No longer would abortion be legal in New York, except for rape or life/death situations.

After the attack on Father Robert, just as the Lord had said, it served to awaken hundreds to join the protests against abortion. Before long, thousands of the 'silent Majority' were protesting until their demands could not be denied. The media covered the protests continuously as support grew more and more each day.

Father Christian was well received by Catholics and Christians alike in England and Ireland but met with much protest from many others. On the positive side, he was warmly greeted by the King of England who was a fierce supporter of the message delivered and an open advocate to the Pro-Life Movement. In fact, after meeting with Father Christen and spending several weekends with him, he vowed to address Parliament in support of the Lord's Message.

Father Jason had a profound influence on the poor and homeless throughout California and most particularly a significant influence on the many dozens and dozens of Catholics and Christian churches he visited over the past five months. Likewise, Father Russel had similar experiences in Canada, but not to the extent of Father Jason.

REPARATION: A STORY OF HOPE

He however, recruited four young men who wanted to be priests of the Holy Order of Reparation. He had already sent two of them to the Seminary and was in the process of sending two more. Additionally, to his amazement, six ordained priests asked to join the Order, eager to help deliver the reparation message.

Josh knew he was sick, as he had experienced more and more migraines and nosebleeds. On the plane back to N.Y. he called and summoned all his priests to meet him back at the Seminary. Several stewardesses attended him throughout the flight as best they could. Kapriel and Lancer prayed for his healing as the Lord had not given them information as to the seriousness of his condition. By the time his plane landed, his migraines worsened, and he had difficulty stopping the blood oozing from his nose.

Father Robert and Father O'Malley met him at the airport and accompanied him by ambulance to the nearest hospital. Conclusive testing revealed that Josh had an inoperative brain tumor. Situated between and among so many intricate and vital nerves and arteries, no operation or treatment would be possible. In fact, the tumor was so large that they did not know how he could still be alive, not to mention functioning normally. Josh later answered that question simply by stating the obvious; it was only through the Will of God.

The official report released to the public said he was suffering from severe fatigue and high blood pressure causing nosebleeds. Rest was recommended. Returning to the seminary, Josh was brought directly to his room to rest. Once everyone had left the room, he knelt and began his usual prayers. Unbeknown to him, all present in the seminary, priests, seminarians, nuns, and lay workers all gathered in the church and were praying for his recovery.

CHAPTER XII

After only a few minutes of prayer, Josh fell asleep. Kapriel gently picked him up and placed him gently in his bed while Lancer pulled the covers over him.

The next morning, Josh was not cured but the medications given to him and no doubt the many prayers, were successful in taking away the painful headaches and bleeding. Exiting from his room, and to the surprise and excitement of everyone, he appeared to be himself again. Father O'Malley and Father Robert knew him too well to be fully convinced but kept their opinions to themselves.

Upon learning that four young men from Canada had joined the seminary in preparation for ordination and an additional six ordained priests had joined their ranks, Josh was overjoyed. Of the five seminarians who Archbishop Nelson ordained, three also chose to join his order. It was hard to imagine that over the past five months, the new order had over a dozen priests, and over two dozen seminarians. Josh said a special Mass for the Priests of his Order and presented each with the red-roped belt.

After two months of resting and with the medications working, Josh was anxious to continue his ministry. Father Robert pleaded with him to continue to rest but useless as it was, Josh prepared for his trip to China as Jesus had instructed him to do. Father Robert would remain in the seminary, coordinating the assignments of the priests while Monsignor Ribson would continue coordinating and serving as head of the seminarians, along with the two deacons he had recruited to assist him in teaching.

Josh was told by Jesus that he had a specific mission to accomplish in China and Russia. However, not knowing exactly what was in store, he trusted and followed instructions as the Lord revealed to him.

REPARATION: A STORY OF HOPE

Upon landing in China, Josh was detained at the airport and told that he would not be able to enter the country. However, no sooner did he arrive then herds of people mobbed him as he was led to a detaining room. Chants of "Donovan, Donovan, Donovan, Donovan" continued to ring out from the crowd which was getting larger and larger. Eventually, after hours of calling out his name, flights being disrupted, and even larger crowds gathering, the authorities were given word to allow him entrance.

Security police quickly escorted him to a nearby hotel where he remained for two days detained in his room. The president of China was very familiar with the message that Josh had been delivering throughout the world. He had pledged that he would never allow that message to be delivered in his country, and what's more, Josh would never be permitted to ever step foot within China's borders.

Nevertheless, here he was. Not to his liking but because of the tremendous pressure placed on him to allow the young Cardinal entrance. Additionally, the President of China was under pressure from human rights groups, advocates for democracy and religious freedom, and not to forget worldwide pressure to de-escalate military and nuclear arms. Uprises were common and despite his military efforts to crush them, more and more were occurring.

During the two days that Josh was detained, the President experienced nightmares that left him not only shaken but petrified. The first night he found himself falling into an endless pit. Falling faster and faster, he tumbled in all directions, often hitting the sides of the cavern and jagged rocks.

What made the dream so real was he literally felt the pain of every object he crashed into and the rising heat of fire upon his flesh, as he kept descending but never

CHAPTER XII

reaching the bottom. Finally, after what seemed like an endless fall, he saw the bottom coming up faster and faster until he smashed into the floor of the pit. Screaming with pain and fright, he jolted awake, sweating and trembling. Standing at the foot of his bed was a man, wearing a red cassock with a red roped belt around his waist. He immediately recognized it to be Josh. As his attendants rushed in, he ordered them to seize Josh, but no one was there.

The second night, the dream began with Josh standing far in the distance, high on a hill, pleading with him. Yet he had no idea what he was saying. Josh kept pleading and pleading. Finally, he threw up his hands in frustration and turned away.

At that moment, the earth shook. The walls began to crumble. Bolts of lightning struck his residence and all the buildings in sight. Thunder roared and the earth separated causing everything to collapse in. Now he was falling again, but this time, everything was falling with him. Buildings, cars, trees, roads, and people.

Everyone and everything were falling and being consumed into the pit of fire until eventually the entire country was consumed. Again, waking up screaming, his attendants rushed in, only to find him alone shaking and petrified. An hour had not passed when he realized what he had to do.

Josh was summoned to the President's residence for a personal meeting. All the President's meetings were canceled, as well as his agenda for the week. Arriving just before noon, Josh was escorted into a small comfortable sitting room where the President was waiting for him. Again, language was no problem, so there was no need for interpreters.

The President immediately stood up as Josh entered. Both shook hands and sat. Staring at Josh intently, the silence finally was broken. The President said four words in English. Four words only and for the next three hours, Josh did all the talking. Those four words would change the course of history.

"TELL ME ABOUT JESUS."

It was in the early morning when Josh arrived in Russia. He had already given notice that he would be meeting with the various Bishops and clergy at the Cathedral of the Immaculate Conception and then later visiting the Russian Orthodox Cathedral of Christ the Savior in Moscow. To his unexpected surprise, dozens of clergy lined up to greet him as he exited the limousine provided for his transportation. Another surprise was the entire Cathedral was full, already waiting hours for his arrival.

After brief introductions, Josh met privately with the Catholic Archbishop and was informed that his message was being delivered throughout Moscow and in many remote parts of the country.

"I can't express the importance and urgency of the message," Josh told the Archbishop. "I feel the Lord's patience is coming to an end. Although there have been numerous efforts and promises to change, still atrocities occur. It is my hope that Jesus will give us more time as, I feel, many people are on the verge of change."

Realizing that the people in the Cathedral had been waiting for hours, he asked if he could address them.

"Of course," the Archbishop gladly responded.

As Josh entered the area where the congregation were waiting, they immediately stood.

"Please, please be seated"

Speaking fluent Russian, he repeated the Lord's plea to repent and to stop the atrocities of the world. Hundreds were on crutches, many in wheelchairs, while more were

CHAPTER XII

hoping beyond hope for the cures they had waited so long for.

Concluding his sermon, Josh reassured them that Jesus loved them and eventually, they would be free to practice their faith openly and without fear. "Because of the Love that Jesus has for you and to show the world his mercy, I ask for the Lord's healing for all those in need."

As it had so often happened before, everyone was instantly healed. Cries of joy, excitement and praise were heard beyond belief. People danced in the aisles. Others cried while many more knelt and praised Jesus. Although they had heard of the miraculous healings occurring throughout the world, the congregation as well as the Archbishop and Bishops looked at each other completely stunned.

The following morning, Josh entered the Cathedral of Christ the Savior, one of the most beautiful Russian Orthodox churches in the country. Although he was openly welcomed, his reception was sparse compared to the reception he received yesterday. However, to his delight, all the Russian Orthodox Bishops and Church Hierarchy were present. They assembled in a large circular conference room, similar to a small theater setting. Josh was introduced and after a brief applause, which totally embarrassed him, he began his address.

"Dear Friends in Christ. I am not here today to preach the message of reparation that Jesus has given me. As you well know, this message is already being delivered throughout this country, and will continue to be proclaimed well after I'm gone. Rather, I have been directed by Jesus and His Mother to deliver two very important messages. Unfortunately, these requests have yet to be fully complied with." Josh could tell there was quite a lot of anxiety after he made that statement.

"As you know, the second secret of Fatima was revealed long ago. On July 13th, 1917, the Virgin Mary appeared to Sister Lucia revealing her request asking for the consecration of Russia to her Immaculate Heart. As history has recorded, Pope Pius XII, John Paul II as well as Pope Francis consecrated the world to the Immaculate Heart of Mary, but not in unity with all the Bishops of the world."

That statement caused much confusion and disagreement. Mumbling and eventually arguments began until there was mass chaos.

"SIT DOWN!" Josh said in a stern voice. "I would like to finish."

Startled and more perplexed as what to say, they all sat down.

"Let me pose a question. Mary promised if her request was honored, Russia would be converted and experience all the spiritual fruits of peace. I ask you, can you say that this indeed has occurred? I believe the answer is 'No'.

"Unless Russia complies fully to our Lady's request, Russia will never experience the true fruits of conversion and there will never be true peace in this world. More wars will come with devastating results. My brothers, Mary's request *must* be honored.

"Secondly, I have come to state that there must be reconciliation and union between all churches. The Russian Orthodox Church and the Roman Catholic Church must unite. Political differences and agenda must stop. It is time to honor these requests. To put aside politics and governmental pressures. Please honor these requests or this is what will occur…"

Josh opened his arms as Jesus had told him to do, and instantly the room was transformed. All present were standing in a circle as the world erupted into chaos. Jesus

CHAPTER XII

was revealing what the annihilation of the world would look like if another war began... a nuclear war.

Just prior to the destruction, as the world waited for the nuclear bombs to strike, chaos occurred. People ran, cried, screamed, and panicked. Mothers hugged their children, others ran to churches, yet no number of prayers or reparation could stop what was about to occur. The world waited for the inevitable. Finally, it happened; a mushroom of destruction moved across countries, across the world. Oceans boiled while everything in sight was destroyed. Fire, explosions, lighting, and earthquakes simultaneously occurred, and then instantly, everything was gone.

Everyone in the room, including Josh, were horrified. They stood there speechless, looking at nothing but smoldering ash, despair, and regret. If only the world had listened. If only they hadn't been so prideful, perhaps this would never have happened. Finally, reality came back.

Nothing was said. No one knew what to say. Josh broke their silence.

"Jesus loves all of us and wants for us to be united with Him and experience His love and peace. He wants His Church to be united and consecrated to the immaculate Heart of His Mother. I came here today not to condemn or to frighten but to plea for you to respond to God's request. I HOPE WITH ALL MY HEART YOU WILL."

Many sat, completely stunned. Others openly cried. There wasn't a person in the room that wasn't affected, yet some, just a few expressed anger. The message had gotten through. The question was, would they act on it? If they would, that indeed would be a miracle.

CHAPTER XIII

RETURN TO ROME

Because both Cathedrals are in the heart of Moscow, it was just about impossible to avoid the crowds. The miracles that occurred just a day ago at the Cathedral of the Immaculate Conception has caused quite a lot of excitement and curiosity. People of various faiths, most of which were non-believers, were waiting outside the Cathedral, hoping to get a glimpse of the healer.

Unfortunately, Josh's headaches were worse than ever, which made it impossible for him to address the crowd. However, spotting a young boy in the distance, leaning up against a building with his crutches at his side, Josh could not resist approaching him. The boy couldn't have been older than five or six. As they talked and the crowd looked on, Josh picked him up and continued to talk, whispering something in his ear.

A closer look at the boy revealed he had a 'clubfoot' deformity. After only a minute or two, he set the boy down and the boy immediately ran off, leaving his crutched behind.

From the crowd came a sharp cry.

"My boy, my boy!" followed by his father running after him.

While on the plane back to Rome, news broke out all over the world:

> IRAN HAS JUST LAUNCHED A NUCLEAR MISSILE TOWARD ISRAEL.

The media was going crazy with all sorts of reports. It was estimated that the missile would strike in about fifteen minutes. Israel was ready to defend themselves and set to intercept the missile and hopefully destroy it. However, minutes after the missile was launched, news reported that it had just been destroyed.

The immediate destruction of the missile was a mystery. Israel had not yet taken any action, nor did any of her allies. The United States quickly determined that the Iranian missile was destroyed from somewhere in space. Only China had that capability to react so quickly, as US defense satellites would have taken too long to reprogram and arm.

Within minutes, news was broadcasted from Beijing:

> 'FROM CHINA: The President of China has just issued a statement that it was their missile from their Space Defense System that destroyed the missile that Iran launched against Israel. Further…. China states, 'It is our hope and belief that no Nation wants war, especially a nuclear holocaust. We all must live in peace. We call for the immediate disarmament of Iran and hope this will lead to the total disarmament of all countries.'

This action by China shocked the world as well as Iran, as they were close allies with each other. No one could reason why China would make such a drastic change so suddenly. Josh however, sat in the plane praising Jesus, for he knew that his meeting with China's president had had a positive impact.

CHAPTER XIII

Iran insisted that the missile did not contain a nuclear warhead and would have exploded before hitting the ground. They felt compelled to act only in desperation, stating it was the only way, they believed, to get the world's attention to remove the blockades and sanctions that had been imposed on them.

Further, their leader contended that his people were starving due to the blockades and sanctions which had been in place for over twenty years. The United States and other countries demanded that they disarm, yet none had offered economic and humanitarian help if they did. Consequently, Iran felt that so long as other countries continued to expand their nuclear arsenal, they had little choice but to do the same.

In another shocking surprise, before Israel had time to retaliate, Iran immediately apologized for their actions. To the immense surprise and delight of the world, Iran reported that if the blockades and sanctions were removed and food was made available, they would immediately dismantle their nuclear arsenal and hopefully be welcomed back into the world community.

Israel was not very happy and had their doubts about Iran's sincerity, as did other countries. They were not convinced that the missile was non-nuclear. Additionally, they were under tremendous pressure to immediately retaliate.

Publicly they protested. However, despite the pressure on them, privately they met with the United States and the United Nations, promising not to retaliate but would agree to join a world effort for humanitarian help if other nations joined in, and of course if Iran's arsenal was immediately dismantled and properly inspected by the United Nations. True to word, Iran not only completely dismantled their nuclear weapons, but in an act of complete compliance, destroyed them as well.

Within a week, all blockades and sanctions were removed and nations all over the globe contributed with aid. Dozens of planes loaded with food and medical supplies were delivered. Numerous truck shipments arrived from European nations as well as dozens of container ships. World tension was at a low. China and Iran were being regarded as world leaders. Josh kept praising Jesus, yet the world said nothing, nor did China, about Josh's influence on the Chinese leader.

Pope Nicholas personally greeted Josh at the Airport. "I thought I would never see you again," the Pontiff said as he warmly put his arm around Josh. Once back at the Vatican, they met for hours and discussed the world situations and all that had occurred with Josh over the past six months or so. The Pope was excited to hear of the miraculous occurrences that the Supreme Leader of North Korea and the President of China experienced. Both him and Josh were hopeful that the leaders would act on the messages given to them. Indeed, they were encouraged as to the decision China made to intervene in the attack Iran made against Israel, thereby avoiding an all-out nuclear war.

After several hours of talk, the Pontiff's mood changed, becoming more serious. He confided in Josh that he believed, despite their efforts to eliminate the corruption and evil that was discovered in the Vatican months ago, there was still an element... a strong element of evil present. However, despite his efforts, he had no clue as to its source.

Josh assured the Pope that he would do all he could to find and eliminate it before more harm occurred to the Church. Additionally, Josh felt that the Pope was not acting like himself. Something was not quite right, but

CHAPTER XIII

although he had no idea, inwardly he sensed that the Pontiff was not well. Before Josh retired to his apartment, the Pope prayed over him asking Jesus for healing.

"I'm so concerned about you, my son...Why do you think the Lord is allowing this?"

"I have no idea, but we both know that God often works in strange ways."

The Pope agreed but nevertheless, he could not change the concern expression he had. "Josh, I want to ask you a favor."

"Anything, your Holiness."

"In the event that I take ill, seriously ill, I do not want you to ask Jesus… well, I think you know what I'm saying. We all know that my health is failing and I'm sure it's time for someone else to shepherd the Church."

Josh looked surprised. "Your Holiness...Only Jesus will determine who will be the next shepherd, but unless I am directly told by the Lord that He wants you to be healed, I will of course respect your wish."

That statement coming from the Pope, confirmed the feeling Josh had about the Pope's health.

"One more thing before you retire for the night."

The Pope reached for a box on the top of his desk. Inside was a beautiful, embroidered hand spun red-roped belt. It was thicker than the one Josh and the others were wearing, and in addition had beautiful golden colored rope fibers interwoven throughout it, with a golden colored tassel at its end.

"This my son is for you. I had it made to signify the distinction between you, as the head of your Order, and the others. Please accept it and wear it proudly." Josh was touched by his gift.

"Your Holiness, I am certainly not worthy of this honor but…"

"Oh, stop," the Pope said as he interrupted Josh and held up his hand. "None of us are worthy. Wear it with pride and always remember that it represents the blood that Jesus shed for all of us."

Of course, Josh accepted it and wore it proudly thereafter.

Surprisingly, major events and changes were occurring worldwide. New York changed their abortion laws and made it illegal with few exceptions. Other states were on the verge to do the same. Congress was feeling tremendous pressure from lobbyists and from pro-life groups. With the recent appointment of a conservative to the Supreme Court, major changes in the abortion laws were expected. North Korea was paying close attention to the recent developments in China and with the disarmament occurring in Iran. Two weeks had hardly gone by, and nations were already referring to China and Iran's leaders as world heroes, not to mention Iran's welcome back to the world community.

Not surprisingly, the Supreme Leader of North Korea was jealous that such honors were being attributed to them. Additionally, he could not get out of his mind his experience of Hell and what Josh had told him if he would disarm and unite with the South. North Korea's economy would flourish, Korean people would be united because of him, the security of his nation would be secure, and he would be accepted into the world community, just as Iran was. Especially pleasing to him was he would be hailed as one of the world's greatest leaders.

Josh's return to Rome was expected to last only for a day or two, just enough time to bring the Pope up to date. The next morning, less than 24 hours after Josh had arrived, he, along with others, including the Pontiff's

CHAPTER XIII

physicians, were summoned to the Pope's chambers. The Pontiff had taken a turn for the worst during the night and was on the verge of death. Evidently, he was in more serious health than he had revealed to Josh.

By the time Josh arrived at the Pontiff's room, the Pope's breathing was extremely weak. Josh knelt and began to pray. Remembering what the Pope had asked of him, and not getting any message from the Lord, Josh did not pray for healing. Pope Nicholas opened his eyes, took Josh's hand, smiled and with that last gesture, passed from this earth to his long-awaited heavenly reward.

News quickly spread throughout the Vatican. Word of the Pontiff's death was passed through the Church's civil service, the Curia. Foreign ambassadors and heads of state were officially informed of his death, and as customary, the Vatican Radio reported the news to the world:

'Pope Nicholas died peacefully this morning in his private apartment at approximately 8:45am. He was surrounded by his physicians and closest Cardinals.'

Likewise, numerous reports were sent throughout the world announcing his death. Churches of many faiths mourned for the Pontiff and offered prayers and condolences. World leaders expressed sorrow over his death and commended him for his many accomplishments, especially regarding Christian unity and world humanitarianism. Bells tolled throughout Italy and in churches throughout the world.

As tradition dictates, the Pontiff was exposed for veneration in St. Peter's Basilica, with thousands paying their respect, as they slowly passed his casket. On Thursday, five days after his death, he was buried under St. Peter's and laid to rest next to his predecessor.

During the nine days of traditional mourning, hundreds of Cardinals began to arrive in preparation for the election of a new Pope. It was then that Josh remembered what Pope Nicholas said about believing that there was still considerable evil within the Church.

To Josh's horror, four Cardinals who recently arrived in Rome had the mark of evil on them - the red glowing mist surrounding their heads. Lancer pointed out a fifth Cardinal and before all the 150 Electoral Conclave of Cardinals, who were eligible to vote, assembled, another two were identified by Kapriel and Lancer. All toll, seven red glowing evil Cardinals were eligible to vote or worse, be elected as the next shepherd of the Catholic Church.

According to years of Church tradition, the election of a new Pope cannot begin until fifteen days, but not more than twenty, after his death. Unfortunately, eight days had already gone by, leaving Josh only one week to expose the evil lurking in the Vatican.

It wasn't long before many Cardinals began to lobby for the position. Alliances were made, along with promises of positions and favors. Josh, on the other hand, prayed with his good friend, Cardinal Mancini, for the Lord's Will to be done in electing a new Pope, and also spent considerable time discussing the dilemma of the evil Cardinals that Josh and his guardians had identified.

Cardinal Mancini wanted Josh to expose them immediately. Unfortunately, the only way Josh had proof of their evilness was by the red glow around their heads. No one, including Satan, knew how Josh was so successful in identifying these evil people. Josh knew there must be another way to expose them without revealing this knowledge.

Not surprising, all seven of the evil Cardinals lingered together as they waited for the election, and when separated, they were lobbying for Cardinal DeBella, one of their own, who they considered the favored due to his popularity, youthful looks, and age.

CHAPTER XIII

During lunch, where all the Cardinals were eating, Cardinal DeBella, who despised Josh, confronted him while he was sitting with Cardinal Mancini.

"Guess you think everyone will vote for you with all the miracles you supposedly have performed."

"Excuse me?" Josh surprisingly said.

"I'm know you heard me," DeBella replied.

Most everyone in the room was now listening intently and staring at both.

"Cardinal DeBella...I'm sure you realize that the Lord Jesus performs all miracles, not I. It sounds like you doubt that they even occurred. Do you?"

Josh waited for an answer, but none came. The question shocked DeBella, as he knew he was in a dilemma. If he said that he did not believe the miracles occurred, then he would be denying what millions of people had witnessed as fact, and therefore discredit himself as a future leader of the Church.

On the other hand, if he said he did believe that the miracles occurred, then he would certainly have known, as any good Catholic clergy would, that Jesus was the one who performed the miracles, not Josh. This would also reveal doubt as to his potential leadership, confirming that he had a vendetta against Josh who was overwhelmingly liked and popular. Either way, he was hard pressed to get himself out of the predicament.

After stammering and trying to find the right words to answer the question, he simply ignored it by saying, "You're being ridiculous and absurd." Trying his best to put the attention back on Josh, he asked him,

"Do you or do you not want to be Pontiff?"

"Although you have avoided answering my question, I will answer yours. No, I have no intention to be the next Pope, unless that is the Lord's Will. You, on the other hand, appear to want it so badly that you have lobbied for it from the moment you have arrived and have not hesitated to promise everything, including the kitchen sink, for support."

"How dare you," DeBella blurted out.

"Do you deny lobbying and promising appointments to those sitting here?"

Before DeBella had a chance to reply, Josh continued. "I'm sure what I have said can easily be verified by those in this room. Shall we ask them?"

DeBella and his associates were fuming.

"You think you're so smart and righteous," DeBella yelled out followed by support from his camp of evil Cardinals. DeBella, once again trying to discredit Josh, went on the attack.

"Tell us Cardinal Donovan, if you did not want to be Pope, why then did you let the Pontiff die. You could have saved him, but no, you did not pray for healing because you had other plans for yourself."

Those remarks created a roar of disagreement and anger among all the Cardinals in the room. Josh stood up and looked directly at DeBella who a few feet from him was now only.

"May I remind you," Josh said with an angry tone, "I do *exactly* as the Lord asks. It is not I who heals nor is it I who determines what miracles will occur and who will receive them. I am faithful to the Lord and do exactly as He asks me, and I can assure you, if Jesus wanted Pope Nicholas to be healed, He would have done so. Unlike you, I love Jesus and serve Him faithfully."

"I do too," DeBella yelled out.

"Great," Josh replied. "Then before God and all of us here, stand and publicly renounce Satan, renounce all evil, renounce all demonic entities, and allow us to lay hands on you and pray for exorcism."

CHAPTER XIII

The room was silent, so very silent. All eyes were on DeBella, even his associates were staring at him waiting for an answer that they knew he would never give. Sweat was visible on their foreheads and some appeared to be trembling.

Josh continued, "Of course, if you truly are a man of God, then you have nothing to fear."

DeBella stood silent for what seemed like an eternity. "I have had just about enough of this. You should be ashamed of yourself for trying to discredit me. It is obvious that you will say anything to win votes. If you are so sure of yourself, prove these unfounded accusations. Otherwise, I suggest you keep your mouth shut"

With those nasty remarks, he turned his back on Josh, and began to storm out of the room. Before DeBella reached the door, Josh yelled out, "You are evil and in league with Satan. Jesus knows it, I know it, you know it... and I intend to prove it."

Several more days passed. Josh, Cardinal Mancini and a few other Cardinals were constantly in prayer seeking the guidance of the Holy Spirit, while others continued to lobby and solicit support for themselves. The comments Josh made about Cardinal DeBella were troublesome to many, and as Josh expected, more than a few came to him inquiring as to the authenticity of his allegations. All he could say, at this time, was to ask those seeking proof to be patient and to trust that what he had said was revealed to him by Jesus. Josh assured them that when the time was right, he would reveal the proof needed to verify all that he had said. This seemed to satisfy some, yet others were not so easily convinced.

On the evening of the fourteenth day after the Pope's death, the night before the Electoral Conclave of Cardinals would be voting for a successor to the Papacy, Josh still had no idea how to verify his comments about DeBella.

Time was running out, yet his faith that Jesus would help him, never faltered. To make matters worse, his migraine headaches had returned.

After hours of private prayer, he fell asleep kneeling at the side of his bed. Then, around 2:00am, he awoke with a startle. Springing to his feet, he said to Kapriel and Lancer that Jesus had revealed to him what he needed to do to prove the validity of his accusations.

"We need to go to DeBella's villa in Wessana. But how? How can I get there and return so quickly?"

Kapriel looked at Josh with a surprised look. "Did you forget?" as he opened his wings. Josh smiled as he and Lancer wrapped their wings around him.

When Josh opened his eyes, they were standing in the private office of DeBella. It was dark, eerie, and the smell of sulfur was everywhere.

"Remember to stay close to us," Kapriel said.

Searching the room, they found nothing. Opening the door into a long dark hallway, lit by a single hanging light, they proceeded slowly toward the winding stairs.

Sulfur was even more putrid than in the office. Josh could sense evil but where? Where were the demonic creatures hiding? Slowly they descended to a stone floor. Josh could hardly see as there were no lights except for two lit candles that sat upon what looked like an altar.

Looking up, Josh stumbled back as he caught sight of a crucifix hanging upside down with icons of evil looking creatures surrounding it. Almost instantly, two small demons shot out from above the crucifix, smashing into the three of them. Lancer sliced one in half, causing it to burst into flames while the other one dashed away.

Kapriel helped Josh up to his feet. "Did you forget you are completely protected?" Kapriel asked with a smile on his face.

"Not used to being frightened so quickly," Josh replied.

CHAPTER XIII

Quietly they continued their search. Soon they discovered a hidden staircase behind the altar. Upon reaching the bottom, they found themselves in a narrow, long room with what appeared to be some kind of sacrifice table in its center. The room was carved out of granite or some very hard stone. It reminded Josh of the tunnels at the seminary in Clarksville. Unlit torches were all around the walls with a huge, circular candle lit chandelier above the sacrifice table. To the far end was a podium set on top of a small stage. Under the podium Josh found what he was searching for.

No sooner did he have it in his hands than literally what seemed like all Hell broke out. The torches instantly lit with the walls covered with clinging demons of all kinds and sizes. Kapriel and Lancer stood with their swords drawn, while a huge sentinel demon stood before them laughing.

"Did you really think you could enter Master DeBella's private home and take what belongs to him?" The sentinel asked. Without waiting for an answer, he shouted, "Now be a good boy and hand it over to me!"

Josh remained frozen between his Guardians. Unfortunately, the pain in his head had returned and Kapriel could sense that he could hardly stand. It would be difficult to let down their guard, wrap their wings around Josh and disappear before the demons attacked. No, Josh had to remain between their wings, standing as still as possible, ready to move with them as they maneuvered if a fight broke out.

Before another word could be spoken, the torches began to flicker, wind came out of nowhere, and a horrific howling noise shook the walls as another huge warrior demon, named Zogan, appeared.

"Didn't you hear the command given to you? Hand over what you are holding," Zogan said looking directly at Josh.

Zogan's eyes were fiery red. His face was scared, badly deformed, and the stench of putrid sulfur was everywhere. "No way will you become Pope, and no way will your pitiful Guardians be able to save you."

Confident about his strength and previous success in battles, he had no idea who he was about to attack. Looking carefully at Josh, his expression changed to reflect a certain amount of bewilderment or perhaps curiosity. "No mortal has ever stood before me so confident. You don't even look afraid, knowing in a few minutes I will rip you to pieces. Tell me, why don't you not fear me?"

Although still in pain, Josh continued to stand between Kapriel and Lancer, confident and smiling.

"My catechism teachers always told me never to speak to demons. However, this time I will make an exception. I don't fear you because there is nothing to fear. Nothing can defeat the Lord Jesus and He is with me. You, on the other hand, should fear Him."

"I fear no one," Zogan shot back, now even more angry than before. Unable to control his fury, he raised his hand and unleashed a blast of fire so strong that the force of it threw the three of them across the room, pinning them against the wall. Flames of fury continued until Zogan was sure that they were destroyed. This was exactly what Josh's guardians were waiting for. Kapriel and Lancer wrapped their wings tightly around Josh and instantly they were back in Josh's room.

When the flames ended and the three were nowhere to be seen, cheers erupted from all the demons present. A smile cracked across Zogan's lips. Unknown to him, though was that Josh was back, safe inside the Vatican. Zogan, on the other hand, thought that he had destroyed

CHAPTER XIII

them. His arrogance would soon end once he reported back to his master only to find out that Josh could not be destroyed when under the protection of his Guardians.

Vatican physicians were called and attended to Josh the best they could as his condition had deteriorated. Medications were increased and he was put on oxygen throughout the night. When morning arrived, the medications had been effective in reducing his pain. Against the wishes of the physicians, Josh removed the oxygen mask and was determined to attend the election.

After breakfast, the Electoral Conclave of Cardinals assembled in the Sistine Chapel. Just before the announcement was made to secure the doors, Josh stood up.

"My brothers, we are still waiting for Cardinal DeBella to respond to my question. In short, who do you serve, Jesus or Satan?"

DeBella looked stunned and soon the anger on his face was evident. "If you don't know by now, I of course, serve Jesus."

With that statement there was complete silence. The doors of the Chapel were still open with others present besides the Cardinals. All eyes turned to Josh. Walking to the center of the room, Josh began to speak.

"If you serve Jesus, how then do you explain what is written in your journal?" DeBella looked carefully at what Josh was holding. Furry shot across his face.

"How did you...? he screamed out, but Josh immediately interrupted him.

"This journal is his account of how he serves Satan, along with Cardinals Philip, Nicoli, Zendori, Jacob, Rasmussen, and Bezek." All seven stood up to protest.

Josh continued. "This journal is handwritten by DeBella himself and was recovered from a hidden room under his private chapel that clearly worships Satan. It is a record of their signed commitment to evil, their pledge to infiltrate the Vatican, and eventually DeBella's plans to assume the role of Bishop of the Church. It is signed by each of these evil men, pretending to be serving the Lord. It describes the atrocities they have committed, including rape, sex trafficking, and human sacrifice."

All eyes were now on the seven who stood silent and fuming with anger.

"Do you deny what you have written and signed in this book? Do you deny serving Satan?"

Silence. Nothing but eerie silence while the six accomplices turned and looked at DeBella.

"You think you are so high and mighty. You think you have won this battle, but I can assure you that Satan will win out in the end... Damn you all!"

With that condemning statement, six Vatican Police entered the Chapel and immediately arrested the seven for their murders and crimes against humanity. Several minutes passed. Cardinals sat looking stunned and not knowing what to do next. Finally, Josh broke the silence.

"My brothers today is a victory for the Lord. The question is should we continue or postpone the election?" It was unanimous, they decided to move forward. The order was given for all those not voting to leave, and the doors were closed and sealed.

Josh was clearly in pain, and his condition was worsening by the minute. Blood began to drip from his nose, but he wiped it off before anyone noticed. Cardinal Mancini recognized his suffering and began to pray for him. Suddenly, Mancini stood up.

"My brothers, clearly there is one among us that the Lord has blessed abundantly. His loyalty and dedication to the Church is unquestionable. I believe that Cardinal Donovan, above all of us here, should be our next Pope. Will you join me in one unanimous vote to elect him?"

CHAPTER XIII

Before Josh could utter a single word, all stood confirming their support for him. Cardinal Mancini walked over to Josh and asked, "Do you accept nomination?" Josh sat silent.

Again, Mancini asked, "Do you accept nomination?"

Outside, there were thousands in St. Peter's square, eagerly waiting for the announcement as to who would be the next leader of the Catholic Church. Priests, Bishops, Nuns, Clergy, and people from all over the globe were present. Of course, everyone had their opinions. Some believed that Cardinal Rosealetti, the oldest of the Cardinals, was the likely choice. Others believed it would be Cardinal Mancini, while most, despite his young age, believed that Josh was a given. Of course, there were some who were strong advocates of Cardinal DeBella, not aware that he, along with six others, had just been arrested.

All eyes were on the Sistine Chapel watching for the white or black smoke to appear. To the crowd's amazement, they were surprised to see white smoke rising from the chimney so quickly. Word was quick to spread that a Pope had been elected in record time.

Now, anxiously waiting for the announcement and his appearance at his balcony window, they prayed and contemplated who he might be.

The new Pontiff was dressed in the traditional white papal vestments. Before exiting the Sistine Chapel, the first official act the new Pope did was to defrock and excommunicate the seven who had just been arrested. The Sistine Chapel doors were opened, and the new Pope was greeted by the many Bishops and Clergy as he headed to his apartment anxious to greet all those awaiting him.

Although Josh's head was throbbing with pain, he continued to walk toward the apartment. Upon reaching it, the double doors to the Pope's balcony were opened. The new pope, Pope Xavier, the name he chose, greeted the crowd. Cheers of Joy and happiness rose as the Pope addressed them.

Josh knew that he could never be the Pope, so when Cardinal Mancini asked him if he accepted the nomination, he responded, "I'm so honored that you all have nominated me, but I believe Jesus has other plans for me. Therefore, I must decline."

Clearly, the Cardinals were upset. However, Josh continued. "I do believe that there is a person in this room that is more than qualified. He is honest, loyal to the Church and to its dogmas. I believe that his wisdom and strength is exactly what the Church needs today. My brothers, I ask you to join me by electing Cardinal Mancini."

After a few minutes of discussion, Cardinal Mancini was unanimously elected as the next leader of the Catholic Church.

Josh stood behind the doors of the Pope's balcony and watched Pope Xavier address the people in Latin, ending with his Papal Blessing. Immediately after his address, Pope Xavier approached Josh.

"It's you who should be Pope."

"No, your Holiness, God has chosen you. May I be one of the first to congratulate you," Pope Xavier thanked Josh and invited him to join him in his private office. Retiring to the Pontiff's office, they continued to talk.

"So, you refused nomination because you said God has other plans for you. May I ask what they are?"

Josh looked deep into the eyes of the new Pope.

"Your Holiness, there are still a few things that I have been led to do. For one, Kirt Williamson, a good friend of mine is finishing up his last year of seminary preparation for the priesthood. He has specifically asked if I would ordain him and become a member of my Order. I would love to be able to accommodate him if possible.

CHAPTER XIII

"Also, Jesus wants me to make one last trip to Russia in hopes of persuading the Russian Orthodox Church to unite with us, and to consecrate themselves to the Immaculate Heart of Mary. Only then, will we have peace in the world."

"I understand," Pope Xavier said, "but you could have done these tasks as Pope."

Josh hesitated and then softly spoke, "Your Holiness, I have a non-operative brain tumor. It grows larger each day, and I'm sure the Lord is calling me home. Time is short for me and more importantly, time is running shorter each day for the world to react to the Lord's Message."

Pope Xavier was shocked.

"Oh, my dear Lord, I am so sorry to hear that. You know I will be praying for you constantly." Josh simply acknowledged with a smile.

The Pope continued, "My son, the world has already reacted to the Lord's message in so many ways. People all over the world are repenting. Abortion laws are changing. There are more Catholic converts who have begun preaching the message of reparation than ever before. More priests are being ordained and so much evil has been exposed and eliminated, thanks to you."

"No, your Holiness, thanks to Jesus." But without sounding too pessimistic, Josh said, "There still is so very much to be done."

"True," the Pope said, "but I don't think Jesus told you that every single person has to repent before forgiveness will be given."

"You're probably right, but only Jesus can answer that question. In the meantime, I'll continue to do as much as I can."

"I'm sure you will," Pope Xavier said, "but for now, I want you to rest." There was no argument from Josh, as he could hardly keep his eyes open.

The World was delighted with the new Pope and extremely optimistic that the new leader of the Catholic Church would be effective in bringing countries together for world peace. Everyone at the Seminary of the Holy Order of Reparation were also thrilled with the selection of the new Pope. However, as excited and pleased as they were, many felt somewhat saddened that Josh was ill and therefore would not serve.

Only Father Robert and Father O'Malley knew the extent of Josh's condition. Although they had not seen him in months, they kept abreast via phone, text, and internet. Prayers were offered up for him and his mission daily. Father O'Malley was particularly saddened as he knew Josh's condition was worsening each day.

On the positive side, more and more young men wanted to join the Order. In fact, so many had applied, that Father Robert, along with the consent of Josh and Pope Xavier, had agreed to establish two more Seminaries of the Holy Order of Reparation.

Weeks passed. Josh's condition improved enough for him to be able to go to Russia. Announcements were made and the date set. He would leave on December 14th early in the morning. The media, and for that matter, the world, had not seen Josh for months since his last visit there. They were shocked to see him leaving the Vatican walking with a cane and breathing through oxygen tubes in his nose.

CHAPTER XIII

Becky was horrified as she watched Josh on TV enter the plane. Frantic and upset, she called him.

"Josh! Are you alright? What's going on? Why didn't you call me?" All three questions came in one breath.

"Calm down," Josh said. "So glad to hear from you too. "Don't be funny, not at a time like this."

"I'm not… just calm down and I'll tell you all about it." Yet immediately after those words slipped out, he didn't quite know how to tell her. Instead, there was only silence on the phone.

"Something is really wrong", she said, but only more silence. "Come on Josh, please tell me."

Summoning up enough courage, Josh finally was able to tell her of his condition. Of course, he exaggerated the effect of the medications he was taking.

"The really good news is I'm taking great medications that are helping."

Becky began to cry. She cried and cried.

"Come on Beck, stop the crying".

"Oh Josh, you should have told me," she managed to say.

"Beck, there's nothing you could do, and I didn't want to worry you." Josh didn't know if she heard him or not as she was still sobbing quite loud. "You hear me? Now, stop your balling and tell me how you and Barry are doing."

Now she began to cry even harder. Finally breaking through the tears, she managed to say, "I'm pregnant."

"That's great!" Josh said, trying his best to uplift the conversation.

Still crying she choked out, "I wanted so much for you to baptize our baby and for you to be there for him as he grows up."

"I will…I will, God willing." Not waiting for a response, he continued. "Do you know if it's a boy or girl?"

"No, it's too early."

Finally, the crying let up.

"Listen. I'm off to Russia. When I return, I'll call you and we can have a long talk, Ok?"

"Ok," she said.

"No crying, you hear me?"

"Ok," she said again as they ended the call. "I love you."

But Josh had already hung up. Deep in his heart he knew, and I'm sure she did too, that there would never be a call.

"Your Eminence, you're bleeding again. Please lie down until we arrive."

Josh did not argue. He quickly grabbed a towel and held it tight against his nose. Lying down, he told his attendant to call Father Robert. Have him meet me at the Vatican when I return.

"I think I'm going to need his help."

Hundreds of people and dozens of news reporters were waiting at the airport as they arrived. Security had a difficult time holding back the crowds. Josh exited the plane without wearing the oxygen device but had to be helped down the stairs until reaching the limousine that was waiting for him. His entourage wanted him to bypass the media and spectators. Josh however, turned toward them and took several questions.

"Your Eminence, we're all are so sorry to see that you are ill. Can you tell us about your illness?" the first reporter asked.

"Yes, I can tell you, but I won't." The crowd laughed. "Just kidding. I have a tumor, but the medications are keeping it under control."

"Is it terminal?" another asked.

CHAPTER XIII

"Only God knows that."

"Why don't you heal yourself?" An arrogant reporter blurted out. Most everyone standing around him appeared to be upset with the question.

However, Josh simply smiled and answered, "As I have always said, Jesus does the healing, not me. And so far, Jesus apparently has other plans for me. Whatever they are, I humbly accept. Now, I hope that answers your question."

Breaking the silence, a small female reporter asked, "Can you tell us why you are here again in Russia?"

"I'm doing the Lord's work; trying my best to unite our beliefs and churches."

More questions were shouted out but no more were answered as Josh got into the Limousine.

Unlike last time when he met with the Russian Orthodox Church Bishops and Archbishops, this visit was quite different. He was met with hundreds of spectators and dozens of Clergy. Every Bishop and Archbishop greeted him personally, kissing his ring and warmly shaking his hand.

Once inside, Josh immediately spoke to his purpose of the visit. This time, due to his weakened condition, he sat while addressing them.

"My brothers, thank you for agreeing to see me once again. My plea is the same. I'm here once again to employ you to unify with the Roman Catholic Church and to dedicate yourselves and Russia to the Immaculate Heart of Mary. It is the Lord's desire that all churches be united."

Josh spoke for over an hour explaining the importance of his visit and answering many questions. Unfortunately, the visit had taken a heavy toll on him. He sat exhausted, clearly out of breath and periodically wiped droplets of blood from his nose.

REPARATION: A STORY OF HOPE

Just before leaving, one of the Archbishops said to him that it is very difficult to change after centuries of tradition.

"It is not tradition that will save mankind, but unity, prayer, and repentance. I wish we had centuries to decide, but we do not. Time, my friend, is now upon us."

Outside the Cathedral, Josh waved and shook hands with dozens of well-wishers, all the while sitting in a wheelchair. Suddenly the young boy that had the clubbed foot that Josh had previously healed, pushed through the crowd. He hugged Josh and thanked him for Jesus's healing. In fact, his entire family came forward, thanking him and announcing that they had converted to the Christian faith.

Josh was overjoyed. Looking around him, he saw hundreds of desperate people, some old, some young but all hoping for his blessing and his healing. Dozens were in wheelchairs and still more were on crutches. Some with deformed bones and others with missing limbs.

"Oh, my dear Jesus," he said in a low voice, "these are your people who need you so much."

Speaking in Russian, he asked them all, "Kneel if you can. If you cannot, please bow your heads and let everyone ask for the Lord's forgiveness and healing." Then, blessing the crowd, he said in a weak voice, "IN THE NAME OF THE FATHER, AND OF THE SON, AND OF THE HOLY SPIRIT, I ask for healing for all those with sincere contrition and faith."

Josh did not wait for the cheers, praises, expressions of joy and bewilderment to occur. In short, hundreds were healed that day. People cried and literally ran into the Cathedral to thank the Lord. People were converted and many repented.

Non-believers looked on in amazement and astonishment as they witnessed legs and arms restored before their very eyes. Many of them began to question

CHAPTER XIII

their own disbelief. The media recorded the entire event and before Josh took off on the plane back to Rome, most of the world was witnessing the miracles that had just occurred.

By the time he arrived in Rome, Josh's condition had worsened even further. His nose bleeds continued and were close to impossible to stop. Blood was now dripping from his eyes due to the pressure that the tumor was causing. As he was placed in a wheelchair, Josh said that he was having trouble seeing and by time he reached the Vatican, he was blind.

Refusing to go to a hospital, he was carried up to his apartment that overlooked St. Peter's square. All this was recorded and millions of people all over the world began to tearfully pray for him. Some fled to churches, believing that the end of God's mercy was near. Still others flocked to their priests, hoping to repent before time ran out. Others just sat and cried.

The news of Josh's condition was broadcasted as fast as they received updated information about his condition. Churches everywhere held vigils desperately praying for his recovery. Especially saddened were all his friends from Clarksville and Jinksville. Many sat glued to their TV's, phones, or radios, hoping and praying for their dear friend who had touched their lives in so many ways.

Pope Xavier, the pope's physicians, nurses, some clergy, and attendants were all trying their best to make Josh as comfortable as possible. Numerous IVs were connected, including transfusions to replace the blood that was so sorely needed. An Oxygen mask was placed over his face, while someone was continuously wiping the blood that was oozing from his nose and eyes. Of course, Kapriel and Lancer knelt, one at each side of his bed, praying for the young man that they had so carefully guarded and loved.

REPARATION: A STORY OF HOPE

News continued to spread quickly that Cardinal Donovan was dying. Father Robert was already on his way to Rome. Father O'Malley and Becky immediately booked nonstop flights and hoped they would arrive before he passed. By the time morning arrived, over two thousand people were holding a vigil for him in St. Peter's Square.

Somehow, Josh lingered, coming in and out of what the doctors called a slight coma. Every once in a while, he was aware of what was happening and would say a few words, although everyone encouraged him not to speak but simply rest. Blood continued to ooze from his nose and eyes.

The first to arrive was Father Robert. It was mid day when Josh recognized Robert's voice.

"Oh Robbie," Josh said in a weak voice as he slipped off his oxygen mask. "I was hoping that we would meet under better circumstances."

Father Robert greeted Josh with a hug and began to cry as the sight of his bleeding face, and all the tubes hooked up to him were more than he could handle.

"Tell me all about our Order?" Josh managed to ask. "How many priests do we have?"

Father Robert, wiping the tears from his face, told him that it was flourishing, and it now had two dozen plus priests, and fifteen seminarians who wanted to be Priests of the Order of Reparation. He also confirmed that two other Seminaries were established.

Josh seemed distant and Father Robert really did not know if he heard him or even comprehend what he had just said. Finally, after a period of silence, Josh mumbled, "Good...that's really good."

Father Robert began to get up, but Josh grabbed him by the arm.

"Wait Robbie. One more thing. This is not official yet, but the Holy Father has approved my request."

CHAPTER XIII

Josh struggled to reach his roped belt that was lying on a night table. Realizing it, the Pope handed it to him.

Robbie, here is my red-roped belt that his Holiness gave me. You are to be head of the Order. Wear it proudly as I have."

Father Robert took the rope, but this time could not stop his tears. Josh began to bleed again, slipping back into a coma. It took twenty minutes to stop the bleeding, but unfortunately due to the loss of blood, it left him extremely weak. Oxygen, morphine, and more blood transfusions were administered, yet the physicians didn't think he would ever come out of his coma. Miraculously his eyes eventually opened. The Pope knelt and thanked Jesus for giving Josh even just a little more time.

Father O'Malley arrived a few hours later. He met Father Robert and Pope Xavier outside Josh's room and was given a full update as to his condition. It would be a miracle if he lasts the night. Pope Xavier agreed with Father Robert.

Father O'Malley asked if he could kneel next to him and pray.

"Of course, you can," replied the Pope. "Let's all go in and pray."

Four hours later, Josh opened his eyes again. Pope Xavier immediately told him to rest, but Josh resisted.

"Holy Father, I want to ask you for a favor."

"Anything, anything you want."

"Would you personally ordain Kirt Williamson? He has just a few more months to go before his preparation is complete. It was Kirt who planned our escape from the seminary when Fr. Gerald controlled it. I promised that I would ordain him, but it looks like Jesus has other plans for me."

"I would be most happy to represent you. Don't think any more about it," the Pontiff said.

Just then, Josh realized that his dear friend and mentor was at his side.

"I'd recognize your voice anywhere," Josh managed to say.

"Don't talk," Father O'Malley said. "Just rest."

Reaching for his oxygen mask, O'Malley tried to put it back on Josh, only for Josh to push it away. "I have all eternity to rest," trying his best to say it jokingly. "I will miss you and Maggie's wonderful dinners."

"I will miss you too, my friend. I will miss our tea together. I will miss…" but O'Malley could not continue. Although Josh could not see his friend, he knew that he was trying his best to conceal his tears.

"It's Ok. Please, please Jamie don't cry. Don't cry for me. I've been so blessed and have been so happy."

Struggling to get air, Father Robert tried to place the oxygen mask back on Josh. Again, pushing it away, he continued to talk. Father O'Malley interrupted, "Stubborn as ever I see." They both chuckled, although Josh's sounded more like choking.

"Let me finish, please. You have been like a father to me. I will never forget…" Now, coughing up some blood, Josh struggled to continue. "And I will always love you…" but the coughing continued without him finishing.

"I will always love you too, Josh. And will never stop," but O'Malley couldn't finish his sentence either. He simply lowered his head on Josh's lap and sobbed and sobbed.

Becky's flight was delayed twice. She finally arrived in Rome around 8:00am the next morning. Frantically, she hailed a cab and rushed toward the Vatican. Josh was awake and miraculously still alive. Thinking no one was in his room, he began to speak to Kapriel and Lancer.

CHAPTER XIII

"I know you are here although I can't see you. I just wanted to thank you for all the protection and love you both have given me. Who would ever believe that I had two wonderful angels constantly at my side?"

Neither one said anything, but each took a hand of Josh, which he clearly could feel, bowed their heads, and prayed. Those in the room could not see his Guardians, but no one doubted who he was talking to or how his hands were mysteriously being held up by two invisible angels.

"Oh," Josh said, "And thanks for those speedy trips to Rome and DeBella's place. What a rush!"

Kapriel and Lancer smiled, while those looking on, wondered exactly what he was talking about. All wondered except for Father Robert and Father O'Malley who knew exactly who he was talking to and what he meant.

Unexpectedly there was a knock on the door. "Your Holiness, a woman named Becky Callaghan is here and says Cardinal Donovan is expecting her."

"Yes, yes, show her in."

Upon hearing her name, Josh said in as loud of a voice as he could, "Thank you, Jesus, for allowing me to say goodbye to her."

Becky politely kissed the ring of the Pontiff and went directly to Josh. She sat on the side of his bed and took his hand in hers.

"Oh Beck, thank you for coming. Give me a hug."

A moment of pure contentment could be seen on Josh's face. "I'm so glad you made it here before I…"

But Becky didn't let him finish because she knew exactly what he was about to say. "Shush", she told him as she released her hug and kissed him on the forehead.

Seeing him in the condition he was, she could not hold the tears back. She placed her head on his lap and began to cry.

REPARATION: A STORY OF HOPE

"No tears, remember?" Josh managed to say as he reached for her face.

Not paying any attention to him, she continued to cry and cry. Josh gently passed his fingers through her hair, "Please Beck...stop." Yet, the more he said it, the more she sobbed. Finally, she was able to choke back her emotions.

"Look at me, blubbering like a baby."

Josh agreed. *"Just* like a baby," which allowed everyone in the room to let out a little laugh and wipe their eyes. "Speaking of babies…" but just then he again began to cough and choke up blood. Blood from his stomach this time, something that has not previously happened.

Father O'Malley reached for a glass of water, but Josh only choked on it. One of the physicians turned to the Pope and whispered in his ear that Josh was now most likely bleeding from the stomach or some internal vessel.

Becky started to get up to allow the physicians to attend him, but Josh managed to grab her, pulling her back to his bed. Josh could hardly speak, and his words were slurred and hard to understand.

"Let me…finish…" Josh said, in an almost unintelligible voice. "Let me touch your baby." Struggling to touch her, Becky assisted him and guided his hand.

Josh smiled. "A boy...it's a boy," he said.

Becky didn't bother asking how he knew the sex of her baby, she knew better. Hugging him she again began to cry. She cried and cried, sobbing her heart out. With tears running down her face, she tried to speak. Finally choking back her tears, she softly said, "I Love you Josh. I will always love you."

Josh found her hand. "Rebecca, I have loved you from the moment I saw you. I have always loved you with all my heart… But I have loved Jesus more…" then he also began to cry.

CHAPTER XIII

"I know," Becky said. We are exactly where Jesus wants us to be."

"Come closer to me," he said, barely audible.

Becky leaned over.

"No...closer."

With that Josh reached up and pulled her close to him, whispering something in her ear. Once again, she began to cry, collapsing her head on his chest. Sobbing more than ever, she kept repeating over and over, "Oh Josh, Oh Josh... Oh, my dear Josh."

By now, even more of the faithful had gathered throughout St. Peter's Square and throughout the world. Every TV station was covering the event. Media were everywhere. Churches throughout the Christian world were continuing to pray. What would have pleased Josh so much was that people of all faiths, religions and beliefs were also praying and offering up well wishes for him, including leaders from the United States, most of the European Countries, as well as China, Russia and Iran.

Another knock on the door interrupted those in the room praying for Josh.

"I hope this is important," Pope Xavier said.

"Your Holiness, we have just received word from representatives of the Russian Orthodox Church that they have officially agreed to unify. What's more, other churches have also agreed to begin a dialect on unification. Although they contend that they have already consecrated themselves to Mary, they have unanimously agreed to reconsecrate Russia to the Immaculate Heart of Mary in the presence of all Bishops throughout the world."

The Pope stood stunned, as was everyone else. Josh smiled, knowing that his mission was complete.

The moment those words were spoken, a brilliant light erupted from the ancient obelisk in the center of St. Peter's Square. The light was so bright that at first, one could not look directly at it. The light grew higher and higher until it could be seen from every corner of the world.

No matter where you were, no matter day or night, the brilliant tower of light could be seen representing the Mercy of Jesus. So long as the world kept true to repentance, love and to the Lord, the light would remain for all to see and for all to be reminded of the mercy of God. All in the room, including Josh, were stunned. Joy and praise were abundant as all present knew that the Lord had accepted the reparation of the world.

Then it happened. Kapriel and Lancer took Josh by the arms and walked him to the window. There were no tubes attached to him. He was once again, full of life looking as handsome and youthful as before.

"I can see. I see the mercy of Jesus. He has given us another chance."

Then turning to everyone in the room, he said, "I see you also. I see the love in your hearts and the friends that I will always be thankful for."

Then looking at Becky, he said, "Love is a beautiful gift. So was our friendship. I will always cherish it and always be with you."

Unbelievably, they also could see. They saw the seven-foot angels standing next to Josh. They were magnificent, just as Josh had explained them to Father's Robert and O'Malley. No one said a word. No one knew what to say. They simply stared at Josh and the two figures, standing in all their glory. Then, wrapping their golden wings around Josh, they all disappeared.

Looking back at the bed, the body of Josh remained. He would have been 28 years old in a month. Becky ran to

CHAPTER XIII

him, crying uncontrollably as she laid her head on his chest and sobbed and sobbed.

"Oh Josh," she said, "Thank you, thank you for all you've done. Thank you for loving me. Thank you for our friendship. I will miss you so much."

Everyone in the room was on their knees, praying and thanking Jesus for his mercy. Bells began to ring throughout St. Peter's, then throughout Vatican City, then throughout the whole of Italy. Soon, as word of Josh's death was announced throughout the world, churches of all denominations were ringing bells in memory of a young man, who faithfully served God to the very end.

Becky slowly stood up and walked to the window. Father Robert and Father O'Malley joined her. All three continued to stare at the miracle of light.

Finally, Father Robert asked Becky, "If I'm not being too forward, would you tell us what Josh whispered in your ear?"

Becky smiled at each.

"He said, 'Your son will be the next Pope.'"

THE END

Or maybe, it is just the beginning…

Made in the USA
Middletown, DE
08 November 2021